IMPACT

FIFTY SHORT SHORT STORIES

SECOND EDITION

HOLT, RINEHART AND WINSTON
Harcourt Brace & Company
Austin • New York • Orlando • Atlanta •
San Francisco • Boston • Dallas • Toronto • London

Staff Credits

Editorial

Editorial Direction: Fannie Safier, Laura Baci
Editorial Staff: Jennifer Osborne, Sally Ahearn
Editorial Permissions: Ann B. Farrar

Design and Production

Pun Nio, *Senior Art Director;* Richard Metzger, *Design Services Supervisor;* Stephen Sharpe, *Designer;* Bob Bretz, *Cover Designer;* Carol Martin, *Electronic Publishing Manager;* Kristy Sprott, *Electronic Publishing Supervisor;* Barbara Hudgens, Maria Veres Homic, *Electronic Publishing Staff;* Beth Prevelige, *Senior Production Manager;* Simira Davis, *Production Assistant;* George Prevelige, *Production Manager;* Rose Degollado, *Production Assistant*

ISBN 0-03-008623-X

4 5 062 98

Curriculum and Writing

Carroll Moulton
Formerly of Duke University
Durham, North Carolina

Critical Readers

John P. Breen
Gordon Technical High School
Chicago, Illinois

Kenneth T. Croswell
Formerly of Towson High School
Towson, Maryland

Ann Luke
The Walker School
Marietta, Georgia

Janice Ollarvia
Fenger Academy for African American Studies
Chicago, Illinois

Linda Sanders
Jenks High School
Jenks, Oklahoma

Susan Wuchter-Stein
Formerly of King Middle School
Portland, Maine

Acknowledgments

For permission to reprint copyrighted material, grateful acknowledgment is made to the following sources:

Agenzia Letteraria Internazionale: Quotation by Dino Buzzati from Introduction and "The Colomber" ("Il Colombre") from *Restless Nights: Selected Stories of Dino Buzzati,* translated by Lawrence Venuti. Copyright © 1966 by Arnoldo Mondadori Editore.

Atheneum Books for Young Readers, an imprint of Simon & Schuster Children's Publishing Division: "The Bracelet" by Yoshiko Uchida from *The Scribner Anthology for Young People,* edited by Anne Diven. Copyright © 1976 by Charles Scribner's Sons.

Susan Bergholz Literary Services, NY: "Three Wise Guys: A Christmas Story" by Sandra Cisneros. Copyright © 1987 by Sandra Cisneros. First published in *Vista* Magazine, December 1987.

Ruskin Bond: Comment about "A Tiger in the House" by Ruskin Bond. Copyright © 1996 by Ruskin Bond.

Gwendolyn Brooks: "Home" from *Maud Martha* by Gwendolyn Brooks. Copyright © 1993 by Gwendolyn Brooks. Published by Third World Press, Chicago, IL.

José Antonio Burciaga: "La Puerta" by José Antonio Burciaga. Copyright © 1992 by José Antonio Burciaga.

Estate of Morley Callaghan: "All the Years of Her Life" by Morley Callaghan. Copyright © 1936 by Morley Callaghan; copyright renewed © 1964.

Chinese Literature Press: "I Confess" by Wei Wenjuan from *One-minute Stories.* Copyright © 1992 by Chinese Literature Press.

Don Congdon Associates, Inc.: "All Summer in a Day" by Ray Bradbury. Copyright © 1954, renewed © 1982 by Ray Bradbury.

Devin-Adair, Publishers, Inc., Old Greenwich, CT 06870: "The Wild Duck's Nest" from *The Game Cock and Other Stories* by Michael McLaverty. Copyright 1947 by Devin-Adair Company. All rights reserved. "The Trout" from *The Man Who Invented Sin and Other Stories* by Sean O'Faolain. Copyright 1949 by Devin-Adair Company. All rights reserved.

Doubleday, a division of Bantam Doubleday Dell Publishing Group, Inc.: "Dead Men's Path" from *Girls at War and Other Stories* by Chinua Achebe. Copyright © 1972, 1973 by Chinua Achebe. "The Panther: A Bedtime Story" from *The Wrecking Yard* by Pinckney Benedict. Copyright © 1992 by Pinckney Benedict. "Half a Day" from *The Time and the Place and Other Stories* by Naguib Mahfouz, translated by Denys Johnson-Davies. Copyright © 1991 by the American University in Cairo Press.

Dutton Signet, a division of Penguin Books USA Inc.: "A Nincompoop" from *Selected Stories of Anton Chekhov* by Anton Chekhov, translated by Ann Dunnigan. Translation copyright © 1960 by Ann Dunnigan.

Farrar, Straus & Giroux, Inc.: "Charles" from *The Lottery* by Shirley Jackson. Copyright © 1948 by Shirley Jackson; copyright renewed © 1976 by Laurence Hyman, Barry Hyman, Mrs. Sarah Webster, and Mrs. Joanne Schnurer.

Gale Research Inc.: Quotation by Ruskin Bond from *Contemporary Authors,* New Revision Series, Vol. 14, Linda Metzger, Editor. Copyright © 1985 by Gale Research Inc. Quotation by

CONTENTS

THE HEART OF THE MATTER

PLOT

CHARACTER

THEME

TOTAL EFFECT

INTRODUCTION TO THE SECOND EDITION

What, exactly, is a short story? According to Edgar Allan Poe, it is a work that yields a single overall "effect" and is short enough to be read in one sitting. Like the novel, though on a smaller scale, the traditional short story takes the time to establish a setting and to develop characters.

Some short stories, however, focus on a pivotal moment between characters or center on a revelation—a flash of insight and understanding—that characters gain through undergoing a powerful experience. These stories are more compressed and are usually more intense than conventional short stories. Here, for example, is a famous tale retold by W. Somerset Maugham:

> **Death speaks:** There was a merchant in Baghdad who sent his servant to market to buy provisions, and in a little while the servant came back, white and trembling, and said, "Master, just now when I was in the marketplace I was jostled by a woman in the crowd, and when I turned I saw it was Death that jostled me. She looked at me and made a threatening gesture; now, lend me your horse, and I will ride away from this city and avoid my fate. I will go to Samarra, and there Death will not find me." The merchant lent him his horse, the servant mounted it, and he dug his spurs in its flanks, and as fast as the horse could gallop he went. Then the merchant went down to the marketplace and he saw me standing in the crowd and he came to me and said, "Why did you make a threatening gesture to my servant when you saw him this morning?" "That was not a threatening gesture," I said, "it was only a start of surprise. I was astonished to see him in Baghdad, for I had an appointment with him tonight in Samarra."
>
> —"Appointment in Samarra"

Part of the appeal of short stories is the *impact* they make on us. In other words, they have the power to move or affect us deeply. Some short stories, such as those in Unit One, achieve this effect by startling us with some kind of twist or surprise. Others, such as "Home" and "The Return" are more subtle and, therefore, moving in a quieter way. Each of the stories in this book is meant to have an impact on the reader.

The stories in this collection also represent a variety of styles: the narrative by Jim Heynen, for example, could be considered a "prose sketch," and the piece by T. Coraghessan Boyle is actually a dramatic monologue. Included are works by writers from a number of different cultures and backgrounds.

Good literature provides both pleasure and insight. We hope you find these stories enjoyable and thought-provoking.

A TIGER IN THE HOUSE
Ruskin Bond

What is the most unusual pet that you have heard of? Write down a few notes about it, and share your notes with the class.

Timothy, the tiger-cub, was discovered by Grandfather on a hunting expedition in the Terai jungle near Dehra.[1]

Grandfather was no *shikari*,[2] but as he knew the forests of the Siwalik hills[3] better than most people, he was persuaded to accompany the party—it consisted of several Very Important Persons from Delhi—to advise on the terrain and the direction the beaters[4] should take once a tiger had been spotted.

The camp itself was sumptuous—seven large tents (one for each *shikari*), a dining-tent, and a number of servants' tents. The dinner was very good, as Grandfather admitted afterwards; it was not often that one saw hot-water plates, finger-glasses, and seven or eight courses, in a tent in the jungle! But that was how things were done in the days of the Viceroys[5]. . . . There were also some fifteen elephants, four of them with howdahs[6] for the *shikaris,* and the others especially trained for taking part in the beat.

The sportsmen never saw a tiger, nor did they shoot anything else, though they saw a number of deer, peacock, and wild boar. They were giving up all hope of finding a tiger, and were beginning to shoot at jackals, when Grandfather, strolling down the forest path at some distance from the rest of the party, discovered a little tiger about eighteen inches long, hiding among the intricate roots of a

---

1. **Terai** (tə-rī′) **jungle near Dehra** (dĕ′rə): the forests at the base of the Himalayan foothills near the town of Dehra Dun in northern India.
2. *shikari* (shĭ-kä′rē): a hunter.
3. **Siwalik hills**: a range of hills running through the Terai.
4. **beaters:** men who drive animals out of cover by beating drums and shouting.
5. **Viceroys:** In colonial times, the Viceroy was the chief official of the ruling British government in India.
6. **howdahs** (hou′dəz): seats placed for riders on elephants' backs.

banyan tree.[7] Grandfather picked him up, and brought him home after the camp had broken up. He had the distinction of being the only member of the party to have bagged any game, dead or alive.

At first the tiger cub, who was named Timothy by Grandmother, was brought up entirely on milk given to him in a feeding-bottle by our cook, Mahmoud.[8] But the milk proved too rich for him, and he was put on a diet of raw mutton and cod liver oil, to be followed later by a more tempting diet of pigeons and rabbits.

Timothy was provided with two companions—Toto the monkey, who was bold enough to pull the young tiger by the tail, and then climb up the curtains if Timothy lost his temper; and a small mongrel puppy, found on the road by Grandfather.

At first Timothy appeared to be quite afraid of the puppy, and darted back with a spring if it came too near. He would make absurd dashes at it with his large forepaws, and then retreat to a ridiculously safe distance. Finally, he allowed the puppy to crawl on his back and rest there!

One of Timothy's favourite amusements was to stalk anyone who would play with him, and so, when I came to live with Grandfather, I became one of the tiger's favourites. With a crafty look in his glittering eyes, and his body crouching, he would creep closer and closer to me, suddenly making a dash for my feet, rolling over on his back and kicking with delight, and pretending to bite my ankles.

He was by this time the size of a full-grown retriever, and when I took him out for walks, people on the road would give us a wide berth. When he pulled hard on his chain, I had difficulty in keeping up with him. His favourite place in the house was the drawing-room, and he would make himself comfortable on the long sofa, reclining there with great dignity, and snarling at anybody who tried to get him off.

Timothy had clean habits, and would scrub his face with his paws exactly like a cat. He slept at night in the cook's quarters, and was always delighted at being let out by him in the morning.

"One of these days," declared Grandmother in her prophetic manner, "we are going to find Timothy sitting on Mahmoud's bed, and no sign of the cook except his clothes and shoes!"

---

7. **banyan tree:** a large, tropical fig tree native to India.
8. **Mahmoud** (mā-mōōd′).

Of course, it never came to that, but when Timothy was about six months old a change came over him; he grew steadily less friendly. When out for a walk with me, he would try to steal away to stalk a cat or someone's pet Pekinese. Sometimes at night we would hear frenzied cackling from the poultry house, and in the morning there would be feathers lying all over the verandah. Timothy had to be chained up more often. And finally, when he began to stalk Mahmoud about the house with what looked like villainous intent, Grandfather decided it was time to transfer him to a zoo.

The nearest zoo was at Lucknow,[9] two hundred miles away. Reserving a first-class compartment for himself and Timothy—no one would share a compartment with them—Grandfather took him to Lucknow where the zoo authorities were only too glad to receive as a gift a well-fed and fairly civilized tiger.

About six months later, when my grandparents were visiting relatives in Lucknow, Grandfather took the opportunity of calling at the zoo to see how Timothy was getting on. I was not there to accompany him, but I heard all about it when he returned to Dehra.

Arriving at the zoo, Grandfather made straight for the particular cage in which Timothy had been interned. The tiger was there, crouched in a corner, full-grown and with a magnificent striped coat.

"Hello Timothy!" said Grandfather and, climbing the railing with ease, he put his arm through the bars of the cage.

The tiger approached the bars, and allowed Grandfather to put both hands around his head. Grandfather stroked the tiger's forehead and tickled his ears, and, whenever he growled, smacked him across the mouth, which was his old way of keeping him quiet.

It licked Grandfather's hands and only sprang away when a leopard in the next cage snarled at him. Grandfather "shooed" the leopard away, and the tiger returned to lick his hands; but every now and then the leopard would rush at the bars, and he would slink back to his corner.

A number of people had gathered to watch the reunion when a keeper pushed his way through the crowd and asked Grandfather what he was doing.

9. **Lucknow** (lŭk′nou): a large city in northern India.

"I'm talking to Timothy," said Grandfather. "Weren't you here when I gave him to the zoo six months ago?"

"I haven't been here very long," said the surprised keeper. "Please continue your conversation. But I have never been able to touch him myself, he is always very bad tempered."

"Why don't you put him somewhere else?" suggested Grandfather. "That leopard keeps frightening him. I'll go and see the Superintendent about it."

Grandfather went in search of the Superintendent of the zoo, but found that he had gone home early; and so, after wandering about the zoo for a little while, he returned to Timothy's cage to say goodbye. It was beginning to get dark.

He had been stroking and slapping Timothy for about five minutes when he found another keeper observing him with some alarm. Grandfather recognized him as the keeper who had been there when Timothy had first come to the zoo.

"*You* remember me," said Grandfather. "Now why don't you transfer Timothy to another cage, away from this stupid leopard?"

"But—sir—" stammered the keeper. "It is not your tiger."

"I know, I know," said Grandfather testily. "I realize he is no longer mine. But you might at least take a suggestion or two from me."

"I remember your tiger very well," said the keeper. "He died two months ago."

"Died!" exclaimed Grandfather.

"Yes, sir, of pneumonia. This tiger was trapped in the hills only last month, and he is very dangerous!"

Grandfather could think of nothing to say. The tiger was still licking his arm, with increasing relish. Grandfather took what seemed to him an age to withdraw his hand from the cage.

With his face near the tiger's he mumbled, "Good night, Timothy," and giving the keeper a scornful look, walked briskly out of the zoo.

First Response: *Were you completely surprised by the story's ending? Why or why not?*

CHECKING UP

1. Why was Grandfather asked to join the hunting expedition?
2. Who were Timothy's two companions?
3. What was Timothy's favorite spot in the house?
4. How old was Timothy when Grandfather took him to the zoo in Lucknow?
5. Why did Grandfather want to see the Superintendent of the zoo?

TALKING IT OVER

1. A situation is considered **ironic** if its outcome is the opposite of what was expected. Why was it ironic that of all those on the hunting expedition, Grandfather was the only one who "bagged any game"? What was ironic about the kind of "game" he caught?
2. What evidence in the story shows that Grandfather was fond of animals and was comfortable with them?
3. Describe Timothy's behavior during his first few months in the house. What kind of change came over him when he reached six months of age?
4. The author's playful attitude toward the characters and events of the story gives the tale a humorous **tone**. For example, the description of the fancy dinner held in a tent in the jungle is almost comical. What other passages contribute to the story's humorous tone?
5. What is the unexpected "twist" at the end of this tale? Did any clues prepare you for the unexpected ending?

FICTION

Any story that is invented or imagined is **fiction**. Fiction may be based on events and experiences that actually happened, but the writer shapes these elements of truth into a narrative that is interesting, insightful and, often, entertaining. In this shaping process, some details are selected, and others are added or deleted. In fact, the word *fiction* comes from the Latin word *fictio,* "the action of shaping." When the writer is finished, the story he or she has to tell is one that people will want to hear.

Ruskin Bond says that he based "A Tiger in the House" on an experience from his childhood. "My maternal grandfather," he writes, "was quite a character, and he had a way with animals." We can assume, therefore, that the narrator in this story speaks for the author and that many of the story's details are true. The story as a whole, however, is fiction.

1. How does the story's opening suggest that the narrator has a knowledge of the places and events he is writing about?
2. Which events and details in the story do you think are true? Which do you think the author may have exaggerated or made up entirely?
3. The narrator was not present at the hunting expedition he describes in the beginning of the story, and he did not accompany his grandfather to the zoo. How does he explain his knowledge of the hunting expedition and the events that took place at the zoo?

UNDERSTANDING THE WORDS IN THE STORY (Multiple-Choice)

1. An expert who advises on the *terrain* knows
   a. how the land lies
   b. how to organize a hunt
   c. how the food should be cooked
2. A person has *distinction* if he or she is
   a. different or special
   b. well liked
   c. lucky
3. The *intricate* roots of a banyan tree are
   a. complex
   b. thick
   c. multicolored

4. When Timothy *stalked* a target, he pursued it
   a. rapidly
   b. stealthily
   c. noisily
5. A *crafty* look in the eye is an indication of
   a. good will
   b. cunning
   c. humor
6. When Timothy *reclined,* he would
   a. groom himself
   b. lash his tail
   c. lie down
7. Grandmother was *prophetic* when she
   a. scolded Timothy
   b. made a prediction
   c. instructed the cook
8. A *villainous* intent is
   a. easily interpreted
   b. evil
   c. benevolent
9. One place an animal might be *interned* is a
   a. sidewalk
   b. meadow
   c. cage
10. The increasing *relish* with which the tiger licked Grandfather's arm was a sign of the animal's
    a. annoyance
    b. playfulness
    c. pleasure

WRITING IT DOWN
Story Materials

Like Ruskin Bond and many other writers, you can take humorous events and experiences from your own life and shape them into fiction.

Think about an amusing experience that you have had with an animal—a family pet, a neighbor's pet, or an animal you saw at the zoo, for example. How could you shape your experience into an entertaining story?

Begin by jotting down some words or phrases that come to mind as you recall the experience. You may find it helpful to fill out a story materials chart like the one below.

STORY MATERIALS CHART
ANIMAL
INCIDENT OR EXPERIENCE
OTHER PERSONS INVOLVED

ABOUT THE AUTHOR

Ruskin Bond was born in 1934 in Kasauli, a rural area of India. A full-time writer since the age of twenty-two, he has published several novels, short stories, and books for children. He has said of his work, "My interests (children, mountains, folklore, nature) are embodied in [these books]. . . . Once you have lived in the Himalayas, you belong to them, and must come back again and again. There is no escape."

Bond contributes short stories and articles to a number of publications. "A Tiger In the House" comes from his best-known collection, *Time Stops at Shamli and Other Stories* (1989).

ROLLS FOR THE CZAR

Robin Kinkead

---

*People sometimes use their courage and quick wit to get out of a
desperate situation. Have you known or heard of any such person?
Discuss your answer with a small group of classmates.*

This is a tale of the days of the Czars, of ermine and gold and
pure white bread.

In Saint Petersburg the Czar held his court with pomp and
ceremony that dazzled peasants and ambassadors alike. His Winter
Palace covered acres by the side of the frozen Neva.[1] It had pillars of
lapis lazuli[2] and of rare stone from the Urals.[3] Its halls held treasures
from all the world.

Once a year the Czar paid a visit of state to Moscow, where the rich
merchants lived, trade center of the Imperial Domain. Here he would
sit in the throne room of the Kremlin,[4] where his ancestors once ruled
warring Muscovy.[5]

There was another great man in Moscow—a baker, Markov by name.
The master bakers of the city were famous, and Markov was prince
among them. His cakes and pastry were renowned throughout all the
Russias, but his rolls were the best of all: pure white, like the driven snow
of the steppes, a crust just hard enough to crunch, the bread not too
soft, but soft enough to hold the melted butter.

Merchant princes from the gold rivers of Siberia, chieftains from the
Caucasus in high fur hats, nobles from their feudal estates in the
country, all came to Moscow to eat Markov's rolls.

The Czar himself was a mighty eater and especially fond of Markov's
delicacies. So one day in February, when it came time for a visit to
Moscow, he was thinking of Markov and his art, anticipating the rolls.
His private car bore the imperial coat of arms. The rest of the train
was filled with grand dukes, princes of the blood, and noble ladies. The

---

1. **Neva** (nē'və, nyĕ-vä'): a river.
2. **lapis lazuli** (lăp'ĭs lăz'yə-lē): a gemstone, azure-blue in color.
3. **Urals:** mountains in Russia that mark the border between Europe and Asia.
4. **Kremlin** (krĕm'lən): the citadel, or fortress, of Moscow.
5. **Muscovy** (mŭs'kə-vē): the Russian Empire.

railroad track ran straight as an arrow five hundred miles through the snow, the white birch forests, and the pines.

The train chuffed into the Moscow station, into a morning of sun and frost. The sun sparkled on the gold domes of churches, it glittered on the cuirasses[6] of a regiment of guards, all men of noble birth. Smoke rose straight up from chimneys. Twin jets of steam snorted from the nostrils of the three horses of the Czar's troika.[7] The Czar had a fine appetite.

The horses' hoofs kicked up gouts of snow as they galloped over the moat and through the gate in the Kremlin wall. The Czar walked up the royal staircase, carpeted in red and lined with bowing servants. He was thinking of the rolls.

He went through the formal greetings with a distracted look, then sat down eagerly at the breakfast table. Not a glance did he give the caviar, the smoked sterlets,[8] the pheasant in aspic. He watched the door. When a royal footman came through carrying a silver platter loaded with rolls, the Czar smiled. All was well.

The Czar rubbed his hands and took a steaming roll. He broke it open and the smile vanished from his face. A dead fly lay embedded in the bread. Courtiers crowded around to look.

"Bring Markov here!" said the Czar, with one of his terrible glances.

The banquet room was silent in tense horror. Markov came in puffing slightly but bearing himself with the pride of a master artist.

"Look at this, Markov," said the Czar, pointing at the fly, "and tell me what it is."

Markov looked and stood frozen for a moment. Princes, nobles, and servants all leaned forward waiting for doom to strike him. The Czar could bend horseshoes in his bare hands. A word from him and the bleak wastes of Siberia lay waiting.

No man could tell what Markov thought, but they knew that a fly had endangered his life. He reached to the platter and picked up the fly. He put it in his mouth and ate it. Every eye watched him swallow.

"It is a raisin, Sire," he said.

---

6. **cuirasses** (kwĭ-răs′əz): armor for the breast and back.
7. **troika** (troi′kə): a small carriage drawn by a team of three horses abreast.
8. **sterlets** (stûr′lĭts): sturgeon, a source of caviar.

Wrath faded from the Czar's face. He broke out laughing and the nobles relaxed.

"Markov," he said, "we grant you a coat of arms with a fly as the motif.[9] A fly imperiled your life and a fly saved your life."

And the Czar went on with his rolls.

9. **motif** (mō-tēf'): main figure in a design.

First Response: *What was your reaction to the story's ending? Did you find it amusing? silly? clever? Explain your answer.*

CHECKING UP

1. At what time of year does the story take place?
2. What form of transportation does the Czar use to travel from St. Petersburg to Moscow?
3. What is in the roll that the Czar breaks open?
4. What does Markov say is in the roll?
5. How does the Czar reward Markov?

TALKING IT OVER

1. The word *czar* comes from the name *Caesar*. How does the story show that the Russian Czar had unlimited power in his empire?
2. Instead of punishing Markov, the Czar rewards him. Why? What does the Czar find admirable in Markov?
3. Is this story merely an entertaining anecdote, or does it reveal insight into human nature?

NARRATIVE

A **narrative** is any story that is told. Narratives in everyday life appear in a variety of forms, both oral and written: for example, news stories; messages in letters or on postcards; jokes; bedtime stories; those family stories retold regularly by your parents, grandparents, or other relatives; and your daily accounts of what happened at school. The element that all these stories have in common is their *telling*. The purpose of a story is to tell about events that happened in a certain time period, in a certain sequence.

To bring the events in a narrative to life, storytellers show their characters acting and speaking just as we might see and hear them if we were witnessing the events ourselves.

1. Look at the passage that describes the czar eagerly awaiting the rolls. How does the storyteller cause you to feel that things are about to go wrong?
2. How does the author make that scene come to life?

UNDERSTANDING THE WORDS IN THE STORY
(Matching Columns)

1. ermine	a. overpowered with brilliance
2. pomp	b. endangered
3. dazzled	c. diverted; turned aside
4. renowned	d. brilliant display
5. moat	e. well known
6. distracted	f. severe; empty
7. embedded	g. violent anger
8. bleak	h. enclosed
9. wrath	i. white fur
10. imperiled	j. deep trench

WRITING IT DOWN
A Narrative

Think of an incident that you either witnessed or participated in, and that could be turned into an interesting story. Write about that incident in the form of a brief narrative.

Begin by jotting down the events that led up to the incident, if necessary, and a few phrases describing the incident itself. Make a list of the people who were involved, and note also where the incident took place. "Shape" your narrative (see pages 5–6) by omitting details that are not important, and by adding any details that might make the story more exciting.

If you have completed the Story Materials Chart on page 8, you might want to use that outline to write your narrative.

A Response

"No man could tell what Markov thought, but they knew that a fly had endangered his life," says the narrator of "Rolls for the Czar." What do you think went through Markov's mind at that crucial moment?

Imagine that you are Markov. The local news team is covering the Czar's visit to Moscow and, fascinated by your episode with the Czar, the reporters want to turn the incident into a news story. As they are interviewing you, they ask, "What went through your mind as the Czar pointed to the fly?" How will you answer?

Prepare to answer the reporters by writing your response in a paragraph or two. Begin by quickly jotting down all the random thoughts that raced through your mind at that critical instant.

THE PANTHER
A BEDTIME STORY
Pinckney Benedict

What kind of story is a "bedtime story"? Jot down some of your thoughts before you read "The Panther." Does this tale fit your idea of a bedtime story?

The boy led his spavined[1] horse through the dwarf brush that grew at the top of the mountain. The gelding's damaged leg was hot with pain, and he held its head close to him by its rope halter. He put his face against its warm brown neck and made soft comforting noises.

There were no roads; the boy followed vague trails that wandered among the trees and petered out and picked up again farther on. He wore a big-brimmed hat that he constantly pushed back from his forehead so he could see. He had a belt full of heavy brass cartridges slung over his shoulder. The cartridges fit the rifle that rode in a leather scabbard on the gelding's offside wither,[2] and they also fit the Colt revolver cinched against the boy's ribs under his jacket.

He had lost the panther he was trailing in the morning of the day. The panther was an aged mountain cat, a hunter gone sheep-stealer. The boy spent the afternoon looking for his way down off the mountain and didn't find it. Now it was evening and he was searching for a clear space to lay out his bedroll, some green forage for the gelding among the sticker bushes and stunted trees. He took a drink from his canteen, wet the palm of his hand, held it against the muzzle of the gelding.

The horse nickered[3] and stepped away from him, dancing on three good legs. The boy gripped the halter tight, reached over the gelding's neck, and unslung the rifle. He scanned the trees for the panther's form. The gelding shunted itself around in a wide half-circle, kicked at the brush, nipped the boy with its long yellow teeth. Hold up there, the boy said, trying to calm the horse. Hold up, he said again.

1. **spavined** (spăv′ĭnd): lame.
2. **wither:** highest part of the back.
3. **nickered:** made a low, whinnying sound.

14

An old woman stepped from the woods onto the narrow path and pushed past the struggling boy and horse. The gelding struck out at her. I'm sorry, the boy said. He was trying to keep the gelding back from the old woman, and it was a hard job. The gelding was trying to climb right over him.

The old woman backed off a couple of steps, watching the two of them for a second. She was dressed all in greasy leathers, and she carried a battered iron stewpot in her hand. He's gone crazy, the boy said. He never did anything like this before with me. The gelding had tangled its tack in a thick gorse[4] bush, and the boy dropped the rifle to try and pull it free. The old woman looked at the rifle and then headed down the path again.

Stand by a minute, the boy called after her. Is it a way down the mountain that you know of? The old woman vanished among the trees. The gelding stood shivering and blowing, still caught fast. It had torn its hide on the thorns as it fought, and the boy's hands were cut and bleeding. He worked to free it—reins, stirrups, mane, tail—and every time the gelding shifted, the boy gashed himself again. You, he said and slapped his fist against the gelding's dusty barrel side. You. The gelding held its lame foot tenderly off the ground, flared its nostrils.

The boy managed after a time to work the horse loose from the briers. He retrieved the rifle and set off down the path after the old woman. The gelding stumbled after him, stopping now and again to crop at the patches of thin yellow grass that grew along the edge of the path.

When it was full dark under the trees, the boy spied a light off to his left. As he approached, he saw the old woman sitting at her campfire in a little clearing. Her hair was wild and glowed orange in the light. The stewpot sat in the hot ashes at the edge of the fire, and the boy smelled lamb and onions and potatoes and pepper. He licked his lips. The gelding started to shy, and the boy tied the reins to a branch when he was still a dozen yards out of the clearing. Stand fast, he said to the gelding, and it pushed its broad head against his middle.

Hey granny, he said to the old woman as he walked into the camp. I'm sorry about the horse trying to bite back there, he said. He held out his arm, where a purple bruise was forming. He got me worse'n he did you, though, the boy said.

The old woman said to him, You got no rifle with you, son.

4. **gorse:** prickly evergreen shrubs.

A man don't carry long-arms into a stranger's camp, the boy said.

You got good manners, the old woman said. Get you some eat.

The boy took the stewpot from the fire and set to, eating with a spoon and metal dish that he carried with him. The stew was hot and filling, and the lamb was cooked tender. The old woman rolled a cigarette and smoked and watched him while he ate.

Thankee, the boy said when he was finished. You live alone all the way up here, do you? he said.

I'll show you a thing, the old woman said. It's a thing nobody else has ever seen, and a thing you'll not see again. I show it to you 'cause you got good manners, and 'cause you brought no rifle into my camp, she said.

Okay, the boy said.

Then you follow the path down the mountain, the old woman said, and she pointed the way out to him. You take it straight down the mountain, straight into the valley. And no more hunting the panther, she said, 'cause it ain't what you think it is, and it's the last one of them left.

Okay, the boy said.

And don't you touch that belly gun you got, the old woman said, and she smiled. You ain't *too* polite.

That's my daddy's lamb there in that pot, ain't it? the boy said.

The old woman threw back her head and her eyes rolled in their sockets. She fell to the ground and writhed in the dirt of the clearing floor, and her body shucked its uncured leathers. The boy touched the revolver at his waist, but the feel of it was foreign to the scene before him and he did not draw the gun.

Something rose on the far side of the fire, and it wasn't the old woman there anymore but the giant catamount.[5] Its great head was blunt, its eyes dark as key slots. Its long narrow body was covered with terrible scars. Some, the boy knew, he had inflicted, and his father and his family and those that peopled the valley. Others were the claw-work of beasts. Still others he imagined were the marks of the darts and spears of ancient savages.

The panther circled the boy, and he thought how he would tell his children and perhaps his grandchildren about the gray-yellow color of that hide and the puckers and tucks in the flesh and of the animal reek that suddenly hung in the air of the clearing.

5. **catamount** (kăt′ə-mount′): another word for a panther.

The panther leapt the fire, and the boy blinked in fear as it stood over him. He could feel its breath on him and hear the beat of its weary heart. Then it leapt again, and though he strove to watch, he did not know if the cat rushed along the ground or hurtled into the boughs of a tree or even if it sped upward and outward and vanished into the clear night sky.

First Response: *Did you suspect that there was something strange about the old woman? If so, at what point in the story?*

CHECKING UP (True/False)

1. The boy has lost the panther he had been trailing.
2. The boy cannot find his way down the mountain.
3. The boy is not surprised that the horse struck out at the old woman.
4. The old woman is wearing a tattered cotton dress.
5. The boy carries his rifle into the old woman's camp.

TALKING IT OVER

1. How do the boy's actions and speech show that he is considerate of others? How are his "good manners" important to the story?
2. **Atmosphere** is the overall mood or feeling that a story creates. What are some of the details that help create an atmosphere of mystery and eeriness?
3. What connection does the boy see between his family's sheep and the lamb in the woman's pot? Why does this connection turn out to be important?
4. What does the old woman mean when she says, "And no more hunting the panther 'cause it ain't what you think it is, and it's the last one of them left"?

5. A number of clues throughout the story serve to hint at, or **foreshadow,** the ending. For example, the horse strikes out at the woman because it recognizes her as the panther. What other examples of foreshadowing can you find?
6. The subtitle of "The Panther" is "A Bedtime Story." Do you consider this tale a kind of bedtime story? Why or why not?

ORAL TRADITION

The passing on of stories from one generation to the next is known as the **oral tradition.** In an oral tradition, stories are handed down by hearing and telling rather than by reading and writing. The author of "The Panther" grew up in West Virginia, one part of America where the tradition of oral storytelling still flourishes.

1. There are at least two references to oral tradition in "The Panther." The first is the subtitle. Where else in the story does Benedict refer to oral tradition?
2. Why do you think Benedict doesn't use quotation marks for the dialogue in this story?
3. What kinds of changes do you think tend to occur as a story is retold numerous times? What elements of such a story might tend to become exaggerated?

UNDERSTANDING THE WORDS IN THE STORY
(Matching Columns)

1.	reek	a.	struggled with great effort
2.	writhed	b.	prickly thorns
3.	forage	c.	strong, offensive smell
4.	cinched	d.	small metal flask
5.	shunted	e.	squirmed in agony
6.	strove	f.	bound or fastened firmly
7.	shy	g.	to move away suddenly
8.	canteen	h.	moved fast with great force
9.	hurtled	i.	moved or turned to one side
10.	briers	j.	food for animals

WRITING IT DOWN
A Well-Known Tale

Get together with your classmates and make a list of well-known stories and fairy tales. Choose one of those stories and write it down the way you remember it.

Reread your tale and then revise it so that it is a polished story. For example, if you were unable to recall specific details, make any changes necessary so that the story will make sense to those hearing it.

SPEAKING AND LISTENING
Retelling the Tale

Have each member of the class read his or her story aloud. To see how the oral tradition works, take note of the various versions of the same narrative. Are there any differences in facts, dialogue, sequence of events, or interpretation? The answers to these questions will probably surprise you.

ABOUT THE AUTHOR

Pinckney Benedict was born in 1964 and grew up on his family's dairy farm in Greenbrier Valley, West Virginia. He received his bachelor's degree from Princeton University, where he studied creative writing with the well-known author Joyce Carol Oates. He holds a master's degree in creative writing from the University of Iowa.

Benedict's tales are spun from the culture of the people of Greenbrier Valley and told in the rhythms of their Appalachian dialect. The rough hills, the barbershop, the farmers and mountain men, and the local banter and storytelling provide inspiration for his fiction.

Benedict published his first book of short stories, *Town Smokes* (1987), when he was twenty-three years old. He has recently completed a novel, *Dogs of God* (1994). "The Panther" is from his second collection of stories, *The Wrecking Yard* (1992).

AN ASTROLOGER'S DAY

R. K. Narayan

What is coincidence? If, say, you are having a conversation about dangerous snakes and a cobra suddenly appears, that is coincidence. Does the use of coincidence give a story an interesting "twist," or does it make a story less believable?

Punctually at midday he opened his bag and spread out his professional equipment, which consisted of a dozen cowrie shells,[1] a square piece of cloth with obscure mystic charts on it, a notebook and a bundle of palmyra[2] writing. His forehead was resplendent with sacred ash and vermilion,[3] and his eyes sparkled with a sharp abnormal gleam which was really an outcome of a continual searching look for customers, but which his simple clients took to be a prophetic light and felt comforted. The power of his eyes was considerably enhanced by their position—placed as they were between the painted forehead and the dark whiskers which streamed down his cheeks: even a half-wit's eyes would sparkle in such a setting. To crown the effect he wound a saffron-coloured turban around his head. This colour scheme never failed. People were attracted to him as bees are attracted to cosmos or dahlia stalks. He sat under the boughs of a spreading tamarind tree which flanked a path running through the Town Hall Park. It was a remarkable place in many ways: a surging crowd was always moving up and down this narrow road morning till night. A variety of trades and occupations was represented all along its way: medicine-sellers, sellers of stolen hardware and junk, magicians and, above all, an auctioneer of cheap cloth, who created enough din all day to attract the whole town. Next to him in vociferousness came a vendor of fried groundnuts, who gave his ware a fancy name each day, calling it Bombay Ice-Cream one day, and on the next Delhi Almond, and on the third Raja's Delicacy, and so on and so forth, and people flocked to him. A

1. **cowrie** (kou′rē) **shells:** glossy, brightly marked seashells.
2. **palmyra** (păl-mī′rə): a tall palm that grows throughout India. Ancient Hindu scholars used strips from its leaves for writing material.
3. **sacred ash and vermilion** (vər-mīl′yən): ashes mixed with a kind of red paint, used by Brahmans, Hindus of the highest caste, to indicate their status as priests.

considerable portion of this crowd dallied before the astrologer too. The astrologer transacted his business by the light of a flare which crackled and smoked up above the groundnut heap nearby. Half the enchantment of the place was due to the fact that it did not have the benefit of municipal lighting. The place was lit up by shop lights. One or two had hissing gaslights, some had naked flares stuck on poles, some were lit up by old cycle lamps and one or two, like the astrologer's, managed without lights of their own. It was a bewildering criss-cross of light rays and moving shadows. This suited the astrologer very well, for the simple reason that he had not in the least intended to be an astrologer when he began life; and he knew no more of what was going to happen to others than he knew what was going to happen to himself next minute. He was as much a stranger to the stars as were his innocent customers. Yet he said things which pleased and astonished everyone: that was more a matter of study, practise and shrewd guesswork. All the same, it was as much an honest man's labour as any other, and he deserved the wages he carried home at the end of a day.

He had left his village without any previous thought or plan. If he had continued there he would have carried on the work of his fore-fathers—namely, tilling the land, living, marrying and ripening in his cornfield and ancestral home. But that was not to be. He had to leave home without telling anyone, and he could not rest till he left it behind a couple of hundred miles. To a villager it is a great deal, as if an ocean flowed between.

He had a working analysis of mankind's troubles: marriage, money and the tangles of human ties. Long practise had sharpened his per-ception. Within five minutes he understood what was wrong. He charged three pies[4] per question and never opened his mouth till the other had spoken for at least ten minutes, which provided him enough stuff for a dozen answers and advices. When he told the person before him, gazing at his palm, "In many ways you are not getting the fullest results for your efforts," nine out of ten were disposed to agree with him. Or he questioned: "Is there any woman in your family, maybe even a distant relative, who is not well disposed towards you?" Or he gave an analysis of character: "Most of your troubles are due to your nature.

4. **pies** (pīs): A pie is a coin of slight value.

How can you be otherwise with Saturn where he is? You have an impetuous nature and a rough exterior." This endeared him to their hearts immediately, for even the mildest of us loves to think that he has a forbidding exterior.

The nuts-vendor blew out his flare and rose to go home. This was a signal for the astrologer to bundle up too, since it left him in darkness except for a little shaft of green light which strayed in from somewhere and touched the ground before him. He picked up his cowrie shells and paraphernalia and was putting them back into his bag when the green shaft of light was blotted out; he looked up and saw a man standing before him. He sensed a possible client and said: "You look so careworn. It will do you good to sit down for a while and chat with me." The other grumbled some vague reply. The astrologer pressed his invitation; whereupon the other thrust his palm under his nose, saying: "You call yourself an astrologer?" The astrologer felt challenged and said, tilting the other's palm towards the green shaft of light: "Yours is a nature . . ." "Oh, stop that," the other said. "Tell me something worthwhile. . . ."

Our friend felt piqued. "I charge only three pies per question, and what you get ought to be good enough for your money. . . ." At this the other withdrew his arm, took out an anna[5] and flung it out to him, saying, "I have some questions to ask. If I prove you are bluffing, you must return that anna to me with interest."

"If you find my answers satisfactory, will you give me five rupees?"

"No."

"Or will you give me eight annas?"

"All right, provided you give me twice as much if you are wrong," said the stranger. This pact was accepted after a little further argument. The astrologer sent up a prayer to heaven as the other lit a cheroot.[6] The astrologer caught a glimpse of his face by the matchlight. There was a pause as cars hooted on the road, *jutka*[7] drivers swore at their horses and the babble of the crowd agitated the semi-darkness of the park. The other sat down, sucking his cheroot, puffing out, sat there

5. **anna:** There are sixteen annas in a rupee. The rupee (roo′pē) is the monetary unit of India.

6. **cheroot** (shĕ-root′): a type of cigar.

7. *jutka* (jŭt′kə): a two-wheeled carriage.

ruthlessly. The astrologer felt very uncomfortable. "Here, take your anna back. I am not used to such challenges. It is late for me today. . . ." He made preparations to bundle up. The other held his wrist and said, "You can't get out of it now. You dragged me in while I was passing." The astrologer shivered in his grip; and his voice shook and became faint. "Leave me today. I will speak to you tomorrow." The other thrust his palm in his face and said, "Challenge is challenge. Go on." The astrologer proceeded with his throat drying up. "There is a woman . . ."

"Stop," said the other. "I don't want all that. Shall I succeed in my present search or not? Answer this and go. Otherwise I will not let you go till you disgorge all your coins." The astrologer muttered a few incantations and replied, "All right. I will speak. But will you give me a rupee if what I say is convincing? Otherwise I will not open my mouth, and you may do what you like." After a good deal of haggling the other agreed. The astrologer said, "You were left for dead. Am I right?"

"Ah, tell me more."

"A knife has passed through you once?" said the astrologer.

"Good fellow!" He bared his chest to show the scar. "What else?"

"And then you were pushed into a well nearby in the field. You were left for dead."

"I should have been dead if some passer-by had not chanced to peep into the well," exclaimed the other, overwhelmed by enthusiasm. "When shall I get at him?" he asked, clenching his fist.

"In the next world," answered the astrologer. "He died four months ago in a far-off town. You will never see any more of him." The other groaned on hearing it. The astrologer proceeded.

"Guru Nayak—"[8]

"You know my name!" the other said, taken aback.

"As I know all other things. Guru Nayak, listen carefully to what I have to say. Your village is two days' journey due north of this town. Take the next train and be gone. I see once again great danger to your life if you go from home." He took out a pinch of sacred ash and held it out to him. "Rub it on your forehead and go home. Never travel southward again, and you will live to be a hundred."

"Why should I leave home again?" the other said reflectively. "I was

---

8. **Guru Nayak** (gōō′rōō nī-yäk′).

only going away now and then to look for him and to choke out his life if I met him." He shook his head regretfully. "He has escaped my hands. I hope at least he died as he deserved." "Yes," said the astrologer. "He was crushed under a lorry."[9] The other looked gratified to hear it.

The place was deserted by the time the astrologer picked up his articles and put them into his bag. The green shaft was also gone, leaving the place in darkness and silence. The stranger had gone off into the night, after giving the astrologer a handful of coins.

It was nearly midnight when the astrologer reached home. His wife was waiting for him at the door and demanded an explanation. He flung the coins at her and said, "Count them. One man gave all that."

"Twelve and a half annas," she said, counting. She was overjoyed. "I can buy some *jaggery*[10] and coconut tomorrow. The child has been asking for sweets for so many days now. I will prepare some nice stuff for her."

"The swine has cheated me! He promised me a rupee," said the astrologer. She looked up at him. "You look worried. What is wrong?"

"Nothing."

After dinner, sitting on the *pyol*,[11] he told her, "Do you know a great load is gone from me today? I thought I had the blood of a man on my hands all these years. That was the reason why I ran away from home, settled here and married you. He is alive."

She gasped. "You tried to kill!"

"Yes, in our village, when I was a silly youngster. We drank, gambled and quarrelled badly one day—why think of it now? Time to sleep," he said, yawning, and stretched himself on the *pyol*.

---

9. **lorry:** a truck.
10. *jaggery* (jăg′ə-rē): brown sugar made from the sap of palm trees.
11. *pyol* (pyôl): a mat spread out for sleeping.

First Response: *Did you feel "tricked" by the author at the end of the story? Or did the ending explain some of the story's puzzling details?*

CHECKING UP (Multiple-Choice)

1. People are attracted to the astrologer because of his
   a. reputation
   b. appearance
   c. reasonable prices
2. The vendors' shops are set up
   a. on a narrow road
   b. on the main street
   c. at the marketplace
3. The astrologer had left his village
   a. with plans to marry
   b. to study philosophy
   c. without a plan
4. The astrologer advises Guru Nayak to
   a. seek a promotion
   b. return home
   c. travel abroad
5. Who was waiting for the astrologer when he returned home?
   a. the customer
   b. his mother
   c. his wife

TALKING IT OVER

1. The story's opening passages form the **exposition,** the part of a story that provides important background information. At what point does the actual **narrative** begin?
2. The astrologer knows nothing about either the stars or the future, yet his customers are always satisfied with the advice he gives. How does he manage to say things that "pleased and astonished everyone"?
3. The author describes in detail the way the various small shops are lit up at night. How is the effect of this lighting advantageous to the astrologer? How is the shop's lighting important to the story?
4. What coincidence becomes apparent to the astrologer when the customer's face is revealed by matchlight? How does the astrologer turn this coincidence to his own advantage?

5. How would you describe the astrologer's character? Is he clever? imaginative? hard-working? reckless? Support your answer with examples from the story.
6. Something said by a character that is the opposite of what readers expect or think appropriate is considered **ironic**. At the end of the story what is ironic about the astrologer's complaint that Guru Nayak has cheated him?

SURPRISE ENDING

Stories with a "twist," or **surprise ending,** have always been popular. These stories are most satisfying when the outcome is not the result of random chance, but the logical conclusion of the events of the story. The use of clues that prepare the reader for the story's ending is called **foreshadowing.**

1. What information in the story hints at, or foreshadows, the story's ending?
2. Early in the story we are told that the astrologer "knew no more of what was going to happen to others than he knew what was going to happen to himself next minute." How, then, does he manage to solve his problem and thus "write" the ending of his own story?

UNDERSTANDING THE WORDS IN THE STORY
(Matching Columns)

1. punctually	a. dangerous; threatening
2. resplendent	b. hasty; impulsive
3. enhanced	c. pleased; satisfied
4. vendor	d. resentful; offended
5. shrewd	e. insight; understanding
6. perception	f. dazzling; shining
7. impetuous	g. on time
8. forbidding	h. seller
9. piqued	i. clever; cunning
10. gratified	j. made greater; improved

WRITING IT DOWN
A Description

Much of the charm of this story comes from the author's vivid **description** of the astrologer. We can picture the gleaming eyes, the dark whiskers, and the colorful turban. The astrologer's character is described as well: he has "a working analysis of mankind's troubles. . . . Long practise had sharpened his perception."

Write a brief description of a character from your own imagination. Be sure to describe his or her appearance and personality. You might want to choose a character from the following list:

an old watchmaker	a librarian
a young athlete	a musician
a clown	a train conductor

SPEAKING AND LISTENING
Discussing a Story

The narrator considers the astrologer a good businessman who deserves the wages he takes home each day. Do you agree with that assessment? Or do you consider the astrologer a fraud and a con artist? Organize a round-table discussion with a small group of classmates to exchange opinions.

ABOUT THE AUTHOR

R. K. Narayan was born in the southern Indian city of Madras in 1906, when India was still a colony of Great Britain. He writes in English and, for the sake of his non-Indian readers, goes by his initials rather than his full name, Rasipuram Krishnaswami.

Narayan's writing depicts the colorful lives of Indians who are uneducated and live just above the poverty line. "An Astrologer's Day" is from the short-story collection *Malgudi Days.* Malgudi is a quaint, fictional place created by Narayan; it is populated by strange and memorable characters.

THE COLOMBER

Dino Buzzati°

People of all ages have imagined that strange sea creatures exist. Some of these fabled creatures, such as mermaids and mermen, are pictured as part human; others, like the Loch Ness Monster, are thought to be huge and terrifying. What kind of creature is the colomber?

When Stefano Roi was twelve years old, he asked his father, a sea captain and the owner of a fine sailing ship, to take him on board as his birthday gift.

"When I am grown up," the boy said, "I want to go to sea with you. And I shall command ships even more beautiful and bigger than yours."

"God bless you, my son," the father answered. And since his vessel had to leave that very day, he took the boy with him.

It was a splendid sunny day, and the sea was calm. Stefano, who had never been on a ship, happily wandered around on deck, admiring the complicated maneuvers of the sails. He asked the sailors about this and that, and they gladly explained everything to him.

When the boy had gone astern, he stopped, his curiosity aroused, to observe something that intermittently rose to the surface at a distance of two to three hundred kilometers,[1] in line with the ship's wake.

Although the ship was indeed moving fast, carried by a great quarter wind, that thing always maintained the same distance. And though the boy did not make out what it was, there was some indefinable air about it which attracted him intensely.

No longer seeing Stefano on deck, the father came down from the bridge after having shouted his name in vain, and went to look for him.

"Stefano, what are you doing there, standing so still?" the captain asked his son, finally perceiving him on the stern as he stared at the waves.

"Papa, come here and see."

The father came, and he too looked in the direction indicated by the boy, but he could not see anything.

° **Dino Buzzati** (dē′nō bōōt-tsä′tē).

1. **two to three hundred kilometers:** a kilometer is five-eighths of a mile; the distance here would be from 125 to 188 miles.

"There's a dark thing that rises in the wake every so often," Stefano said, "and it follows behind us."

"Despite my forty years," said the father, "I believe I still have good eyesight. But I see absolutely nothing."

After the boy insisted, the father went to get a telescope, and he scrutinized the surface of the sea, in line with the wake. Stefano saw him turn pale.

"What is it? Why do you make that face?"

"Oh, I wish I had never listened to you," the captain exclaimed. "Now I'm worried about you. What you see rising from the water and following us is not some object. That is a colomber. It's the fish that sailors fear above all others, in every sea in the world. It is a tremendous, mysterious shark, more clever than man. For reasons that perhaps no one will ever know, it chooses its victim, and when it has chosen, it pursues him for years and years, for his entire life, until it has succeeded in devouring him. And the strange thing is this: no one can see the colomber except the victim himself and his blood relations."

"It's not a story?"

"No. I have never seen it. But from descriptions I have heard many times, I immediately recognized it. That bison-like muzzle, that mouth continually opening and closing, those terrible teeth. Stefano, there's no doubt, the colomber has ominously chosen you, and as long as you go to sea, it will give you no peace. Listen to me: we are going back to land now, immediately; you will go ashore and never leave it again, not for any reason whatsoever. You must promise me you won't. Seafaring is not for you, my son. You must resign yourself. After all, you will be able to make your fortune on land too."

Having said this, he immediately reversed his course, reentered the port, and on the pretext of a sudden illness, he put his son ashore. Then he left again without him.

Deeply troubled, the boy remained on the shore until the last tip of the masts sank behind the horizon. Beyond the pier that bounded the port, the sea was completely deserted. But looking carefully, Stefano could perceive a small black point which intermittently surfaced on the water: it was "his" colomber, slowly moving back and forth, obstinately waiting for him.

From then on, with every expedient the boy was dissuaded from his desire to go to sea. His father sent him to study at an inland city, hundreds of kilometers away. And for some time, distracted by his new surroundings, Stefano no longer thought about the sea monster.

Still, he returned home for summer vacations, and the first thing he did, as soon as he had some free time, was hurry to the end of the pier for a kind of verification, although he fundamentally considered it unnecessary. After so many years, even supposing that all the stories his father told him were true, the colomber had certainly given up its siege.

But Stefano stood there, astonished, his heart pounding. At a distance of two to three hundred meters from the pier, in the open sea, the sinister fish was moving back and forth, slowly, raising its muzzle from the water every now and then and turning toward land, as if it anxiously watched for whether Stefano was coming at last.

So, the idea of that hostile creature waiting for him day and night became a secret obsession for Stefano. And even in the distant city it cropped up to wake him with worry in the middle of the night. He was safe, of course; hundreds of kilometers separated him from the colomber. And yet he knew that beyond the mountains, beyond the forests and the plains, the shark was waiting for him. He might have moved even to the most remote continent, and still the colomber would have appeared in the mirror of the nearest sea, with the inexorable obstinacy of a fatal instrument.

Stefano, who was a serious and eager boy, profitably continued his studies, and as soon as he was a man, he found a dignified and well-paying position at an emporium[2] in that inland city. Meanwhile, his father died through illness, his magnificent ship was sold by his widow, and his son found himself the heir to a modest fortune. Work, friends, diversions, first love affairs—Stefano's life was now well under way, but the thought of the colomber nonetheless tormented him like a mirage that was fatal and fascinating at the same time; and as the days passed, rather than disappear, it seemed to become more insistent.

Great are the satisfactions of an industrious, well-to-do, and quiet life, but greater still is the attraction of the abyss. Stefano was hardly twenty-two years old when, having said good-bye to his inland friends

---

2. **emporium** (ĕm-pôr′ē-əm): trading center; large store.

and resigned from his job, he returned to his native city and told his mother of his firm intention to follow his father's trade. The woman, to whom Stefano had never mentioned the mysterious shark, joyfully welcomed his decision. To have her son abandon the sea for the city had always seemed to her, in her heart, a betrayal of the family's tradition.

Stefano began to sail, giving proof of his seaworthiness, his resistance to fatigue, and his intrepid spirit. He sailed and sailed, and in the wake of his ship, day and night, in good weather and in storms, the colomber trudged along. He knew that this was his curse and his penalty, and precisely for this reason, perhaps, he did not find the strength to sever himself from it. And no one on board, except him, perceived the monster.

"Don't you see anything over there?" he asked his companions from time to time, pointing at the wake.

"No, we don't see anything at all. Why?"

"I don't know. It seemed to me . . ."

"You didn't see a colomber, by any chance, did you?" the sailors asked, laughing and touching wood.

"Why are you laughing? Why are you touching wood?"

"Because the colomber is an animal that spares no one. And if it has begun to follow this ship, it means that one of us is doomed."

But Stefano did not slacken. The uninterrupted threat that followed on his heels seemed in fact to strengthen his will, his passion for the sea, his courage in times of strife and danger.

When he felt that he was master of his trade, he used his modest patrimony to acquire a small steam freighter with a partner, then he became the sole proprietor of it, and thanks to a series of successful shipments, he could subsequently buy a true merchantman, setting out with always more ambitious aims. But the successes, and the millions, were unable to remove that continual torment from his soul; nor did he ever try, on the other hand, to sell the ship and retire to undertake different enterprises on land.

To sail and sail was his only thought. Just as soon as he set foot on land in some port after a long journey, the impatience to depart again immediately pricked him. He knew that outside the colomber was waiting for him, and that the colomber was synonymous with ruin. With nothingness. An indomitable impulse dragged him without rest, from one ocean to another.

Until, one day, Stefano suddenly realized that he had grown old, very old; and no one around him could explain why, rich as he was, he did not finally leave the cursed life of the sea. He was old, and bitterly unhappy, because his entire existence had been spent in that mad flight across the seas, to escape his enemy. But the temptation of the abyss had always been greater for him than the joys of a prosperous and quiet life.

One evening, while his magnificent ship was anchored offshore the port where he was born, he felt close to death. He then called his second officer, in whom he had great trust, and ordered him not to oppose what he was about to do. The other man promised, on his honor.

Having gotten this assurance, Stefano revealed to the second officer the story of the colomber that continued to pursue him uselessly for nearly fifty years. The officer listened to him, frightened.

"It has escorted me from one end of the world to the other," Stefano said, "with a faithfulness that not even the noblest friend could have shown. Now I am about to die. The colomber too will be terribly old and weary by now. I cannot betray it."

Having said this, he took his leave of the crew, ordered a small boat to be lowered into the sea, and boarded it, after he made them give him a harpoon.

"Now I am going to meet it," he announced. "It isn't right to disappoint it. But I shall struggle, with all my might."

With a few weary strokes of the oars, he drew away from the side of the ship. Officers and sailors saw him disappear down below, on the placid sea, shrouded in the nocturnal shadows. In the sky was a crescent moon.

He did not have to work very hard. Suddenly the colomber's horrible snout emerged at the side of the boat.

"Here I am with you, finally," Stefano said. "Now it's just the two of us." And gathering his remaining strength, he raised the harpoon to strike.

"Uh," the colomber groaned, imploringly, "what a long journey it's taken to find you. I too am wasted with fatigue. How much you made me swim. And you kept on fleeing. You never understood at all."

"What?" asked Stefano, with the point of his harpoon over the colomber's heart.

"I have not pursued you around the world to devour you, as you thought. I was charged by the King of the Sea only to deliver this to you."

And the shark stuck out its tongue, offering the old captain a small phosphorescent[3] sphere.

Stefano picked it up and examined it. It was a pearl of disproportionate size. And he recognized it as the famous *Perla del Mare*,[4] which brought luck, power, love, and peace of mind to whoever possessed it. But now it was too late.

"Alas!" said the captain, shaking his head sadly. "How wrong it all is. I managed to condemn myself, and I have ruined your life."

"Good-bye, poor man," answered the colomber. And it sank into the black waters forever.

Two months later, pushed by an undertow, a small boat came alongside an abrupt reef. It was sighted by several fishermen who drew near, curious. In the boat, still seated, was a sun-bleached skeleton: between the little bones of its fingers it grasped a small round stone.

The colomber is a huge fish, frightening to behold and extremely rare. Depending on the sea, and the people who live by its shores, the fish is also called the kolombrey, kahloubrha, kalonga, kalu-balu, chalung-gra. Naturalists strangely ignore it. Some even maintain that it does not exist.

3. **phosphorescent** (fäs′fə-rĕs′ənt): glowing.
4. *Perla del Mare* (pĕr′lä dĕl mä′rā): pearl of the sea.

First Response: *How did you feel at the end of the story, when the colomber's true mission was revealed?*

CHECKING UP

1. When Stefano turns twelve, what does he ask of his father as a birthday gift?
2. According to Stefano's father, for how long does the colomber pursue its victim?
3. What decision does Stefano make when he is twenty-two years old?
4. To whom does Stefano reveal the story of the colomber?
5. What does the colomber give Stefano before it sinks into the black waters forever?

TALKING IT OVER

1. After his father's death, Stefano decides to ignore the advice his father had given him and become a sea captain. Why does he make this decision?
2. In the "twist" that ends this story, how does the colomber turn out to be quite different from what Stefano had been led to expect?
3. Which passages depict the colomber as an animal waiting for its master? Which passages in the story show that Stefano, in a sense, identifies with the colomber? Could these passages be considered clues to the story's ending?
4. What evidence in the story suggests that the colomber may really be a part of Stefano's own nature? If the colomber exists only in Stefano's mind, is it any less "real," in your view?
5. The narrator says of Stefano that "The temptation of the abyss had always been greater for him than the joys of a prosperous and quiet life." What does this comment reveal about Stefano's character? How does this statement relate to the colomber's gift of the pearl at the end of the story?
6. Even when Stefano is in an inland city hundreds of kilometers from the sea, he worries about the colomber. Why is the colomber a source of torment for him even when he is far away from it? How has Stefano been "devoured" by the colomber even though he has lived out his life?

7. Do you think Stefano could have led a life of contentment and satisfaction? Or does the story suggest that some people are singled out by destiny and their own natures to lead lives of restless searching? Support your answer with details from the text.

FANTASY AND MAGICAL REALISM

Literature that is highly imaginative and makes use of unrealistic settings and characters is known as **fantasy**. Fantasy deals with imaginary worlds, such as societies beneath the sea and enchanted forests, and creatures like dragons, elves, ghosts, and talking animals. Fairy tales and science fiction are two well-known types of fantasy literature.

"The Colomber" takes place in the real world and its characters are ordinary people, yet the story seems just slightly unreal. The story is a special type of fantasy called **magical realism**, which has become popular among contemporary writers. In this type of fiction, the author uses settings that are realistic, but also slips in fantastic elements in an almost casual way.

In the fifth paragraph, for example, Buzzati describes Stefano peering into the distance from the stern of his father's ship. This description is entirely realistic, except that Stefano is observing something "at a distance of two to three hundred kilometers," a length about ten times greater than the distance at which an object can be seen with the naked eye.

In realistic literature, the presence of a "colomber" would cause quite a stir. In magical realism, such a creature is an accepted part of a strange and different reality.

1. What are some of the other elements of fantasy in the story?
2. How does the story's final paragraph blend fantasy with reality?
3. Authors often use magical realism to write thought-provoking fantasies on serious themes. What do you think is the underlying message of this fantasy? How is the colomber fantastic on one level and possibly very "real" on another?

UNDERSTANDING THE WORDS IN THE STORY
(Matching Columns)

1. astern	a. at intervals
2. wake	b. means to an end
3. pretext	c. examined carefully
4. dissuaded	d. persisting concern or idea
5. intermittently	e. excuse
6. indefinable	f. at or to the rear of a ship
7. scrutinized	g. turned aside
8. expedient	h. ship's trail in the water
9. obsession	i. threateningly
10. ominously	j. vague; unclear

(Multiple-Choice)

1. Stefano's career shows the great attraction of the *abyss* for certain people.
   a. marketplace
   b. bottomless gulf
   c. sea
2. The colomber kept appearing with *inexorable* obstinacy.
   a. unrelenting
   b. noisy
   c. savage
3. Despite his crew's remarks, Stefano's will did not *slacken*.
   a. harden
   b. weaken
   c. alter
4. Stefano used his *patrimony* to acquire a freighter.
   a. bargaining skill
   b. credit
   c. inheritance
5. An *indomitable* impulse dragged Stefano from ocean to ocean.
   a. imaginary
   b. interesting
   c. unconquerable

6. Stefano proved his seaworthiness and his *intrepid* spirit.
   a. strong
   b. joking
   c. fearless
7. When Stefano set out in the rowboat, the sea was *placid*.
   a. calm
   b. misty
   c. choppy
8. The rowboat disappeared in the *nocturnal* shadows.
   a. nighttime
   b. thin
   c. nightmarish
9. The colomber's horrible *snout* suddenly appeared.
   a. tail
   b. muzzle
   c. fin
10. When Stefano raised his harpoon, the colomber groaned *imploringly*.
    a. loudly
    b. faintly
    c. pleadingly

WRITING IT DOWN
Notes for a Story

In "The Colomber" you have seen how a writer can blend fantasy and realism to create a striking tale.

Freewrite for ten minutes to develop ideas for a story of your own. You can use real-life experiences and settings as a basis for your story, or you can use imaginary, even fantastic events. Remember that anything can be fuel for your imagination when you write a story: a difficult test, a movie you saw recently, a conversation with a family member, or a humorous episode involving a pet. When you have completed your freewriting, get together with a small group of classmates to share and discuss story ideas.

If you wish, use these notes to write a short short story.

ABOUT THE AUTHOR

Dino Buzzati (1906–1972) was born in Belluno, a small city in northern Italy. He spent most of his life in Milan, where he earned a law degree and worked as a writer and journalist.

Buzzati published two novels in the 1930s, but it was his third, *Il deserto dei Tartari* (1940, translated as *The Tartar Steppe*) that brought him international recognition. The novel tells of a young lieutenant who is stationed at a fortress to await the invasion of the Tartars and, along with his fellow officers, becomes obsessed with the desire to display his military prowess. The threatened attack, while giving meaning to their lives, never comes. Years pass, and the waiting soldiers grow old and die or are sent to other posts. They have lost the real battle, the one against time.

Buzzati's writing is steeped in existentialist philosophy, which was widespread in Europe during the 1940s and 1950s. Like *The Tartar Steppe*, the many short stories he wrote at that time reflect the existentialist view of the meaninglessness of life and the absurdity of human existence.

Buzzati is known for his unusual approach to fantasy; he uses journalistic devices to blur the distinction between the bizarre and the real. In "The Colomber," for example, he relates fantastic incidents as if they were everyday events. He once said, "When I relate something of a fantastic nature, I must make the greatest effort to render it plausible and convincing . . . it seems to me, fantasy should be as close as possible to journalism . . . the effectiveness of a fantastic story will depend on its being told in the most simple and practical terms."

THREE WISE GUYS
UN CUENTO DE NAVIDAD/
A CHRISTMAS STORY
Sandra Cisneros

The "Day of the Kings," observed on January 6, celebrates the journey of the Three Wise Men who brought gifts to the stable where the Christ child was born. In many countries, people exchange gifts on this day, rather than on Christmas. Make a short list of some holiday celebrations from cultures other than your own.

The big box came marked DO NOT OPEN TILL XMAS, but the mama said not until the Day of the Three Kings. Not until Día de los Reyes, the sixth of January, do you hear? That is what the mama said exactly, only she said it all in Spanish. Because in Mexico where she was raised, it is the custom for boys and girls to receive their presents on January sixth, and not Christmas, even though they were living on the Texas side of the river[1] now. Not until the sixth of January.

Yesterday the mama had risen in the dark same as always to reheat the coffee in a tin saucepan and warm the breakfast tortillas.[2] The papa had gotten up coughing and spitting up the night, complaining how the evening before the buzzing of the chicharras[3] had kept him from sleeping. By the time the mama had the house smelling of oatmeal and cinnamon, the papa would be gone to the fields, the sun already tangled in the trees and the urracas[4] screeching their rubber-screech cry. The boy Ruben and the girl Rosalinda would have to be shaken awake for school. The mama would give the baby Gilberto his bottle and then she would go back to sleep before getting up again to the

---

1. **river:** the Rio Grande, which separates Mexico and Texas.
2. **tortillas** (tôr-tē′yäs): thin, flat cakes of cornmeal or flour, cooked on a griddle.
3. **chicharras** (chē-chä′räs): cicadas, insects that make a loud, shrill sound.
4. **urracas** (ōō-rä′käs): magpies, black and white birds of the crow family, known for their noisy chattering.

chores that were always waiting. That is how the world had been.

But today the big box had arrived. When the boy Ruben and the girl Rosalinda came home from school, it was already sitting in the living room in front of the television set that no longer worked. Who had put it there? Where had it come from? A box covered with red paper with green Christmas trees and a card on top that said "Merry Christmas to the Gonzales Family. Frank, Earl, and Dwight Travis. P.S. DO NOT OPEN TILL XMAS." That's all.

Two times the mama was made to come into the living room, first to explain to the children and later to their father how the brothers Travis had arrived in the blue pickup, and how it had taken all three of those big men to lift the box off the back of the truck and bring it inside, and how she had had to nod and say thank-you thank-you thank-you over and over because those were the only words she knew in English. Then the brothers Travis had nodded as well, the way they always did when they came and brought the boxes of clothes, or the turkey each November, or the canned ham on Easter, ever since the children had begun to earn high grades at the school where Dwight Travis was the principal.

But this year the Christmas box was bigger than usual. What could be in a box so big? The boy Ruben and the girl Rosalinda begged all afternoon to be allowed to open it, and that is when the mama had said the sixth of January, the Day of the Three Kings. Not a day sooner.

It seemed the weeks stretched themselves wider and wider since the arrival of the big box. The mama got used to sweeping around it because it was too heavy for her to push in a corner. But since the television no longer worked ever since the afternoon the children had poured iced tea through the little grates in the back, it really didn't matter if the box obstructed the view. Visitors that came inside the house were told and told again the story of how the box had arrived, and then each was made to guess what was inside.

It was the comadre[5] Elodia who suggested over coffee one afternoon that the big box held a portable washing machine that could be rolled away when not in use, the kind she had seen in her Sears Roebuck catalog. The mama said she hoped so because the wringer washer she had used for the last ten years had finally gotten tired and quit. These past few weeks

5. **comadre** (kō-mä′*th*rā): literally, "co-mother," a woman who is a relative or close friend of the family.

she had had to boil all the clothes in the big pot she used for cooking the Christmas tamales. Yes. She hoped the big box was a portable washing machine. A washing machine, even a portable one, would be good. But the neighbor man Cayetano said, What foolishness, comadre. Can't you see the box is too small to hold a washing machine, even a portable one. Most likely God has heard your prayers and sent a new color TV. With a good antenna you could catch all the Mexican soap operas, the neighbor man said. You could distract yourself with the complicated troubles of the rich and then give thanks to God for the blessed simplicity of your poverty. A new TV would surely be the end to all your miseries.

Each night when the papa came home from the fields, he would spread newspapers on the cot in the living room, where the boy Ruben and the girl Rosalinda slept, and sit facing the big box in the center of the room. Each night he imagined the box held something different. The day before yesterday he guessed a new record player. Yesterday an ice chest filled with beer. Today the papa sat with his bottle of beer, fanning himself with a magazine, and said in a voice as much a plea as a prophecy: air conditioner.

But the boy Ruben and the girl Rosalinda were sure the big box was filled with toys. They had even punctured it in one corner with a pencil when their mother was busy cooking, but they could see nothing inside but blackness.

Only the baby Gilberto remained uninterested in the contents of the big box and seemed each day more fascinated with the exterior of the box rather than the interior. One afternoon he tore off a fistful of paper, which he was chewing when his mother swooped him up with one arm, rushed him to the kitchen sink, and forced him to swallow handfuls of lukewarm water in case the red dye of the wrapping paper might be poisonous.

When Christmas Eve finally came, the family Gonzalez put on their good clothes and went to Midnight Mass. They came home to a house that smelled of tamales[6] and atole,[7] and everyone was allowed to open one present before going to sleep. But the big box was to remain untouched until the sixth of January.

On New Year's Eve the little house was filled with people, some

---

6. **tamales** (tä-mä′läs): meat, tomato sauce, and red peppers rolled in cornmeal and cooked in a corn husk.
7. **atole** (ä-tō′lä): broth made from corn flour.

related, some not, coming in and out. The friends of the papa came with bottles, and the mama set out a bowl of grapes to count off the New Year. That night the children did not sleep in the living room cot as they usually did, because the living room was crowded with big-fannied ladies and fat-stomached men sashaying to the accordion music of the midget twins from McAllen.[8] Instead the children fell asleep on a lump of handbags and crumpled suit jackets on top of the mama and the papa's bed, dreaming of the contents of the big box.

Finally, the fifth of January. And the boy Ruben and the girl Rosalinda could hardly sleep. All night they whispered last-minute wishes. The boy thought perhaps if the big box held a bicycle, he would be the first to ride it, since he was the oldest. This made his sister cry until the mama had to yell from her bedroom on the other side of the plastic curtains, Be quiet or I'm going to give you each the stick, which sounds worse in Spanish than it does in English. Then no one said anything. After a very long time, long after they heard the mama's wheezed breathing and the papa's piped snoring, the children closed their eyes and remembered nothing.

The papa was already in the bathroom coughing up the night before from his throat when the urracas began their clownish chirping. The boy Ruben awoke and shook his sister. The mama, frying the potatoes and beans for breakfast, nodded permission for the box to be opened.

With a kitchen knife the boy Ruben cut a careful edge along the top. The girl Rosalinda tore the Christmas wrapping with her fingernails. The papa and the mama lifted the cardboard flaps and everyone peered inside to see what it was the brothers Travis had brought them on the Day of the Three Kings.

There were layers of balled newspaper packed on top. When these had been cleared away the boy Ruben looked inside. The girl Rosalinda looked inside. The papa and the mama looked.

This is what they saw: the complete Britannica Junior Encyclopaedia, twenty-four volumes in red imitation leather with gold-embossed letters, beginning with Volume I, Aar–Bel and ending with Volume XXIV, Yel–Zyn. The girl Rosalinda let out a sad cry, as if her hair was going to be cut again. The boy Ruben pulled out Volume IV, Ded–Fem. There were

8. **McAllen:** a city in southeast Texas, near the Mexican border.

many pictures and many words, but there were more words than pictures. The papa flipped through Volume XXII, but because he could not read English words, simply put the book back and grunted, What can we do with this? No one said anything, and shortly after, the screen door slammed.

Only the mama knew what to do with the contents of the big box. She withdrew Volumes VI, VII, and VIII, marched off to the dinette set in the kitchen, placed two on Rosalinda's chair so she could better reach the table, and put one underneath the plant stand that danced.

When the boy and the girl returned from school that day they found the books stacked into squat pillars against one living room wall and a board placed on top. On this were arranged several plastic doilies and framed family photographs. The rest of the volumes the baby Gilberto was playing with, and he was already rubbing his sore gums along the corners of Volume XIV.

The girl Rosalinda also grew interested in the books. She took out her colored pencils and painted blue on the eyelids of all the illustrations of women and with a red pencil dipped in spit she painted their lips and fingernails red-red. After a couple of days, when all the pictures of women had been colored in this manner, she began to cut out some of the prettier pictures and paste them on looseleaf paper.

One volume suffered from being exposed to the rain when the papa improvised a hat during a sudden shower. He forgot it on the hood of the car when he drove off. When the children came home from school they set it on the porch to dry. But the pages puffed up and became so fat, the book was impossible to close.

Only the boy Ruben refused to touch the books. For several days he avoided the principal because he didn't know what to say in case Mr. Travis were to ask how they were enjoying the Christmas present.

On the Saturday after New Year's the mama and the papa went into town for groceries and left the boy in charge of watching his sister and baby brother. The girl Rosalinda was stacking books into spiral staircases and making her paper dolls descend them in a fancy manner.

Perhaps the boy Ruben would not have bothered to open the volume left on the kitchen table if he had not seen his mother wedge her name-day[9] corsage in its pages. On the page where the mama's

---

9. **name-day:** the feast day of the saint for whom a person is named.

carnation lay pressed between two pieces of Kleenex was a picture of a dog in a space ship. FIRST DOG IN SPACE the caption said. The boy turned to another page and read where cashews came from. And then about the man who invented the guillotine. And then about Bengal tigers. And about clouds. All afternoon the boy read, even after the mama and the papa came home. Even after the sun set, until the mama said time to sleep and put the light out.

In their bed on the other side of the plastic curtain the mama and the papa slept. Across from them in the crib slept the baby Gilberto. The girl Rosalinda slept on her end of the cot. But the boy Ruben watched the night sky turn from violet. To blue. To gray. And then from gray. To blue. To violet once again.

First Response: *How did you feel when the gift turned out to be a set of encyclopedias? Were you surprised? disappointed? amused?*

CHECKING UP

1. Who are the brothers Travis?
2. When did the brothers first begin bringing gifts to the Gonzalez family?
3. What does the comadre Elodia think the box contains?
4. What does Rosalinda do with the books?
5. Why does Ruben avoid Mr. Travis for several days after opening the gift?

TALKING IT OVER

1. Why does the mother insist that the family wait until January sixth to open the box?
2. What details in the story show that, although the mother and father work hard, the family is not well off?

3. Each member of the family is hoping that the box contains something different. How do these wishes reflect the needs and longings of each one?
4. Why does the neighbor Cayetano think that a color television would be a good gift?
5. How does the story suggest that the gift is a "turning point" in the life of Ruben?
6. What do you think is the significance of the story's title? Who are the "three wise guys"?

PARABLE

A **parable** is a short, simple tale—usually about an everyday event—from which a moral or spiritual lesson can be drawn. Some well-known parables are those in the New Testament of the Bible, such as the story of the Good Samaritan (Luke 10:30–37).

The subtitle "A Christmas Story," as well as the style of the tale and the allusion to the Biblical narrative of the wise men, suggests that "Three Wise Guys" may be read as a parable.

The moral of a parable is usually left unstated. How would you state the lesson of "Three Wise Guys" in your own words?

UNDERSTANDING THE WORDS IN THE STORY (Multiple-Choice)

1. obstructed	a. prediction
2. portable	b. columns
3. distract	c. short and thick
4. plea	d. go downward
5. prophecy	e. request
6. sashaying	f. blocked
7. squat	g. created on the spot
8. pillars	h. divert the attention of
9. improvised	i. gliding
10. descend	j. movable

WRITING IT DOWN
A Report on an Interview

Ask an older member of your family to describe the memory of a holiday, a family reunion, or a special gift. As you hold your interview, take note of interesting details that could form the basis of a short story.

To prepare for your interview, make a list of questions you will ask. After the interview, organize your results by filling out a chart such as the one below:

INTERVIEW CHART

PERSON INTERVIEWED:

_____

EVENT/OBJECT DESCRIBED:

_____

WHO WAS INVOLVED? (Characters)

_____

_____

_____

WHAT HAPPENED? (Plot)

_____

_____

_____

WHEN AND WHERE DID THE EPISODE HAPPEN? (Setting)

_____

_____

Sandra Cisneros was born in Chicago in 1954. She often felt displaced and homeless growing up, moving frequently between Mexico and the United States with her Mexican father, Chicana mother, and six brothers.

Cisneros experienced a turning point during a classroom discussion at the University of Iowa Writers Workshop. Realizing for the first time that her background and upbringing set her apart from the rest of her classmates, she decided to turn to her own childhood memories for the subject matter of her writing.

Cisneros is best known for *The House on Mango Street* (1983), a collection of fictional sketches featuring a young Hispanic girl named Esperanza. She writes in a style that is a blend of prose and poetry and emphasizes dialogue and imagery rather than traditional narrative forms. Cisneros has also published a short-story collection called *Woman Hollering Creek* (1991) and three volumes of poetry.

THE TROUT

Sean O'Faolain°

Have you ever solved a problem or fixed a bad situation by taking matters into your own hands? If so, write a sentence or two about the experience.

One of the first places Julia always ran to when they arrived in G—— was The Dark Walk. It is a laurel walk, very old; almost gone wild, a lofty midnight tunnel of smooth, sinewy branches. Underfoot the tough brown leaves are never dry enough to crackle: there is always a suggestion of damp and cool trickle.

She raced right into it. For the first few yards she always had the memory of the sun behind her, then she felt the dusk closing swiftly down on her so that she screamed with pleasure and raced on to reach the light at the far end; and it was always just a little too long in coming so that she emerged gasping, clasping her hands, laughing, drinking in the sun. When she was filled with the heat and glare she would turn and consider the ordeal again.

This year she had the extra joy of showing it to her small brother, and of terrifying him as well as herself. And for him the fear lasted longer because his legs were so short and she had gone out at the far end while he was still screaming and racing.

When they had done this many times they came back to the house to tell everybody that they had done it. He boasted. She mocked. They squabbled.

"Cry babby!"

"You were afraid yourself, so there!"

"I won't take you anymore."

"You're a big pig."

"I hate you."

Tears were threatening so somebody said, "Did you see the well?" She opened her eyes at that and held up her long, lovely neck suspiciously and decided to be incredulous. She was twelve and at that age little girls are beginning to suspect most stories: they have already found

---

° **Sean O'Faolain** (shôn ō-fə-lôn', -līn').

out too many, from Santa Claus to the Stork. How could there be a well! In The Dark Walk? That she had visited year after year? Haughtily she said, "Nonsense."

But she went back, pretending to be going somewhere else, and she found a hole scooped in the rock at the side of the walk, choked with damp leaves, so shrouded by ferns that she uncovered it only after much searching. At the back of this little cavern there was about a quart of water. In the water she suddenly perceived a panting trout. She rushed for Stephen and dragged him to see, and they were both so excited that they were no longer afraid of the darkness as they hunched down and peered in at the fish panting in his tiny prison, his silver stomach going up and down like an engine.

Nobody knew how the trout got there. Even old Martin in the kitchen garden laughed and refused to believe that it was there, or pretended not to believe, until she forced him to come down and see. Kneeling and pushing back his tattered old cap he peered in.

"You're right. How did that fella get there?"

She stared at him suspiciously.

"You knew?" she accused; but he said, "The divil a know"; and reached down to lift it out. Convinced, she hauled him back. If she had found it then it was her trout.

Her mother suggested that a bird had carried the spawn. Her father thought that in the winter a small streamlet might have carried it down there as a baby, and it had been safe until the summer came and the water began to dry up. She said, "I see," and went back to look again and consider the matter in private. Her brother remained behind, wanting to hear the whole story of the trout, not really interested in the actual trout but much interested in the story which his mummy began to make up for him on the lines of, "So one day Daddy Trout and Mammy Trout . . ." When he retailed[1] it to her she said, "Pooh."

It troubled her that the trout was always in the same position; he had no room to turn; all the time the silver belly went up and down; otherwise he was motionless. She wondered what he ate and in between visits to Joey Pony, and the boat and a bathe to get cool, she thought of his hunger. She brought him down bits of dough; once she brought him a

1. **retailed** (rĭ-tāld′): retold.

worm. He ignored the food. He just went on panting. Hunched over him she thought how, all the winter, while she was at school he had been there. All the winter, in The Dark Walk, all day, all night, floating around alone. She drew the leaf of her hat down around her ears and chin and stared. She was thinking of it as she lay in bed.

It was late in June, the longest days of the year. The sun had sat still for a week, burning up the world. Although it was after ten o'clock it was still bright and still hot. She lay on her back under a single sheet, with her long legs spread, trying to keep cool. She could see the D of the moon through the fir tree—they slept on the ground floor. Before they went to bed her mummy had told Stephen the story of the trout again, and she, in her bed, had resolutely presented her back to them and read her book. But she had kept one ear cocked.

"And so, in the end, this naughty fish who would not stay at home got bigger and bigger and bigger, and the water got smaller and smaller. . . ."

Passionately she had whirled and cried, "Mummy, don't make it a horrible old moral story!" Her mummy had brought in a Fairy God-mother, then, who sent lots of rain, and filled the well, and a stream poured out and the trout floated away down to the river below. Staring at the moon she knew that there are no such things as Fairy Godmothers and that the trout, down in The Dark Walk, was panting like an engine. She heard somebody unwind a fishing reel. Would the *beasts* fish him out!

She sat up. Stephen was a hot lump of sleep, lazy thing. The Dark Walk would be full of little scraps of moon. She leaped up and looked out the window, and somehow it was not so lightsome now that she saw the dim mountains far away and the black firs against the breathing land and heard a dog say bark-bark. Quietly she lifted the ewer of water, and climbed out the window and scuttled along the cool but cruel gravel down to the maw[2] of the tunnel. Her pajamas were very short so that when she splashed water it wet her ankles. She peered into the tunnel. Something alive rustled inside there. She raced in, and up and down she raced, and flurried, and cried aloud, "Oh, gosh, I can't find it," and then at last she did. Kneeling down in the damp she put her hand into the slimy hole. When the body lashed they were both mad

---

2. **maw** (mô): here, a large opening.

with fright. But she gripped him and shoved him into the ewer and raced, with her teeth ground, out to the other end of the tunnel and down the steep paths to the river's edge.

All the time she could feel him lashing his tail against the side of the ewer. She was afraid he would jump right out. The gravel cut into her soles until she came to the cool ooze of the river's bank where the moon-mice on the water crept into her feet. She poured out watching until he plopped. For a second he was visible in the water. She hoped he was not dizzy. Then all she saw was the glimmer of the moon in the silent-flowing river, the dark firs, the dim mountains, and the radiant pointed face laughing down at her out of the empty sky.

She scuttled up the hill, in the window, plonked down the ewer and flew through the air like a bird into bed. The dog said bark-bark. She heard the fishing reel whirring. She hugged herself and giggled. Like a river of joy her holiday spread before her.

In the morning Stephen rushed to her, shouting that "he" was gone, and asking "where" and "how." Lifting her nose in the air she said superciliously,[3] "Fairy Godmother, I suppose?" and strolled away patting the palms of her hands.

---

3. **superciliously** (soo'pər-sĭl'ē-əs-lē): pridefully; scornfully.

First Response: *How did you feel as Julia struggled with the trout in The Dark Walk?*

CHECKING UP

1. Who is the main character of the story?
2. At what time of year does the story take place?
3. Who discovers the trout?
4. What story does Julia's mother tell about the trout?
5. How does Julia rescue the trout?

TALKING IT OVER

1. Why does Julia enjoy racing through The Dark Walk? How do you know that she feels possessive about this place?
2. In what way does Stephen serve as a contrast to Julia?
3. Julia becomes preoccupied with the trout. How does the trout interfere with her vacation?
4. Julia's mother tells Stephen a make-believe story about the trout. How does this story provide an incentive for Julia to act?
5. At the end of the story, why do you think Julia doesn't give her little brother a straight answer?
6. How does Julia, in effect, write her own ending to the story of the trout? How might this episode be taken as a "turning point," or sign of her growing up?
7. Are the games and stories of childhood a preparation for life? Consider the events of O'Faolain's story in your answer.

UNDERSTANDING THE WORDS IN THE STORY
(Matching Columns)

1. lofty	a. trial
2. sinewy	b. arrogantly
3. ordeal	c. jug
4. squabbled	d. tough
5. incredulous	e. steadily
6. haughtily	f. moved swiftly
7. spawn	g. rising high in the air
8. resolutely	h. not ready to believe
9. ewer	i. eggs
10. scuttled	j. quarreled noisily

WRITING IT DOWN
Updating a Fairy Tale

In many popular fairy tales, someone in trouble is rescued by a character such as a handsome prince, a nearby woodsman, or a fairy godmother. The stories of Sleeping Beauty, Little Red Riding

Hood, and Cinderella are examples. Can you think of any others? Imagine yourself as a character in one of these fairy tales. Write a modern version of that story with yourself in the role of rescuer. Which character is in trouble? What steps will you take to rescue him or her?

A Narrative

Have you ever rescued an animal that was in trouble? A lost puppy, a cat up a tree, or an injured bird, for example? If so, relate your experience in a brief narrative. If you prefer, base your writing on an episode about a rescued animal that you have read about or seen on television or in the movies.

ABOUT THE AUTHOR

Sean O'Faolain (1900–1991) was born John Francis Whelan in Cork, Ireland. As a boy, he loved watching plays performed at the Cork Opera House. He was especially moved by *The Patriot*, a play by Lennox Robinson, about the kind of simple Irish life young Whelan was familiar with.

At the age of eighteen, Whelan learned Gaelic and changed his name to the Gaelic form, O'Faolain. Like many others of his generation, he became involved in the Irish Civil War. During this time, also, he began writing stories.

O'Faolain was educated at University College Dublin. He studied at Harvard and taught Gaelic there from 1926 to 1929. In 1932 he published *A Nest of Simple Folk*, a partly autobiographical novel that describes the long and painful struggle of the Irish people for independence.

O'Faolain's works include a history of Ireland; a biography of Eamon De Valera, the twentieth-century patriot and prime minister; and an autobiography with the amusing title *Vive Moi!* ("Long Live Me!") His short stories, which are compassionate and subtle, have been compared with those of Guy de Maupassant and Anton Chekhov.

THE NO-GUITAR BLUES

Gary Soto

Read the first two paragraphs of this story. Then try to recall a time when you wanted something as badly as Fausto did. Explain in a sentence or two why the item was so important to you.

The moment Fausto[1] saw the group Los Lobos[2] on "American Bandstand,"[3] he knew exactly what he wanted to do with his life—play guitar. His eyes grew large with excitement as Los Lobos ground out a song while teenagers bounced off each other on the crowded dance floor.

He had watched "American Bandstand" for years and had heard Ray Camacho and the Teardrops at Romain Playground, but it had never occurred to him that he too might become a musician. That afternoon Fausto knew his mission in life: to play guitar in his own band; to sweat out his songs and prance around the stage; to make money and dress weird.

Fausto turned off the television set and walked outside, wondering how he could get enough money to buy a guitar. He couldn't ask his parents because they would just say, "Money doesn't grow on trees" or "What do you think we are, bankers?" And besides, they hated rock music. They were into the *conjunto*[4] music of Lydia Mendoza, Flaco Jimenez, and Little Joe and La Familia. And, as Fausto recalled, the last album they bought was *The Chipmunks Sing Christmas Favorites*.

But what the heck, he'd give it a try. He returned inside and watched his mother make tortillas.[5] He leaned against the kitchen counter, trying to work up the nerve to ask her for a guitar. Finally, he couldn't hold back any longer.

"Mom," he said, "I want a guitar for Christmas."

1. **Fausto** (fou′stō).
2. **Los Lobos:** a rock band.
3. **"American Bandstand":** a long-running television show that featured popular bands and live dancing.
4. *conjunto* (kōn-hoōn′tō): polka music from northern Mexico, played with accordion, bass guitar, and drums.
5. **tortillas** (tôr-tē′yäs): thin, flat cakes made of cornmeal or flour that are cooked on a griddle.

She looked up from rolling tortillas. "Honey, a guitar costs a lot of money."

"How 'bout for my birthday next year," he tried again.

"I can't promise," she said, turning back to her tortillas, "but we'll see."

Fausto walked back outside with a buttered tortilla. He knew his mother was right. His father was a warehouseman at Berven Rugs, where he made good money but not enough to buy everything his children wanted. Fausto decided to mow lawns to earn money, and was pushing the mower down the street before he realized it was winter and no one would hire him. He returned the mower and picked up a rake. He hopped onto his sister's bike (his had two flat tires) and rode north to the nicer section of Fresno[6] in search of work. He went door-to-door, but after three hours he managed to get only one job, and not to rake leaves. He was asked to hurry down to the store to buy a loaf of bread, for which he received a grimy, dirt-caked quarter.

He also got an orange, which he ate sitting at the curb. While he was eating, a dog walked up and sniffed his leg. Fausto pushed him away and threw an orange peel skyward. The dog caught it and ate it in one gulp. The dog looked at Fausto and wagged his tail for more. Fausto tossed him a slice of orange, and the dog snapped it up and licked his lips.

"How come you like oranges, dog?"

The dog blinked a pair of sad eyes and whined.

"What's the matter? Cat got your tongue?" Fausto laughed at his joke and offered the dog another slice.

At that moment a dim light came on inside Fausto's head. He saw that it was sort of a fancy dog, a terrier or something, with dog tags and a shiny collar. And it looked well fed and healthy. In his neighborhood, the dogs were never licensed, and if they got sick they were placed near the water heater until they got well.

This dog looked like he belonged to rich people. Fausto cleaned his juice-sticky hands on his pants and got to his feet. The light in his head grew brighter. It just might work. He called the dog, patted its muscular back, and bent down to check the license.

6. **Fresno:** a city in central California.

"Great," he said. "There's an address."

The dog's name was Roger, which struck Fausto as weird because he'd never heard of a dog with a human name. Dogs should have names like Bomber, Freckles, Queenie, Killer, and Zero.

Fausto planned to take the dog home and collect a reward. He would say he had found Roger near the freeway. That would scare the daylights out of the owners, who would be so happy that they would probably give him a reward. He felt bad about lying, but the dog *was* loose. And it might even really be lost, because the address was six blocks away.

Fausto stashed the rake and his sister's bike behind a bush, and, tossing an orange peel every time Roger became distracted, walked the dog to his house. He hesitated on the porch until Roger began to scratch the door with a muddy paw. Fausto had come this far, so he figured he might as well go through with it. He knocked softly. When no one answered, he rang the doorbell. A man in a silky bathrobe and slippers opened the door and seemed confused by the sight of his dog and the boy.

"Sir," Fausto said, gripping Roger by the collar. "I found your dog by the freeway. His dog license says he lives here." Fausto looked down at the dog, then up to the man. "He does, doesn't he?"

The man stared at Fausto a long time before saying in a pleasant voice, "That's right." He pulled his robe tighter around him because of the cold and asked Fausto to come in. "So he was by the freeway?"

"Uh-huh."

"You bad, snoopy dog," said the man, wagging his finger. "You probably knocked over some trash cans, too, didn't you?"

Fausto didn't say anything. He looked around, amazed by this house with its shiny furniture and a television as large as the front window at home. Warm bread smells filled the air and music full of soft tinkling floated in from another room.

"Helen," the man called to the kitchen. "We have a visitor." His wife came into the living room wiping her hands on a dish towel and smiling. "And who have we here?" she asked in one of the softest voices Fausto had ever heard.

"This young man said he found Roger near the freeway."

Fausto repeated his story to her while staring at a perpetual clock with a bell-shaped glass, the kind his aunt got when she celebrated her twenty-fifth anniversary. The lady frowned and said, wagging a finger at Roger, "Oh, you're a bad boy."

"It was very nice of you to bring Roger home," the man said. "Where do you live?"

"By that vacant lot on Olive," he said. "You know, by Brownie's Flower Place."

The wife looked at her husband, then Fausto. Her eyes twinkled triangles of light as she said, "Well, young man, you're probably hungry. How about a turnover?"

"What do I have to turn over?" Fausto asked, thinking she was talking about yard work or something like turning trays of dried raisins.

"No, no, dear, it's a pastry." She took him by the elbow and guided him to a kitchen that sparkled with copper pans and bright yellow wallpaper. She guided him to the kitchen table and gave him a tall glass of milk and something that looked like an *empanada*.[7] Steamy waves of heat escaped when he tore it in two. He ate with both eyes on the man and woman who stood arm-in-arm smiling at him. They were strange, he thought. But nice.

"That was good," he said after he finished the turnover. "Did you make it, ma'am?"

"Yes, I did. Would you like another?"

"No, thank you. I have to go home now."

As Fausto walked to the door, the man opened his wallet and took out a bill. "This is for you," he said. "Roger is special to us, almost like a son."

Fausto looked at the bill and knew he was in trouble. Not with these nice folks or with his parents but with himself. How could he have been so deceitful? The dog wasn't lost. It was just having a fun Saturday walking around.

"I can't take that."

"You have to. You deserve it, believe me," the man said.

"No, I don't."

"Now don't be silly," said the lady. She took the bill from her husband and stuffed it into Fausto's shirt pocket. "You're a lovely child. Your parents are lucky to have you. Be good. And come see us again, please."

7. *empanada* (ĕm-pä-nä′ thä): meat pie.

Fausto went out, and the lady closed the door. Fausto clutched the bill through his shirt pocket. He felt like ringing the doorbell and begging them to please take the money back, but he knew they would refuse. He hurried away, and at the end of the block, pulled the bill from his shirt pocket: it was a crisp twenty-dollar bill.

"Oh, man, I shouldn't have lied," he said under his breath as he started up the street like a zombie. He wanted to run to church for Saturday confession,[8] but it was past four-thirty, when confession stopped.

He returned to the bush where he had hidden the rake and his sister's bike and rode home slowly, not daring to touch the money in his pocket. At home, in the privacy of his room, he examined the twenty-dollar bill. He had never had so much money. It was probably enough to buy a secondhand guitar. But he felt bad, like the time he stole a dollar from the secret fold inside his older brother's wallet.

Fausto went outside and sat on the fence. "Yeah," he said. "I can probably get a guitar for twenty. Maybe at a yard sale—things are cheaper."

His mother called him to dinner.

The next day he dressed for church without anyone telling him. He was going to go to eight o'clock mass.

"I'm going to church, Mom," he said. His mother was in the kitchen cooking *papas*[9] and *chorizo con huevos*.[10] A pile of tortillas lay warm under a dishtowel.

"Oh, I'm so proud of you, Son." She beamed, turning over the crackling *papas*.

His older brother, Lawrence, who was at the table reading the funnies, mimicked, "Oh, I'm so proud of you, my son," under his breath.

At Saint Theresa's he sat near the front. When Father Jerry began by saying that we are all sinners, Fausto thought he looked right at him. Could he know? Fausto fidgeted with guilt. No, he thought. I only did it yesterday.

---

8. **confession:** in some churches, a ritual in which a person tells of his or her wrong-doing before a priest and seeks forgiveness.

9. *papas* (pä′päs): potatoes.

10. *chorizo con huevos* (chô-rē′sō kōn hwä′bōs): sausage with eggs.

Fausto knelt, prayed, and sang. But he couldn't forget the man and the lady, whose names he didn't even know, and the *empanada* they had given him. It had a strange name but tasted really good. He wondered how they got rich. And how that dome clock worked. He had asked his mother once how his aunt's clock worked. She said it just worked, the way the refrigerator works. It just did.

Fausto caught his mind wandering and tried to concentrate on his sins. He said a Hail Mary[11] and sang, and when the wicker basket came his way, he stuck a hand reluctantly in his pocket and pulled out the twenty-dollar bill. He ironed it between his palms, and dropped it into the basket. The grown-ups stared. Here was a kid dropping twenty dollars in the basket while they gave just three or four dollars.

There would be a second collection for Saint Vincent de Paul, the lector[12] announced. The wicker baskets again floated in the pews, and this time the adults around him, given a second chance to show their charity, dug deep into their wallets and purses and dropped in fives and tens. This time Fausto tossed in the grimy quarter.

Fausto felt better after church. He went home and played football in the front yard with his brother and some neighbor kids. He felt cleared of wrongdoing and was so happy that he played one of his best games of football ever. On one play, he tore his good pants, which he knew he shouldn't have been wearing. For a second, while he examined the hole, he wished he hadn't given the twenty dollars away.

Man, I coulda bought me some Levi's, he thought. He pictured his twenty dollars being spent to buy church candles. He pictured a priest buying an armful of flowers with *his* money.

Fausto had to forget about getting a guitar. He spent the next day playing soccer in his good pants, which were now his old pants. But that night during dinner, his mother said she remembered seeing an old bass guitarron[13] the last time she cleaned out her father's garage.

"It's a little dusty," his mom said, serving his favorite enchiladas,[14] "But I think it works. Grandpa says it works."

---

11. **Hail Mary:** a special prayer addressed to the Virgin Mary.
12. **lector:** a person who reads a lesson from the Bible during a church service.
13. **guitarron** (gē-tä′rōn): a type of large guitar.
14. **enchiladas** (ĕn-chē-lä′*th*äs): tortillas wrapped around meat and usually served with chili sauce.

Fausto's ears perked up. That was the same kind the guy in Los Lobos played. Instead of asking for the guitar, he waited for his mother to offer it to him. And she did, while gathering the dishes from the table. "No, Mom, I'll do it," he said, hugging her. "I'll do the dishes forever if you want."

It was the happiest day of his life. No, it was the second-happiest day of his life. The happiest was when his grandfather Lupe[15] placed the guitarron, which was nearly as huge as a washtub, in his arms. Fausto ran a thumb down the strings, which vibrated in his throat and chest. It sounded beautiful, deep and eerie. A pumpkin smile widened on his face.

"OK, *hijo*,[16] now you put your fingers like this," said his grandfather, smelling of tobacco and aftershave. He took Fausto's fingers and placed them on the strings. Fausto strummed a chord on the guitarron, and the bass resounded in their chests.

The guitarron was more complicated than Fausto imagined. But he was confident that after a few more lessons he could start a band that would someday play on "American Bandstand" for the dancing crowds.

15. **Lupe** (lo͞o′pä).
16. *hijo* (ē′hō): son.

First Response: *What was your reaction when Fausto decided to tell a lie?*

CHECK-UP (True/False)

1. Fausto mowed lawns to earn money for a guitar.
2. Fausto fed the dog pieces of orange peel.
3. Fausto thought the dog belonged to rich people.
4. Fausto felt guilty about having deceived the couple.
5. Fausto's grandfather bought him a new guitar.

TALKING IT OVER

1. Why did Fausto think his parents would not want to get him a guitar?
2. How did Fausto try to earn the money to buy a guitar? What idea came to him when he saw the "fancy" dog?
3. **Internal conflict** is a character's struggle within himself or herself. At what points in the story does Fausto face internal conflict?
4. A statement is considered ironic when it points out the difference between appearance and reality. Why is it ironic that the woman calls Fausto a "lovely child?" Why is it ironic that Fausto's mother is proud of him for going to church?
5. How might this episode be a "turning point" in Fausto's life?

REALISM

Many popular stories are fanciful and imaginative and are based on extraordinary characters and events. "The Panther" and "The Colomber" (pages 14 and 28) are examples of fanciful stories. "The No-Guitar Blues," on the other hand, is an example of a type of writing called **realism**, which depicts everyday life and ordinary people.

1. How is Fausto presented as an ordinary teenager? In what way are his thoughts and actions realistic?
2. The use of **dialogue**, or conversation between characters, contributes to the realistic quality of a story. Is the dialogue between Fausto and his mother believable? Did you consider the dialogue between Fausto and the husband and wife to be realistic? Explain your answers.
3. What details about the setting help make the story true to life?

UNDERSTANDING THE WORDS IN THE STORY (Completion)

Choose one of the words in the following list to complete the sentences below. A word may be used only once.

distracted   reluctantly
deceitful   charity
fidgeted

1. The baby started to cry, but I _____ him with a cookie.
2. He always said that the best kind of _____ is giving without being asked.
3. Since he remembered the pain from the last shot he received, Pablo entered the doctor's office _____.
4. Ludmila _____ so much that her mother couldn't fasten the back of her dress.
5. Since there was no other explanation for the disappearance of the trunk, we realized that the porter had been _____.

WRITING IT DOWN
A Journal Entry

Imagine that you are Fausto and that you want to write about your recent experience in your journal. In your journal entry you might want to describe the following:

Why you wanted the guitar so badly
How you felt once you were in the couple's house
How you felt after you went to church
What you plan to do with the guitar

A Dialogue

Think of an interesting conversation you either heard or took part in recently, and write it down, using bits of actual dialogue. Remember to enclose the speaker's actual words in quotation marks, and to set them off with proper punctuation. For example:

> The teacher was checking our assignments. I said to myself, "Oh, no."
> "Where is your essay?" he demanded.
> "The dog ate it," I responded.

ABOUT THE AUTHOR

Gary Soto was born in 1952 in Fresno, California. He grew up in the industrial side of that city, in a neighborhood that allowed him freedom to explore and discover. Discarded objects such as bathtubs, chicken wire, plumbing, and bricks fed his imagination.

Soto was not a highly motivated student in high school. However, in junior college he discovered poetry, and that experience proved a turning point. He devoured James Wright, W. S. Merwin, and Pablo Neruda, his favorite, and he went on to read everything he could get his hands on. His love of reading led him to try writing.

In his writing, Soto tries to see the world through the imagination of a child. He has published a number of books, including poetry collections, the novels *Taking Sides* and *Pacific Crossing*, and the short-story collections *Baseball in April* (1990) and *Local News* (1993). Soto teaches occasionally at the University of California at Berkeley.

I CONFESS . . .

Wei Wenjuan

"Admitting one's mistakes and changing one's ways is the sign of a good student," says the teacher in this story. Do you agree? Discuss your reaction to that statement with a small group of classmates.

"May I come in?" rang out a clear voice.

"Come in." I knew it was the boy who monitored discipline in my class. "What is it?"

"Mr. Wei, Wang Wei has carved characters in his desk top."

"What? Send him to me at once! What nonsense is this?"

I quickly stood up, paced up and down and considered how I should handle this. It was a case of severe damage to public property.

I had only recently graduated from teacher training college and had been assigned to work at the same high school that I myself had attended—Linhu Junior High. The school had shown great faith in me and had put me in charge of the eighth graders. I had drawn on all my reserves of strength and had vowed to myself not to let my superiors down. I had set myself strict standards and, as I had hoped, my hard work had begun to pay off. After only half a term, the school's splendid red flag of citation had been brought in to decorate the wall of my classroom. I had felt the same sense of happy satisfaction that I got when eating an ice cream on a hot summer's day. Content, I nevertheless worked even harder. The last thing I expected was an incident like this.

"May I come in?" Wang Wei asked shyly, standing awkwardly in the doorway.

"Yes. Come in!" I roared fiercely. In all the time I had been there I had never used such a harsh voice to chastise a student. "Wang Wei . . . stand up straight!"

Other, more experienced teachers had told me that it was important to exert one's authority at first in order to let the naughtier children know who was in charge; if you gave them an inch, they would take a yard. Wang Wei was obviously terrified. He was trembling from head to foot, while awkwardly standing at attention. A combination of terror and guilt flashed in his eyes.

"I want an explanation! Why did you feel it necessary to carve characters in the desk top?" I was too angry to employ the investigative method I had originally intended to use. Instead I came straight to the point.

"I . . . I didn't do it." He raised his head. "If you don't believe me, sir, you can go and . . ."

"Go and what?" I interrupted abruptly. More than two months of teaching experience had taught me that I should not let him argue. If the atmosphere relaxed, it would be even harder to sort him out. "Why would anyone accuse you for no reason? Out of a class of more than fifty, why would they pick on you out of the blue?"

Wang Wei's lips trembled and he clearly was unable to articulate what he wanted to say. Instead, he dropped his eyes, and with great effort stammered, "I . . . I . . ." But before he could finish his sentence tears were rolling down his cheeks.

"Admitting one's mistakes and changing one's ways is the sign of a good student." Then I said, in a slightly softened tone, "I want you to consider for yourself how this matter should be resolved. The school rules state that you must confess to all the teachers and students, and reimburse the cost of the damage done. Prepare yourself for this."

"Sir, I . . . I really did not do it."

Since he was still trying to deny it, I tried another angle. In an attempt to trap him, I suddenly asked, "What is carved into the desk?"

"I don't know. The characters are all twisted. I can't read them."

"What do you mean 'twisted'? Do you mean the sort of characters you find on a seal?" I wanted to laugh; at the same time I thought it rather odd. Normally, eighth graders don't know how to write seal characters. A more thorough investigation into the matter seemed necessary.

Between classes, I took Wang Wei, puffy-faced, back to his own classroom. Tension immediately settled over the whole class. The pupils looked at me steadily and the air in the classroom was still.

I went directly to Wang Wei's desk and looked at it carefully. Indistinct carvings were just visible in the left-hand corner. They had obviously been inscribed there a long time ago.

"These are ancient characters, aren't they, sir?" one pupil asked curiously.

I bent over and tried to identify them. I read them aloud, without registering their meaning: "Wei . . ." Suddenly, I felt the blood rush to my head! Wasn't that my own name carved in those elongated seal characters? The style was so familiar, the characters had to have been carved by my own hand. Beneath them was another line of characters written in the Song-dynasty[1] style: "In memory of my graduation." The date followed. Oh no, how dreadful! Now I remembered.

"The same last name as you, sir?"

"What are the last two characters?"

I felt quite dizzy, and at a loss for words. I was ashamed to show my face. "Eh . . . um . . . They're . . ."

"What's the matter, sir?"

"Mr. Wei is ill."

"Mr. Wei, let me take you to rest."

"No, no! I'm not ill. Children, I . . ." I could not go on. I turned and went up to the blackboard. I picked up a piece of chalk and copied the characters from the desk onto the blackboard, then turned and looked anxiously at the pupils. "Class, I want to confess."

"Confess? Our teacher is going to make a confession?"

"Yes, I confess . . ."

---

1. **Song-dynasty:** The Song (sōong), or Sung, dynasty was a period in Chinese history (960–1279) noted for its cultural achievements.

First Response: *How would you have responded if you had been in Wang Wei's predicament?*

CHECKING UP (True/False)

1. Mr. Wei had been teaching for many years.
2. Mr. Wei had been encouraged to be firm with the children.
3. Wang Wei is terrified as Mr. Wei questions him.
4. Wang Wei identifies the characters carved on the desk.
5. Mr. Wei is ashamed when he realizes that he had carved the characters himself.

TALKING IT OVER

1. Why is Mr. Wei so upset about the carvings on the desk?
2. How does Wang Wei react to Mr. Wei's questioning? Why do you think he responds as he does?
3. Why doesn't Mr. Wei allow Wang Wei to defend himself?
4. What evidence in the story **foreshadows,** or hints at, the story's conclusion?
5. An experience that causes a person to admit a mistake and change his or her ways can be considered a "turning point." How might the incident with Wang Wei be a turning point in Mr. Wei's teaching career?

UNDERSTANDING THE WORDS IN THE STORY (Completion)

Choose one of the words in the following list to complete each of the sentences below. A word may be used only once.

monitored	stammered
reserves	resolved
chastise	reimburse
abruptly	indistinct
articulate	registering

1. We _____ the problem by leaving a day earlier.
2. It was easy for him to _____ what was on his mind.
3. The amount was incorrect by hundreds of dollars, but I was not _____ that fact.

4. Paco had to _____ his sister for the money he had borrowed.
5. Sally tried to write in the snow, but her letters were _____.
6. Mother left the table _____ when she heard the baby cry.
7. The nurse _____ the patient's progress.
8. The teacher was careful to keep _____ of pens in her desk.
9. Surprised and unable to speak, he _____ for a few moments.
10. Father did not _____ the children for getting home late.

WRITING IT DOWN
A Personal Essay

How do you think Mr. Wei will change as a result of this experience? Will he treat his students any differently? Will he alter his approach to discipline in the classroom? Write down your thoughts in a brief essay.

A Play

Working with a group of two or three other classmates, adapt "I Confess . . ." as a short play for the stage or for television. Think about the opening scene. Do you want it to take place in Mr. Wei's office, in the teachers' lounge, or in another classroom? How will you convey background information about Mr. Wei to your audience? Will you divide the play into scenes? Will you create additional dialogue for the students in Wang Wei's classroom?

If you are writing a screenplay, be sure to include shooting instructions on techniques such as camera angles, close-ups, and long shots.

Pool your ideas with those of other group members and come up with a plan for a stage play or a shooting script for a teleplay. Use a chart like the one on page 69 to record your notes.

ACTORS:
COSTUMES:
SCENERY:
LIGHTING:
SOUND EFFECTS:
PROPS:

In writing dialogue, remember to use *stage directions* that tell how a line should be spoken or what kind of action, movement, or facial expression should be used when the line is delivered. For example:

MR. WEI (angrily): What? Send him to me at once! What nonsense is this?

[He stands up and begins pacing.]

WAR

Luigi Pirandello

Some people think of war as a heroic fight for a noble cause, whereas others see it only as a source of misery and loss. Write down four or five words that you associate with war. What does your list suggest about your own view of war?

The passengers who had left Rome by the night express had had to stop until dawn at the small station of Fabriano in order to continue their journey by the small old-fashioned local joining the main line with Sulmona.

At dawn, in a stuffy and smoky second-class carriage in which five people had already spent the night, a bulky woman in deep mourning was hoisted in—almost like a shapeless bundle. Behind her, puffing and moaning, followed her husband—a tiny man, thin and weakly, his face death-white, his eyes small and bright and looking shy and uneasy.

Having at last taken a seat he politely thanked the passengers who had helped his wife and who had made room for her; then he turned round to the woman trying to pull down the collar of her coat, and politely inquired:

"Are you all right, dear?"

The wife, instead of answering, pulled up her collar again to her eyes, so as to hide her face.

"Nasty world," muttered the husband with a sad smile.

And he felt it his duty to explain to his traveling companions that the poor woman was to be pitied, for the war was taking away from her her only son, a boy of twenty to whom both had devoted their entire life, even breaking up their home at Sulmona to follow him to Rome, where he had to go as a student, then allowing him to volunteer for war with an assurance, however, that at least for six months he would not be sent to the front and now, all of a sudden, receiving a wire saying that he was due to leave in three days' time and asking them to go and see him off.

The woman under the big coat was twisting and wriggling, at times growling like a wild animal, feeling certain that all those explanations

70

would not have aroused even a shadow of sympathy from those people who—most likely—were in the same plight as herself. One of them, who had been listening with particular attention, said:

"You should thank God that your son is only leaving now for the front. Mine was sent there the first day of the war. He has already come back twice wounded and been sent back again to the front."

"What about me? I have two sons and three nephews at the front," said another passenger.

"Maybe, but in our case it is our *only* son," ventured the husband.

"What difference can it make? You may spoil your only son with excessive attentions, but you cannot love him more than you would all your other children if you had any. Paternal love is not like bread that can be broken into pieces and split amongst the children in equal shares. A father gives *all* his love to each one of his children without discrimination, whether it be one or ten, and if I am suffering now for my two sons, I am not suffering half for each of them but double . . ."

"True . . . true . . ." sighed the embarrassed husband, "but suppose (of course we all hope it will never be your case) a father has two sons at the front and he loses one of them, there is still one left to console him . . . while . . ."

"Yes," answered the other, getting cross, "a son left to console him but also a son left for whom he must survive, while in the case of the father of an only son if the son dies the father can die too and put an end to his distress. Which of the two positions is the worse? Don't you see how my case would be worse than yours?"

"Nonsense," interrupted another traveler, a fat, red-faced man with bloodshot eyes of the palest gray.

He was panting. From his bulging eyes seemed to spurt inner violence of an uncontrolled vitality which his weakened body could hardly contain.

"Nonsense," he repeated, trying to cover his mouth with his hand so as to hide the two missing front teeth. "Nonsense. Do we give life to our children for our own benefit?"

The other travelers stared at him in distress. The one who had had his son at the front since the first day of the war sighed: "You are right. Our children do not belong to us, they belong to the Country. . . ."

"Bosh," retorted the fat traveler. "Do we think of the Country when

we give life to our children? Our sons are born because . . . well, because
they must be born and when they come to life they take our own life
with them. This is the truth. We belong to them but they never belong
to us. And when they reach twenty they are exactly what we were at their
age. We too had a father and mother, but there were so many other
things as well . . . girls, cigarettes, illusions, new ties . . . and the Country,
of course, whose call we would have answered—when we were twenty—
even if father and mother had said no. Now at our age, the love of our
Country is still great, of course, but stronger than it is the love for our
children. Is there any one of us here who wouldn't gladly take his son's
place at the front if he could?"

There was a silence all round, everybody nodding as to approve.

"Why then," continued the fat man, "shouldn't we consider the
feelings of our children when they are twenty? Isn't it natural that at
their age they should consider the love for their Country (I am speaking of decent boys, of course) even greater than the love for us? Isn't it
natural that it should be so, as after all they must look upon us as upon
old boys who cannot move any more and must stay at home? If Country
exists, if Country is a natural necessity, like bread, of which each of us
must eat in order not to die of hunger, somebody must go to defend it.
And our sons go, when they are twenty, and they don't want tears,
because if they die, they die inflamed and happy (I am speaking, of
course, of decent boys). Now, if one dies young and happy, without
having the ugly sides of life, the boredom of it, the pettiness, the bitterness of disillusion . . . what more can we ask for him? Everyone should
stop crying; everyone should laugh, as I do . . . or at least thank God—
as I do—because my son, before dying, sent me a message saying that
he was dying satisfied at having ended his life in the best way he could
have wished. That is why, as you see, I do not even wear mourning. . . ."
He shook his light fawn coat as to show it; his livid lip over his missing
teeth was trembling, his eyes were watery and motionless, and soon
after he ended with a shrill laugh which might well have been a sob.

"Quite so . . . quite so . . ." agreed the others.

The woman who, bundled in a corner under her coat, had been
sitting and listening had—for the last three months—tried to find in
the words of her husband and her friends something to console her in
her deep sorrow, something that might show her how a mother should

resign herself to send her son not even to death but to a probably dangerous life. Yet not a word had she found amongst the many which had been said . . . and her grief had been greater in seeing that nobody—as she thought—could share her feelings.

But now the words of the traveler amazed and almost stunned her. She suddenly realized that it wasn't the others who were wrong and could not understand her but herself who could not rise up to the same height of those fathers and mothers willing to resign themselves, without crying, not only to the departure of their sons but even to their death.

She lifted her head, she bent over from her corner trying to listen with great attention to the details which the fat man was giving to his companions about the way his son had fallen as a hero, for his King and his Country, happy and without regrets. It seemed to her that she had stumbled into a world she had never dreamt of, a world so far unknown to her and she was so pleased to hear everyone joining in congratulating that brave father who could so stoically speak of his child's death.

Then suddenly, just as if she had heard nothing of what had been said and almost as if waking up from a dream, she turned to the old man, asking him:

"Then . . . is your son really dead?"

Everybody stared at her. The old man, too, turned to look at her, fixing his great, bulging, horribly watery light gray eyes deep in her face. For some little time he tried to answer, but words failed him. He looked and looked at her, almost as if only then—at that silly, incongruous question—he had suddenly realized at last that his son was really dead . . . gone forever . . . forever. His face contracted, became horribly distorted, then he snatched in haste a handkerchief from his pocket and, to the amazement of everyone, broke into harrowing, heart-rending, uncontrollable sobs.

First Response: *What was your reaction to the woman's question?*

CHECK-UP (True/False)

1. The people in this story are being evacuated from Rome during wartime.
2. The couple who board the train at the opening of the story have just lost their only son.
3. The characters present different points of view about losing sons in warfare.
4. The fat man argues that a parent should be comforted by a son's heroic death.
5. At the end of the story, the fat man is overwhelmed by grief.

TALKING IT OVER

1. What is the **setting** of this story? How does it serve to bring together the different characters?
2. The major **conflict** in the story is the differing attitudes toward a specific subject. What is the subject of discussion? What are the different points of view of the characters?
3. How does the fat man's description of his son's noble and heroic death affect the woman whose only son has gone to war?
4. The **climax,** or point of greatest intensity, occurs when the woman asks a "silly" question. What does the fat man realize at that moment? How does his reaction to the question suggest that this episode may be a "turning point" in his life?
5. Why do you suppose the author did not identify his characters by name? Is the story's impact heightened or lessened by this anonymity?
6. Do you think the author has chosen a good title for his story? Give reasons to support your answer.

UNDERSTANDING THE WORDS IN THE STORY
(Matching Columns)

1. plight
2. excessive
3. paternal
4. console
5. spurt
6. livid
7. stoically
8. incongruous
9. distorted
10. harrowing

a. comfort or help
b. unflinchingly
c. gush forth
d. too much
e. distressing
f. not fitting
g. unfortunate condition
h. twisted
i. characteristic of a father
j. grayish or pale

WRITING IT DOWN
A Monologue

The fat traveler delivers a **monologue,** or extended speech, in which he makes interesting claims about the relationship between parents and children, about patriotism, and about the glory in dying for one's country. Do you agree or disagree with him?

Imagine that you are a character in the story and that all eyes have turned to you; your fellow travelers want to hear your opinion on the issues they have been discussing. What will you say to the group in the railway car? Write your response in the form of a brief monologue.

SPEAKING AND LISTENING
Evaluating the Impact of War

Pirandello's story explores the effects of war on one group of people who do not take part in the actual fighting—the parents of soldiers. Get together with a small group of classmates and discuss some ways in which war affects people other than those on the battlefield. Take notes on the discussion.

ABOUT THE AUTHOR

Luigi Pirandello (1867–1936) was not a well-disciplined student when he attended the University of Rome, but he was inspired by one of his professors, from whom he learned about the traditions and customs of his native Sicily. As a young man, Pirandello wrote poetry; later he turned to plays, novels, and short stories. His first play, *Right You Are If You Think You Are* (1916), was a success. Five years later his most famous play, *Six Characters in Search of an Author,* was produced.

Pirandello was intrigued by the themes of despair, jealousy, and death. He also explored the contradictions between appearance and reality. In 1934, one year after the dictator Mussolini condemned his plays for their "introspective, moody and unrealistic" style, Pirandello was awarded the Nobel Prize for Literature. "War" is from a collection called *The Medals and Other Stories.*

HOME

Gwendolyn Brooks

If you suddenly had to move from your home, what are the things you would miss most? Write down a short list.

What had been wanted was this always, this always to last, the talking softly on this porch, with the snake plant in the jardiniere[1] in the southwest corner, and the obstinate slip from Aunt Eppie's magnificent Michigan fern at the left side of the friendly door. Mama, Maud Martha, and Helen rocked slowly in their rocking chairs, and looked at the late afternoon light on the lawn and at the emphatic iron of the fence and at the poplar tree. These things might soon be theirs no longer. Those shafts and pools of light, the tree, the graceful iron, might soon be viewed possessively by different eyes.

Papa was to have gone that noon, during his lunch hour, to the office of the Home Owners' Loan. If he had not succeeded in getting another extension, they would be leaving this house in which they had lived for more than fourteen years. There was little hope. The Home Owners' Loan was hard. They sat, making their plans.

"We'll be moving into a nice flat somewhere," said Mama. "Somewhere on South Park, or Michigan, or in Washington Park Court." Those flats, as the girls and Mama knew well, were burdens on wages twice the size of Papa's. This was not mentioned now.

"They're much prettier than this old house," said Helen. "I have friends I'd just as soon not bring here. And I have other friends that wouldn't come down this far for anything, unless they were in a taxi."

Yesterday, Maud Martha would have attacked her. Tomorrow she might. Today she said nothing. She merely gazed at a little hopping robin in the tree, her tree, and tried to keep the fronts of her eyes dry.

---

1. **jardiniere** (järd′dn-îr′): a decorative pot for plants.

"Well, I do know," said Mama, turning her hands over and over, "that I've been getting tireder and tireder of doing that firing.[2] From October to April, there's firing to be done."

"But lately we've been helping, Harry and I," said Maud Martha. "And sometimes in March and April and in October, and even in November, we could build a little fire in the fireplace. Sometimes the weather was just right for that."

She knew, from the way they looked at her, that this had been a mistake. They did not want to cry.

But she felt that the little line of white, sometimes ridged with smoked purple, and all that cream-shot saffron[3] would never drift across any western sky except that in back of this house. The rain would drum with as sweet a dullness nowhere but here. The birds on South Park were mechanical birds, no better than the poor caught canaries in those "rich" women's sun parlors.

"It's just going to kill Papa!" burst out Maud Martha. "He loves this house! He *lives* for this house!"

"He lives for us," said Helen. "It's us he loves. He wouldn't want the house, except for us."

"And he'll have us," added Mama, "wherever."

"You know," Helen sighed, "if you want to know the truth, this is a relief. If this hadn't come up, we would have gone on, just dragged on, hanging out here forever."

"It might," allowed Mama, "be an act of God. God may just have reached down and picked up the reins."

"Yes," Maud Martha cracked in, "that's what you always say—that God knows best."

Her mother looked at her quickly, decided the statement was not suspect, looked away.

Helen saw Papa coming. "There's Papa," said Helen.

They could not tell a thing from the way Papa was walking. It was that same dear little staccato walk, one shoulder down, then the other, then repeat, and repeat. They watched his progress. He passed the Kennedys', he passed the vacant lot, he passed Mrs. Blakemore's. They wanted to hurl themselves over the fence, into the street, and shake the

2. **firing:** starting a coal fire.
3. **saffron:** a yellow-orange color.

truth out of his collar. He opened his gate—the gate—and still his stride and face told them nothing.

"Hello," he said.

Mama got up and followed him through the front door. The girls knew better than to go in too.

Presently Mama's head emerged. Her eyes were lamps turned on. "It's all right," she exclaimed. "He got it. It's all over. Everything is all right."

The door slammed shut. Mama's footsteps hurried away.

"I think," said Helen, rocking rapidly, "I think I'll give a party. I haven't given a party since I was eleven. I'd like some of my friends to just casually see that we're homeowners."

First Response: *Were you surprised by the ending of the story? pleased? Why or why not?*

CHECKING UP (True/False)

1. Maud Martha is unhappy about leaving the old house.
2. The family plans to rent out rooms in the house.
3. Papa wants to move into a better neighborhood.
4. Helen is tired of starting the fire in the house.
5. Papa gets an extension on his loan.

TALKING IT OVER

1. In this story we see how the members of a family react to the threat of losing their home. How do Mama and Helen react? What defenses do these characters use against disappointment?
2. How does Maud Martha's reaction differ from the reactions of Mama and Helen? What are the things she feels she will miss?

3. What evidence is there that Maud Martha and Helen value different things?
4. How does the author heighten suspense at the end of the story?
5. How is the problem the family faces resolved?
6. If Papa had not been successful, which family member do you think would have taken the blow hardest of all? Explain your answer.
7. Reread the first paragraph of the story. What things about their home are at "the heart of the matter" for Maud Martha and her family?

SKETCH

A **sketch** is a short, informal piece of writing that presents a single setting, episode, or character. A sketch can take the form of a poem, an essay, a story, or a play. "Home" is an example of a sketch.

1. How do the details in the opening paragraph of "Home" quickly establish a sense of place?
2. What is the atmosphere, or mood, in most of this sketch?
3. Explain how the subject matter of this sketch makes the scene important and memorable.

UNDERSTANDING THE WORDS IN THE STORY
(Matching Columns)

1. obstinate	a. arousing suspicion
2. emphatic	b. came out
3. shafts	c. troubles
4. possessively	d. short and abrupt
5. extension	e. slender rays
6. flat	f. as an owner
7. burdens	g. hard to control
8. suspect	h. apartment
9. staccato	i. striking
10. emerged	j. additional time

WRITING IT DOWN
A Description

Reread the first paragraph of "Home," noting the vivid, concrete details Brooks uses to describe the family's house. Also note the way the description follows *spatial order:* we move outward from the house and the porch to the lawn, and then to the fence at the border of the property.

Choose a subject for a descriptive paragraph of your own. Collect as many vivid details about your subject as you can. Filling out an observation chart like the one below will help you focus on concrete, sensory details that appeal to each of the five senses.

OBSERVATION CHART

SUBJECT: _____

SIGHT	SOUND	TOUCH	SMELL	TASTE

After you have completed your chart, arrange your details in spatial order: that is, in the order in which an observer would see them. Some examples of spatial order include the following:

> near to far (or far to near)
> top to bottom (or bottom to top)
> outside to inside (or inside to outside)
> left to right (or right to left)

Now use the details on your outline to write your descriptive paragraph. When you have finished, share your writing with a small group of classmates.

ABOUT THE AUTHOR

Gwendolyn Brooks was born in 1917 in Topeka, Kansas, and has spent most of her life in Chicago. Brooks is considered one of America's outstanding poets. Many of her poems are set in Chicago's South Side, in an African American community she calls Bronzeville. Brooks's second poetry collection, *Annie Allen*, won the Pulitzer Prize in 1950.

The story "Home" is taken from *Maud Martha* (1953), Brooks's novel about a young black girl growing up in Chicago. Of that book she wrote, "My novel is not autobiographical in the usual sense. . . . But it is true that much in the 'story' was taken out of my own life, and twisted, highlighted or dulled, dressed up or down. . . . 'Home' is indeed fact-bound. The Home Owners' Loan Corporation was a sickening reality."

Brooks advises young writers to get as much education as possible, read widely, and "live richly with eyes open, and heart, too."

SUCCESS STORY

James Gould Cozzens

How would you define success? What qualities does a person need most to be successful? Before you read the following story, get together with a small group of classmates to exchange ideas.

I met Richards ten years or more ago when I first went down to Cuba. He was a short, sharp-faced, agreeable chap, then about twenty-two. He introduced himself to me on the boat and I was surprised to find that Panamerica Steel & Structure was sending us both to the same job.

Richards was from some not very good state university engineering school. Being the same age myself, and just out of tech,[1] I was prepared to patronize him if I needed to; but I soon saw I didn't need to. There was really not the faintest possibility of anyone supposing that Richards was as smart as I was. In fact, I couldn't then imagine how he had managed to get his job. I have an idea now. It came to me when I happened to read a few weeks ago that Richards had been made a vice-president and director of Panamerica Steel when the Prossert interests bought the old firm.

Richards was naturally likable, and I liked him a lot, once I was sure that he wasn't going to outshine me. The firm had a contract for the construction of a private railroad, about seventeen miles of it, to give United Sugar a sea terminal at a small deepwater Caribbean port. For Richards and me it was mostly an easy job of inspections and routine paperwork. At least it was easy for me. It was harder for Richards, because he didn't appear ever to have mastered the use of a slide rule.[2] When he asked me to check his figures I found it was no mere formality. "Boy," I was at last obliged to say, "you are undoubtedly the dumbest man in Santa Clara province. If you don't buck up, Farrell will see you never get another job down here."

Richards grinned and said, "I never want another one. Not a job like this, anyway. I'm the executive type."

---

1. **tech:** short for "technical." The narrator has just graduated from a leading engineering school.
2. **slide rule:** an instrument used for rapid calculation. It looks like a ruler and has a sliding strip in the center.

"Oh, you are!"

"Sure, I am. And what do I care what Farrell thinks? What can he do for me?"

"Plenty. If he thinks you're any good, he can see you get something that pays money."

"He doesn't know anything that pays money, my son."

"He knows things that would pay enough for me," I answered, annoyed.

"Oh," said Richards, "if that's all you want, when Farrell's working for me I'll make him give you a job. A good one."

"Go to the devil!" I said. I was still checking his trial figures for an extra concrete pouring at the Nombre de Dios viaduct.[3] "Look, stupid," I said, "didn't you ever take arithmetic? How much are seven times thirteen?"

"Work that out," Richards said, "and let me have a report tomorrow."

When I had time, I continued to check his figures for him, and Farrell only caught him in a bad mistake about twice; but Farrell was the best man Panamerica Steel had. He'd been managing construction jobs both in Cuba and Mexico for twenty years. After the first month or so he simply let Richards alone and devoted himself to giving me the whole benefit of his usually sharp and scornful criticism. He was at me every minute he could spare, telling me to forget this or that and use my head, showing me little tricks of figuring and method. He said it would be a good plan to take some Spanish lessons from a clerk he named in the sugar company's office.

"Spanish?" said Richards, when I told him he'd better join the class. "Not for me! Say, it took me twenty-two years to learn English. People who want to talk to me have to know it, or they'd better bring an interpreter with them."

"All right," I said. "I don't mind telling you the idea is Farrell's. He spoke to me about it."

"Well, he didn't speak to me," said Richards. "I guess he thinks I'm perfect the way I am. And now, if you'll excuse me, I have a date with a beer bottle."

I could easily see that he was coming to no good end.

---

3. **viaduct** (vī′ə-dŭkt′): a long bridge carrying a road or railroad over a valley or ravine.

In January several directors of the United Sugar Company came down on their annual jaunt—nominally business, but mostly pleasure; a good excuse to get south on a vacation. They came on a yacht.

The yacht belonged to Mr. Joseph Prossert, who was, I think, chairman of United Sugar's board then. It was the first time I'd ever seen at close quarters one of these really rich and powerful financial figures whose name everyone knows. He was an inconspicuous, rather stout man, with little hair on his head and a fussy, ponderous way of speaking. He dressed in some dark thin cloth that looked like alpaca.[4] His interest in sugar and in Cuba was purely financial—he didn't know anything about it from the practical standpoint. I really saw him at close quarters, too, for he was delayed on his boat when the directors went up to Santa Inez and Farrell left Richards and me and two or three armed guards to come up that afternoon.

Mr. Prossert was very affable. He asked me a number of questions. I knew the job well enough and could have answered almost any intelligent question—I mean, the sort that a trained engineer would be likely to ask. As it was, I suppose I'd said for perhaps the third time, "I'm afraid I wouldn't know, sir. We haven't any calculations on that," getting a glance of mildly surprised disbelief, when Richards suddenly spoke up. "I think, about nine million cubic feet, sir," he said. He looked boyishly embarrassed. "I just happened to be working it out last night. Just for my own interest, that is. Not officially." He blushed.

"Oh," said Mr. Prossert, turning in his seat and giving him a sharp look. "That's very interesting, Mr.—er—Richards, isn't it? Well, now, maybe you could tell me about——"

Richards could. He knew everything. He knew to the last car the capacity of every switch and yard; he knew the load limits of every bridge and culvert;[5] he knew the average rainfall for the last twenty years; he knew the population of the various straggling villages we passed through; he knew the heights of the distant blue peaks to the west. He had made himself familiar with local labor costs and wage scales. He had the statistics on accidents and unavoidable delays. He had figured out the costs of moving a cubic yard of earth at practically

4. **alpaca** (ăl-păk′ə): a thin cloth of blended cotton, rayon, and wool, made to look like the wool of the alpaca.
5. **culvert** (kŭl′vərt): sewer or drain.

every cut and fill. All the way up Mr. Prossert fired questions at him and he fired answers right back.

When we reached the railhead,[6] a motor was waiting to take Mr. Prossert on. Getting out of the gas car, he nodded absent-mindedly to me, shook hands with Richards. "Very interesting indeed," he said. "Very interesting indeed, Mr. Richards. Goodbye and thank you."

"Not at all, sir," Richards said. "Glad if I could be of service to you."

As soon as the motor moved off, I exploded. "Of all the asinine tricks! A little honest bluff doesn't hurt; but some of your so-called figures——"

"I aim to please," Richards said, grinning. "If a man like Prossert wants to know something, who am I to hold out on him?"

"I suppose you think you're smart," I told him. "What's he going to think when he looks up the figures or asks somebody who does know?"

"Listen, my son," said Richards kindly. "He wasn't asking for any information he was going to use. He doesn't want to know those figures. If he ever does, he has plenty of people to get him the right ones. He won't remember these. I don't even remember them myself. What he is going to remember is you and me."

"Oh, yes?"

"Oh, yes," said Richards firmly. "He's going to remember that Panamerica Steel & Structure has a bright young man named Richards who could tell him everything he wanted to know when he wanted to know it—just the sort of chap he can use; not like that other fellow who took no interest in his job, couldn't answer the simplest question, and who's going to be doing small-time contracting in Cuba all his life."

"Oh, yeah?" I said. But it is true that I am still in Cuba, still doing a little work in the construction line.

6. **railhead:** the farthest point to which rails for a railroad have been laid.

First Response: *Which character did you find yourself rooting for—Richards or the narrator? Why?*

CHECKING UP (True/False)

1. The narrator and Richards both worked for United Sugar.
2. Farrell was construction manager for Panamerica Steel.
3. The narrator impressed Prossert with his intelligence and training.
4. Prossert easily saw through Richards' bluffing.
5. Richards was a poor engineer but a good judge of characer.

TALKING IT OVER

1. This story gives us a picture of two young engineers at the start of their careers. How are they different in attitude and ability?
2. Richards claims that he is the "executive type." How does the incident with Prossert demonstrate what he means?
3. When the outcome of a situation is the opposite of what we were expecting, we say that it is **ironic**. In what way is the outcome of "Success Story" ironic? Why is Richards a success?
4. Consider the author's attitude toward the characters and events in the story. Do you think his attitude is realistic? pessimistic? scornful? Give reasons for your answer.
5. In the second paragraph of the story, the narrator says about Richards, ". . . I couldn't then imagine how he had managed to get his job. I have an idea now." What has the narrator figured out?

THE AUTHOR AND THE NARRATOR

The **narrator** of a short story is the person who tells the events of the story from his or her own point of view. This person is either a character in the story or an outside observer of the events. The **author,** who is the writer of the story, usually remains in the background. When you read a story, it is important to distinguish the narrator from the author.

1. The narrator of "Success Story" says about Richards, "I liked him a lot, once I was sure that he wasn't going to outshine me." What does this remark suggest about the narrator's confidence in his ability?
2. The narrator says to Richards, "Boy, you are undoubtedly the dumbest man in Santa Clara province. If you don't buck up, Farrell will see you never get another job down here." What does this comment reveal about the narrator's attitude toward interacting with other people?
3. Richards' faults are obvious because the narrator points them out to us. By allowing the narrator to speak and think in a certain way, however, the author indirectly points to the narrator's shortcomings. What are these shortcomings?

UNDERSTANDING THE WORDS IN THE STORY (Completion)

Choose one of the words in the following list to complete each of the sentences below. A word may be used only once.

affable	inconspicuous
nominally	stout
scornful	jaunt
ponderous	formality
patronize	asinine

1. The children liked to visit the old man because he didn't _____ them or talk down to them.

2. Since Fiona had already been hired for the job, she knew that the next interview would be a mere _____.

3. We were _____ of those who disagreed with us.

4. Everyone knew that Allie's father considered all politicians stupid, so it came as no surprise when he pronounced the mayor's speech _____ from beginning to end.

5. Because the director had such a _____ way of answering questions, everyone tried to avoid asking them.

6. Even though Ronan feared meeting Spaulding's mother, her _____ manner set him at ease right away.

7. He was a short, _____ man with a hearty appetite.

8. On a weekend _____ through Michigan, they stopped to visit some friends.

9. _____ at work on an urban renewal project, Cheever took advantage of the city's numerous movie theaters.

10. Magda hung her poster in such a(n) _____ spot that weeks passed before her family noticed it.

WRITING IT DOWN
A Persuasive Essay

Persuasive speaking or writing attempts to influence the beliefs or actions of its audience. Good persuasive discourse uses arguments that appeal to logic—people's sense of reason—and also to emotion. If, for example, you need to persuade members of the school board to increase the budget for your school's athletic program, you will support your opinion with logical arguments: The parallel bars need to be replaced; more equipment is needed for the rising student population. You will also use emotional argument: New equipment will boost school pride and spirit! Don't you want the best for your students?

Using both logical and emotional arguments, write an outline for a persuasive essay about success in a job or career. Your **purpose** will be to convince your readers to agree with your opinion about what qualities are most important to success. To organize your ideas, you may find it helpful to fill out an outline such as the one on the following page.

PERSUASIVE ESSAY

INTRODUCTION: _____
_____

PURPOSE OF ESSAY: _____
_____
_____

OPENING SENTENCE: _____
_____
_____

SUPPORT
  Logical Arguments: _____
_____
_____
_____

  Emotional Arguments: _____
_____
_____
_____

A Personal Essay

In "Success Story," the narrator and Richards take different approaches toward achieving success. Which approach do you think you might apply some day to your own job or career?

Write a brief essay about how you plan to achieve success. For example, will you try to acquire any special skills? Will you work hard? Will you try to prove to others—or to yourself—that you know your job well?

SPEAKING AND LISTENING
A Group Discussion

In a round-table discussion with a small group of classmates, compare and contrast the personalities of Richards and the narrator. For each character, what values and goals were at "the heart of the matter"?

ABOUT THE AUTHOR

James Gould Cozzens (1903–1978) was, from an early age, dedicated to becoming a writer. As a teenager he recorded his thoughts and activities in detailed diaries, and while a student at Harvard he had his first book published. Cozzens went on to publish thirteen more novels and one collection of short stories, *Children and Others*. In 1948 he received the Pulitzer Prize for *Guard of Honor*.

In his writings Cozzens explores the necessity of conforming to society's values and norms. His characters, primarily middle- and upper-class men, represent, to Cozzens, the backbone of contemporary American life. "Success Story" first appeared in *Collier's* magazine.

THE MAN TO SEND RAINCLOUDS

Leslie Marmon Silko

The Southwest, because of its history, has a rich legacy of various cultural traditions that exist side by side. Think of how you have been affected by cultures other than your own — in the foods you eat, the clothes you wear, and the music you enjoy.

They found him under a big cottonwood tree. His Levi jacket and pants were faded light blue so that he had been easy to find. The big cottonwood tree stood apart from a small grove of winter bare cottonwoods which grew in the wide, sandy arroyo.[1] He had been dead for a day or more, and the sheep had wandered and scattered up and down the arroyo. Leon and his brother-in-law, Ken, gathered the sheep and left them in the pen at the sheep camp before they returned to the cottonwood tree. Leon waited under the tree while Ken drove the truck through the deep sand to the edge of the arroyo. He squinted up at the sun and unzipped his jacket—it sure was hot for this time of year. But high and northwest the blue mountains were still in snow. Ken came sliding down the low, crumbling bank about fifty yards down, and he was bringing the red blanket.

Before they wrapped the old man, Leon took a piece of string out of his pocket and tied a small gray feather in the old man's long white hair. Ken gave him the paint. Across the brown wrinkled forehead he drew a streak of white and along the high cheekbones he drew a strip of blue paint. He paused and watched Ken throw pinches of corn meal and pollen into the wind that fluttered the small gray feather. Then Leon painted with yellow under the old man's broad nose, and finally, when he had painted green across the chin, he smiled.

"Send us rain clouds, Grandfather." They laid the bundle in the back of the pickup and covered it with a heavy tarp before they started back to the pueblo.[2]

---

1. **arroyo** (ə-roi'ō): a deep, dry gully cut by a stream that flows intermittently.
2. **pueblo** (pwĕb'lō): a communal village inhabited by the Pueblo peoples. The Pueblos comprise various Native American groups who live in the southwestern United States.

They turned off the highway onto the sandy pueblo road. Not long after they passed the store and post office they saw Father Paul's car coming toward them. When he recognized their faces he slowed his car and waved for them to stop. The young priest rolled down the car window.

"Did you find old Teofilo?" he asked loudly.

Leon stopped the truck. "Good morning, Father. We were just out to the sheep camp. Everything is O.K. now."

"Thank God for that. Teofilo is a very old man. You really shouldn't allow him to stay at the sheep camp alone."

"No, he won't do that any more now."

"Well, I'm glad you understand. I hope I'll be seeing you at Mass this week—we missed you last Sunday. See if you can get old Teofilo to come with you." The priest smiled and waved at them as they drove away.

Louise and Teresa were waiting. The table was set for lunch, and the coffee was boiling on the black iron stove. Leon looked at Louise and then at Teresa.

"We found him under a cottonwood tree in the big arroyo near sheep camp. I guess he sat down to rest in the shade and never got up again." Leon walked toward the old man's bed. The red plaid shawl had been shaken and spread carefully over the bed, and a new brown flannel shirt and pair of stiff new Levi's were arranged neatly beside the pillow. Louise held the screen door open while Leon and Ken carried in the red blanket. He looked small and shriveled, and after they dressed him in the new shirt and pants he seemed more shrunken.

It was noontime now because the church bells rang the Angelus.[3] They ate the beans with hot bread, and nobody said anything until after Teresa poured the coffee.

Ken stood up and put on his jacket. "I'll see about the gravediggers. Only the top layer of soil is frozen. I think it can be ready before dark."

Leon nodded his head and finished his coffee. After Ken had been gone for a while, the neighbors and clanspeople came quietly to embrace Teofilo's family and to leave food on the table because the gravediggers would come to eat when they were finished.

3. **Angelus** (an′jə-ləs): a prayer named for its opening word, "angel," in Latin and said at morning, noon, and evening.

The sky in the west was full of pale yellow light. Louise stood outside with her hands in the pockets of Leon's green army jacket that was too big for her. The funeral was over, and the old men had taken their candles and medicine bags and were gone. She waited until the body was laid into the pickup before she said anything to Leon. She touched his arm, and he noticed that her hands were still dusty from the corn meal that she had sprinkled around the old man. When she spoke, Leon could not hear her.

"What did you say? I didn't hear you."

"I said that I had been thinking about something."

"About what?"

"About the priest sprinkling holy water for Grandpa. So he won't be thirsty."

Leon stared at the new moccasins that Teofilo had made for the ceremonial dances in the summer. They were nearly hidden by the red blanket. It was getting colder, and the wind pushed gray dust down the narrow pueblo road. The sun was approaching the long mesa where it disappeared during the winter. Louise stood there shivering and watching his face. Then he zipped up his jacket and opened the truck door. "I'll see if he's there."

Ken stopped the pickup at the church, and Leon got out; and then Ken drove down the hill to the graveyard where people were waiting. Leon knocked at the old carved door with its symbols of the Lamb.[4] While he waited he looked up at the twin bells from the king of Spain with the last sunlight pouring around them in their tower.

The priest opened the door and smiled when he saw who it was. "Come in! What brings you here this evening?"

The priest walked toward the kitchen, and Leon stood with his cap in his hand, playing with the earflaps and examining the living room—the brown sofa, the green armchair, and the brass lamp that hung down from the ceiling by links of chain. The priest dragged a chair out of the kitchen and offered it to Leon.

"No thank you, Father. I only came to ask you if you would bring your holy water to the graveyard."

The priest turned away from Leon and looked out the window at

---

4. **symbols of the Lamb:** Jesus Christ is often referred to as the "Lamb of God."

the patio full of shadows and the dining-room windows of the nuns' cloister[5] across the patio. The curtains were heavy, and the light from within faintly penetrated; it was impossible to see the nuns inside eating supper. "Why didn't you tell me he was dead? I could have brought the Last Rites[6] anyway."

Leon smiled. "It wasn't necessary, Father."

The priest stared down at his scuffed brown loafers and the worn hem of his cassock.[7] "For a Christian burial it was necessary."

His voice was distant, and Leon thought that his blue eyes looked tired.

"It's OK, Father, we just want him to have plenty of water."

The priest sank down into the green chair and picked up a glossy missionary magazine. He turned the colored pages full of lepers and pagans without looking at them.

"You know I can't do that, Leon. There should have been the Last Rites and a funeral Mass at the very least."

Leon put on his green cap and pulled the flaps down over his ears. "It's getting late, Father. I've got to go."

When Leon opened the door Father Paul stood up and said, "Wait." He left the room and came back wearing a long brown overcoat. He followed Leon out the door and across the dim churchyard to the adobe steps in front of the church. They both stooped to fit through the low adobe entrance. And when they started down the hill to the graveyard only half of the sun was visible above the mesa.

The priest approached the grave slowly, wondering how they had managed to dig into the frozen ground; and then he remembered that this was New Mexico, and saw the pile of cold loose sand beside the hole. The people stood close to each other with little clouds of steam puffing from their faces. The priest looked at them and saw a pile of jackets, gloves, and scarves in the yellow, dry tumbleweeds that grew in the graveyard. He looked at the red blanket, not sure that Teofilo was so small, wondering if it wasn't some perverse Indian trick—something they did in March to ensure a good harvest—wondering if maybe old

---

5. **cloister** (kloi′stər): a monastery or convent; a place for religious seclusion.
6. **Last Rites:** in the Roman Catholic Church, the final rites and prayers for a person who is close to death.
7. **cassock** (kăs′ək): a robe worn by members of the clergy.

Teofilo was actually at sheep camp corralling the sheep for the night. But there he was, facing into a cold dry wind and squinting at the last sunlight, ready to bury a red wool blanket while the faces of his parishioners were in shadow with the last warmth of the sun on their backs.

His fingers were stiff, and it took him a long time to twist the lid off the holy water. Drops of water fell on the red blanket and soaked into dark icy spots. He sprinkled the grave and the water disappeared almost before it touched the dim, cold sand; it reminded him of something— he tried to remember what it was, because he thought if he could remember he might understand this. He sprinkled more water; he shook the container until it was empty, and the water fell through the light from sundown like August rain that fell while the sun was still shining, almost evaporating before it touched the wilted squash flowers.

The wind pulled at the priest's brown Franciscan[8] robe and swirled away the corn meal and pollen that had been sprinkled on the blanket. They lowered the bundle into the ground, and they didn't bother to untie the stiff pieces of new rope that were tied around the ends of the blanket. The sun was gone, and over on the highway the eastbound lane was full of headlights. The priest walked away slowly. Leon watched him climb the hill, and when he had disappeared within the tall, thick walls, Leon turned to look up at the high blue mountains in the deep snow that reflected a faint red light from the west. He felt good because it was finished, and he was happy about the sprinkling of the holy water; now the old man could send them big thunderclouds for sure.

8. **Franciscan:** a Roman Catholic religious order named for St. Francis of Assisi, who founded it in the thirteenth century.

First Response: *Who do you think is "the man to send rainclouds"?*

CHECKING UP (True/False)

1. Teofilo had been herding sheep before he died.
2. Leon and Ken wrapped Teofilo's body in an old sheet.
3. Leon and Ken wanted holy water for Teofilo's grave.
4. The priest offered to sprinkle holy water on the grave.
5. The neighbors and clanspeople came to comfort Teofilo's family and leave food on the table.

TALKING IT OVER

1. The season of the year in which a story takes place is sometimes an important part of the story's **setting.** At what time of year does "The Man to Send Rainclouds" take place? How is the season important to the story?
2. To prepare Teofilo's body for burial, Leon and Ken perform a traditional ceremony. Why do they perform this ritual?
3. Father Paul tells Leon and Ken that they shouldn't allow Teofilo to stay at the sheep camp alone. Why is their response **ironic,** or the opposite of what we would expect? Why do you think they mislead the priest?
4. For both the Native American people and the Franciscan priest, water is an important part of the burial ceremony. Why do Leon and Ken change their minds about involving Father Paul?
5. When Father Paul sprinkles the holy water on the grave, it falls "through the light from sundown like August rain. . . ." How does this image **symbolize,** or represent, the events of the story?
6. What evidence in the story suggests that the Native Americans in this story move in two worlds—the world of the Christian workers and that of their traditional culture? What does the story suggest lies at "the heart of the matter" for the Native American characters?
7. What is the narrator's attitude toward these characters and their differing cultures? Do you think the story is told with sympathy for all the characters?

UNDERSTANDING THE WORDS IN THE STORY (Multiple-Choice)

1. A *tarp* is used to
   a. start an engine
   b. cover and protect something
   c. decorate a building
2. To *embrace* is to
   a. visit
   b. move
   c. hug
3. A *mesa* is a
   a. high, flat plateau
   b. heavy downpour
   c. sharp rock
4. A *glossy* magazine is
   a. filled with pictures
   b. large and colorful
   c. smooth and shiny
5. A *perverse* trick might be described as
   a. improper and contrary
   b. amusing and ingenious
   c. grim and repulsive

WRITING IT DOWN
An Outline for a Personal Narrative

When you write a **personal narrative,** you focus on an experience that happened to you, and you explore the meaning of that experience. A personal narrative is different from a short story because it tells about events that have actually taken place. However, a personal narrative has many of the elements of a short story, including plot, characters, and setting.

Write an outline for a personal narrative about your participation in a ceremony. Focus on the meaning that this participation held for you. Here are some examples of ceremonies from which you might choose:

religious ceremonies	holiday meals
awards ceremonies	weddings
graduations	funerals

To outline your narrative, you may find it helpful to fill out a chart such as the one below.

PERSONAL NARRATIVE CHART

NATURE OF CEREMONY: _____

SETTING: _____

PEOPLE INVOLVED: _____

EVENTS/ACTIONS IN TIME ORDER

1. _____
2. _____
3. _____
4. _____

MEMORABLE WORDS/QUOTATIONS:

_____

_____

IMPORTANT OBJECTS: _____

_____

YOUR FEELINGS/OPINIONS

Before Experience: _____

After Experience: _____

ABOUT THE AUTHOR

Leslie Marmon Silko was born in 1948 in Albuquerque, New Mexico. She grew up on the Laguna Pueblo Reservation there, in a community with a strong sense of Native American history and tradition.

Silko first received critical attention in 1977 with the publication of her novel *Ceremony*, which focuses on the lives of Laguna veterans of World War II. Silko is probably best known for her numerous short stories and poems, which reflect her Native American consciousness. Joseph Bruchac, who has edited anthologies of Native American literature, has said of her writing, "These stories are both recent personal reminiscences and very old myths and, at times, the two blend. The boundary lines between the 'real' world and the world of legends and between 'today' and the ancient, though continuing past are very thin in all of her work." One of Silko's most recent works is an ambitious novel called *Almanac of the Dead* (1991).

"The Man to Send Rainclouds" has appeared in an anthology of the same title, and also in *Storyteller*, an unusual collection of old photographs, stories, and story-poems.

DEAD MEN'S PATH
Chinua Achebe

Is change always for the better? Have you ever seen—or heard about—a situation in which one group of people wanted to try out new ideas while another group wanted to "stick to the way we've always done it"? What happened? Discuss the episode with a few of your classmates.

Michael Obi's hopes were fulfilled much earlier than he had expected. He was appointed headmaster of Ndume[1] Central School in January 1949. It had always been an unprogressive school, so the Mission authorities decided to send a young and energetic man to run it. Obi accepted this responsibility with enthusiasm. He had many wonderful ideas and this was an opportunity to put them into practice. He had had sound secondary school education which designated him a "pivotal teacher" in the official records and set him apart from the other headmasters in the mission field. He was outspoken in his condemnation of the narrow views of these older and often less-educated ones.

"We shall make a good job of it, shan't we?" he asked his young wife when they first heard the joyful news of his promotion.

"We shall do our best," she replied. We shall have such beautiful gardens and everything will be just *modern* and delightful . . ." In their two years of married life she had become completely infected by his passion for "modern methods" and his denigration of "these old and superannuated[2] people in the teaching field who would be better employed as traders in the Onitsha[3] market." She began to see herself already as the admired wife of the young headmaster, the queen of the school.

The wives of the other teachers would envy her position. She would set the fashion in everything . . . Then, suddenly, it occurred to her that there might not be other wives. Wavering between hope and fear, she

---

1. **Ndume** (n-dōō′mē).
2. **superannuated** (sōō′pər-ăn′yōō-ā-tĭd): too old to be useful.
3. **Onitsha** (ō-nĭch′ə): a commercial center in Nigeria.

asked her husband, looking anxiously at him.

"All our colleagues are young and unmarried," he said with enthusiasm which for once she did not share. "Which is a good thing," he continued.

"Why?"

"Why? They will give all their time and energy to the school."

Nancy was downcast. For a few minutes she became skeptical about the new school; but it was only for a few minutes. Her little personal misfortune could not blind her to her husband's happy prospects. She looked at him as he sat folded up in a chair. He was stoop-shouldered and looked frail. But he sometimes surprised people with sudden bursts of physical energy. In his present posture, however, all his bodily strength seemed to have retired behind his deep-set eyes, giving them an extraordinary power of penetration. He was only twenty-six, but looked thirty or more. On the whole, he was not unhandsome.

"A penny for your thoughts, Mike," said Nancy after a while, imitating the woman's magazine she read.

"I was thinking what a grand opportunity we've got at last to show these people how a school should be run."

Ndume School was backward in every sense of the word. Mr. Obi put his whole life into the work, and his wife hers too. He had two aims. A high standard of teaching was insisted upon, and the school compound[4] was to be turned into a place of beauty. Nancy's dream-gardens came to life with the coming of the rains, and blossomed. Beautiful hibiscus and allemande hedges in brilliant red and yellow marked out the carefully tended school compound from the rank neighbourhood bushes.

One evening as Obi was admiring his work he was scandalized to see an old woman from the village hobble right across the compound, through a marigold flower-bed and the hedges. On going up there he found faint signs of an almost disused path from the village across the school compound to the bush on the other side.

"It amazes me," said Obi to one of his teachers who had been three years in the school, "that you people allowed the villagers to make use

---

4. **compound:** an enclosed area for a group of buildings.

of this footpath. It is simply incredible." He shook his head.

"The path," said the teacher apologetically, "appears to be very important to them. Although it is hardly used, it connects the village shrine with their place of burial."

"And what has that got to do with the school?" asked the headmaster.

"Well, I don't know," replied the other with a shrug of the shoulders. "But I remember there was a big row[5] some time ago when we attempted to close it."

"That was some time ago. But it will not be used now," said Obi as he walked away. "What will the Government Education Officer think of this when he comes to inspect the school next week? The villagers might, for all I know, decide to use the schoolroom for a pagan ritual during the inspection."

Heavy sticks were planted closely across the path at the two places where it entered and left the school premises. These were further strengthened with barbed wire.

Three days later the village priest of *Ani* called on the headmaster. He was an old man and walked with a slight stoop. He carried a stout walking-stick which he usually tapped on the floor, by way of emphasis, each time he made a new point in his argument.

"I have heard," he said after the usual exchange of cordialities, "that our ancestral footpath has recently been closed . . ."

"Yes," replied Mr. Obi. 'We cannot allow people to make a highway of our school compound."

"Look here, my son," said the priest bringing down his walking-stick, "this path was here before you were born and before your father was born. The whole life of this village depends on it. Our dead relatives depart by it and our ancestors visit us by it. But most important, it is the path of children coming in to be born . . ."

Mr. Obi listened with a satisfied smile on his face.

"The whole purpose of our school," he said finally, "is to eradicate just such beliefs as that. Dead men do not require footpaths. The whole idea is just fantastic. Our duty is to teach your children to laugh at such ideas."

---

5. **row** (rou): a noisy quarrel.

"What you say may be true," replied the priest, "but we follow the practices of our fathers. If you reopen the path we shall have nothing to quarrel about. What I always say is: let the hawk perch and let the eagle perch." He rose to go.

"I am sorry," said the young headmaster. "But the school compound cannot be a thoroughfare. It is against our regulations. I would suggest your constructing another path, skirting our premises. We can even get our boys to help in building it. I don't suppose the ancestors will find the little detour too burdensome."

"I have no more words to say," said the old priest, already outside.

Two days later a young woman in the village died in childbed. A diviner[6] was immediately consulted and he prescribed heavy sacrifices to propitiate[7] ancestors insulted by the fence.

Obi woke up next morning among the ruins of his work. The beautiful hedges were torn up not just near the path but right round the school, the flowers trampled to death and one of the school buildings pulled down . . . That day, the white Supervisor came to inspect the school and wrote a nasty report on the state of the premises but more seriously about the "tribal-war situation developing between the school and the village, arising in part from the misguided zeal of the new headmaster."

6. **diviner:** one who interprets omens or foretells the future.
7. **propitiate** (prō-pĭsh′ē-āt′): to regain the good will of or to pacify.

First Response: *Did you feel sorry for Michael Obi at the end of the story, or did you feel that he "got what he deserved"?*

CHECKING UP

1. What does Michael Obi hope to accomplish as headmaster of Ndume Central School?
2. What news comes as a disappointment to his wife?

3. Why is Obi anxious to close the path right away?
4. What event causes the villagers to seek revenge?
5. How do the villagers take revenge?

TALKING IT OVER

1. What is Michael Obi's attitude toward the beliefs of the villagers?
2. In the discussion between Obi and the village priest, which of the two shows more tolerance for the other's beliefs? What is the meaning of the proverb the priest recites to Obi?
3. According to the priest, why is the path important to the life of the village? Why is the death of the young woman so significant?
4. A situation is **ironic** when the outcome is the opposite of what was expected. What is ironic about Obi's closing the path with heavy sticks and barbed wire? In light of Obi's ambitions, why is the conclusion of the story ironic?
5. In what sense was the headmaster's zeal "misguided"?
6. Is the main conflict in this story a clash between characters, between generations, or between ideas? Explain.

UNDERSTANDING THE WORDS IN THE STORY
(Matching Columns)

1. thoroughfare	a. deviation from the direct way
2. pivotal	b. named; appointed
3. designated	c. overgrown; coarse
4. skirting	d. intense enthusiasm
5. downcast	e. to root out; eliminate
6. cordialities	f. passing along the edge of
7. detour	g. public way or passage
8. rank	h. central; crucial
9. zeal	i. friendly warmth
10. eradicate	j. sad; depressed

WRITING IT DOWN
A Letter to a Colleague

Imagine that you are Michael Obi and that the school has finally been rebuilt. You now hear that a fellow teacher at another school—who is as enthusiastic as yourself—is also at odds with the people of his village. You decide to write a letter to your friend to help him avoid suffering the consequences of "misguided zeal" as you did.

Before you begin your letter, you might want to jot down a few thoughts about what you should have done differently in your own situation. For example, should you have shown respect for the beliefs of the people around you? How could your enthusiasm have been put to better use? You might want to begin your letter by briefly describing the events that took place in your village.

SPEAKING AND LISTENING
Improvising a Scene

To *improvise* is to make something up as you go along. Improvise the scene that might have followed if a local news team had decided to cover the story breaking at the Ndume School. Assign one student to play the role of "investigative reporter," and others to play the roles of the characters in the story, including Michael and Nancy Obi and the priest. You might want to create roles for related characters such as the Supervisor and the people of the village.

Begin by compiling a list of questions for the reporter to ask. Give each person playing the role of a character a few minutes to decide how he or she will respond to those questions.

Comparing Two Stories

Join with a small group of classmates to compare Leslie Marmon Silko's "The Man to Send Rainclouds" (page 92) with Chinua Achebe's "Dead Men's Path." Begin by discussing how the idea of conflict between cultures is treated in each story. Then think about each author's attitude toward the subject, or the story's tone. Finally, discuss the values that, according to these stories, form "the heart of the matter."

ABOUT THE AUTHOR

Chinua Achebe (chĭn'wä' ä-chä'bē) is widely regarded as one of Africa's leading writers. He was born in 1930 in the southeastern, Ibo (ē'bō) region of Nigeria. The son of Christian missionaries, he attended the local missionary school where his father taught. He began to learn English at the age of eight. In 1948 he was among the first students admitted to the University College at Ibadan, in western Nigeria. He studied English literature, history, and religion.

While working as a broadcaster in Lagos, the nation's capital, Achebe wrote his first four novels, *Things Fall Apart* (1958), *No Longer at Ease* (1960), *Arrow of God* (1964), and *A Man of the People* (1966). During the Nigerian civil war (1967–1970), in which the Eastern Region fought unsuccessfully for independence, Achebe supported the short-lived Ibo state of Biafra.

Achebe has taught and lectured all over the world, and has edited collections of fiction and poetry by modern African writers. His recent works include a novel, *Anthills of the Savannah* (1987), and a collection of essays, *Hopes and Impediments* (1988).

THE BRACELET

Yoshiko Uchida°

---

*Shortly after the bombing of Pearl Harbor on December 7, 1941, all
people of Japanese descent living on the West Coast of the United
States were evacuated to internment camps.*

*If your family had to move to another part of the country, how
would you feel about leaving your best friend? Take a minute to write
down a few thoughts.*

"Mama, is it time to go?"

I hadn't planned to cry, but the tears came suddenly, and I wiped them away with the back of my hand. I didn't want my older sister to see me crying.

"It's almost time, Ruri," my mother said gently. Her face was filled with a kind of sadness I had never seen before.

I looked around at my empty room. The clothes that Mama always told me to hang up in the closet, the junk piled on my dresser, the old rag doll I could never bear to part with; they were all gone. There was nothing left in my room, and there was nothing left in the rest of the house. The rugs and furniture were gone, the pictures and drapes were down, and the closets and cupboards were empty. The house was like a gift box after the nice thing inside was gone; just a lot of nothingness.

It was almost time to leave our home, but we weren't moving to a nicer house or to a new town. It was April 21, 1942. The United States and Japan were at war, and every Japanese person on the West Coast was being evacuated by the government to a concentration camp. Mama, my sister Keiko and I were being sent from our home, and out of Berkeley, and eventually, out of California.

The doorbell rang, and I ran to answer it before my sister could. I thought maybe by some miracle, a messenger from the government might be standing there, tall and proper and buttoned into a uniform, come to tell us it was all a terrible mistake; that we wouldn't have to leave after all. Or maybe the messenger would have a telegram from

°**Yoshiko Uchida** (yō-shē′kō ōo-chē′dä).

108

Papa, who was interned in a prisoner-of-war camp in Montana because he had worked for a Japanese business firm.

The FBI had come to pick up Papa and hundreds of other Japanese community leaders on the very day that Japanese planes had bombed Pearl Harbor. The government thought they were dangerous enemy aliens. If it weren't so sad, it would have been funny. Papa could no more be dangerous than the mayor of our city, and he was every bit as loyal to the United States. He had lived here since 1917.

When I opened the door, it wasn't a messenger from anywhere. It was my best friend, Laurie Madison, from next door. She was holding a package wrapped up like a birthday present, but she wasn't wearing her party dress, and her face drooped like a wilted tulip.

"Hi," she said. "I came to say good-bye."

She thrust the present at me and told me it was something to take to camp. "It's a bracelet," she said before I could open the package. "Put it on so you won't have to pack it." She knew I didn't have one inch of space left in my suitcase. We had been instructed to take only what we could carry into camp, and Mama had told us that we could each take only two suitcases.

"Then how are we ever going to pack the dishes and blankets and sheets they've told us to bring with us?" Keiko worried.

"I don't really know," Mama said, and she simply began packing those big impossible things into an enormous duffel bag—along with umbrellas, boots, a kettle, hot plate, and flashlight.

"Who's going to carry that huge sack?" I asked.

But Mama didn't worry about things like that. "Someone will help us," she said. "Don't worry." So I didn't.

Laurie wanted me to open her package and put on the bracelet before she left. It was a thin gold chain with a heart dangling on it. She helped me put it on, and I told her I'd never take it off, ever.

"Well, good-bye then," Laurie said awkwardly. "Come home soon."

"I will," I said, although I didn't know if I would ever get back to Berkeley again.

I watched Laurie go down the block, her long blond pigtails bouncing as she walked. I wondered who would be sitting in my desk at Lincoln Junior High now that I was gone. Laurie kept turning and waving, even walking backwards for a while, until she got to the corner. I didn't want to watch anymore, and I slammed the door shut.

The next time the doorbell rang, it was Mrs. Simpson, our other neighbor. She was going to drive us to the Congregational church, which was the Civil Control Station where all the Japanese of Berkeley were supposed to report.

It was time to go. "Come on, Ruri. Get your things," my sister called to me.

It was a warm day, but I put on a sweater and my coat so I wouldn't have to carry them, and I picked up my two suitcases. Each one had a tag with my name and our family number on it. Every Japanese family had to register and get a number. We were Family Number 13453.

Mama was taking one last look around our house. She was going from room to room, as though she were trying to take a mental picture of the house she had lived in for fifteen years, so she would never forget it.

I saw her take a long last look at the garden that Papa loved. The irises beside the fish pond were just beginning to bloom. If Papa had been home, he would have cut the first iris blossom and brought it inside to Mama. "This one is for you," he would have said. And Mama would have smiled and said, "Thank you, Papa San,"[1] and put it in her favorite cut-glass vase.

But the garden looked shabby and forsaken now that Papa was gone and Mama was too busy to take care of it. It looked the way I felt, sort of empty and lonely and abandoned.

When Mrs. Simpson took us to the Civil Control Station, I felt even worse. I was scared, and for a minute I thought I was going to lose my breakfast right in front of everybody. There must have been over a thousand Japanese people gathered at the church. Some were old and some were young. Some were talking and laughing, and some were crying. I guess everybody else was scared too. No one knew exactly what was going to happen to us. We just knew we were being taken to the Tanforan Racetracks, which the army had turned into a camp for the Japanese. There were fourteen other camps like ours along the West Coast.

---

1. **Papa San:** In Japan, the suffix *san* is added to a name as a mark of respect.

What scared me most were the soldiers standing at the doorway of the church hall. They were carrying guns with mounted bayonets. I wondered if they thought we would try to run away, and whether they'd shoot us or come after us with their bayonets if we did.

A long line of buses waited to take us to camp. There were trucks, too, for our baggage. And Mama was right; some men were there to help us load our duffel bag. When it was time to board the buses, I sat with Keiko and Mama sat behind us. The bus went down Grove Street and passed the small Japanese food store where Mama used to order her bean-curd cakes and pickled radish. The windows were all boarded up, but there was a sign still hanging on the door that read, "We are loyal Americans."

The crazy thing about the whole evacuation was that we were all loyal Americans. Most of us were citizens because we had been born here. But our parents, who had come from Japan, couldn't become citizens because there was a law that prevented any Asian from becoming a citizen. Now everybody with a Japanese face was being shipped off to concentration camps.

"It's stupid," Keiko muttered as we saw the racetrack looming up beside the highway. "If there were any Japanese spies around, they'd have gone back to Japan long ago."

"I'll say," I agreed. My sister was in high school and she ought to know, I thought.

When the bus turned into Tanforan, there were more armed guards at the gate, and I saw barbed wire strung around the entire grounds. I felt as though I were going into a prison, but I hadn't done anything wrong.

We streamed off the buses and poured into a huge room, where doctors looked down our throats and peeled back our eyelids to see if we had any diseases. Then we were given our housing assignments. The man in charge gave Mama a slip of paper. We were in Barrack 16, Apartment 40.

"Mama!" I said. "We're going to live in an apartment!" The only apartment I had ever seen was the one my piano teacher lived in. It was in an enormous building in San Francisco with an elevator and thick carpeted hallways. I thought how wonderful it would be to have our own elevator. A house was all right, but an apartment seemed elegant and special.

We walked down the racetrack looking for Barrack 16. Mr. Noma, a friend of Papa's, helped us carry our bags. I was so busy looking around, I slipped and almost fell on the muddy track. Army barracks had been built everywhere, all around the racetrack and even in the center oval.

Mr. Noma pointed beyond the track toward the horse stables. "I think your barrack is out there."

He was right. We came to a long stable that had once housed the horses of Tanforan, and we climbed up the wide ramp. Each stall had a number painted on it, and when we got to 40, Mr. Noma pushed open the door.

"Well, here it is," he said, "Apartment 40."

The stall was narrow and empty and dark. There were two small windows on each side of the door. Three folded army cots were on the dust-covered floor and one light bulb dangled from the ceiling. That was all. This was our apartment, and it still smelled of horses.

Mama looked at my sister and then at me. "It. won't be so bad when we fix it up," she began. "I'll ask Mrs. Simpson to send me some material for curtains. I could make some cushions too, and . . . well . . . " She stopped. She couldn't think of anything more to say.

Mr. Noma said he'd go get some mattresses for us. "I'd better hurry before they're all gone." He rushed off. I think he wanted to leave so that he wouldn't have to see Mama cry. But he needn't have run off, because Mama didn't cry. She just went out to borrow a broom and began sweeping out the dust and dirt. "Will you girls set up the cots?" she asked.

It was only after we'd put up the last cot that I noticed my bracelet was gone. " I've lost Laurie's bracelet! " I screamed. "My bracelet's gone!"

We looked all over the stall and even down the ramp. I wanted to run back down the track and go over every inch of ground we'd walked on, but it was getting dark and Mama wouldn't let me.

I thought of what I'd promised Laurie. I wasn't ever going to take the bracelet off, not even when I went to take a shower. And now I had lost it on my very first day in camp. I wanted to cry.

I kept looking for it all the time we were in Tanforan. I didn't stop looking until the day we were sent to another camp, called Topaz, in the middle of a desert in Utah. And then I gave up.

But Mama told me never mind. She said I didn't need a bracelet to remember Laurie, just as I didn't need anything to remember Papa or our home in Berkeley or all the people and things we loved and had left behind.

"Those are things we can carry in our hearts and take with us no matter where we are sent," she said.

And I guess she was right. I've never forgotten Laurie, even now.

First Response: *Do you agree with Mama's statement at the end of the story? Why or why not?*

CHECKING UP

1. How long had Ruri's mother lived in the house?
2. Which family members are leaving with Ruri?
3. Where had Ruri's father been sent?
4. Why does Ruri wear the bracelet instead of packing it?
5. Who drives Ruri and her family to the Civil Control Station?

TALKING IT OVER

1. How do Ruri's descriptions of her empty room and the abandoned garden help establish the mood of the story?
2. A **symbol** can be an object or a place that stands for a larger idea. How is the garden a symbol of Ruri's feelings?
3. **Irony** is a situation or idea that is the reverse of our expectations. Why is there irony in the message of the sign hanging on the Japanese food store that the family passes?
4. Why is Ruri excited at first about living in an apartment? How are her hopes cruelly disappointed?
5. Despite the sadness in this story, Mama manages to comfort Ruri by reminding her of what things are truly valuable. Why, according to Mama, are physical "things" not necessary for remembering people and places we have loved?

UNDERSTANDING THE WORDS IN THE STORY (Jumbles)

Use the clues to solve the jumble items. The solutions are drawn from the glossary word bank below.

Glossary Word Bank

interned	evacuated	looming
bayonets	eventually	forsaken

1. L E E L T V A N Y U   In the course of time

2. D N R I E N T E   Imprisoned

3. G O I L M N O   Appearing threateningly

4. K R A N F S E O   Abandoned

5. C A T U V E E D A   Forced to move from

WRITING IT DOWN
A Book Review

Many newspapers and magazines have a section in which books are reviewed. Book reviews help inform people of current issues, and they help readers decide which books may be of interest to them.

Often, when two or more books on the same subject have been published, they are reviewed together. The writer of the review examines the way each author has treated that subject and may compare the books. If, for example, two books about basketball are published this month, a reviewer may read both and write a review comparing the books. Although one might focus on a young girl's desire to become a professional basketball player and the other might talk about a teenage boy's ambition to own a basketball team, the books will probably address some similar issues.

Imagine that you are the book-review editor of a well-known magazine. The five stories in this unit have come to you (in book form), and you are to review two of them. The subject of all the stories is, of course, "the heart of the matter"—what is truly important in life. In "Home," for example, everyday activities and family closeness are what Maud Martha values most.

Begin by thinking about the characters in each story. What troublesome situation does each one face? How does that situation reveal the heart of the matter? Which characters have a clear understanding of what is valuable to them and which characters come to such an understanding as a result of their experiences? What is the theme, or underlying message, of each story? What is at the heart of the matter for the characters in each story? You might find it helpful to organize your thoughts into a chart such as the one below.

STORY	CHARACTERS	PROBLEM	"HEART OF THE MATTER"

Begin your review with an introduction that tells your readers what you will be writing about. For example:

> When people of different cultures live side by side, some type of conflict is likely to arise. This type of conflict is illustrated in two stories: "The Man to Send Rainclouds," by Leslie Marmon Silko, and "Dead Men's Path," by Chinua Achebe.

Be sure to develop your review with specific references to the stories.

ABOUT THE AUTHOR

Yoshiko Uchida (1921–1992) saw her own family split apart during the Second World War. On the day that Pearl Harbor was bombed, her father was taken away, and she and her mother and brother were sent to an internment camp in Topaz, Utah. Uchida wrote about her internment experience in *Journey to Topaz* (1971).

Uchida wrote a number of books for young people, including *The Dancing Kettle and Other Japanese Folk Tales* (1949) and *The Invisible Thread: A Memoir* (1991). She tried to increase Asian American people's sense of personal history while addressing universal concerns. She once said that she wrote "to celebrate our common humanity, for the basic elements of humanity are present in all our strivings."

THE REVOLT OF THE EVIL FAIRIES

Ted Poston

What is a "no-win" situation? Have you ever come across one?
Think about these questions for a moment and then discuss them
with your classmates.

The grand dramatic offering of the Booker T. Washington Colored Grammar School was the biggest event of the year in our social life in Hopkinsville, Kentucky. It was the one occasion on which they let us use the old Cooper Opera House, and even some of the white folks came out yearly to applaud our presentation. The first two rows of the orchestra were always reserved for our white friends, and our leading colored citizens sat right behind them—with an empty row intervening, of course.

Mr. Ed Smith, our local undertaker, invariably occupied a box to the left of the house and wore his cutaway coat[1] and striped breeches. This distinctive garb was usually reserved for those rare occasions when he officiated at the funerals of our most prominent colored citizens. Mr. Thaddeus Long, our colored mailman, once rented a tuxedo and bought a box too. But nobody paid him much mind. We knew he was just showing off.

The title of our play never varied. It was always Prince Charming and the Sleeping Beauty, but no two presentations were ever the same. Miss H. Belle LaPrade, our sixth-grade teacher, rewrote the script every season, and it was never like anything you read in the storybooks.

Miss LaPrade called it "a modern morality play[2] of conflict between

---

1. **cutaway coat:** a man's formal coat, with the front edges cut out away from the waist.
2. **morality play:** a type of drama popular during the Middle Ages, in which battling characters represented different virtues and vices.

the forces of good and evil." And the forces of evil, of course, always came off second best.

The Booker T. Washington Colored Grammar School was in a state of ferment from Christmas until February, for this was the period when parts were assigned. First there was the selection of the Good Fairies and the Evil Fairies. This was very important, because the Good Fairies wore white costumes and the Evil Fairies black. And strangely enough most of the Good Fairies usually turned out to be extremely light in complexion, with straight hair and white folks' features. On rare occasions a darkskinned girl might be lucky enough to be a Good Fairy, but not one with a speaking part.

There never was any doubt about Prince Charming and the Sleeping Beauty. They were always lightskinned. And though nobody ever discussed those things openly, it was an accepted fact that a lack of pigmentation was a decided advantage in the Prince Charming and Sleeping Beauty sweepstakes.

And therein lay my personal tragedy. I made the best grades in my class, I was the leading debater, and the scion of a respected family in the community. But I could never be Prince Charming, because I was black.

In fact, every year when they started casting our grand dramatic offering my family started pricing black cheesecloth at Franklin's Department Store. For they knew that I would be leading the forces of darkness and skulking back in the shadows—waiting to be vanquished in the third act. Mamma had experience with this sort of thing. All my brothers had finished Booker T. before me.

Not that I was alone in my disappointment. Many of my classmates felt it too. I probably just took it more to heart. Rat Joiner, for instance, could rationalize the situation. Rat was not only black; he lived on Billy Goat Hill. But Rat summed it up like this:

"If you black, you black."

I should have been able to regard the matter calmly too. For our grand dramatic offering was only a reflection of our daily community life in Hopkinsville. The yallers[3] had the best of everything. They held most of the teaching jobs in Booker T. Washington Colored Grammar

---

3. **yallers:** a term for light-skinned blacks.

School. They were the Negro doctors, the lawyers, the insurance men. They even had a "Blue Vein Society,"[4] and if your dark skin obscured your throbbing pulse you were hardly a member of the elite. Yet I was inconsolable the first time they turned me down for Prince Charming. That was the year they picked Roger Jackson. Roger was not only dumb; he stuttered. But he was light enough to pass for white, and that was apparently sufficient.

In all fairness, however, it must be admitted that Roger had other qualifications. His father owned the only colored saloon in town and was quite a power in local politics. In fact, Mr. Clinton Jackson had a lot to say about just who taught in the Booker T. Washington Colored Grammar School. So it was understandable that Roger should have been picked for Prince Charming.

My real heartbreak, however, came the year they picked Sarah Williams for Sleeping Beauty. I had been in love with Sarah since kindergarten. She had soft light hair, bluish-gray eyes, and a dimple which stayed in her left cheek whether she was smiling or not.

Of course Sarah never encouraged me much. She never answered any of my fervent love letters, and Rat was very scornful of my one-sided love affairs. "As long as she don't call you a big baboon," he sneered, "you'll keep on hanging around."

After Sarah was chosen for Sleeping Beauty, I went out for the Prince Charming role with all my heart. If I had declaimed boldly in previous contests, I was matchless now. If I had bothered Mamma with rehearsals at home before, I pestered her to death this time. Yes, and I purloined my sister's can of Palmer's Skin Success.[5]

I knew the Prince's role from start to finish, having played the Head Evil Fairy opposite it for two seasons. And Prince Charming was one character whose lines Miss LaPrade never varied much in her many versions. But although I never admitted it, even to myself, I knew I was doomed from the start. They gave the part to Leonardius Wright. Leonardius, of course, was yarrler.

The teachers sensed my resentment. They were almost apologetic. They pointed out that I had been such a splendid Head Evil Fairy for

4. **"Blue Vein Society":** a group of blacks who felt superior because their skin color was light enough to show blue veins.
5. **Palmer's Skin Success:** a commercial product for lightening the skin.

two seasons that it would be a crime to let anybody else try the role. They reminded me that Mamma wouldn't have to buy any more cheesecloth because I could use my same old costume. They insisted that the Head Evil Fairy was even more important than Prince Charming because he was the one who cast the spell on Sleeping Beauty. So what could I do but accept?

I had never liked Leonardius Wright. He was a goody-goody, and even Mamma was always throwing him up to me. But, above all, he too was in love with Sarah Williams. And now he got a chance to kiss Sarah every day in rehearsing the awakening scene.

Well, the show must go on, even for little black boys. So I threw my soul into my part and made the Head Evil Fairy a character to be remembered. When I drew back from the couch of Sleeping Beauty and slunk away into the shadows at the approach of Prince Charming, my facial expression was indeed something to behold. When I was vanquished by the shining sword of Prince Charming in the last act, I was a little hammy perhaps—but terrific!

The attendance at our grand dramatic offering that year was the best in its history. Even the white folks overflowed the two rows reserved for them, and a few were forced to sit in the intervening one. This created a delicate situation, but everybody tactfully ignored it.

When the curtain went up on the last act, the audience was in fine fettle.[6] Everything had gone well for me too—except for one spot in the second act. That was where Leonardius unexpectedly rapped me over the head with his sword as I slunk off into the shadows. That was not in the script, but Miss LaPrade quieted me down by saying it made a nice touch anyway. Rat said Leonardius did it on purpose.

The third act went on smoothly, though, until we came to the vanquishing scene. That was where I slunk from the shadows for the last time and challenged Prince Charming to mortal combat. The hero reached for his shining sword—a bit unsportsmanlike, I always thought, since Miss LaPrade consistently left the Head Evil Fairy unarmed—and then it happened!

Later I protested loudly—but in vain—that it was a case of self-defense. I pointed out that Leonardius had a mean look in his eye. I

6. **in fine fettle:** in good spirits.

cited the impromptu rapping he had given my head in the second act. But nobody would listen. They just wouldn't believe that Leonardius really intended to brain me when he reached for his sword.

Anyway, he didn't succeed. For the minute I saw that evil gleam in his eye—or was it my own?—I cut loose with a right to the chin, and Prince Charming dropped his shining sword and staggered back. His astonishment lasted only a minute, though, for he lowered his head and came charging in, fists flailing. There was nothing yellow about Leonardius but his skin.

The audience thought the scrap was something new Miss LaPrade had written in. They might have kept on thinking so if Miss LaPrade hadn't been screaming so hysterically from the sidelines. And if Rat Joiner hadn't decided that this was as good a time as any to settle old scores. So he turned around and took a sock at the male Good Fairy nearest him.

When the curtain rang down, the forces of Good and Evil were locked in combat. And Sleeping Beauty was wide awake and streaking for the wings.

They rang the curtain back up fifteen minutes later, and we finished the play. I lay down and expired according to specifications but Prince Charming will probably remember my sneering corpse to his dying day. They wouldn't let me appear in the grand dramatic offering at all the next year. But I didn't care. I couldn't have been Prince Charming anyway.

First Response: *If you had been the narrator, would you have chosen a different course of action? Explain your answer.*

CHECKING UP (True/False)

1. Miss LaPrade used the same script each year.
2. The narrator made the best grades in his class.
3. The narrator's disappointment was shared by his classmates.

4. The teachers were unaware of the narrator's resentment.
5. The audience thought that the fight was part of the play.

TALKING IT OVER

1. What is the narrator's "personal tragedy"?
2. What do you think the character of Rat Joiner contributes to the story? How does he serve as a contrast to the narrator?
3. The **climax** of a story is its turning point, or moment of greatest intensity. What is the climax of this story? Explain your answer.
4. How does the narrator prolong the **suspense,** or feeling of tension and excitement, as he describes the third act?
5. Miss LaPrade refers to the production as a "modern morality play." How could this description apply to the story itself?
6. The **tone** of this story—its overall mood, or atmosphere— is humorous. What examples of humor can you find in the story?

PLOT
Exposition and Conflict

Plot is the carefully worked-out sequence of events in a story. A plot has a structure—that is, all the individual parts of the story are arranged and interrelated in order to lead to a satisfying conclusion.

A traditional plot structure has a section of **exposition,** which gives the reader important background information. Most stories also have a **conflict**—a problem or struggle of some kind. Conflict is the most important element in a plot.

There are two major kinds of conflict, external and internal. **External conflict** is a character's struggle with another person, with society as a whole, or with an outside force (such as a force of nature or an animal). **Internal conflict** is the character's struggle to subdue or come to terms with his or her own inner feelings, attitudes, or desires.

1. Reread the exposition in the first five paragraphs of "The Revolt of the Evil Fairies." Where does the story take place? What event is at the center of the story? Who is telling the story?

2. What external conflict does the narrator face? How does this conflict reflect the larger conflict within the community?
3. What internal conflict does the narrator experience?

UNDERSTANDING THE WORDS IN THE STORY (Multiple-Choice)

1. An *intervening* row is one that is
   a. off to the side
   b. between other rows
   c. blocked off
2. Mr. Ed Smith's *garb* refers to his
   a. clothing
   b. facial expression
   c. prudent behavior
3. A *scion* of a family is one of the family's
   a. friends
   b. critics
   c. descendants
4. If you *rationalize* a situation, you
   a. find ways to explain it
   b. reject it
   c. get angry at it
5. If you are a member of the *elite*, you are in
   a. trouble
   b. the top rank of society
   c. a dilemma
6. You *declaim* when you
   a. apologize
   b. back down
   c. speak eloquently
7. To *purloin* something is to
   a. analyze it
   b. steal it
   c. respect it

8. If people behave *tactfully,* they may be said to act
   a. diplomatically
   b. outrageously
   c. shyly
9. Leonardius' *impromptu* rapping in the second act was
   a. improper
   b. unrehearsed
   c. malicious
10. When the narrator *expired* on stage, he pretended to
    a. catch his breath
    b. fight back
    c. die

WRITING IT DOWN
A List of Story Conflicts

At the heart of every good story is some kind of conflict. Think of some situations that could be developed into short-story conflicts. Begin by filling in a chart like the one below, which lists the four types of conflict used in fiction. For example, for "character vs. character" you might write "baseball players arguing about whether the runner is safe or out"; for "character vs. force of nature," you could enter "hikers battle a sudden storm."

CHARACTER vs. CHARACTER
CHARACTER vs. SOCIETY
CHARACTER vs. FORCE OF NATURE
CHARACTER vs. SELF

ABOUT THE AUTHOR

Ted Poston (1906–1974), who was born Theodore Roosevelt Augustus Major Poston in Hopkinsville, Kentucky, was one of the first African Americans to work as a full-time staff reporter for a white-owned daily newspaper. As a teenager Poston worked as a copy clerk on his family's controversial weekly, the *Contender.* After receiving his bachelor's degree, he joined the staff of the *Amsterdam News,* an important black weekly in New York City. He was promoted to city editor in 1934, but lost the job after leading a strike to unionize the paper.

A few years later Poston was hired as a reporter for the *New York Post;* he kept that position until he retired in 1972. In addition to covering City Hall, he traveled frequently to the South during the 1940s and 1950s to report on the racial turmoil there. Those assignments, dangerous for an African American reporter, earned Poston several awards.

Poston also contributed short stories, articles, and reviews to a number of periodicals. "The Revolt of the Evil Fairies" was published in *New Republic* in 1942.

THE DINNER PARTY

Mona Gardner

People react differently to tense situations. Some remain calm and collected while others panic. Think about whom you would most like to have nearby in a crisis.

The country is India. A colonial official[1] and his wife are giving a large dinner party. They are seated with their guests—army officers and government attachés[2] and their wives, and a visiting American naturalist[3]—in their spacious dining room, which has a bare marble floor, open rafters and wide glass doors opening onto a veranda.

A spirited discussion springs up between a young girl who insists that women have outgrown the jumping-on-a-chair-at-the-sight-of-a-mouse era and a colonel who says that they haven't.

"A woman's unfailing reaction in any crisis," the colonel says, "is to scream. And while a man may feel like it, he has that ounce more of nerve control than a woman has. And that last ounce is what counts."

The American does not join in the argument but watches the other guests. As he looks, he sees a strange expression come over the face of the hostess. She is staring straight ahead, her muscles contracting slightly. With a slight gesture she summons the native boy standing behind her chair and whispers to him. The boy's eyes widen: he quickly leaves the room.

Of the guests, none except the American notices this or sees the boy place a bowl of milk on the veranda just outside the open doors.

The American comes to with a start. In India, milk in a bowl means only one thing—bait for a snake. He realizes there must be a cobra in the room. He looks up at the rafters—the likeliest place—but they are bare. Three corners of the room are empty, and in the fourth the servants are waiting to serve the next course. There is only one place left—under the table.

---

1. **colonial official:** At this time India was a British colony.
2. **attachés** (ăt′ə-shāz′, ă-tă′shāz′): officials on the staff of a diplomatic mission.
3. **naturalist:** a person who studies animals and plants.

His first impulse is to jump back and warn the others, but he knows the commotion would frighten the cobra into striking. He speaks quickly, the tone of his voice so arresting that it sobers everyone.

"I want to know just what control everyone at this table has. I will count to three hundred—that's five minutes—and not one of you is to move a muscle. Those who move will forfeit fifty rupees.[4] Ready!"

The twenty people sit like stone images while he counts. He is saying ". . . two hundred and eighty . . ." when, out of the corner of his eye, he sees the cobra emerge and make for the bowl of milk. Screams ring out as he jumps to slam the veranda doors safely shut.

"You were right, Colonel!" the host exclaims. "A man has just shown us an example of perfect control."

"Just a minute," the American says, turning to his hostess. "Mrs. Wynnes, how did you know that cobra was in the room?"

A faint smile lights up the woman's face as she replies: "Because it was crawling across my foot."

---

4. **rupees** (roo'-pēz): The rupee is the basic monetary unit of India, like the dollar in the United States.

First Response: *In this crisis, who do you think showed more self-control—the American naturalist or Mrs. Wynnes?*

CHECKING UP (Multiple-Choice)

1. Which of the following statements would the colonel agree with?
   a. "Women never show courage."
   b. "Men show greater self-control than women."
   c. "Men do not experience fear."

2. The naturalist knows that there is a snake in the room because
   a. he sees a strange expression on his hostess' face
   b. the native boy's eyes widen in alarm
   c. a bowl of milk is placed on the veranda
3. The naturalist gets everyone to sit still by
   a. warning them about the snake
   b. challenging the guests to test their self-control
   c. offering to pay each guest money
4. We can assume that the cobra did not strike Mrs. Wynnes because
   a. she kept her body absolutely still
   b. cobras do not attack women
   c. it wasn't hungry

TALKING IT OVER

1. The first sentence of the story tells us that the action takes place in India. Why is this information important to the story?
2. The American is identified as a *naturalist*. How does his training as a scientist show itself in his behavior?
3. The colonel believes that men always show greater self-control than women. What do the events of the story show about his belief?
4. A situation is said to be **ironic** when the outcome of events is the opposite of what is expected or believed to be true. Why is the twist at the end of this story ironic?

PLOT
Climax and Resolution

Once the major conflict of a story is established, the plot generally moves toward a **climax,** the point of greatest intensity. The climax determines how the story will turn out.

The final part of a story is its **resolution,** in which the conflict is resolved, or worked out. The resolution makes clear the outcome of events.

1. What is the climax of this story?
2. How is the conflict resolved? Do you think that the resolution is a fitting conclusion to the story?

UNDERSTANDING THE WORDS IN THE STORY (Multiple-Choice)

1. A *spacious* dining room is
   a. large and comfortable
   b. well decorated
   c. huge and impressive
2. The *rafters* of a house are
   a. tiles decorating the walls
   b. beams supporting the roof
   c. ceiling fans
3. A *veranda* is
   a. an open porch
   b. a screen door
   c. a circular staircase
4. A *spirited* discussion is
   a. an angry quarrel
   b. a lively conversation
   c. a seance with a medium
5. An *unfailing* reaction is one that is
   a. unfavorable
   b. certain
   c. unfeeling
6. When the muscles of her face *contract,* the hostess
   a. smiles broadly
   b. opens her eyes in alarm
   c. draws her brows together

7. When the hostess *summons* the native boy, she
   a. orders him to approach
   b. criticizes him
   c. reports him to the police
8. A *commotion* is
   a. noisy
   b. quiet
   c. stealthy
9. If the guests who move *forfeit* fifty rupees, they will
   a. surrender the money as a penalty
   b. lend the money to the hostess
   c. give the money as a reward to the native boy
10. When the American sees the cobra *emerge,* the snake
   a. rises up to strike
   b. becomes visible
   c. weaves across the room

WRITING IT DOWN
An Incident for a Story Plot

Think of an incident that could be turned into the climax, or turning point, of a short story: for example, an argument between two people, a crucial examination, or an athletic event. Begin building a plot around this event by entering notes onto a chart like the one below.

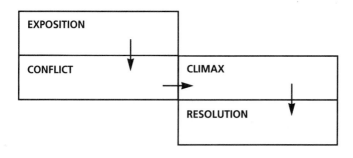

A Dialogue

Imagine the conversation between the colonel and the young girl *following* the events of the dinner party. Write the dialogue for that scene. To begin the dialogue, you might have the young girl say, "Colonel, do you still believe that a woman always screams in a crisis?" Use the dialogue in "The Dinner Party" as a model for paragraphing and punctuating your writing.

ABOUT THE AUTHOR

Mona Gardner (1900–1981), who was born in Seattle, Washington, chose the settings for many of her novels and short stories from the places she visited. Hong Kong, Malaysia, and Thailand are among the countries in which she traveled. In fact, one of her novels is called *Hong Kong*. Gardner's stories were published in several magazines, including *The New Yorker, Saturday Review of Literature,* and *Reader's Digest.*

STOLEN DAY

Sherwood Anderson

A "stolen day" is a day spent away from one's normal duties and responsibilities. How would you spend such a day? Jot down a few ideas before you read the story.

It must be that all children are actors. The whole thing started with a boy on our street named Walter, who had inflammatory rheumatism.[1] That's what they called it. He didn't have to go to school.

Still he could walk about. He could go fishing in the creek or the waterworks pond. There was a place up at the pond where in the spring the water came tumbling over the dam and formed a deep pool. It was a good place. Sometimes you could get some good big ones there.

I went down that way on my way to school one spring morning. It was out of my way but I wanted to see if Walter was there.

He was, inflammatory rheumatism and all. There he was, sitting with a fish pole in his hand. He had been able to walk down there all right.

It was then that my own legs began to hurt. My back too. I went on to school but, at the recess time, I began to cry. I did it when the teacher, Sarah Suggett, had come out into the schoolhouse yard.

She came right over to me.

"I ache all over," I said. I did, too.

I kept on crying and it worked all right.

"You'd better go on home," she said.

So I went. I limped painfully away. I kept on limping until I got out of the schoolhouse street.

Then I felt better. I still had inflammatory rheumatism pretty bad but I could get along better.

I must have done some thinking on the way home.

"I'd better not say I have inflammatory rheumatism," I decided. "Maybe if you've got that you swell up."

I thought I'd better go around to where Walter was and ask him about that, so I did—but he wasn't there.

---

1. **inflammatory rheumatism** (ro͞oʹmə-tĭzʹəm): a painful disease affecting the joints and muscles.

"They must not be biting today," I thought.

I had a feeling that, if I said I had inflammatory rheumatism, Mother or my brothers and my sister Stella might laugh. They did laugh at me pretty often and I didn't like it at all.

"Just the same," I said to myself, "I have got it." I began to hurt and ache again.

I went home and sat on the front steps of our house. I sat there a long time. There wasn't anyone at home but Mother and the two little ones. Ray would have been four or five then and Earl might have been three.

It was Earl who saw me there. I had got tired sitting and was lying on the porch. Earl was always a quiet, solemn little fellow.

He must have said something to Mother for presently she came.

"What's the matter with you? Why aren't you in school?" she asked.

I came pretty near telling her right out that I had inflammatory rheumatism but I thought I'd better not. Mother and Father had been speaking of Walter's case at the table just the day before. "It affects the heart," Father had said. That frightened me when I thought of it. "I might die," I thought. "I might just suddenly die right here; my heart might stop beating."

On the day before I had been running a race with my brother Irve. We were up at the fairgrounds after school and there was a half-mile track.

"I'll bet you can't run a half-mile," he said. "I bet you I could beat you running clear around the track."

And so we did it and I beat him, but afterwards my heart did seem to beat pretty hard. I remembered that lying there on the porch. "It's a wonder, with my inflammatory rheumatism and all, I didn't just drop down dead," I thought. The thought frightened me a lot. I ached worse than ever.

"I ache, Ma," I said. "I just ache."

She made me go in the house and upstairs and get into bed.

It wasn't so good. It was spring. I was up there for perhaps an hour, maybe two, and then I felt better.

I got up and went downstairs. "I feel better, Ma," I said.

Mother said she was glad. She was pretty busy that day and hadn't paid much attention to me. She had made me get into bed upstairs and then hadn't even come up to see how I was.

I didn't think much of that when I was up there but when I got downstairs where she was, and when, after I had said I felt better and she only said she was glad and went right on with her work, I began to ache again.

I thought, "I'll bet I die of it. I bet I do."

I went out to the front porch and sat down. I was pretty sore at Mother.

"If she really knew the truth, that I have the inflammatory rheumatism and I may just drop down dead any time, I'll bet she wouldn't care about that either," I thought.

I was getting more and more angry the more thinking I did.

"I know what I'm going to do," I thought; "I'm going to go fishing."

I thought that, feeling the way I did, I might be sitting on the high bank just above the deep pool where the water went over the dam, and suddenly my heart would stop beating.

And then, of course, I'd pitch forward, over the bank into the pool and, if I wasn't dead when I hit the water, I'd drown sure.

They would all come home to supper and they'd miss me.

"But where is he?"

Then Mother would remember that I'd come home from school aching.

She'd go upstairs and I wouldn't be there. One day during the year before, there was a child got drowned in a spring. It was one of the Wyatt children.

Right down at the end of the street there was a spring under a birch tree and there had been a barrel sunk in the ground.

Everyone had always been saying the spring ought to be kept covered, but it wasn't.

So the Wyatt child went down there, played around alone, and fell in and got drowned.

Mother was the one who had found the drowned child. She had gone to get a pail of water and there the child was, drowned and dead.

This had been in the evening when we were all at home, and Mother had come running up the street with the dead, dripping child in her arms. She was making for the Wyatt house as hard as she could run, and she was pale.

She had a terrible look on her face, I remembered then.

"So," I thought, "they'll miss me and there'll be a search made. Very likely there'll be someone who has seen me sitting by the pond fishing, and there'll be a big alarm and all the town will turn out and they'll drag the pond."

I was having a grand time, having died. Maybe, after they found me and had got me out of the deep pool, Mother would grab me up in her arms and run home with me as she had run with the Wyatt child.

I got up from the porch and went around the house. I got my fishing pole and lit out for the pool below the dam. Mother was busy—she always was—and didn't see me go. When I got there I thought I'd better not sit too near the edge of the high bank.

By this time I didn't ache hardly at all, but I thought.

"With inflammatory rheumatism you can't tell," I thought.

"It probably comes and goes," I thought.

"Walter has it and he goes fishing," I thought.

I had got my line into the pool and suddenly I got a bite. It was a regular whopper. I knew that. I'd never had a bite like that.

I knew what it was. It was one of Mr. Fenn's big carp.

Mr. Fenn was a man who had a big pond of his own. He sold ice in the summer and the pond was to make the ice. He had bought some big carp and put them into his pond and then, earlier in the spring when there was a freshet,[2] his dam had gone out.

So the carp had got into our creek and one or two big ones had been caught—but none of them by a boy like me.

The carp was pulling and I was pulling and I was afraid he'd break my line, so I just tumbled down the high bank, holding onto the line and got right into the pool. We had it out, there in the pool. We struggled. We wrestled. Then I got a hand under his gills and got him out.

He was a big one all right. He was nearly half as big as I was myself. I had him on the bank and I kept one hand under his gills and I ran.

I never ran so hard in my life. He was slippery, and now and then he wriggled out of my arms; once I stumbled and fell on him, but I got him home.

So there it was. I was a big hero that day. Mother got a washtub and filled it with water. She put the fish in it and all the neighbors came to

2. **freshet:** a sudden overflowing of a stream from a heavy rain or thaw.

look. I got into dry clothes and went down to supper—and then I made a break that spoiled my day.

There we were, all of us, at the table, and suddenly Father asked what had been the matter with me at school. He had met the teacher, Sarah Suggett, on the street and she had told him how I had become ill.

"What was the matter with you?" Father asked, and before I thought what I was saying I let it out.

"I had the inflammatory rheumatism," I said—and a shout went up. It made me sick to hear them, the way they all laughed.

It brought back all the aching again, and like a fool I began to cry.

"Well, I *have* got it—I *have*, I *have*," I cried, and I got up from the table and ran upstairs.

I stayed there until Mother came up. I knew it would be a long time before I heard the last of the inflammatory rheumatism. I was sick all right, but the aching I now had wasn't in my legs or in my back.

First Response: *As you read the story, did you sense that the narrator's day would not end happily? Explain your answer.*

CHECKING UP

Arrange the following events in the order in which they occur in the story.

> The narrator begins to cry during recess.
> Mother puts the big carp in the washtub.
> The narrator sees Walter fishing at the pond.
> The narrator's mother sends him upstairs to bed.
> The narrator tells his family that he has inflammatory rheumatism.
> The narrator's father asks him why he left school.

The narrator's legs and back begin to hurt.

The narrator gets his fishing pole and heads for the pool.

The narrator wrestles with the fish.

The narrator gets a bite on his line.

TALKING IT OVER

1. This story is told by an adult who remembers an episode in his childhood. He opens the narrative by saying, "It must be that all children are actors." How do the events of the story show this to have been true in his own case?
2. How does the narrator convince himself that he has inflammatory rheumatism? What do you suppose is his motivation?
3. Why does the narrator become angry at his mother? What dramatic scene does he imagine as punishment for her?
4. In what way is the narrator's day "stolen"?
5. What kind of ache does the narrator have at the end of the story?

PLOT
Flashback

The sequence of events in a story usually follows chronological order. Sometimes, however, an author will interrupt a narrative to relate an incident that has already occurred. Such an interruption is called a **flashback**. In "Stolen Day," for example, the narrator tells about a drowning accident that had occurred a year earlier.

1. What causes the narrator to remember the death of the Wyatt child?
2. How does this memory stimulate him to imagine the effect of his own death?

WRITING IT DOWN
An Anecdote

The narrator of "Stolen Day" says, "It must be that all children are actors." Do you agree with him? Think of an episode from your own childhood in which you—or one of your friends—could have been considered an "actor." What happened? Was the motivation for the "acting" the same as that of the narrator in the story? Write about the episode in the form of an **anecdote,** a brief, entertaining account that illustrates a point.

ABOUT THE AUTHOR

Sherwood Anderson (1867–1941) was born in Camden, Ohio. When he was fourteen, he left school and worked at various jobs. Finally he moved to Chicago, where he met a number of intellectuals, including Theodore Dreiser and Carl Sandburg. Encouraged by them, he gave up his work in order to write. He felt that his experiences had given him a sense of the aspirations of small-town Americans.

One of Anderson's most important themes was the impact of industrialization on the long-held values and traditions of rural America. *Winesburg, Ohio* (1919), a collection of stories about the inhabitants of a small Midwestern town, is his most famous work. Its theme of self-discovery and its psychological exploration of the unhappy lives of Winesburg's residents influenced several writers, including Ernest Hemingway.

WHO'S THERE?

Arthur C. Clarke

Have you ever been in a frightening situation, one in which you were you afraid you "might not make it"? Describe the episode in a sentence or two.

When Satellite Control called me, I was writing up the day's progress report in the Observation Bubble—the glass-domed office that juts out from the axis of the Space Station like the hubcap of a wheel. It was not really a good place to work, for the view was too overwhelming. Only a few yards away I could see the construction teams performing their slow-motion ballet as they put the station together like a giant jigsaw puzzle. And beyond them, twenty thousand miles below, was the blue-green glory of the full Earth, floating against the raveled star clouds of the Milky Way.

"Station Supervisor here," I answered. "What's the trouble?"

"Our radar's showing a small echo two miles away, almost stationary, about five degrees west of Sirius.[1] Can you give us a visual report on it?"

Anything matching our orbit so precisely could hardly be a meteor; it would have to be something we'd dropped—perhaps an inadequately secured piece of equipment that had drifted away from the station. So I assumed; but when I pulled out my binoculars and searched the sky around Orion,[2] I soon found my mistake. Though this space traveler was man-made, it had nothing to do with us.

"I've found it," I told Control. "It's someone's test satellite—cone-shaped, four antennas, and what looks like a lens system in its base. Probably U.S. Air Force, early nineteen-sixties, judging by the design. I know they lost track of several when their transmitters failed. There were quite a few attempts to hit this orbit before they finally made it."

After a brief search through the files, Control was able to confirm

---

1. **Sirius** (sĭr'ē-əs): the "Dog Star," in the constellation Canis Major (kā'nĭs mā'jər) in the Southern Hemisphere. It is the brightest star in the sky.
2. **Orion** (ō-rī'ən): a constellation that the ancient Greeks named for the hunter Orion, because the stars in the constellation form the figure of a man with a belt and a sword.

my guess. It took a little longer to find out that Washington wasn't in the least bit interested in our discovery of a twenty-year-old stray satellite, and would be just as happy if we lost it again.

"Well, we can't do *that*," said Control. "Even if nobody wants it, the thing's a menace to navigation. Someone had better go out and haul it aboard."

That someone, I realized, would have to be me. I dared not detach a man from the closely knit construction teams, for we were already behind schedule—and a single day's delay on this job cost a million dollars. All the radio and TV networks on Earth were waiting impatiently for the moment when they could route their programs through us, and thus provide the first truly global service, spanning the world from Pole to Pole.

"I'll go out and get it," I answered, snapping an elastic band over my papers so that the air currents from the ventilators wouldn't set them wandering around the room. Though I tried to sound as if I was doing everyone a great favor, I was secretly not at all displeased. It had been at least two weeks since I'd been outside; I was getting a little tired of stores schedules, maintenance reports, and all the glamorous ingredients of a Space Station Supervisor's life.

The only member of the staff I passed on my way to the air lock³ was Tommy, our recently acquired cat. Pets mean a great deal to men thousands of miles from Earth, but there are not many animals that can adapt themselves to a weightless environment. Tommy mewed plaintively at me as I clambered into my spacesuit, but I was in too much of a hurry to play with him.

At this point, perhaps I should remind you that the suits we use on the station are completely different from the flexible affairs men wear when they want to walk around on the moon. Ours are really baby spaceships, just big enough to hold one man. They are stubby cylinders, about seven feet long, fitted with low-powered propulsion jets, and have a pair of accordion-like sleeves at the upper end for the operator's arms. Normally, however, you keep your hands drawn inside the suit, working the manual controls in front of your chest.

As soon as I'd settled down inside my very exclusive spacecraft, I

---

3. **air lock:** an airtight compartment with adjustable pressure.

switched on power and checked the gauges on the tiny instrument panel. There's a magic word, "FORB," that you'll often hear spacemen mutter as they climb into their suits; it reminds them to test fuel, oxygen, radio, batteries. All my needles were well in the safety zone, so I lowered the transparent hemisphere over my head and sealed myself in. For a short trip like this, I did not bother to check the suit's internal lockers, which were used to carry food and special equipment for extended missions.

As the conveyor belt decanted[4] me into the air lock, I felt like an Indian papoose being carried along on its mother's back. Then the pumps brought the pressure down to zero, the outer door opened, and the last traces of air swept me out into the stars, turning very slowly head over heels.

The station was only a dozen feet away, yet I was now an independent planet—a little world of my own. I was sealed up in a tiny, mobile cylinder, with a superb view of the entire universe, but I had practically no freedom of movement inside the suit. The padded seat and safety belts prevented me from turning around, though I could reach all the controls and lockers with my hands or feet.

In space, the great enemy is the sun, which can blast you to blindness in seconds. Very cautiously, I opened up the dark filters on the "night" side of my suit, and turned my head to look out at the stars. At the same time I switched the helmet's external sunshade to automatic, so that whichever way the suit gyrated my eyes would be shielded from that intolerable glare.

Presently, I found my target—a bright fleck of silver whose metallic glint distinguished it clearly from the surrounding stars. I stamped on the jet-control pedal, and felt the mild surge of acceleration as the low-powered rockets set me moving away from the station. After ten seconds of steady thrust, I estimated that my speed was great enough, and cut off the drive. It would take me five minutes to coast the rest of the way, and not much longer to return with my salvage.

And it was at that moment, as I launched myself out into the abyss, that I knew that something was horribly wrong.

---

4. **decanted** (dĭ-kănt'əd): unloaded.

It is never completely silent inside a spacesuit; you can always hear the gentle hiss of oxygen, the faint whirr of fans and motors, the susurration[5] of your own breathing—even, if you listen carefully enough, the rhythmic thump that is the pounding of your heart. These sounds reverberate through the suit, unable to escape into the surrounding void; they are the unnoticed background of life in space, for you are aware of them only when they change.

They had changed now; to them had been added a sound which I could not identify. It was an intermittent, muffled thudding, sometimes accompanied by a scraping noise, as of metal upon metal.

I froze instantly, holding my breath and trying to locate the alien sound with my ears. The meters on the control board gave no clues; all the needles were rock-steady on their scales, and there were none of the flickering red lights that would warn of impending disaster. That was some comfort, but not much. I had long ago learned to trust my instincts in such matters; their alarm signals were flashing now, telling me to return to the station before it was too late. . . .

Even now, I do not like to recall those next few minutes, as panic slowly flooded into my mind like a rising tide, overwhelming the dams of reason and logic which every man must erect against the mystery of the universe. I knew then what it was like to face insanity; no other explanation fitted the facts.

For it was no longer possible to pretend that the noise disturbing me was that of some faulty mechanism. Though I was in utter isolation, far from any other human being or indeed any material object, I was not alone. The soundless void was bringing to my ears the faint but unmistakable stirrings of life.

In that first, heart-freezing moment it seemed that something was trying to get into my suit—something invisible, seeking shelter from the cruel and pitiless vacuum of space. I whirled madly in my harness, scanning the entire sphere of vision around me except for the blazing, forbidden cone toward the sun. There was nothing there, of course. There could not be—yet that purposeful scrabbling was clearer than ever.

Despite the nonsense that has been written about us, it is not true

---

5. **susurration** (so͞o′sə-rā′shən): soft sound, as a murmur, whisper, or rustle.

that spacemen are superstitious. But can you blame me if, as I came to the end of logic's resources, I suddenly remembered how Bernie Summers had died, no farther from the station than I was at this very moment?

It was one of those "impossible" accidents; it always is. Three things had gone wrong at once. Bernie's oxygen regulator had run wild and sent the pressure soaring, the safety valve had failed to blow—and a faulty joint had given way instead. In a fraction of a second, his suit was open to space.

I had never known Bernie, but suddenly his fate became of overwhelming importance to me—for a horrible idea had come into my mind. One does not talk about these things, but a damaged spacesuit is too valuable to be thrown away, even if it has killed its wearer. It is repaired, renumbered—and issued to someone else. . . .

What happens to the soul of a man who dies between the stars, far from his native world? Are you still here, Bernie, clinging to the last object that linked you to your lost and distant home?

As I fought the nightmares that were swirling around me—for now it seemed that the scratchings and soft fumblings were coming from all directions—there was one last hope to which I clung. For the sake of my sanity, I had to prove that this wasn't Bernie's suit—that the metal walls so closely wrapped around me had never been another man's coffin.

It took me several tries before I could press the right button and switch my transmitter to the emergency wave length. "Station!" I gasped. "I'm in trouble! Get records to check my suit history and—"

I never finished; they say my yell wrecked the microphone. But what man alone in the absolute isolation of a spacesuit would *not* have yelled when something patted him softly on the back of the neck?

I must have lunged forward, despite the safety harness, and smashed against the upper edge of the control panel. When the rescue squad reached me a few minutes later, I was still unconscious, with an angry bruise across my forehead.

And so I was the last person in the whole satellite relay system to know what had happened. When I came to my senses an hour later, all our medical staff was gathered around my bed, but it was quite a while before the doctors bothered to look at me. They were much too busy playing with the three cute little kittens our badly misnamed Tommy had been rearing in the seclusion of my spacesuit's Number Five Storage Locker.

First Response: *How did you feel as the narrator was panicking inside his spacesuit? Were you eager to find out how the story was going to end?*

CHECKING UP

1. Why does the narrator leave the space station?
2. Why doesn't the narrator check the suit's internal lockers?
3. Why is the sun an enemy to those traveling in space?
4. What causes the narrator to yell into the microphone?
5. What are the doctors busy doing when the narrator regains consciousness?

TALKING IT OVER

1. The **exposition** of a story gives the reader important background information. Where does the action of this story take place? What details are used to create a sense of place?
2. Why does the narrator decide that he is the person to retrieve the space traveler?
3. What preparations are necessary for using the spacesuit? What omission in the narrator's preparations has frightening consequences?
4. What possibilities does the narrator consider and reject in attempting to explain the noise in his spacesuit?
5. The action in a story is often built around some kind of **conflict.** What is the major conflict in this story?

PLOT
Suspense and Foreshadowing

When the narrator launches himself out into deep space, he becomes aware that something is wrong inside his spacesuit. As he tries to identify the strange sounds, you want to know what the alien presence is. As he struggles to control his panic, you want to know what is going to happen to him.

In a story, **suspense** is that element that keeps you guessing about the outcome of events. The author's purpose is to keep you excited and interested, so that you will read on to learn what happens next.

Writers often provide hints of what is to come later in a story. This method of building in clues to the outcome of the action is called **foreshadowing.**

1. What details in "Who's There?" create suspense?
2. At what point in the story did you experience the greatest suspense?
3. What hints does Clarke use to prepare you for the ending of the story?

UNDERSTANDING THE WORDS IN THE STORY
(Matching Columns)

1. confirm	a. an increase in speed
2. plaintively	b. moved in a circular path
3. clambered	c. about to happen
4. gyrated	d. total emptiness
5. acceleration	e. climbed clumsily
6. reverberate	f. plunged forward
7. void	g. establish as true
8. impending	h. isolation from others
9. lunged	i. sadly or sorrowfully
10. seclusion	j. re-echo

WRITING IT DOWN
A Critical Review

Think of a suspenseful episode from a book you have read or a movie or television show you have seen. Were you tense or nervous as the episode unfolded? Were you eager to find out what the outcome would be? Or did you find the situation silly, forced, and unbelievable?

Write a critical review of that episode. Explain why it kept you in suspense—or why it did not. Support your opinion with examples from the story or show.

SPEAKING AND LISTENING
Focusing on Suspenseful Details

Working in pairs, prepare an oral summary of a suspenseful movie or television show that you and your partner have enjoyed. Jot down some notes, focusing especially on details or plot twists that contributed to the show's suspense.

Get together with another group of partners and take turns presenting your summaries orally. Offer each other suggestions on how to make your summaries clearer and more interesting.

ABOUT THE AUTHOR

Arthur C. Clarke was born in Minehead, England in 1917. His interest in science developed early. At the age of thirteen, he constructed a telescope from an old lens and a cardboard tube.

A prolific writer, Clarke has been called "the colossus of science fiction." His collections of short stories include *Across the Sea of Stars, The Other Side of the Sky, The Nine Billion Names of God,* and *Tales of Ten Worlds.* Some well-known novels are *Childhood's End, Earthlight,* and *Islands in the Sky.* In 1969 Clarke was nominated for an Academy Award for the screenplay *2001: A Space Odyssey,* which he wrote with Stanley Kubrick. He collaborated on *First on the Moon* with the astronauts who made that milestone journey, and on *Mars and the Mind of Man* with Ray Bradbury and Carl Sagan. As an underwater photographer, Clarke has explored the Great Barrier Reef off Australia and the coast of Sri Lanka (Ceylon), where he has lived for many years.

THE INTERLOPERS

Saki (H. H. Munro)

A feud is a bitter, long-standing quarrel between two individuals, two families, or two clans. The most famous example in literature is that of the Capulets and Montagues, the warring families in Shakespeare's Romeo and Juliet. *What other feuds can you name, in either fact or fiction?*

In a forest of mixed growth somewhere on the eastern spurs of the Carpathians,[1] a man stood one winter night watching and listening, as though he waited for some beast of the woods to come within the range of his vision, and, later, of his rifle. But the game for whose presence he kept so keen an outlook was none that figured in the sportsman's calendar as lawful and proper for the chase; Ulrich von Gradwitz patrolled the dark forest in quest of a human enemy.

The forest lands of Gradwitz were of wide extent and well stocked with game; the narrow strip of precipitous[2] woodland that lay on its outskirt was not remarkable for the game it harboured or the shooting it afforded, but it was the most jealously guarded of all its owner's territorial possessions. A famous lawsuit, in the days of his grandfather, had wrested it from the illegal possession of a neighbouring family of petty landowners; the dispossessed party had never acquiesced in the judgment of the Courts, and a long series of poaching affrays[3] and similar scandals had embittered the relationships between the families for three generations. The neighbour feud had grown into a personal one since Ulrich had come to be head of his family; if there was a man in the world whom he detested and wished ill to it was Georg Znaeym, the inheritor of the quarrel and the tireless game-snatcher and raider of the disputed border-forest. The feud might, perhaps, have died down or been compromised if the personal ill-will of the two men had not stood in the way; as boys they had thirsted for one another's blood, as men each prayed that misfortune might fall on the other, and this

---

1. **Carpathians** (kär-pā′thē-ənz): mountains in central and eastern Europe.
2. **precipitous** (prĭ-sĭp′ə-təs): steep and hazardous.
3. **poaching affrays:** quarrels over trespassing for the purpose of illegal hunting.

wind-scourged winter night Ulrich had banded together his foresters to watch the dark forest, not in quest of four-footed quarry, but to keep a look-out for the prowling thieves whom he suspected of being afoot from across the land boundary. The roebuck, which usually kept in the sheltered hollows during a storm-wind, were running like driven things tonight, and there was movement and unrest among the creatures that were wont[4] to sleep through the dark hours. Assuredly there was a disturbing element in the forest, and Ulrich could guess the quarter from whence it came.

He strayed away by himself from the watchers whom he had placed in ambush on the crest of the hill, and wandered far down the steep slopes amid the wild tangle of undergrowth, peering through the tree-trunks and listening through the whistling and skirling[5] of the wind and the restless beating of the branches for sight or sound of the marauders. If only on this wild night, in this dark, lone spot, he might come across Georg Znaeym, man to man, with none to witness—that was the wish that was uppermost in his thoughts. And as he stepped round the trunk of a huge beech he came face to face with the man he sought.

The two enemies stood glaring at one another for a long silent moment. Each had a rifle in his hand, each had hate in his heart and murder uppermost in his mind. The chance had come to give full play to the passions of a lifetime. But a man who has been brought up under the code of a restraining civilization cannot easily nerve himself to shoot down his neighbour in cold blood and without word spoken, except for an offence against his hearth and honour. And before the moment of hesitation had given way to action a deed of Nature's own violence overwhelmed them both. A fierce shriek of the storm had been answered by a splitting crash over their heads, and ere they could leap aside a mass of falling beech tree had thundered down on them. Ulrich von Gradwitz found himself stretched on the ground, one arm numb beneath him and the other held almost as helplessly in a tight tangle of forked branches, while both legs were pinned beneath the fallen mass. His heavy shooting-boots had saved his feet from being crushed to pieces, but if his fractures were not as serious as they might

4. **wont:** accustomed.
5. **skirling:** making a shrill, piercing sound.

have been, at least it was evident that he could not move from his present position till someone came to release him. The descending twigs had slashed the skin of his face, and he had to wink away some drops of blood from his eyelashes before he could take in a general view of the disaster. At his side, so near that under ordinary circumstances he could almost have touched him, lay Georg Znaeym, alive and struggling, but obviously as helplessly pinioned down[6] as himself. All round them lay a thick-strewn wreckage of splintered branches and broken twigs.

Relief at being alive and exasperation at his captive plight brought a strange medley of pious thank-offerings and sharp curses to Ulrich's lips. Georg, who was nearly blinded with the blood which trickled across his eyes, stopped his struggling for a moment to listen, and then gave a short, snarling laugh.

"So you're not killed, as you ought to be, but you're caught, anyway," he cried; "caught fast. Ho, what a jest, Ulrich von Gradwitz snared in his stolen forest. There's real justice for you!"

And he laughed again, mockingly and savagely.

"I'm caught in my own forest-land," retorted Ulrich. "When my men come to release us you will wish, perhaps, that you were in a better plight than caught poaching on a neighbour's land, shame on you."

Georg was silent for a moment; then he answered quietly:

"Are you sure that your men will find much to release? I have men, too, in the forest tonight, close behind me, and *they* will be here first and do the releasing. When they drag me out from under these damned branches it won't need much clumsiness on their part to roll this mass of trunk right over on the top of you. Your men will find you dead under a fallen beech tree. For form's sake I shall send my condolences to your family."

"It is a useful hint," said Ulrich fiercely. "My men had orders to follow in ten minutes' time, seven of which must have gone by already, and when they get me out—I will remember the hint. Only as you will have met your death poaching on my lands I don't think I can decently send any message of condolence to your family."

"Good," snarled Georg, "good. We fight this quarrel out to the death,

6. **pinioned down:** immobilized.

you and I and our foresters, with no cursed interlopers to come between us. Death and damnation to you, Ulrich von Gradwitz."

"The same to you, Georg Znaeym, forest-thief, game-snatcher."

Both men spoke with the bitterness of possible defeat before them, for each knew that it might be long before his men would seek him out or find him; it was a bare matter of chance which party would arrive first on the scene.

Both had now given up the useless struggle to free themselves from the mass of wood that held them down; Ulrich limited his endeavours to an effort to bring his one partially free arm near enough to his outer coat-pocket to draw out his wine-flask. Even when he had accomplished that operation it was long before he could manage the unscrewing of the stopper or get any of the liquid down his throat. But what a Heaven-sent draught[7] it seemed! It was an open winter, and little snow had fallen as yet, hence the captives suffered less from the cold than might have been the case at that season of the year; nevertheless, the wine was warming and reviving to the wounded man, and he looked across with something like a throb of pity to where his enemy lay, just keeping the groans of pain and weariness from crossing his lips.

"Could you reach this flask if I threw it over to you?" asked Ulrich suddenly; "there is good wine in it, and one may as well be as comfortable as one can. Let us drink, even if tonight one of us dies."

"No, I can scarcely see anything; there is so much blood caked round my eyes," said Georg, "and in any case I don't drink wine with an enemy."

Ulrich was silent for a few minutes, and lay listening to the weary screeching of the wind. An idea was slowly forming and growing in his brain, an idea that gained strength every time that he looked across at the man who was fighting so grimly against pain and exhaustion. In the pain and languor that Ulrich himself was feeling the old fierce hatred seemed to be dying down.

"Neighbour," he said presently, "do as you please if your men come first. It was a fair compact. But as for me, I've changed my mind. If my men are the first to come you shall be the first to be helped, as though

---

7. **draught** (drăft): amount taken in a single swallow.

you were my guest. We have quarrelled like devils all our lives over this stupid strip of forest, where the trees can't even stand upright in a breath of wind. Lying here tonight, thinking, I've come to think we've been rather fools; there are better things in life than getting the better of a boundary dispute. Neighbour, if you will help me to bury the old quarrel I—I will ask you to be my friend."

Georg Znaeym was silent for so long that Ulrich thought, perhaps, he had fainted with the pain of his injuries. Then he spoke slowly and in jerks.

"How the whole region would stare and gabble if we rode into the market-square together. No one living can remember seeing a Znaeym and a von Gradwitz talking to one another in friendship. And what peace there would be among the forester folk if we ended our feud tonight. And if we choose to make peace among our people there is none other to interfere, no interlopers from outside. . . . You would come and keep the Sylvester night[8] beneath my roof, and I would come and feast on some high day at your castle. . . . I would never fire a shot on your land, save when you invited me as a guest; and you should come and shoot with me down in the marshes where the wildfowl are. In all the countryside there are none that could hinder if we willed to make peace. I never thought to have wanted to do other than hate you all my life, but I think I have changed my mind about things too, this last half-hour. And you offered me your wine-flask. . . . Ulrich von Gradwitz, I will be your friend."

For a space both men were silent, turning over in their minds the wonderful changes that this dramatic reconciliation would bring about. In the cold, gloomy forest, with the wind tearing in fitful gusts through the naked branches and whistling round the tree-trunks, they lay and waited for the help that would now bring release and succour to both parties. And each prayed a private prayer that his men might be the first to arrive, so that he might be the first to show honourable attention to the enemy that had become a friend.

Presently, as the wind dropped for a moment, Ulrich broke silence.

"Let's shout for help," he said; "in this lull our voices may carry a little way."

8. **Sylvester night:** New Year's Eve.

"They won't carry far through the trees and undergrowth," said Georg, "but we can try. Together, then."

The two raised their voices in a prolonged hunting call.

"Together again," said Ulrich a few minutes later, after listening in vain for an answering halloo.

"I heard something that time, I think," said Ulrich.

"I heard nothing but the pestilential wind," said Georg hoarsely.

There was silence again for some minutes, and then Ulrich gave a joyful cry.

"I can see figures coming through the wood. They are following in the way I came down the hillside."

Both men raised their voices in as loud a shout as they could muster.

"They hear us! They've stopped. Now they see us. They're running down the hill towards us," cried Ulrich.

"How many of them are there?" asked Georg.

"I can't see distinctly," said Ulrich; "nine or ten."

"Then they are yours," said Georg; "I had only seven out with me."

"They are making all the speed they can, brave lads," said Ulrich gladly.

"Are they your men?" asked Georg, "Are they your men?" he repeated impatiently as Ulrich did not answer.

"No," said Ulrich with a laugh, the idiotic chattering laugh of a man unstrung with hideous fear.

"Who are they?" asked Georg quickly, straining his eyes to see what the other would gladly not have seen.

"*Wolves.*"

First Response: *Were you completely surprised by the outcome of the story? Describe your reaction.*

CHECKING UP

1. What is the reason for the quarrel between Ulrich von Gradwitz and Georg Znaeym?
2. Why do the enemies hesitate to shoot each other down when they meet?
3. At what point does Ulrich experience a change of feeling toward his old enemy?
4. What plans do the men make for resolving their conflict?
5. Who are the interlopers?

TALKING IT OVER

1. The **exposition** at the opening of the story gives readers important background information. What do you learn about the conflict between the main characters?
2. Given the time and place of the story, is the accident in the woods believable?
3. Did you find the sudden change of heart in the two enemies believable? If they had been rescued, would they have remained friends?
4. Note the number of times the word *interlopers* appears in the story. How does this word become ironic at the end of the story?
5. Suppose the story had been called "The Feud." Would that have been as effective a title as "The Interlopers"?

PLOT
Coincidence

Coincidence is the accidental coming together of things or events in a way that seems planned or arranged rather than natural. When things happen in a story, they happen for good reasons. If events seem to be the result of coincidence rather than cause and effect, we may no longer believe in the characters and their actions.

Some writers have made skillful use of coincidence. O. Henry, whose story "The Gift of the Magi" appears on page 403, uses coincidence as a plot device in many of his stories. Consider the events at the opening of "The Interlopers." Do you think the meeting of Ulrich and Georg in the woods happens by chance, or is it the logical outcome of events that have gone before? If this is a case of coincidence, does it make the story even more effective?

UNDERSTANDING THE WORDS IN THE STORY (Analogy)

Some vocabulary questions, called *analogies,* involve two pairs of words. You must decide what relationship exists between the words in the first pair. The same relationship applies to the second pair. An analogy has a special format and uses special symbols. Analogy questions may test synonym and antonym relationships, grammatical and verbal relationships, cause-and-effect relationships, and the like. Here is an example of one type of analogy question:

> hot : cold :: simple : _____
> a. easy   c. clever
> b. complex   d. fundamental

The two dots (:) stand for "is to"; the four dots (::) stand for "as." The example reads "Hot *is to* cold *as* simple *is to* _____." Since the first two words are antonyms, the correct answer is b. The word *complex* is the opposite of *simple*. Complete the following analogies.

1. joy : sadness :: languor : _____
   a. happiness   c. weariness
   b. effort   d. energy

2. eat : devour :: acquiesce : _____
   a. assent   c. assist
   b. attack   d. fix

3. thief : steal :: marauder : _____
   a. villain   c. flee
   b. raid   d. citizen

4. obstacle : barrier :: succour : _____
   a. hindrance   c. encouragement
   b. relief   d. justice

5. mean : cruel :: pious : _____
   a. angry   c. anxious
   b. fascinated   d. devout

WRITING IT DOWN
A Radio Play

Adapt "The Interlopers" as a short radio play. Think about how you will create a sense of place and mood. Will you use background music or other sound effects? How will you convey the background of the feuding families to your audience? Will you create additional dialogue or give speaking parts to the men patrolling the forest?

In writing dialogue, remember to include directions that tell how a line should be spoken. For example:

ULRICH (fiercely): It is a useful hint.

ABOUT THE AUTHOR

Saki is the pen name of Hector Hugh Munro (1870–1916), who was born in Burma, where his father served in the police force. After his mother's death, he was brought up very strictly by two English aunts. He served a year with the Burmese police, then turned to journalism. He took the pen name Saki from *The Rubáiyát* by Omar Khayyám. It means "wine-bearer" or "bringer of joy."

Saki became famous for his whimsical, ironic short stories. He delighted in surprising his readers with unexpected endings. "The Interlopers" is from his best-known book of stories, *Beasts and Superbeasts.* Frequently anthologized stories include "The Storyteller," "The Open Window," "Sredni Vashtar," and "The Schartz-Metterklume Method." During the First World War, Munro enlisted as a private in the royal Fusiliers. He was killed in action in France on November 13, 1916.

GENTLEMAN OF RÍO EN MEDIO

Juan A. A. Sedillo

Have you ever heard of someone passing up a chance to make money rather than do something he or she didn't believe in? Discuss your answer with a small group of classmates.

It took months of negotiation to come to an understanding with the old man. He was in no hurry. What he had the most of was time. He lived up in Río en Medio, where his people had been for hundreds of years. He tilled the same land they had tilled. His house was small and wretched, but quaint. The little creek ran through his land. His orchard was gnarled and beautiful.

The day of the sale he came into the office. His coat was old, green and faded. I thought of Senator Catron,[1] who had been such a power with these people up there in the mountains. Perhaps it was one of his old Prince Alberts.[2] He also wore gloves. They were old and torn and his fingertips showed through them. He carried a cane, but it was only the skeleton of a worn-out umbrella. Behind him walked one of his innumerable kin—a dark young man with eyes like a gazelle.

The old man bowed to all of us in the room. Then he removed his hat and gloves, slowly and carefully. Chaplin[3] once did that in a picture, in a bank—he was the janitor. Then he handed his things to the boy, who stood obediently behind the old man's chair.

There was a great deal of conversation, about rain and about his family. He was very proud of his large family. Finally we got down to business. Yes, he would sell, as he had agreed, for twelve hundred dollars, in

1. **Senator Catron:** Thomas Benton Catron, Senator from New Mexico (1912–1917).
2. **Prince Alberts:** The Prince Albert was a long, double-breasted coat named after the English Prince Albert, who later became Edward VII.
3. **Chaplin:** Charlie Chaplin (1889–1977), known for his great comic performances in silent movies.

cash. We would buy, and the money was ready. "Don[4] Anselmo," I said to him in Spanish, "we have made a discovery. You remember that we sent that surveyor, that engineer, up there to survey your land so as to make the deed. Well, he finds that you own more than eight acres. He tells us that your land extends across the river and that you own almost twice as much as you thought." He didn't know that. "And now, Don Anselmo," I added, "these Americans are *buena gente,* they are good people, and they are willing to pay you for the additional land as well, at the same rate per acre, so that instead of twelve hundred dollars you will get almost twice as much, and the money is here for you."

The old man hung his head for a moment in thought. Then he stood up and stared at me. "Friend," he said, "I do not like to have you speak to me in that manner." I kept still and let him have his say. "I know these Americans are good people, and that is why I have agreed to sell my house to them. But I do not care to be insulted. I have agreed to sell my house and land for twelve hundred dollars and that is the price."

I argued with him but it was useless. Finally he signed the deed and took the money but refused to take more than the amount agreed upon. Then he shook hands all around, put on his ragged gloves, took his stick and walked out with the boy behind him.

A month later my friends had moved into Río en Medio. They had replastered the old adobe house, pruned the trees, patched the fence, and moved in for the summer. One day they came back to the office to complain. The children of the village were overrunning their property. They came every day and played under the trees, built little play fences around them, and took blossoms. When they were spoken to they only laughed and talked back good-naturedly in Spanish.

I sent a messenger up to the mountains for Don Anselmo. It took a week to arrange another meeting. When he arrived he repeated his previous preliminary performance. He wore the same faded cutaway,[5] carried the same stick and was accompanied by the boy again. He shook hands all around, sat down with the boy behind his chair, and talked about the weather. Finally I broached the subject. "Don Anselmo, about

4. **Don:** a title of respect, formerly used for Spaniards of high rank, now used as a title of courtesy.
5. **cutaway:** a long coat used for formal occasions, so named because part of its lower front is cut away.

the ranch you sold to these people. They are good people and want to be your friends and neighbors always. When you sold to them you signed a document, a deed, and in that deed you agreed to several things. One thing was that they were to have the complete possession of the property. Now, Don Anselmo, it seems that every day the children of the village overrun the orchard and spend most of their time there. We would like to know if you, as the most respected man in the village, could not stop them from doing so in order that these people may enjoy their new home more in peace."

Don Anselmo stood up. "We have all learned to love these Americans," he said, "because they are good people and good neighbors. I sold them my property because I knew they were good people, but I did not sell them the trees in the orchard."

This was bad. "Don Anselmo," I pleaded, "when one signs a deed and sells real property one sells also everything that grows on the land, and those trees, every one of them, are on the land and inside the boundaries of what you sold."

"Yes, I admit that," he said. "You know," he added, "I am the oldest man in the village. Almost everyone there is my relative and all the children of Río en Medio are my *sobrinos* and *nietos,*[6] my descendants. Every time a child has been born in Río en Medio since I took possession of that house from my mother I have planted a tree for that child. The trees in that orchard are not mine, *Señor,* they belong to the children of the village. Every person in Río en Medio born since the railroad came to Santa Fe owns a tree in that orchard. I did not sell the trees because I could not. They are not mine."

There was nothing we could do. Legally we owned the trees but the old man had been so generous, refusing what amounted to a fortune for him. It took most of the following winter to buy the trees, individually, from the descendants of Don Anselmo in the valley of Río en Medio.

---

6. *sobrinos* (sō-brē′nōs) **and** *nietos* (nyĕ′tōs): Spanish for "nephews and nieces" and "grandchildren."

First Response: *Was Don Anselmo foolish for refusing the extra money for his land? Explain your answer.*

CHECKING UP (True/False)

1. Don Anselmo has no intention of selling his land.
2. Don Anselmo demands an outrageous price for his land.
3. Good manners are important to Don Anselmo.
4. The lawyer tries to cheat Don Anselmo and the Americans who wish to buy his property.
5. Don Anselmo is a shrewd and practical businessman.
6. Don Anselmo lives in the mountains.
7. The children of the village come every day to play under the trees.
8. The children of the village are rude to the new owners of the orchard.
9. Don Anselmo offers to keep the children of Río en Medio out of the orchard.
10. The owners feel they have been tricked by Don Anselmo.

TALKING IT OVER

1. What details describe Don Anselmo's appearance when he first comes to the office? What details describe his behavior? How does his behavior contrast with his appearance?
2. Look up the word *gentleman* in a dictionary. In what way is this word an accurate description of Don Anselmo's character and manners?
3. Don Anselmo lives by a code that the Americans find surprising. Why does he refuse to accept more money for his property? Why does he believe that he does not own the trees in the orchard?
4. Despite his new wealth, Don Anselmo is still wearing the same old clothes a month after the sale of his land. What does this reveal about him?
5. Are the descendants of Don Anselmo entitled to the money they receive for the trees? Give reasons for your answer.

CHARACTER
Direct and Indirect Characterization

Although a short story may focus on several characters, there is usually one main character who is at the center of the story. In "Gentleman of Río en Medio," the main character, or **protagonist,** is Don Anselmo.

The way a writer presents a character in a story is known as **characterization.** In **direct characterization** the writer reveals the character directly to the reader. For example, at one point in the story, Don Anselmo is identified as "the most respected man in the village." Later on, he is described as "generous." These are direct comments from the author that reveal Don Anselmo's character.

It is more common, however, for a writer to develop a character through **indirect characterization.** With this method, the writer allows you to draw your own conclusions about a character by

> describing the character's physical appearance
> showing the character's actions and words
> revealing the character's thoughts
> showing how the character is thought of and treated
>   by others

A writer may, of course, use both direct and indirect methods of characterization in presenting a character.

In "Gentleman of Río en Medio," we are not told directly that Don Anselmo is a person of great dignity. The writer reveals this trait indirectly in describing Don Anselmo's manners:

> The old man bowed to all of us in the room. Then he removed his hat and gloves, slowly and carefully. . . . Then he handed his things to the boy, who stood obediently behind the old man's chair.

Find other passages in the story that reveal the character of Don Anselmo indirectly. In each case, tell what conclusion you have drawn.

UNDERSTANDING THE WORDS IN THE STORY
(Matching Columns)

1. quaint
2. kin
3. broached
4. survey
5. adobe
6. innumerable
7. gnarled
8. negotiation
9. preliminary
10. real property

a. without number
b. introductory
c. pleasingly old-fashioned
d. land and houses
e. blood relatives
f. mentioned
g. knotty and twisted
h. sun-dried brick
i. determine land boundaries
j. bargaining

WRITING IT DOWN
A Character Sketch

A good way to explore a character for a character sketch or a short story is to make a *character wheel*. Write the character's name in the center of a piece of paper. Then, draw a wheel like the one on page 165, or use one provided by your teacher, with wide and narrow spaces between the spokes. Around the wheel, write a few of the character's important traits in the wider sections. Underneath each trait, list details and events from the story that illustrate the trait.

Page 165 shows a sample character wheel for Don Anselmo. Using this wheel as a model, create a character wheel for a fictional character of your own, filling out the spokes as shown.

Expand the information on your wheel into a **character sketch**, a three- or four-paragraph description of your fictional character. When you have finished writing, exchange papers with a partner. Read each other's work and offer suggestions for revision.

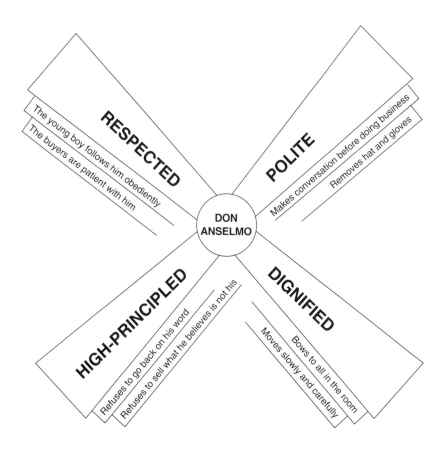

DON ANSELMO

RESPECTED
- The young boy follows him obediently
- The buyers are patient with him

POLITE
- Makes conversation before doing business
- Removes hat and gloves

HIGH-PRINCIPLED
- Refuses to go back on his word
- Refuses to sell what he believes is not his

DIGNIFIED
- Bows to all in the room
- Moves slowly and carefully

ABOUT THE AUTHOR

Juan A. A. Sedillo (1902–1982) was born in New Mexico, a descendant of early Spanish colonists. He was a lawyer and judge, and held several public offices. While he was practicing law in Santa Fe, an incident took place in his office that inspired Sedillo to write the story "Gentleman of Río en Medio." The tale reflects the compassion that Sedillo felt for the Spanish-speaking people of the Southwest.

THANK YOU, M'AM

Langston Hughes

"When I get through with you, sir, you are going to remember Mrs. Luella Bates Washington Jones," says a character in this story. Can you recall anybody's particular behavior or advice that made a lasting impression on you? If so, write a description of it in a sentence or two.

She was a large woman with a large purse that had everything in it but hammer and nails. It had a long strap and she carried it slung across her shoulder. It was about eleven o'clock at night, and she was walking alone, when a boy ran up behind her and tried to snatch her purse. The strap broke with the single tug the boy gave it from behind. But the boy's weight, and the weight of the purse combined caused him to lose his balance so, instead of taking off full blast as he had hoped, the boy fell on his back on the sidewalk, and his legs flew up. The large woman simply turned around and kicked him right square in his blue-jeaned sitter. Then she reached down, picked the boy up by his shirt front, and shook him until his teeth rattled.

After that the woman said, "Pick up my pocketbook, boy, and give it here."

She still held him. But she bent down enough to permit him to stoop and pick up her purse. Then she said, "Now ain't you ashamed of yourself?"

Firmly gripped by his shirt front, the boy said, "Yes'm."

The woman said, "What did you want to do it for?"

The boy said, "I didn't aim to."

She said, "You a lie!"

By that time two or three people passed, stopped, turned to look, and some stood watching.

"If I turn you loose, will you run?" asked the woman.

"Yes'm," said the boy.

"Then I won't turn you loose," said the woman. She did not release him.

"I'm very sorry, lady, I'm sorry," whispered the boy.

"Um-hum! And your face is dirty. I got a great mind to wash your face for you. Ain't you got nobody home to tell you to wash your face?"

"No'm," said the boy.

"Then it will get washed this evening," said the large woman starting up the street, dragging the frightened boy behind her.

He looked as if he were fourteen or fifteen, frail and willow-wild, in tennis shoes and blue jeans.

The woman said, "You ought to be my son. I would teach you right from wrong. Least I can do right now is to wash your face. Are you hungry?"

"No'm," said the being-dragged boy. "I just want you to turn me loose."

"Was I bothering *you* when I turned that corner?" asked the woman.

"No'm."

"But you put yourself in contact with *me*," said the woman. "If you think that that contact is not going to last awhile, you got another thought coming. When I get through with you, sir, you are going to remember Mrs. Luella Bates Washington Jones."

Sweat popped out on the boy's face and he began to struggle. Mrs. Jones stopped, jerked him around in front of her, put a half nelson about his neck, and continued to drag him up the street. When she got to her door, she dragged the boy inside, down a hall, and into a large kitchenette-furnished room at the rear of the house. She switched on the light and left the door open. The boy could hear other roomers laughing and talking in the large house. Some of their doors were open, too, so he knew he and the woman were not alone. The woman still had him by the neck in the middle of her room.

She said, "What is your name?"

"Roger," answered the boy.

"Then, Roger, you go to that sink and wash your face," said the woman, whereupon she turned him loose—at last. Roger looked at the door—looked at the woman—looked at the door—*and went to the sink*.

"Let the water run until it gets warm," she said. "Here's a clean towel."

"You gonna take me to jail?" asked the boy, bending over the sink.

"Not with that face, I would not take you nowhere," said the woman. "Here I am trying to get home to cook me a bite to eat and you snatch my pocketbook! Maybe you ain't been to your supper either, late as it be. Have you?"

"There's nobody home at my house," said the boy.

"Then we'll eat," said the woman. "I believe you're hungry—or been hungry—to try to snatch my pocketbook."

"I wanted a pair of blue suede shoes," said the boy.

"Well, you didn't have to snatch *my* pocketbook to get some suede shoes," said Mrs. Luella Bates Washington Jones. "You could of asked me."

"M'am?"

The water dripping from his face, the boy looked at her. There was a long pause. A very long pause. After he had dried his face and not knowing what else to do dried it again, the boy turned around, wondering what next. The door was open. He could make a dash for it down the hall. He could run, run, run, run, *run!*

The woman was sitting on the daybed. After awhile she said, "I were young once and I wanted things I could not get."

There was another long pause. The boy's mouth opened. Then he frowned, but not knowing he frowned.

The woman said, "Um-hum! You thought I was going to say, *but,* didn't you? You thought I was going to say, *but I didn't snatch people's pocketbooks.* Well, I wasn't going to say that." Pause. Silence. "I have done things, too, which I would not tell you, son—neither tell God, if he didn't already know. So you set down while I fix us something to eat. You might run that comb through your hair so you will look presentable."

In another corner of the room behind a screen was a gas plate and an icebox. Mrs. Jones got up and went behind the screen. The woman did not watch the boy to see if he was going to run now, nor did she watch her purse which she left behind her on the daybed. But the boy took care to sit on the far side of the room where he thought she could easily see him out of the corner of her eye, if she wanted to. He did not trust the woman *not* to trust him. And he did not want to be mistrusted now.

"Do you need somebody to go to the store," asked the boy, "maybe to get some milk or something?"

"Don't believe I do," said the woman, "unless you just want sweet milk yourself. I was going to make cocoa out of this canned milk I got here."

"That will be fine," said the boy.

She heated some lima beans and ham she had in the icebox, made the cocoa, and set the table. The woman did not ask the boy anything about where he lived, or his folks, or anything else that would embarrass him. Instead, as they ate, she told him about her job in a hotel beauty shop that stayed open late, what the work was like, and how all kinds of women came in and out, blondes, redheads, and Spanish. Then she cut him a half of her ten-cent cake.

"Eat some more, son," she said.

When they were finished eating she got up and said, "Now, here, take this ten dollars and buy yourself some blue suede shoes. And next time, do not make the mistake of latching onto *my* pocketbook *nor nobody else's*—because shoes come by devilish like that will burn your feet. I got to get my rest now. But I wish you would behave yourself, son, from here on in."

She led him down the hall to the front door and opened it. "Goodnight! Behave yourself, boy!" she said, looking out into the street.

The boy wanted to say something else other than, "Thank you, m'am," to Mrs. Luella Bates Washington Jones, but he couldn't do so as he turned at the barren stoop and looked back at the large woman in the door. He barely managed to say, "Thank you," before she shut the door. And he never saw her again.

First Response: *If you had been Roger, would you have run away when you saw the open door?*

CHECKING UP

Arrange the following events in the order in which they occur in the story.

The woman drags the boy up the street.
The boy washes his face.
The woman turns the boy loose.

The boy snatches the woman's purse.

The boy thanks the woman.

The woman grabs the boy by his shirt front.

The woman gives the boy money to buy a pair of blue suede shoes.

The woman cooks dinner.

The boy offers to go to the store.

The woman tells the boy about her job in a hotel beauty shop.

TALKING IT OVER

1. Why do you think Mrs. Jones takes Roger home with her instead of calling the police?
2. After she releases Roger, Mrs. Jones leaves her door open and the purse on the bed. Why does she do this? Why doesn't Roger take the purse and run?
3. How does Mrs. Jones show that she does not want to embarrass Roger or hurt his feelings?
4. Why do you think Mrs. Jones gives Roger the ten dollars?
5. What do you think Roger has learned from Mrs. Jones?

CHARACTER
Credibility, Consistency, and Motivation

In fairy tales and stories written for children, it is common for characters to be one-sided and simple. The wicked witch is always evil; the selfish sister is always mean; the good and obedient child never has a temper tantrum. Real people, of course, are a good deal more complicated. They are neither all good nor all bad, and they cannot be reduced to a single trait.

In order for the characters in a story to have **credibility,** or believability, they must behave like real people. We need to feel that they are true to life.

To be believable, characters must behave with **consistency.** If a character undergoes a change, there must be sufficient reason to explain it. A character who is presented as shy and awkward cannot suddenly become bold and confident unless there is some crucial experience that makes such a change possible.

Finally, there must be **motivation,** or reason, to account for a character's actions. People can be motivated by outside forces or by inner needs.

1. How does Langston Hughes make Mrs. Jones a true-to-life character?
2. While he is in Mrs. Jones's apartment, Roger has an opportunity to steal her purse and run, but he does not do so. Is his behavior consistent? Give reasons for your answer.
3. Why does Mrs. Jones take Roger into her home? Why does she cook for him and give him money? Are her motives believable? Give reasons for your answer.

WRITING IT DOWN
Notes for a Retelling

Imagine that you are Roger twenty years after the episode with Mrs. Jones and that you have decided to tell your own children about that encounter. What will you say? What about the episode do you want them to know? What is your reason for telling them—do you have a point to make?

Jot down some notes about what you would like to say. Begin by thinking about how you felt that night and about the impression that Mrs. Jones made on you.

SPEAKING AND LISTENING
Relating an Incident

Using your notes, present your retelling of the episode before a small group of classmates.

ABOUT THE AUTHOR

Langston Hughes (1902–1967), who was born in Joplin, Missouri, is associated with the Harlem Renaissance of the 1920s, a cultural awakening of remarkable creativity among African American writers and artists. In his novels, short stories, and plays, Hughes describes both the bitterness and the triumph of the black experience in America. His most famous character is Jess B. Semple, whose struggles and achievements Hughes portrays with humor and dignity. Hughes was the first African American to earn a living by writing and public speaking. His enduring themes—the joys of love and the closeness of family life—have universal appeal. His works have been translated into a number of languages.

ALL THE YEARS OF HER LIFE

Morley Callaghan

What do we mean when we refer to a person's "true colors?" Can you think of a person whom you knew for a long time before you saw his or her true colors? Freewrite your answer for a minute or two.

They were closing the drugstore, and Alfred Higgins, who had just taken off his white jacket, was putting on his coat and getting ready to go home. The little gray-haired man, Sam Carr, who owned the drugstore, was bending down behind the cash register, and when Alfred Higgins passed him, he looked up and said softly, "Just a moment, Alfred. One moment before you go."

The soft, confident, quiet way in which Sam Carr spoke made Alfred start to button his coat nervously. He felt sure his face was white. Sam Carr usually said, "Good night," brusquely, without looking up. In the six months he had been working in the drugstore Alfred had never heard his employer speak softly like that. His heart began to beat so loud it was hard for him to get his breath. "What is it, Mr. Carr?" he asked.

"Maybe you'd be good enough to take a few things out of your pocket and leave them here before you go," Sam Carr said.

"What things? What are you talking about?"

"You've got a compact and a lipstick and at least two tubes of toothpaste in your pockets, Alfred."

"What do you mean? Do you think I'm crazy?" Alfred blustered. His face got red and he knew he looked fierce with indignation. But Sam Carr, standing by the door with his blue eyes shining brightly behind his glasses and his lips moving underneath his gray mustache, only nodded his head a few times, and then Alfred grew very frightened and he didn't know what to say. Slowly he raised his hand and dipped it into his pocket, and with his eyes never meeting Sam Carr's eyes, he took out a blue compact and two tubes of toothpaste and a lipstick, and he laid them one by one on the counter.

"Petty thieving, eh, Alfred?" Sam Carr said. "And maybe you'd be good enough to tell me how long this has been going on."

"This is the first time I ever took anything."

"So now you think you'll tell me a lie, eh? What kind of a sap do I look like, huh? I don't know what goes on in my own store, eh? I tell you you've been doing this pretty steady," Sam Carr said as he went over and stood behind the cash register.

Ever since Alfred had left school he had been getting into trouble wherever he worked. He lived at home with his mother and his father, who was a printer. His two older brothers were married and his sister had got married last year, and it would have been all right for his parents now if Alfred had only been able to keep a job.

While Sam Carr smiled and stroked the side of his face very delicately with the tips of his fingers, Alfred began to feel that familiar terror growing in him that had been in him every time he had got into such trouble.

"I liked you," Sam Carr was saying. "I liked you and would have trusted you, and now look what I got to do." While Alfred watched with his alert, frightened blue eyes, Sam Carr drummed with his fingers on the counter. "I don't like to call a cop in point-blank," he was saying as he looked very worried. "You're a fool, and maybe I should call your father and tell him you're a fool. Maybe I should let them know I'm going to have you locked up."

"My father's not at home. He's a printer. He works nights," Alfred said.

"Who's at home?"

"My mother, I guess."

"Then we'll see what she says." Sam Carr went to the phone and dialed the number. Alfred was not so much ashamed, but there was that deep fright growing in him, and he blurted out arrogantly, like a strong, full-grown man, "Just a minute. You don't need to draw anybody else in. You don't need to tell her." He wanted to sound like a swaggering, big guy who could look after himself, yet the old, childish hope was in him, the longing that someone at home would come and help him. "Yeah, that's right, he's in trouble," Mr. Carr was saying. "Yeah, your boy works for me. You'd better come down in a hurry." And when he was finished Mr. Carr went over to the door and looked out at the street and watched the people passing in the late summer night. "I'll keep my eye out for a cop," was all he said.

Alfred knew how his mother would come rushing in; she would rush in with her eyes blazing, or maybe she would be crying, and she would push him away when he tried to talk to her, and make him feel her dreadful contempt; yet he longed that she might come before Mr. Carr saw the cop on the beat passing the door.

While they waited—and it seemed a long time—they did not speak, and when at last they heard someone tapping on the closed door, Mr. Carr, turning the latch, said crisply, "Come in, Mrs. Higgins." He looked hard-faced and stern.

Mrs. Higgins must have been going to bed when he telephoned, for her hair was tucked in loosely under her hat, and her hand at her throat held her light coat tight across her chest so her dress would not show. She came in, large and plump, with a little smile on her friendly face. Most of the store lights had been turned out and at first she did not see Alfred, who was standing in the shadow at the end of the counter. Yet as soon as she saw him she did not look as Alfred thought she would look: she smiled, her blue eyes never wavered, and with a calmness and dignity that made them forget that her clothes seemed to have been thrown on her, she put out her hand to Mr. Carr and said politely, "I'm Mrs. Higgins. I'm Alfred's mother."

Mr. Carr was a bit embarrassed by her lack of terror and her simplicity, and he hardly knew what to say to her, so she asked, "Is Alfred in trouble?"

"He is. He's been taking things from the store. I caught him red-handed. Little things like compacts and toothpaste and lipsticks. Stuff he can sell easily," the proprietor said.

As she listened Mrs. Higgins looked at Alfred sometimes and nodded her head sadly, and when Sam Carr had finished she said gravely, "Is it so, Alfred?"

"Yes."

"Why have you been doing it?"

"I been spending money, I guess."

"On what?"

"Going around with the guys, I guess," Alfred said.

Mrs. Higgins put out her hand and touched Sam Carr's arm with an understanding gentleness, and speaking as though afraid of disturbing him, she said, "If you would only listen to me before doing anything." Her simple earnestness made her shy; her humility made her falter and look away, but in a moment she was smiling gravely again, and she said with a kind of patient dignity, "What did you intend to do, Mr. Carr?"

"I was going to get a cop. That's what I ought to do."

"Yes, I suppose so. It's not for me to say, because he's my son. Yet I sometimes think a little good advice is the best thing for a boy when he's at a certain period in his life," she said.

Alfred couldn't understand his mother's quiet composure, for if they had been at home and someone had suggested that he was going to be arrested, he knew she would be in a rage and would cry out against him. Yet now she was standing there with that gentle, pleading smile on her face, saying, "I wonder if you don't think it would be better just to let him come home with me. He looks like a big fellow, doesn't he? It takes some of them a long time to get any sense," and they both stared at Alfred, who shifted away with a bit of light shining for a moment on his thin face and the tiny pimples over his cheekbone.

But even while he was turning away uneasily Alfred was realizing that Mr. Carr had become aware that his mother was really a fine woman; he knew that Sam Carr was puzzled by his mother, as if he had expected her to come in and plead with him tearfully, and instead he was being made to feel a bit ashamed by her vast tolerance. While there was only the sound of the mother's soft, assured voice in the store, Mr. Carr began to nod his head encouragingly at her. Without being alarmed, while being just large and still and simple and hopeful, she was becoming dominant there in the dimly lit store. "Of course, I don't want to be harsh," Mr. Carr was saying. "I'll tell you what I'll do. I'll just fire him and let it go at that. How's that?" and he got up and shook hands with Mrs. Higgins, bowing low to her in deep respect.

There was such warmth and gratitude in the way she said, "I'll never forget your kindness," that Mr. Carr began to feel warm and genial himself.

"Sorry we had to meet this way," he said. "But I'm glad I got in touch with you. Just wanted to do the right thing, that's all," he said.

"It's better to meet like this than never, isn't it?" she said. Suddenly they clasped hands as if they liked each other, as if they had known each other a long time. "Good night, sir," she said.

"Good night, Mrs. Higgins. I'm truly sorry," he said.

The mother and son walked along the street together, and the mother was taking a long, firm stride as she looked ahead with her stern face full of worry. Alfred was afraid to speak to her, he was afraid of the silence that was between them, so he only looked ahead too, for the excitement and relief was still pretty strong in him; but in a little while, going along like that in silence made him terribly aware of the strength and the sternness in her; he began to wonder what she was thinking of as she stared ahead so grimly; she seemed to have forgotten that he walked beside her; so when they were passing under the Sixth Avenue elevated[1] and the rumble of the train seemed to break the silence, he said in his old, blustering way, "Thank God it turned out like that. I certainly won't get in a jam like that again."

"Be quiet. Don't speak to me. You've disgraced me again and again," she said bitterly.

"That's the last time. That's all I'm saying."

"Have the decency to be quiet," she snapped. They kept on their way, looking straight ahead.

When they were at home and his mother took off her coat, Alfred saw that she was really only half-dressed, and she made him feel afraid again when she said, without even looking at him, "You're a bad lot. God forgive you. It's one thing after another and always has been. Why do you stand there stupidly? Go to bed, why don't you?" When he was going, she said, "I'm going to make myself a cup of tea. Mind, now, not a word about tonight to your father."

While Alfred was undressing in his bedroom, he heard his mother moving around the kitchen. She filled the kettle and put it on the stove. She moved a chair. And as he listened there was no shame in him, just wonder and a kind of admiration of her strength and repose. He could still see Sam Carr nodding his head encouragingly to her; he could hear her talking simply and earnestly, and as he sat on his bed he felt a pride in her strength. "She certainly was smooth," he thought. "Gee, I'd like to tell her she sounded swell."

And at last he got up and went along to the kitchen, and when he was at the door he saw his mother pouring herself a cup of tea. He watched and he didn't move. Her face, as she sat there, was a frightened, broken face utterly unlike the face of the woman who had been

---

1. **elevated:** a railway that runs above street level.

so assured a little while ago in the drugstore. When she reached out and lifted the kettle to pour hot water in her cup, her hand trembled and the water splashed on the stove. Leaning back in the chair, she sighed and lifted the cup to her lips, and her lips were groping loosely as if they would never reach the cup. She swallowed the hot tea eagerly, and then she straightened up in relief, though her hand holding the cup still trembled. She looked very old.

It seemed to Alfred that this was the way it had been every time he had been in trouble before, that this trembling had really been in her as she hurried out half-dressed to the drugstore. He understood why she had sat alone in the kitchen the night his young sister had kept repeating doggedly that she was getting married. Now he felt all that his mother had been thinking of as they walked along the street together a little while ago. He watched his mother, and he never spoke, but at that moment his youth seemed to be over; he knew all the years of her life by the way her hand trembled as she raised the cup to her lips. It seemed to him that this was the first time he had ever looked upon his mother.

First Response: *Would you have handled the situation any differently if you had been Albert?*

CHECKING UP (Multiple-Choice)

1. Alfred Higgins has been working for Sam Carr
   a. since he left school
   b. for six months
   c. for a few weeks
2. When he is questioned by his employer, Alfred
   a. at first denies that he has anything in his pockets
   b. calls Mr. Carr a liar
   c. immediately returns the stolen items

3. Alfred is guilty of
   a. robbery
   b. burglary
   c. petty theft
4. From evidence in the story we know that Alfred
   a. is bored with his job
   b. enjoys getting into trouble
   c. can't keep a job
5. From Mr. Carr's actions we can conclude that he
   a. is hesitant to call the police
   b. is eager to have Alfred locked up
   c. will let Alfred have his job back
6. Alfred expects his mother to
   a. rush into the drugstore in a rage
   b. beg Mr. Carr to give her son another chance
   c. urge Mr. Carr to call the police
7. Mrs. Higgins surprises both Alfred and Mr. Carr by
   a. her calm manner
   b. her stern looks
   c. the way she is dressed
8. Mrs. Higgins convinces Mr. Carr that
   a. she will punish Alfred severely
   b. Alfred is innocent
   c. what Alfred needs is good advice
9. Alfred's reaction to the incident is
   a. anger at Mr. Carr
   b. admiration for his mother's strength
   c. shame and guilt
10. At the end of the story, Alfred realizes that his mother is
    a. fatally ill
    b. filled with self-pity
    c. broken in spirit

TALKING IT OVER

1. What do we learn about Alfred's life since he left school? How does his behavior reveal that he is immature and irresponsible?

2. Why is Mr. Carr reluctant to call the police?
3. Alfred is surprised by his mother's behavior in the drugstore. What has he come to expect?
4. How does Mrs. Higgins win Mr. Carr's respect and confidence?
5. At what point in the story does Alfred become aware of the consequences of his actions?
6. What does Alfred finally realize about his mother? How is he changed by this new understanding?

CHARACTER
Static and Dynamic Characters

Some characters in short stories do not change in any meaningful way. At the end of their stories, they have essentially the same personalities that they had at the beginning. Such characters are referred to as **static**. Don Anselmo in "Gentleman of Río en Medio" (page 159) is a static character. He does not undergo any visible change during the course of the story.

Characters who undergo some important change are referred to as **dynamic**. In "All the Years of Her Life," Alfred is a dynamic character because he experiences an important change.

How does his understanding of his mother cause Alfred to change? Find the passage that tells you.

UNDERSTANDING THE WORDS IN THE STORY (Multiple-Choice)

1. When one speaks *brusquely,* one
   a. hesitates over each word
   b. shouts angrily
   c. is blunt to the point of rudeness

2. The person most likely to *bluster* is
   a. an infant
   b. a bully
   c. a librarian
3. *Indignation* results from
   a. anger at some injustice
   b. jealousy over possessions
   c. rivalry in sports
4. Something that is *blurted out* is
   a. spoken before thinking
   b. expressed calmly
   c. whispered brokenly
5. To behave *arrogantly* is to
   a. pay attention to other people's ideas
   b. act superior to other people
   c. submit willingly to criticism
6. To *swagger* is to
   a. drink thirstily
   b. stagger along
   c. show off
7. One feels *contempt* for someone or something that is
   a. despised
   b. far away
   c. precious
8. When one speaks *crisply,* one's words are
   a. harsh and angry
   b. short and forceful
   c. gentle and flattering
9. Eyes that *waver*
   a. stare fixedly at an object
   b. grow tearful
   c. show indecision
10. The *proprietor* of a store is
    a. its owner
    b. a janitor
    c. the salesperson

(Matching Columns)

1. gravely	a. respect for others' beliefs
2. humility	b. stubbornly
3. falter	c. calmness
4. composure	d. seriously
5. tolerance	e. hesitate
6. assured	f. reaching for uncertainly
7. dominant	g. quietness
8. repose	h. most important
9. groping	i. confident
10. doggedly	j. modesty

WRITING IT DOWN
An Opinion

How do you suppose this episode will affect Alfred Higgins? Do you expect that he will turn over a new leaf? Examine the evidence in the story and present your opinion in a paragraph or two.

A Conversation

If you have read "Thank You M'am" (page 166), imagine a meeting between either Roger and Albert or Mrs. Jones and Mrs. Higgins. Under what circumstances would they meet? How would they discover that they have undergone a similar experience? What would they say to each other? Write the imaginary conversation in the form of a dialogue.

A Comparison

If you have read "Thank You M'am," write a paragraph or two comparing and contrasting either Mrs. Jones and Mrs. Higgins or Roger and Albert. You might find it helpful to begin by filling in a chart such as the one on page 183.

CHARACTER	APPEARANCE	PERSONALITY	ACTIONS	STATIC OR DYNAMIC
MRS. JONES				
MRS. HIGGINS				
ROGER				
ALFRED				

ABOUT THE AUTHOR

Morley Callaghan (1903–1990), one of Canada's most distinguished writers, was born in Toronto. During his college years, Callaghan worked part time at the *Toronto Daily Star,* where Ernest Hemingway was a reporter. Hemingway was impressed with Callaghan's work and encouraged the young reporter to write fiction.

Callaghan and Hemingway met again in the late 1920s, when Callaghan traveled to Paris to join the "lost generation"—expatriate writers and artists searching for new ways to express ideas in art and literature.

Shortly after Callaghan arrived in Paris, Hemingway challenged him to a boxing match. That match became a literary event associated with Callaghan for the next sixty years. F. Scott Fitzgerald, like Hemingway a well-known American writer, kept time during the fight, and he became so engrossed in the match that he let it run two minutes overtime. Callaghan beat Hemingway, who did not like to lose. The match ended relations between the three writers, each one of whom was later to publish his own version of the event. Callaghan described the incident in his popular memoir entitled *That Summer in Paris* (1963).

Callaghan continued writing fiction well into his eighties. His stories have been collected in *A Native Argosy* and *Now That April's Here*. He wrote several novels, including *Broken Journey, More Joy in Heaven,* and *The Many-Colored Coat*. Some of his best-known stories are "Luke Baldwin's Vow," "The Snob," and "A Cap for Steve."

THE RIFLES OF
THE REGIMENT
Eric Knight

This story takes place in France during World War II, shortly after British troops had been rescued from the French seaport of Dunkirk.
 Can you recall any episodes—either fictional or historic—in which a military leader faced a perilous situation? Discuss your answer with a small group of classmates.

Colonel Heathergall has become a bit of a regimental legend already. In the mess[1] of the Loyal Rifles, they say, "Ah, but old Glass-eye! He was a one for one. A pukka sahib![2] I'll never forget once . . ."

Then off they go on some story or other about "Old Glass-eye."

But the regiment doesn't know the finest and truest story of all: when he fought all night with Fear—and won.

Colonel Heathergall met Fear in a little shack atop a cliff near the French village of Ste. Marguerite-en-Vaux.[3] He had never met Fear before—not on the Somme[4] nor in India nor in Palestine—because he was the type brought up not to know Fear. Fear is a cad—you just don't recognize the bounder.

The system has its points. Not being even on nodding acquaintance with Fear had allowed the colonel to keep the Loyal Rifle Regiment going in France long after all other British troops had gone—they were still fighting, working their way westward toward the Channel,[5] nearly two weeks after Dunkirk[6] was all over.

---

1. **mess:** the place where soldiers eat meals together.
2. **pukka sahib:** In Anglo-Indian, *pukka* means "genuine or good." *Sahib* is a respectful title formerly used by Indians in addressing Europeans.
3. **Ste. Marguerite-en-Vaux** (săn mär′gə-rēt′ än vō).
4. **Somme** (sôm): a river in northern France. A major battle was fought there during World War I. The French and British tried to break through the German line along the Somme River. They lost over half a million men.
5. **Channel:** The English Channel, which lies between England and France.
6. **Dunkirk** (dŭn′kûrk′): a seaport in northern France. In May of 1940, the British army was trapped at Dunkirk by Hitler's armies. English civilians sent their boats across the English Channel to help evacuate the British troops.

185

The men—those that were left—were drunk with fatigue. When they marched between fights, they slept. When they rested, they went into a sort of coma, and the sergeants had to slap them to waken them.

"They're nearly done," the adjutant[7] said. "Shouldn't we jettison[8] equipment?"

"All right," the colonel said, finally. "Equipment can be destroyed and left behind. But not rifles! Regiment's never failed to carry its rifles in—and carry 'em out. We'll take our rifles with us—every last single rifle."

The adjutant saluted.

"Er—and tell 'em we'll cut through soon," the colonel added. "Tell 'em I say we'll find a soft spot and cut through soon."

But the Loyal Rifles never did cut through. For there was then no British Army left in France to cut through to. But the regiment didn't know that. It marched west and north and attacked, and went west and north again. Each time it brought out its rifles and left its dead. First the sergeants were carrying two rifles, and then the men, and then the officers.

The Loyal Rifles went on until—they could go no farther. For they had reached the sea. It was on a headland looking out over the Channel, beside the fishing port of Ste. Marguerite-en-Vaux.

In the late afternoon the colonel used the regiment's last strength in an attempt to take Ste. Marguerite, for there might be boats there, fishing smacks,[9] something that could carry them all back to England. He didn't find boats. He found the enemy with tanks and artillery, and the regiment withdrew. They left their dead, but they left no rifles.

The colonel sent out scouts. They brought him the report. They were cut off by the Germans—ringed about with their backs to the sea; on a cliff top with a two-hundred-foot drop to the beach below.

The regiment posted pickets, and dug foxholes,[10] and fought until darkness came. Then they waited through the night for the last attack that was sure to come.

---

7. **adjutant** (ăj′o͞o-tənt): officer who serves as an assistant to a commanding officer.
8. **jettison** (jĕt′ĭ-sən, -zən): cast off (unwanted articles), generally in an emergency.
9. **smacks:** boats, also called *well smacks*, used to transport live fish to market.
10. **foxholes:** shallow pits dug in the ground for shelter against enemy gunfire.

And it was that night, in his headquarters at the cliff top shack, that Colonel Heathergall, for the first time in his well-bred, British, military life, met Fear.

Fear had a leprous face. Its white robes were damp, and it smelled of stale sweat.

Colonel Heathergall, who had not heard the door close, saw the figure standing there in the darkness.

"Who—who is it?"

Fear bowed and said, "You know me, really, Colonel. All your arrogant, aristocratic, British life you've snubbed me and pretended you didn't know me, but really you do, don't you? Let us be friends."

The colonel adjusted his monocle.[11] "What do you want?" he asked.

"I've come to tell you," Fear said, "that it's time for you to surrender the regiment. You're finished."

"You're a slimy brute," the colonel said. "I won't surrender. There must be some way out! That R.A.F.[12] plane this morning! I'm sure it saw us—the way the chap waggled[13] his wings. He'd go get help. The navy—they'll come!"

Fear laughed. "And if they come, then what? How would you get down that cliff? . . . You *can't* get down—and you know it!"

"We could cut south and find a better spot—the men still have fight left," the colonel said desperately.

"The men," Fear said, "they'll leave their broken bodies wherever you choose. They've got the stuff. And oh, yes, you, too, have courage, in your way. The huntin'-shootin'-fishin' sort of courage. The well-bred polo-field kind of courage. But that's got nothing to do with *this* kind of war. You haven't the right to ask your men to die to preserve that sort of record. Have you?"

The colonel sat still, not answering.

Fear spoke again. "The enemy will be here soon. Your men are exhausted. They can't do any more. Really, you'd be saving their lives if you surrender. No one would blame you. . . ."

The colonel shook his head. "No," he said. "We can't do that. You see—we never have done that. And we can't now. Perhaps we are outmoded.

11. **monocle** (mŏn′ə-kəl): an eyeglass for one eye.
12. **R.A.F.:** Royal Air Force.
13. **waggled** (wăg′əld): moved rapidly up and down.

I and my kind may be out-of-date—incompetent—belonging to a bygone day. But . . ." He looked around him as if for help. Then he went on desperately: "But—we've brought out all the rifles."

"Is that all?" mocked Fear.

"All?" the colonel echoed. "Is that all?"

Then at last he squared his shoulders. "All? Why, you bloody civilian, it's everything! I may die—and my men may die—but the regiment! It doesn't. The regiment goes on living. It's bigger than me—it's bigger than the men. Why, you slimy dugout king of a base-wallah[14]—it's bigger than you!"

And exactly as he said that, Fear fled. And there came a rap on the door, and the adjutant's voice sounded.

"Come in," the colonel said quietly.

"Are you alone, sir?" the adjutant asked.

"Yes," the colonel said. "Quite alone. What is it?"

"Report from the signal officer, sir. He has carried an ordinary torch with him, and he feels the colonel will be interested to know that he's in visual communication with the navy—destroyers or something. They say they're ready to put off boats to take us off."

"Tell him my thanks to C.O.[15] of whatever naval force there is there. Message to company commanders: Withdraw pickets quietly. Rendezvous[16] cliff top north of this H.Q.[17] at three-fifty-five ack emma.[18] Er—pretty good chaps in the navy—I've heard."

"Indeed, sir," the adjutant said.

So they assembled the men of the Loyal Rifle Regiment on the cliff top, where they could see out and below them the brief dots and dashes of light that winked.[19] And there, too, in the night wind, they could feel the space and know the vast drop to the beach. Some of the men lay flat and listened for the sound of the sailors two hundred feet below them.

---

14. **wallah:** Anglo-Indian for someone who is associated with a particular occupation or function.

15. **C.O.:** Commanding Officer.

16. **Rendezvous** (rän′dā-vōō′, -də-): Assemble troops.

17. **H.Q.:** Headquarters.

18. **ack emma:** A.M.

19. **dots . . . winked:** The message was transmitted in Morse code.

The officers waited, looking toward the colonel. It was the major who spoke: "But—how on earth are we going to get down there, Colonel?"

Colonel Heathergall smiled privately within himself. "The rifles," he said softly. "The rifles, of course. I think we'll just about have enough." And that's how the regiment escaped. They made a great chain of linked rifle slings, and went down it one at a time. The colonel came last, of course, as custom dictated.

Below, they picked up the rifles, whole and shattered, that they had thrown from the cliff top, and wading out into the sea, carried them to the boats.

By this time the Germans were awake, and they let loose with everything they had. The sailors used fine naval language, and said that Dunkirk was a picnic compared to this so-and-so bloody mess. But they got the men into the boats. The navy got in and got them out.

That's the way the Loyal Rifle Regiment came home nearly two weeks after the last troops from Dunkirk had landed in Blighty.[20] . . .

In the mess they still talk of the colonel. "Old Glass-eye," they say. "Ah, there was a colonel for you. Saved the outfit, he did. Knew the only way it'd ever get out would be down a cliff—so he made 'em carry all the rifles halfway across France. Knew he'd need the slings for that cliff. Foresight, eh? . . . Great Chap, Old Glass-eye. Never knew the meaning of Fear."

20. **Blighty:** British slang for "England."

First Response: *Did you find the story suspenseful even though you had an idea of the outcome? Explain your answer.*

CHECKING UP (True/False)

1. Colonel Heathergall has only one eye.
2. The colonel will not permit the regiment to get rid of its equipment.
3. The regiment is trapped on a cliff beside the English Channel.
4. The men use the rifles to escape from the Germans.
5. The British troops are rescued by American soldiers.

TALKING IT OVER

1. How did Colonel Heathergall get the nickname "Old Glass-eye"? Does this name show the men's affection or disrespect for their leader? Explain your answer.
2. We are told early in the story that Colonel Heathergall was the "type brought up not to know Fear." Explain what this statement means, using what you know about the colonel's background, education, and military career.
3. The colonel insists that the men carry out all their rifles. What does this tell you about his feeling for army tradition?
4. At what point does the colonel first experience fear? Why do you think the author represents the colonel's inner conflict as a conversation between two characters? How does the colonel master his fear?
5. How is the colonel's escape solution logical and consistent with his character?
6. Why do you think Knight chose the title "The Rifles of the Regiment" for this story instead of naming it for Colonel Heathergall, the hero?

CHARACTER
Stock Characters

Some characters appear so often in literature that they can be recognized immediately as **types**. Instead of existing as individual or original creations, they conform to a set pattern. For example, in fairy tales, a familiar character type is the handsome prince. His behavior is predictable because it is based on a pattern that remains the same from one story to another. Other familiar character types are the evil villain, the beautiful princess, and the absent-minded professor. These characters are known as **stock characters** or **stereotypes.**

Sometimes a writer will choose to individualize a stock character, creating a new personality out of a familiar pattern. The colonel in Knight's story has many of the characteristics associated with the British military officer who prizes devotion to duty and tradition above all else. One conventional feature of this type is keeping a "stiff upper lip," that is, not showing fear or discouragement. This character is typically efficient and unemotional. Even the physical detail of the monocle helps establish the type.

In his confrontation with Fear, however, the colonel becomes a human being who experiences serious misgivings about his principles and his judgment.

1. What details in the story make the colonel's experience of fear vivid and persuasive?
2. How does the colonel show his desperation?
3. What doubts does he express about his abilities as a leader?

Personification

In the story Knight represents an emotion—fear—as a person who converses with the colonel. The presentation of an abstract quality or idea as a human being is called **personification.**

This technique is sometimes used to intensify the importance of some event or condition.

1. What physical characteristics are given to Fear?
2. How do these characteristics suggest a nightmarish vision?

3. How does the personification of Fear make the colonel's experience of terror convincing?

UNDERSTANDING THE WORDS IN THE STORY (Jumbles)

Use the clues to solve the jumble items. All the solutions are drawn from the glossary word bank below.

Glossary Word Bank

headland	outmoded
snubbed	incompetent
arrogant	bygone
aristocratic	foresight

1. P O T T N I E M C E N   Incapable, unskillful

2. T H I S O R G E F   Plan for the future

3. T R O C I S T R A C I A   Of a privileged class

4. T A R A G O R N   Scornful

5. D U M D O E T O   No longer in fashion

FOR WRITING
A Character Analysis

Think of some of your favorite characters from books, movies, and television programs. Which of them could be considered character types? Choose one of those characters and explain in a paragraph or two why he or she functions as a stock character.

ABOUT THE AUTHOR

Eric Knight (1897–1943) was born in Yorkshire, England, the setting for his most famous story, "Lassie Come-Home." This story has also appeared as a novel, a movie, and a television series. Another well-known work, *The Flying Yorkshireman*, contains the humorous adventures of Sam Small, a colorful character.

Knight fought in the Canadian Army during the First World War. During the Second World War, he was a major in the United States Army. He lost his life in an airplane crash while on an official mission. "The Rifles of the Regiment" appeared in *Collier's* magazine the year before his death.

CHARLES

Shirley Jackson

In movies, television programs, and comic strips, children are often portrayed as bold, clever, mischievous characters. Can you think of any examples? Think of one such child and describe him or her in a sentence or two.

The day my son Laurie started kindergarten he renounced corduroy overalls with bibs and began wearing blue jeans with a belt; I watched him go off the first morning with the older girl next door, seeing clearly that an era of my life was ended, my sweet-voiced nursery-school tot replaced by a long-trousered, swaggering character who forgot to stop at the corner and wave goodbye to me.

He came home the same way, the front door slamming open, his cap on the floor, and the voice suddenly become raucous shouting, "Isn't anybody *here?*"

At lunch he spoke insolently to his father, spilled his baby sister's milk, and remarked that his teacher said we were not to take the name of the Lord in vain.

"How *was* school today?" I asked, elaborately casual.

"All right," he said.

"Did you learn anything?" his father asked.

Laurie regarded his father coldly. "I didn't learn nothing," he said.

"Anything," I said. "Didn't learn anything."

"The teacher spanked a boy, though," Laurie said, addressing his bread and butter. "For being fresh," he added, with his mouth full.

"What did he do?" I asked. "Who was it?"

Laurie thought. "It was Charles," he said. "He was fresh. The teacher spanked him and made him stand in a corner. He was awfully fresh."

"What did he do?" I asked again, but Laurie slid off his chair, took a cookie, and left, while his father was still saying, "See here, young man."

The next day Laurie remarked at lunch, as soon as he sat down, "Well, Charles was bad again today." He grinned enormously and said, "Today Charles hit the teacher."

"Good heavens," I said, mindful of the Lord's name, "I suppose he got spanked again?"

"He sure did," Laurie said. "Look up," he said to his father.

"What?" his father said, looking up.

"Look down," Laurie said. "Look at my thumb. Gee, you're dumb." He began to laugh insanely.

"Why did Charles hit the teacher?" I asked quickly.

"Because she tried to make him color with red crayons," Laurie said. "Charles wanted to color with green crayons so he hit the teacher and she spanked him and said nobody play with Charles but everybody did."

The third day—it was Wednesday of the first week—Charles bounced a seesaw onto the head of a little girl and made her bleed, and the teacher made him stay inside all during recess. Thursday Charles had to stand in a corner during story time because he kept pounding his feet on the floor. Friday Charles was deprived of blackboard privileges because he threw chalk.

On Saturday I remarked to my husband, "Do you think kindergarten is too unsettling for Laurie? All this toughness, and bad grammar, and this Charles boy sounds like such a bad influence."

"It'll be all right," my husband said reassuringly. "Bound to be people like Charles in the world. Might as well meet them now as later."

On Monday Laurie came home late, full of news. "Charles," he shouted as he came up the hill; I was waiting anxiously on the front steps. "Charles," Laurie yelled all the way up the hill, "Charles was bad again."

"Come right in," I said, as soon as he came close enough. "Lunch is waiting."

"You know what Charles did?" he demanded, following me through the door. "Charles yelled so in school they sent a boy in from first grade to tell the teacher she had to make Charles keep quiet, and so Charles had to stay after school. And so all the children stayed to watch him."

"What did he do?" I asked.

"He just sat there," Laurie said, climbing into his chair at the table. "Hi, Pop, y'old dust mop."

"Charles had to stay after school today," I told my husband. "Everyone stayed with him."

"What does this Charles look like?" my husband asked Laurie. "What's his other name?"

"He's bigger than me," Laurie said. "And he doesn't have any rubbers and he doesn't ever wear a jacket."

Monday night was the first Parent-Teachers meeting, and only the fact that the baby had a cold kept me from going; I wanted passionately to meet Charles's mother. On Tuesday Laurie remarked suddenly, "Our teacher had a friend come to see her in school today."

"Charles's mother?" my husband and I asked simultaneously.

"Naaah," Laurie said scornfully. "It was a man who came and made us do exercises, we had to touch our toes. Look." He climbed down from his chair and squatted down and touched his toes. "Like this," he said. He got solemnly back into his chair and said, picking up his fork, "Charles didn't even *do* exercises."

"That's fine," I said heartily. "Didn't Charles want to do exercises?"

"Naaah," Laurie said, "Charles was so fresh to the teacher's friend he wasn't *let* do exercises."

"Fresh again?" I said.

"He kicked the teacher's friend," Laurie said. "The teacher's friend told Charles to touch his toes like I just did and Charles kicked him."

"What are they going to do about Charles, do you suppose?" Laurie's father asked him.

Laurie shrugged elaborately. "Throw him out of school, I guess," he said.

Wednesday and Thursday were routine; Charles yelled during story hour and hit a boy in the stomach and made him cry. On Friday Charles stayed after school again and so did all the other children.

With the third week of kindergarten Charles was an institution in our family; the baby was being a Charles when she cried all afternoon; Laurie did a Charles when he filled his wagon full of mud and pulled it through the kitchen; even my husband, when he caught his elbow in the telephone cord and pulled telephone, ashtray, and a bowl of flowers off the table, said, after the first minute, "Looks like Charles."

During the third and fourth weeks it looked like a reformation in Charles; Laurie reported grimly at lunch on Thursday of the third week, "Charles was so good today the teacher gave him an apple."

"What?" I said, and my husband added warily, "You mean Charles?"

"Charles," Laurie said. "He gave the crayons around and he picked up the books afterward and the teacher said he was her helper."

"What happened?" I asked incredulously.

"He was her helper, that's all," Laurie said, and shrugged.

"Can this be true, about Charles?" I asked my husband that night. "Can something like this happen?"

"Wait and see," my husband said cynically. "When you've got a Charles to deal with, this may mean he's only plotting."

He seemed to be wrong. For over a week Charles was the teacher's helper; each day he handed things out and he picked things up; no one had to stay after school.

"The P.T.A. meeting's next week again," I told my husband one evening. "I'm going to find Charles's mother there."

"Ask her what happened to Charles," my husband said. "I'd like to know."

"I'd like to know myself," I said.

On Friday of that week things were back to normal. "You know what Charles did today?" Laurie demanded at the lunch table, in a voice slightly awed. "He told a little girl to say a word and she said it and the teacher washed her mouth out with soap and Charles laughed."

"What word?" his father asked unwisely, and Laurie said, "I'll have to whisper it to you, it's so bad." He got down off his chair and went around to his father. His father bent his head down and Laurie whispered joyfully. His father's eyes widened.

"Did Charles tell the little girl to say *that?*" he asked respectfully.

"She said it *twice,*" Laurie said. "Charles told her to say it *twice.*"

"What happened to Charles?" my husband asked.

"Nothing," Laurie said, "He was passing out the crayons."

Monday morning Charles abandoned the little girl and said the evil word himself three or four times, getting his mouth washed out with soap each time. He also threw chalk.

My husband came to the door with me that evening as I set out for the P.T.A. meeting. "Invite her over for a cup of tea after the meeting," he said. "I want to get a look at her."

"If only she's there," I said prayerfully.

"She'll be there," my husband said. "I don't see how they could hold a P.T.A. meeting without Charles's mother."

At the meeting I sat restlessly, scanning each comfortable matronly face, trying to determine which one hid the secret of Charles. None of them looked to me haggard enough. No one stood up in the meeting and apologized for the way her son had been acting. No one mentioned Charles.

After the meeting I identified and sought out Laurie's kindergarten teacher. She had a plate with a cup of tea and a piece of chocolate cake; I had a plate with a cup of tea and a piece of marshmallow cake. We maneuvered up to one another cautiously, and smiled.

"I've been so anxious to meet you," I said. "I'm Laurie's mother."

"We're all so interested in Laurie," she said.

"Well, he certainly likes kindergarten," I said. "He talks about it all the time."

"We had a little trouble adjusting, the first week or so," she said primly, "but now he's a fine little helper. With occasional lapses, of course."

"Laurie usually adjusts very quickly," I said. "I suppose this time it's Charles's influence."

"Charles?"

"Yes," I said, laughing, "you must have your hands full in that kindergarten, with Charles."

"Charles?" she said. "We don't have any Charles in the kindergarten."

First Response: *Why do you think Laurie invented "Charles"?*

CHECKING UP (True/False)

1. When he begins attending kindergarten, Laurie becomes bold and disrespectful.
2. Laurie claims that Charles is his best friend in school.
3. According to Laurie, Charles is the teacher's pet.
4. Laurie's parents are eager to meet Charles's mother.
5. The teacher says there is no Charles in the kindergarten.

TALKING IT OVER

1. Laurie tells a great many stories about Charles's behavior in kindergarten. Whose behavior is he describing? Is it likely that all these stories are true?
2. Why do you suppose Laurie enjoys telling his family stories about Charles?
3. At what point in the story did you begin to suspect the true identity of Charles? Why do you suppose Laurie's parents never catch on?
4. Why do you think the author does not move the action to the school until the end of the story?
5. How does the author create humor in this story?
6. In what way is the outcome of this story ironic?

CHARACTER
Methods of Characterization

The way an author presents a character in a short story is called **characterization.** Sometimes an author tells you directly what a character is like. More often, the author lets you draw your own conclusions about a character from information in the story.

Shirley Jackson uses several **methods of characterization** to reveal what Laurie is like.

Details of Physical Appearance. At the opening of the story, Laurie's mother makes a point of saying that Laurie has given up bibbed corduroy overalls for blue jeans with a belt.

What Other Characters Think. We see very clearly how Laurie is thought of by his mother and father. Despite his bad behavior, they continue to regard him as an innocent little boy. In fact, Laurie's mother fears that kindergarten itself, along with the bad influence of Charles, might be the cause of her son's rudeness.

How the Character Behaves. Laurie has become rude and insolent. He slams the door, drops his cap on the floor, and spills his sister's milk. In each conversation with his mother and father, he is very disrespectful.

1. How does Laurie's style of dress reflect a change in his behavior and attitude?
2. There is a sharp contrast between the way Laurie's mother and father think of him and the way he actually is. How does this contrast serve as a clue to the outcome of the story?
3. How is Laurie's behavior strikingly similar to Charles's?

**UNDERSTANDING THE WORDS IN THE STORY
(Matching Columns)**

1. renounced
2. raucous
3. swaggering
4. insolently
5. deprived of
6. warily
7. incredulously
8. cynically
9. haggard
10. primly

a. cautiously
b. denied
c. in a way that shows distrust
d. neatly and properly
e. tired
f. gave up utterly
g. disrespectfully
h. bold and self-important
i. in an unbelieving way
j. loud and rowdy

**WRITING IT DOWN
Another Point of View**

The story "Charles" is told by Laurie's mother. How would the story change if it were told from the point of view of a different character—one of Laurie's classmates, the kindergarten teacher, or even Laurie himself? Imagine that you are one of these characters and retell the story from your point of view.

A Comparison

According to the narrator of "Stolen Day" (page 132), "all children are actors." Is this true of the character Laurie? What are his motives for behaving as he does? Is he aware that he is, in a sense, performing? If you have read "Stolen Day," write a brief essay comparing the narrator of that story with Laurie from "Charles."

A Cartoon

Create a cartoon or a comic strip about Charles. Use one of the episodes in the story or make up one of your own.

ABOUT THE AUTHOR

Shirley Jackson (1919–1965) was born in San Francisco. She is known chiefly for her horror stories. Her novel *The Haunting of Hill House* (1959) was made into a movie called *The Haunting*. In her macabre novels and tales, human life is troubled by evil and unpredictability. Her most famous story, "The Lottery," appeared in *The New Yorker* in 1948 and created quite a stir. This story is a chilling tale about modern-day ritual sacrifice. Not all of Jackson's works emphasize the sinister elements in human life, however. Her stories of family life, like "Charles," are highly entertaining. More stories about her family can be found in *Life Among the Savages* and *Raising Demons*.

ALL SUMMER IN A DAY

Ray Bradbury

Imagine trying to describe the sun to someone who had never seen it. What comparison would you use?

"Ready?"

"Ready."

"Now?"

"Soon."

"Do the scientists really know? Will it happen today, will it?"

"Look, look; see for yourself!"

The children pressed to each other like so many roses, so many weeds, intermixed, peering out for a look at the hidden sun.

It rained.

It had been raining for seven years; thousands upon thousands of days compounded and filled from one end to the other with rain, with the drum and gush of water, with the sweet crystal fall of showers and the concussion of storms so heavy they were tidal waves come over the islands. A thousand forests had been crushed under the rain and grown up a thousand times to be crushed again. And this was the way life was forever on the planet Venus, and this was the schoolroom of the children of the rocket men and women who had come to a raining world to set up civilization and live out their lives.

"It's stopping, it's stopping!"

"Yes, yes!"

Margot stood apart from them, from these children who could never remember a time when there wasn't rain and rain and rain. They were all nine years old, and if there had been a day, seven years ago, when the sun came out for an hour and showed its face to the stunned world, they could not recall. Sometimes, at night, she heard them stir, in remembrance, and she knew they were dreaming and remembering gold or a yellow crayon or a coin large enough to buy the world with. She knew they thought they remembered a warmness, like a blushing in the face, in the body, in the arms and legs and trembling hands. But then they always awoke to the tatting drum, the endless shaking down of clear bead necklaces upon the roof, the walk, the gardens, the forests, and their dreams were gone.

All day yesterday they had read in class about the sun. About how like a lemon it was, and how hot. And they had written small stories or essays or poems about it:

> *I think the sun is a flower,*
> *That blooms for just one hour.*

That was Margot's poem, read in a quiet voice in the still classroom while the rain was falling outside.

"Aw, you didn't write that!" protested one of the boys.

"I did," said Margot. "I did."

"William!" said the teacher.

But that was yesterday. Now the rain was slackening, and the children were crushed in the great thick windows.

"Where's teacher?"

"She'll be back."

"She'd better hurry, we'll miss it!"

They turned on themselves, like a feverish wheel, all tumbling spokes.

Margot stood alone. She was a very frail girl who looked as if she had been lost in the rain for years and the rain had washed out the blue from her eyes and the red from her mouth and the yellow from her hair. She was an old photograph dusted from an album, whitened away, and if she spoke at all her voice would be a ghost. Now she stood, separate, staring at the rain and the loud wet world beyond the huge glass.

"What're *you* looking at?" said William.

Margot said nothing.

"Speak when you're spoken to." He gave her a shove. But she did not move; rather she let herself be moved only by him and nothing else.

They edged away from her, they would not look at her. She felt them go away. And this was because she would play no games with them in the echoing tunnels of the underground city. If they tagged her and ran, she stood blinking after them and did not follow. When the class sang songs about happiness and life and games her lips barely moved. Only when they sang about the sun and the summer did her lips move as she watched the drenched windows.

And then, of course, the biggest crime of all was that she had come here only five years ago from Earth, and she remembered the sun and the way the sun was and the sky was when she was four in Ohio. And they, they had been on Venus all their lives, and they had been only two years old when last the sun came out and had long since forgotten the color and heat of it and the way it really was. But Margot remembered.

"It's like a penny," she said once, eyes closed.

"No, it's not!" the children cried.

"It's like a fire," she said, "in the stove."

"You're lying, you don't remember!" cried the children.

But she remembered and stood quietly apart from all of them and watched the patterning[1] windows. And once, a month ago, she had refused to shower in the school shower rooms, had clutched her hands to her ears and over her head, screaming the water mustn't touch her head. So after that, dimly, dimly, she sensed it, she was different and they knew her difference and kept away.

There was talk that her father and mother were taking her back to Earth next year; it seemed vital to her that they do so, though it would mean the loss of thousands of dollars to her family. And so, the children hated her for all these reasons of big and little consequence. They hated her pale snow face, her waiting silence, her thinness, and her possible future.

"Get away!" The boy gave her another push. "What're you waiting for?"

Then, for the first time, she turned and looked at him. And what she was waiting for was in her eyes.

"Well, don't wait around here!" cried the boy savagely. "You won't see nothing!"

Her lips moved.

"Nothing!" he cried. "It was all a joke, wasn't it?" He turned to the other children. "Nothing's happening today. *Is* it?"

They all blinked at him and then, understanding, laughed and shook their heads. "Nothing, nothing!"

---

1. **patterning** (păt′ər-nĭng): forming a pattern (of raindrops).

"Oh, but," Margot whispered, her eyes helpless. "But this is the day, the scientists predict, they say, they *know*, the sun . . ."

"All a joke!" said the boy, and seized her roughly. "Hey, everyone, let's put her in a closet before teacher comes!"

"No," said Margot, falling back.

They surged about her, caught her up and bore her, protesting, and then pleading, and then crying, back into a tunnel, a room, a closet, where they slammed and locked the door. They stood looking at the door and saw it tremble from her beating and throwing herself against it. They heard her muffled cries. Then, smiling, they turned and went out and back down the tunnel, just as the teacher arrived.

"Ready, children?" She glanced at her watch.

"Yes!" said everyone.

"Are we all here?"

"Yes!"

The rain slackened still more.

They crowded to the huge door.

The rain stopped.

It was as if, in the midst of a film concerning an avalanche, a tornado, a hurricane, a volcanic eruption, something had, first, gone wrong with the sound apparatus, thus muffling and finally cutting off all noise, all of the blasts and repercussions and thunders, and then, second, ripped the film from the projector and inserted in its place a peaceful tropical slide which did not move or tremor. The world ground to a standstill. The silence was so immense and unbelievable that you felt your ears had been stuffed or you had lost your hearing altogether. The children put their hands to their ears. They stood apart. The door slid back and the smell of the silent, waiting world came in to them.

The sun came out.

It was the color of flaming bronze and it was very large. And the sky around it was a blazing blue tile color. And the jungle burned with sunlight as the children, released from their spell, rushed out, yelling, into the springtime.

"Now, don't go too far," called the teacher after them.

"You've only two hours, you know. You wouldn't want to get caught out!"

But they were running and turning their faces up to the sky and feeling the sun on their cheeks like a warm iron; they were taking off their jackets and letting the sun burn their arms.

"Oh, it's better than the sunlamps, isn't it?"

"Much, much better!"

They stopped running and stood in the great jungle that covered Venus, that grew and never stopped growing, tumultuously, even as you watched it. It was a nest of octopi, clustering up great arms of fleshlike weed, wavering, flowering in this brief spring. It was the color of rubber and ash, this jungle, from the many years without sun. It was the color of stones and white cheeses and ink, and it was the color of the moon.

The children lay out, laughing, on the jungle mattress, and heard it sigh and squeak under them, resilient and alive. They ran among the trees, they slipped and fell, they pushed each other, they played hide-and-seek and tag, but most of all they squinted at the sun until tears ran down their faces, they put their hands up to that yellowness and that amazing blueness and they breathed of the fresh, fresh air and listened and listened to the silence which suspended them in a blessed sea of no sound and no motion. They looked at everything and savored everything. Then, wildly, like animals escaped from their caves, they ran and ran in shouting circles. They ran for an hour and did not stop running.

And then——

In the midst of their running one of the girls wailed.

Everyone stopped.

The girl, standing in the open, held out her hand.

"Oh, look, look," she said, trembling.

They came slowly to look at her opened palm.

In the center of it, cupped and huge, was a single raindrop.

She began to cry, looking at it.

They glanced quietly at the sky.

"Oh. Oh."

A few cold drops fell on their noses and their cheeks and their mouths. The sun faded behind a stir of mist. A wind blew cool around them. They turned and started to walk back toward the underground house, their hands at their sides, their smiles vanishing away.

A boom of thunder startled them and like leaves before a new hurricane, they tumbled upon each other and ran. Lightning struck ten miles away, five miles away, a mile, a half mile. The sky darkened into midnight in a flash.

They stood in the doorway of the underground for a moment until it was raining hard. Then they closed the door and heard the gigantic sound of the rain falling in tons and avalanches, everywhere and forever.

"Will it be seven more years?"

"Yes. Seven."

Then one of them gave a little cry.

"Margot!"

"What?"

"She's still in the closet where we locked her."

"Margot."

They stood as if someone had driven them, like so many stakes, into the floor. They looked at each other and then looked away. They glanced out at the world that was raining now and raining and raining steadily. They could not meet each other's glances. Their faces were solemn and pale. They looked at their hands and feet, their faces down.

"Margot."

One of the girls said, "Well . . . ?"

No one moved.

"Go on," whispered the girl.

They walked slowly down the hall in the sound of cold rain. They turned through the doorway to the room in the sound of the storm and thunder, lightning on their faces, blue and terrible. They walked over to the closet door slowly and stood by it.

Behind the closet door was only silence.

They unlocked the door, even more slowly, and let Margot out.

First Response: *How did you feel at the end of the story, as Margot was about to walk out of the closet?*

CHECKING UP (Multiple-Choice)

1. The author of this story imagines the planet Venus to be
   a. covered with forests and lakes
   b. a wetter place than Earth
   c. pitted with craters
2. The other children in the class resent Margot because she
   a. is the teacher's pet
   b. is a crybaby
   c. was born on Earth
3. The events of the story suggest that Margot probably will
   a. never adjust to life on Venus
   b. get even with her classmates
   c. make friends with the other children
4. The children lock Margot in the closet
   a. by accident
   b. to keep her from seeing the sun
   c. as a game
5. At the end of the story, the children feel
   a. ashamed of their behavior
   b. affection for Margot
   c. angry at their teacher

TALKING IT OVER

1. What are the climatic conditions the author imagines to exist on the planet Venus? What places on earth does the planet Venus most closely resemble?
2. Although the story takes place in an alien world, the characters behave much the same way human beings behave on Earth. Why do the children pick on Margot? In what ways is she different from them?
3. Why do you suppose Margot makes no effort to join the children in their games or to respond to their taunts?
4. How are the children affected by their first experience of the sun?
5. Do you think that the children have a better understanding of Margot at the end of the story? Explain your answer.

SETTING
Background in a Story

A painting or a photograph is said to have a **foreground** and a **background.** The foreground is the part of the scene that is nearest to you, the viewer, and therefore most noticeable. The background is the part of the scene that is toward the back and that forms the surroundings for the images in the foreground.

A short story, too, may be said to have a foreground and a background. The foreground consists of the main characters and the actions that are of greatest interest to the reader. The background of the story—the time and place in which the events occur, and the circumstances that surround these events—is known as the story's **setting.**

Setting is an important element in many short stories. Clearly, the action of Ray Bradbury's story depends upon its physical background. The events he describes are tied to the setting.

Find details in the story that describe the climatic conditions and environment Bradbury imagines to exist on the planet Venus. How does the author make the setting convincing?

UNDERSTANDING THE WORDS IN THE STORY
(Matching Columns)

1. concussion
2. consequence
3. muffling
4. repercussions
5. resilient
6. savored
7. slackening
8. solemn
9. suspended
10. tumultuously

a. reflections of sound
b. enjoyed
c. slowing down
d. held in position
e. importance
f. serious
g. springing back
h. violent shaking
i. in a riotous way
j. deadening

FOR WRITING
Notes to Describe a Setting

Think of a place—either real or imaginary—that could provide an interesting setting for a story. What does the place look like? How does it feel to be there? To organize your thoughts, you might find it helpful to fill in a chart like the one below. Try to make your details as specific and vivid as possible.

SETTING CHART

PLACE: _____

WEATHER: _____

TIME OF YEAR: _____

TIME OF DAY: _____

OBJECTS: _____
_____
_____
_____
_____
_____

SIGHTS/SOUNDS/SMELLS: _____
_____
_____
_____
_____

212 ALL SUMMER IN A DAY

ABOUT THE AUTHOR

Ray Bradbury was born in Waukegan, Illinois, in 1920. When he was twelve he wrote a sequel to an Edgar Rice Burroughs novel. "Burroughs was a sly character," he told an interviewer. "He wrote one of his Martian novels and left his heroine trapped in the Sun Prison, and you had to buy the next book to find out how she got out. I had no money, so I wrote the sequel and got her out." By the time Bradbury was fifteen, he was sending science-fiction stories to magazines.

Bradbury's interest in fantasy and space travel has led him to become a science-fiction writer—but of an unusual sort. He has been more concerned with creating poetic images and examining the impact of technology on everyday life than with describing interplanetary battles. He believes, in fact, that the exploration of space should result in a better understanding of human nature.

Bradbury's works have attained a wide following. His books include the *Martian Chronicles, The Golden Apples of the Sun,* and *Fahrenheit 451.* Several of his works have been adapted for the screen and for television. During the 1985 season, "All Summer in a Day" was dramatized for a television series called *Wonderworks.*

THE SNIPER

Liam O'Flaherty

How is a civil war different from an international conflict? In what ways is it more tragic? Discuss these questions with your classmates.

The long June twilight faded into night. Dublin lay enveloped in darkness but for the dim light of the moon that shone through fleecy clouds, casting a pale light as of approaching dawn over the streets and the dark waters of the Liffey. Around the beleaguered Four Courts the heavy guns roared. Here and there through the city machine guns and rifles broke the silence of the night, spasmodically,[1] like dogs barking on lone farms. Republicans and Free Staters were waging civil war.[2]

On a rooftop near O'Connell Bridge, a Republican sniper lay watching. Beside him lay his rifle and over his shoulders were slung a pair of field glasses. His face was the face of a student—thin and ascetic, but his eyes had the cold gleam of the fanatic. They were deep and thoughtful, the eyes of a man who is used to looking at death.

He was eating a sandwich hungrily. He had eaten nothing since morning. He had been too excited to eat. He finished the sandwich, and taking a flask of whiskey from his pocket, he took a short draft. Then he returned the flask to his pocket. He paused for a moment, considering whether he should risk a smoke. It was dangerous. The flash might be seen in the darkness and there were enemies watching. He decided to take the risk. Placing a cigarette between his lips, he struck a match, inhaled the smoke hurriedly and put out the light. Almost immediately, a bullet flattened itself against the parapet of the roof. The sniper took another whiff and put out the cigarette. Then he swore softly and crawled away to the left.

Cautiously he raised himself and peered over the parapet. There was a flash and a bullet whizzed over his head. He dropped immediately. He had seen the flash. It came from the opposite side of the street.

1. **spasmodically** (spăz-mŏd′ĭk-lē): fitfully; happening at irregular intervals.
2. **civil war:** Civil war followed the founding of the Irish Free State in 1921. The Free State forces supported dominion status in the British Empire. The Republicans aimed at overthrowing English rule in Ireland.

213

He rolled over the roof to a chimney stack in the rear, and slowly drew himself up behind it, until his eyes were level with the top of the parapet. There was nothing to be seen—just the dim outline of the opposite housetop against the blue sky. His enemy was under cover.

Just then an armored car came across the bridge and advanced slowly up the street. It stopped on the opposite side of the street fifty yards ahead. The sniper could hear the dull panting of the motor. His heart beat faster. It was an enemy car. He wanted to fire, but he knew it was useless. His bullets would never pierce the steel that covered the gray monster.

Then round the corner of a side street came an old woman, her head covered by a tattered shawl. She began to talk to the man in the turret of the car. She was pointing to the roof where the sniper lay. An informer.

The turret opened. A man's head and shoulders appeared, looking towards the sniper. The sniper raised his rifle and fired. The head fell heavily on the turret wall. The woman darted toward the side street. The sniper fired again. The woman whirled around and fell with a shriek into the gutter.

Suddenly from the opposite roof a shot rang out and the sniper dropped his rifle with a curse. The rifle clattered to the roof. The sniper thought the noise would wake the dead. He stopped to pick the rifle up. He couldn't lift it. His forearm was dead. "I'm hit," he muttered.

Dropping flat onto the roof, he crawled back to the parapet. With his left hand he felt the injured right forearm. The blood was oozing through the sleeve of his coat. There was no pain—just a deadened sensation, as if the arm had been cut off.

Quickly he drew his knife from his pocket, opened it on the breastwork[3] of the parapet and ripped open the sleeve. There was a small hole where the bullet had entered. On the other side there was no hole. The bullet had lodged in the bone. It must have fractured it. He bent the arm below the wound. The arm bent back easily. He ground his teeth to overcome the pain.

---

3. **breastwork** (brĕst′wûrk′): a low wall.

Then, taking out his field dressing, he ripped open the packet with his knife. He broke the neck of the iodine bottle and let the bitter fluid drip into the wound. A paroxysm[4] of pain swept through him. He placed the cotton wadding over the wound and wrapped the dressing over it. He tied the end with his teeth.

Then he lay still against the parapet, and closing his eyes, he made an effort of will to overcome the pain.

In the street beneath all was still. The armored car had retired speedily over the bridge, with the machine gunner's head hanging lifeless over the turret. The woman's corpse lay still in the gutter.

The sniper lay for a long time nursing his wounded arm and planning escape. Morning must not find him wounded on the roof. The enemy on the opposite roof covered his escape. He must kill that enemy and he could not use his rifle. He had only a revolver to do it. Then he thought of a plan.

Taking off his cap, he placed it over the muzzle of his rifle. Then he pushed the rifle slowly upwards over the parapet, until the cap was visible from the opposite side of the street. Almost immediately there was a report,[5] and a bullet pierced the center of the cap. The sniper slanted the rifle forward. The cap slipped down into the street. Then, catching the rifle in the middle, the sniper dropped his left hand over the roof and let it hang, lifelessly. After a few moments he let the rifle drop to the street. Then he sank to the roof, dragging his hand with him.

Crawling quickly to the left, he peered up at the corner of the roof. His ruse had succeeded. The other sniper, seeing the cap and rifle fall, thought that he had killed his man. He was now standing before a row of chimney pots, looking across, with his head clearly silhouetted[6] against the western sky.

The Republican sniper smiled and lifted his revolver above the edge of the parapet. The distance was about fifty yards—a hard shot in the dim light, and his right arm was paining him like a thousand devils. He took a steady aim. His hand trembled with eagerness. Pressing his lips together, he took a deep breath through his nostrils and fired. He

4. **paroxysm** (păr'ək-sĭz'əm): sudden attack or spasm.
5. **report:** an explosive noise.
6. **silhouetted** (sĭl'ōō-ĕt'əd): outlined.

was almost deafened with the report and his arm shook with the recoil. Then, when the smoke cleared, he peered across and uttered a cry of joy. His enemy had been hit. He was reeling over the parapet in his death agony. He struggled to keep his feet, but he was slowly falling forward, as if in a dream. The rifle fell from his grasp, hit the parapet, fell over, bounded off the pole of a barber's shop beneath and then cluttered[7] onto the pavement.

Then the dying man on the roof crumpled up and fell forward. The body turned over and over in space and hit the ground with a dull thud. Then it lay still.

The sniper looked at his enemy falling and he shuddered. The lust of battle died in him. He became bitten by remorse. The sweat stood out in beads on his forehead. Weakened by his wound and the long summer day of fasting and watching on the roof, he revolted from the sight of the shattered mass of his dead enemy. His teeth chattered. He began to gibber[8] to himself, cursing the war, cursing himself, cursing everybody.

He looked at the smoking revolver in his hand and with an oath he hurled it to the roof at his feet. The revolver went off with the concussion, and the bullet whizzed past the sniper's head. He was frightened back to his senses by the shock. His nerves steadied. The cloud of fear scattered from his mind and he laughed.

Taking the whiskey flask from his pocket, he emptied it at a draft. He felt reckless under the influence of the spirits. He decided to leave the roof and look for his company commander to report. Everywhere around was quiet. There was not much danger in going through the streets. He picked up his revolver and put it in his pocket. Then he crawled down through the skylight to the house underneath.

When the sniper reached the laneway on the street level, he felt a sudden curiosity as to the identity of the enemy sniper whom he had killed. He wondered if he knew him. Perhaps he had been in his own company before the split in the army. He decided to risk going over to have a look at him. He peered around the corner into O'Connell Street. In the upper part of the street there was heavy firing, but around here all was quiet.

7. **cluttered:** clattered.
8. **gibber** (jĭb′ər, gĭb′-): talk senselessly.

The sniper darted across the street. A machine gun tore up the ground around him with a hail of bullets, but he escaped. He threw himself face downwards beside the corpse. The machine gun stopped.

Then the sniper turned over the dead body and looked into his brother's face.

First Response: *How did you feel when the sniper discovered his enemy's identity?*

CHECKING UP

Arrange the following events in the order in which they occur in the story.

The sniper is wounded.
The sniper crawls down through the skylight.
The sniper eats a sandwich.
An armored car advances up the street.
The sniper strikes a match.
The sniper shoots the informer.
The sniper turns over the body of his enemy.
The sniper kills the machine gunner.
The sniper lets his rifle drop to the street.
The sniper feels remorse.

TALKING IT OVER

1. In this story O'Flaherty gives us a realistic account of the fighting in the Irish Civil War. What conclusions can you draw about the war from the events in the story?

2. The sniper is referred to as a *fanatic.* How do his actions show that he is obsessed with a cause? How does he show both courage and cunning?
3. What change becomes apparent in the sniper after he succeeds in killing his opponent? How do you explain this change?
4. What is the ironic twist at the end of the story? Do you consider this ending a logical outcome of the events? Explain.
5. The characters in this story are not identified by name, but by function. The old woman wearing a shawl is referred to as an informer, and the central character is known only as the sniper. What do you think is O'Flaherty's purpose in making his characters anonymous?
6. What do the events of the story lead you to conclude about the author's attitude toward war?

SETTING
Verisimilitude

In the story "All Summer in a Day" (page 203), Ray Bradbury imaginatively creates the climatic conditions and environment of the planet Venus. Although this world is fictional, it is so well realized that while we read the story we are convinced that Venus is a place of rain and storms where the sun comes out only once every seven years.

A short story may be given a setting that is true to a specific time and place. This appearance of reality in a work of fiction is called **verisimilitude** (věr′ə-sĭm-ĭl′ə-to͞od′, -tyo͞od′). For example, "The Sniper" takes place in a real city, Dublin, during the period of the Irish Civil War in the early 1920s. O'Flaherty's story shows accurately how this war was fought in small skirmishes on rooftops and in the streets, often between members of the same family.

Identify at least five details that establish the historical setting of "The Sniper."

UNDERSTANDING THE WORDS IN THE STORY (Completion)

1. A person who gives information against others for pay is a(n) _____. (fanatic, informer)
2. To stagger or sway is to _____. (reel, revolt)
3. Regret for one's past actions is _____. (agony, remorse)
4. To deny oneself comforts is to be _____. (ascetic, reckless)
5. A low protective railing or wall is a _____. (parapet, turret)
6. The kick of a gun when it is fired is known as its _____. (concussion, recoil)
7. To look intently is to _____. (bound, peer)
8. To besiege with armed forces is to _____ the enemy. (beleaguer, envelop)
9. An action intended to mislead someone is a _____. (recoil, ruse)
10. The light in someone's eyes is a _____. (gleam, ruse)

WRITING IT DOWN
The Setting of a Historic Event

Choose a notable historic event, such as the March on Washington on August 28, 1963, when Dr. Martin Luther King, Jr., delivered his famous "I Have a Dream" speech, or the first moon landing in July of 1969. Read about the event in old magazines, history books, or other reference works. Make a list of details about the setting of the event. If possible, find photographs, drawings, or other illustrations. Share your information with a small group of classmates.

ABOUT THE AUTHOR

Liam O'Flaherty (1896–1984) grew up on the Aran Islands off the western coast of Ireland. He studied at a Dublin seminary until he decided against entering the priesthood. He enrolled in University College, Dublin, but left when the First World War broke out. While fighting in France he became shell shocked. After his discharge, he spent three years traveling, and then returned to Ireland, where he became involved in politics. He was arrested when he and a group of unemployed workers seized a building in Dublin. Forced to leave Ireland, he settled in England, where he wrote his first novel. O'Flaherty's most famous work is *The Informer* (1926), about a man who betrays his friends for money. The novel was later made into a movie. "The Sniper" is one of O'Flaherty's best-known stories.

TOO SOON A WOMAN

Dorothy M. Johnson

What do you know about the lives of women in the Old West? What did they do—cook, sew, farm, raise children? Freewrite for a minute or two about your impression of the role of women in the Old West.

We left the home place behind, mile by slow mile, heading for the mountains, across the prairie where the wind blew forever.

At first there were four of us with the one-horse wagon and its skimpy load. Pa and I walked, because I was a big boy of eleven. My two little sisters romped and trotted until they got tired and had to be boosted up into the wagon bed.

That was no covered Conestoga,[1] like Pa's folks came West in, but just an old farm wagon, drawn by one weary horse, creaking and rumbling westward to the mountains, toward the little woods town where Pa thought he had an old uncle who owned a little two-bit sawmill.

Two weeks we had been moving when we picked up Mary, who had run away from somewhere that she wouldn't tell. Pa didn't want her along, but she stood up to him with no fear in her voice.

"I'd rather go with a family and look after kids," she said, "but I ain't going back. If you won't take me, I'll travel with any wagon that will."

Pa scowled at her, and her wide blue eyes stared back.

"How old are you?" he demanded.

"Eighteen," she said. "There's teamsters come this way sometimes. I'd rather go with you folks. But I won't go back."

"We're prid'near out of grub," my father told her. "We're clean out of money. I got all I can handle without taking anybody else." He turned away as if he hated the sight of her. "You'll have to walk," he said.

So she went along with us and looked after the little girls, but Pa wouldn't talk to her.

On the prairie, the wind blew. But in the mountains, there was rain. When we stopped at little timber claims along the way, the homesteaders

---

1. **Conestoga** (kŏn′ĭ-stō′gə): a covered wagon with broad wheels, used by pioneers crossing the American prairies.

said it had rained all summer. Crops among the blackened stumps
were rotted and spoiled. There was no cheer anywhere, and little hos-
pitality. The people we talked to were past worrying. They were scared
and desperate.

So was Pa. He traveled twice as far each day as the wagon, ranging
through the woods with his rifle, but he never saw game. He had been
depending on venison.[2] But we never got any except as a grudging gift
from the homesteaders.

He brought in a porcupine once, and that was fat meat and good.
Mary roasted it in chunks over the fire, half crying with the smoke. Pa
and I rigged up the tarp[3] sheet for shelter to keep the rain from putting
the fire clean out.

The porcupine was long gone, except for some of the tried-out fat[4]
that Mary had saved, when we came to an old, empty cabin. Pa said we'd
have to stop. The horse was wore out, couldn't pull anymore up those
grades on the deep-rutted roads in the mountains.

At the cabin, at least there was shelter. We had a few potatoes left
and some corn meal. There was a creek that probably had fish in it, if
a person could catch them. Pa tried it for half a day before he gave up.
To this day I don't care for fishing. I remember my father's sunken eyes
in his gaunt, grim face.

He took Mary and me outside the cabin to talk. Rain dripped on us
from branches overhead.

"I think I know where we are," he said. "I calculate to get to old
John's and back in about four days. There'll be grub in the town, and
they'll let me have some whether old John's still there or not."

He looked at me. "You do like she tells you," he warned. It was the
first time he had admitted Mary was on earth since we picked her up
two weeks before.

"You're my pardner," he said to me, "but it might be she's got more
brains. You mind what she says."

He burst out with bitterness. "There ain't anything good left in the
world, or people to care if you live or die. But I'll get grub in the town
and come back with it."

---

2. **venison** (vĕn'ə-sən, -zən): deer meat.
3. **tarp:** tarpaulin (tär-pô'lĭn, tär'pə-lĭn), waterproof canvas.
4. **tried-out fat:** fat that is rendered, or melted down.

He took a deep breath and added, "If you get too all-fired hungry, butcher the horse. It'll be better than starvin'."

He kissed the little girls goodbye and plodded off through the woods with one blanket and the rifle.

The cabin was moldy and had no floor. We kept a fire going under a hole in the roof, so it was full of blinding smoke, but we had to keep the fire so as to dry out the wood.

The third night we lost the horse. A bear scared him. We heard the racket, and Mary and I ran out, but we couldn't see anything in the pitch-dark.

In gray daylight I went looking for him, and I must have walked fifteen miles. It seemed like I had to have that horse at the cabin when Pa came or he'd whip me. I got plumb[5] lost two or three times and thought maybe I was going to die there alone and nobody would ever know it, but I found the way back to the clearing.

That was the fourth day, and Pa didn't come. That was the day we ate up the last of the grub.

The fifth day, Mary went looking for the horse. My sisters whimpered, huddled in a quilt by the fire, because they were scared and hungry.

I never did get dried out, always having to bring in more damp wood and going out to yell to see if Mary would hear me and not get lost. But I couldn't cry like the little girls did, because I was a big boy, eleven years old.

It was near dark when there was an answer to my yelling, and Mary came into the clearing.

Mary didn't have the horse—we never saw hide nor hair of that old horse again—but she was carrying something big and white that looked like a pumpkin with no color to it.

She didn't say anything, just looked around and saw Pa wasn't there yet, at the end of the fifth day.

"What's that thing?" my sister Elizabeth demanded.

"Mushroom," Mary answered. "I bet it hefts[6] ten pounds."

"What are you going to do with it now?" I sneered. "Play football here?"

5. **plumb** (plŭm): completely.
6. **hefts:** weighs.

"Eat it—maybe," she said, putting it in a corner. Her wet hair hung over her shoulders. She huddled by the fire.

My sister Sarah began to whimper again. "I'm hungry!" she kept saying.

"Mushrooms ain't good eating," I said. "They can kill you."

"Maybe," Mary answered. "Maybe they can. I don't set up to know all about everything, like some people."

"What's that mark on your shoulder?" I asked her. "You tore your dress on the brush."

"What do you think it is?" she said, her head bowed in the smoke.

"Looks like scars," I guessed.

" 'Tis scars. They whipped me. Now mind your own business. I want to think."

Elizabeth whimpered, "Why don't Pa come back?"

"He's coming," Mary promised. "Can't come in the dark. Your pa'll take care of you soon's he can."

She got up and rummaged around in the grub box.

"Nothing there but empty dishes," I growled. "If there was anything, we'd know it."

Mary stood up. She was holding the can with the porcupine grease. "I'm going to have something to eat," she said coolly. "You kids can't have any yet. And I don't want any squalling, mind."

It was a cruel thing, what she did then. She sliced that big, solid mushroom and heated grease in a pan.

The smell of it brought the little girls out of their quilt, but she told them to go back in so fierce a voice that they obeyed. They cried to break your heart.

I didn't cry. I watched, hating her.

I endured the smell of the mushroom frying as long as I could. Then I said, "Give me some."

"Tomorrow," Mary answered. "Tomorrow, maybe. But not tonight." She turned to me with a sharp command: "Don't bother me! Just leave me be."

She knelt there by the fire and finished frying the slice of mushroom.

If I'd had Pa's rifle, I'd have been willing to kill her right then and there.

She didn't eat right away. She looked at the brown, fried slice for a while and said, "By tomorrow morning, I guess you can tell whether you want any."

The little girls stared at her as she ate. Sarah was chewing an old leather glove.

When Mary crawled into the quilts with them, they moved away as far as they could get.

I was so scared that my stomach heaved, empty as it was.

Mary didn't stay in the quilts long. She took a drink out of the water bucket and sat down by the fire and looked through the smoke at me.

She said in a low voice, "I don't know how it will be if it's poison. Just do the best you can with the girls. Because your pa will come back, you know. . . . You better go to bed. I'm going to sit up."

And so would you sit up. If it might be your last night on earth and the pain of death might seize you at any moment, you would sit up by the smoky fire, wide-awake, remembering whatever you had to remember, savoring life.

We sat in silence after the girls had gone to sleep. Once I asked, "How long does it take?"

"I never heard," she answered. "Don't think about it."

I slept after a while, with my chin on my chest. Maybe Peter[7] dozed that way at Gethsemane[8] as the Lord knelt praying.

Mary's moving around brought me wide-awake. The black of night was fading.

"I guess it's all right," Mary said. "I'd be able to tell by now, wouldn't I?"

I answered gruffly, "I don't know."

Mary stood in the doorway for a while, looking out at the dripping world as if she found it beautiful. Then she fried slices of the mushroom while the little girls danced with anxiety.

We feasted, we three, my sisters and I, until Mary ruled, "That'll hold you," and would not cook any more. She didn't touch any of the mushroom herself.

That was a strange day in the moldy cabin. Mary laughed and was gay; she told stories, and we played "Who's Got the Thimble?" with a pine cone.

7. **Peter:** one of the twelve apostles, also called Simon Peter or Saint Peter.
8. **Gethsemane** (gĕth-sĕm′ə-nē): the garden outside Jerusalem where Jesus was arrested (Matthew 26:36–57).

In the afternoon we heard a shout, and my sisters screamed and I ran ahead of them across the clearing.

The rain had stopped. My father came plunging out of the woods leading a pack horse—and well I remember the treasures of food in that pack.

He glanced at us anxiously as he tore at the ropes that bound the pack.

"Where's the other one?" he demanded.

Mary came out of the cabin then, walking sedately. As she came toward us, the sun began to shine.

My stepmother was a wonderful woman.

First Response: *Would you have had the courage to eat the mushroom if you had been Mary?*

CHECKING UP

1. Why doesn't Pa want Mary to travel with the family?
2. Why does the group stop at the cabin?
3. Where does Pa go when he leaves Mary and the children at the cabin?
4. Why does Mary refuse at first to give any of the mushroom to the children?
5. How do you know that Mary stays on with the family?

TALKING IT OVER

1. Writers often use details of setting to establish an overall **atmosphere,** or **mood.** In the first part of this story, up to the

point where the travelers come to the old, empty cabin, what mood does the setting create?

2. Pa makes it clear that he doesn't want to take anyone else along on the trip. Why, then, does he allow Mary to join the family?

3. How does Mary save the children from starving?

4. How does Mary show that she is courageous and strong-willed? How does she show that she can be gentle?

5. At the end of the story, what change occurs in the family's attitude toward Mary?

SETTING
Setting and Plot

In some stories, **setting** is incidental to the characters and action. "Success Story," (page 83) does not need to take place in the Caribbean; it would be just as effective if it were set in a large city in Europe or in a small town in Japan. It could take place in any season of the year. The **plot** of that story depends upon the values and personalities of human beings, not upon their environment. In other stories, setting is a crucial element. "A Tiger in the House" (page 1), for example, would not be believable if the action were set in England rather than in India, because people do not hunt tigers in Great Britain.

The events in "Too Soon a Woman" take place in a setting unique to American history. Although no specific time or place is mentioned in the story, we can guess that the background is the Old West and that the characters are pioneers. References to the prairie, to homesteaders, to the great distances traveled, and to the hardships endured by the settlers are typical in Western stories. The main action of the story tells of the desperate courage that was necessary in this vast, uninhabited land.

Find at least five details in the story that give you a sense of what life was like on the frontier.

UNDERSTANDING THE WORDS IN THE STORY
(Matching Columns)

1. anxiety	a. cried softly
2. gaunt	b. roughly
3. grim	c. loud crying
4. whimpered	d. calmly
5. squalling	e. frowned
6. scowled	f. restlessness
7. savoring	g. thin
8. rummaged	h. searched thoroughly
9. sedately	i. enjoying
10. gruffly	j. severe

WRITING IT DOWN
A Sketch of Time and Place

The narrator of "Too Soon a Woman" seems to be describing events from his past. As his story unfolds, a way of life during a particular time and place in history is revealed as well.

Ask an older person—such as a neighbor, friend, or grand-parent—to tell you about his or her childhood. Where did the person grow up? What historic events were taking place at the time? What was life like back then? Listen carefully and take notes.

Write a brief sketch about the setting that the person has described to you. Use specific details to create a sense of time and place. You may find it helpful to fill out a chart similar to the one on page 211.

ABOUT THE AUTHOR

Dorothy M. Johnson (1905–1984) was born in McGregor, Iowa, and grew up in Montana. She wrote a number of works about the American

West. The films *The Man Who Shot Liberty Valence, The Hanging Tree,* and *A Man Called Horse* were based on her stories. Her *Warrior for a Lost Nation: A Biography of Sitting Bull* (1969) is about the life of the Sioux chief and resistance fighter. She was an honorary member of the Blackfoot tribe in Montana.

THE WILD DUCK'S NEST

Michael McLaverty

What wild animals are you familiar with? Do you know them from
reading books or watching television, or from your own backyard?
Write a sentence or two about your favorite wild animal.

The sun was setting, spilling gold light on the low western hills of
Rathlin Island.[1] A small boy walked jauntily along a hoof-printed
path that wriggled between the folds of these hills and opened
out into a craterlike valley on the clifftop. Presently he stopped as if
remembering something, then suddenly he left the path, and began
running up one of the hills. When he reached the top he was out of
breath and stood watching streaks of light radiating from golden-edged
clouds, the scene reminding him of a picture he had seen of the
Transfiguration.[2] A short distance below him was the cow standing at
the edge of a reedy lake. Colm[3] ran down to meet her, waving his stick
in the air, and the wind rumbling in his ears made him give an exultant
whoop which splashed upon the hills in a shower of echoed sound. A
flock of gulls lying on the short grass near the lake rose up languidly,
drifting like blown snowflakes over the rim of the cliff.

The lake faced west and was fed by a stream, the drainings of the
semicircling hills. One side was open to the winds from the sea and in
winter a little outlet trickled over the cliffs making a black vein in their
gray sides. The boy lifted stones and began throwing them into the lake,
weaving web after web on its calm surface. Then he skimmed the water
with flat stones, some of them jumping the surface and coming to rest
on the other side. He was delighted with himself and after listening to
his echoing shouts of delight he ran to fetch his cow. Gently he tapped
her on the side and reluctantly she went towards the brown-mudded
path that led out of the valley. The boy was about to throw a final stone
into the lake when a bird flew low over his head, its neck astrain, and
its orange-colored legs clear in the soft light. It was a wild duck. It

---

1. **Rathlin Island:** an island a few miles off the coast of Northern Ireland.
2. **the Transfiguration:** an event in the life of Jesus Christ, told in Matthew 17:1–8.
3. **Colm** (kŭl′əm).

circled the lake twice, thrice, coming lower each time and then with a nervous flapping of wings it skidded along the surface, its legs breaking the water into a series of silvery arcs. Its wings closed, it lit silently, gave a slight shiver, and began pecking indifferently at the water. Colm with dilated eyes eagerly watched it making for the farther end of the lake. It meandered between tall bulrushes[4], its body black and solid as stone against the graying water. Then as if it had sunk it was gone. The boy ran stealthily along the bank looking away from the lake, pretending indifference. When he came opposite to where he had last seen the bird he stopped and peered through the sighing reeds whose shadows streaked the water in a maze of black strokes. In front of him was a soddy islet[5] guarded by the spears of sedge[6] and separated from the bank by a narrow channel of water. The water wasn't too deep—he could wade across with care.

Rolling up his short trousers he began to wade, his arms outstretched, and his legs brown and stunted in the mountain water. As he drew near the islet, his feet sank in the cold mud and bubbles winked up at him. He went more carefully and nervously. Then one trouser fell and dipped into the water; the boy dropped his hands to roll it up, he unbalanced, made a splashing sound, and the bird arose with a squawk and whirred away over the cliffs. For a moment the boy stood frightened. Then he clambered onto the wet-soaked sod of land, which was spattered with sea gulls' feathers and bits of wind-blown rushes.

Into each hummock[7] he looked, pulling back the long grass. At last he came on the nest, facing seawards. Two flat rocks dimpled the face of the water and between them was a neck of land matted with coarse grass containing the nest. It was untidily built of dried rushes, straw and feathers, and in it lay one solitary egg. Colm was delighted. He looked around and saw no one. The nest was his. He lifted the egg, smooth and green as the sky, with a faint tinge of yellow like the reflected light from a buttercup; and then he felt he had done wrong. He put it back. He knew he shouldn't have touched it and he wondered would the bird forsake the nest. A vague sadness stole over him and he felt in his heart

---

4. **bulrushes** (bool'rŭsh'ĭz): grasslike plants.
5. **soddy islet** (ī'lĭt'): small, turf-covered island.
6. **sedge:** a grasslike plant with pointed leaves.
7. **hummock** (hŭm'ək): a small mound of earth.

he had sinned. Carefully smoothing out his footprints he hurriedly left the islet and ran after his cow. The sun had now set and the cold shiver of evening enveloped him, chilling his body and saddening his mind.

In the morning he was up and away to school. He took the grass rut that edged the road for it was softer on the bare feet. His house was the last on the western headland and after a mile or so he was joined by Paddy McFall; both boys dressed in similar hand-knitted blue jerseys and gray trousers carried homemade schoolbags. Colm was full of the nest and as soon as he joined his companion he said eagerly: "Paddy, I've a nest—a wild duck's with one egg."

"And how do you know it's a wild duck's?" asked Paddy slightly jealous.

"Sure I saw her with my own two eyes, her brown speckled back with a crow's patch on it, and her yellow legs——"

"Where is it?" interrupted Paddy in a challenging tone.

"I'm not going to tell you, for you'd rob it!"

"Aach! I suppose it's a tame duck's you have or maybe an old gull's."

Colm put out his tongue at him. "A lot you know!" he said, "for a gull's egg has spots and this one is greenish-white, for I had it in my hand."

And then the words he didn't want to hear rushed from Paddy in a mocking chant, "You had it in your hand! . . . She'll forsake it! She'll forsake it! She'll forsake it!" he said, skipping along the road before him.

Colm felt as if he would choke or cry with vexation.

His mind told him that Paddy was right, but somehow he couldn't give in to it and he replied: "She'll not forsake it! She'll not! I know she'll not!"

But in school his faith wavered. Through the windows he could see moving sheets of rain—rain that dribbled down the panes filling his mind with thoughts of the lake creased and chilled by wind; the nest sodden and black with wetness; and the egg cold as a cave stone. He shivered from the thoughts and fidgeted with the inkwell cover, sliding it backwards and forwards mechanically. The mischievous look had gone from his eyes and the school day dragged on interminably. But at last they were out in the rain, Colm rushing home as fast as he could.

He was no time at all at his dinner of potatoes and salted fish until he was out in the valley now smoky with drifts of slanting rain. Opposite the islet he entered the water. The wind was blowing into his face, rustling noisily the rushes heavy with the dust of rain. A moss cheeper,[8] swaying on a reed like a mouse, filled the air with light cries of loneliness.

The boy reached the islet, his heart thumping with excitement, wondering did the bird forsake. He went slowly, quietly onto the strip of land that led to the nest. He rose on his toes, looking over the ledge to see if he could see her. And then every muscle tautened. She was on, her shoulders hunched up, and her bill lying on her breast as if she were asleep. Colm's heart hammered wildly in his ears. She hadn't forsaken. He was about to turn stealthily away. Something happened. The bird moved, her neck straightened, twitching nervously from side to side. The boy's head swam with lightness. He stood transfixed. The wild duck with a panicky flapping, rose heavily, and flew off towards the sea. . . . A guilty silence enveloped the boy. . . . He turned to go away, hesitated, and glanced back at the bare nest; it'd be no harm to have a look. Timidly he approached it, standing straight, and gazing over the edge. There in the nest lay two eggs. He drew in his breath with delight, splashed quickly from the island, and ran off whistling in the rain.

8. **moss cheeper:** a type of songbird.

First Response: *Did you think Colm was silly for worrying about the egg he had touched? Or did he have reason to be concerned?*

CHECKING UP (Multiple-Choice)

1. The period of time covered by this story is
   a. a little more than a week
   b. approximately twenty-four hours
   c. one afternoon and one evening

2. Colm follows the bird in order to
   a. catch and tame it
   b. rob its nest
   c. discover its nesting place
3. Paddy is Colm's
   a. cousin
   b. older brother
   c. schoolmate
4. Colm's chief fear is that
   a. the bird will desert its nest
   b. Paddy will steal the duck's egg
   c. the rain will destroy the nest
5. Colm is relieved when
   a. the bird moves on the nest
   b. he sees a second egg in the nest
   c. the wild duck flies off toward the sea

TALKING IT OVER

1. In the first part of the story, we get a sense that Colm lives in harmony with nature. Which details express his delight in the beauty and wonder of nature?
2. Colm is unusually sensitive to the natural world. Why, then, does he pursue the wild duck and lift its egg from the nest?
3. You have seen that in some stories the central conflict is internal. Although Colm comes into brief conflict with Paddy, the more important conflict in this story is the psychological conflict within Colm. Explain why he is torn by guilt.
4. How is Colm's conflict resolved at the end of the story?
5. Do you think Colm will visit the nest again? Give reasons for your answer.

SETTING
Setting and Character

When the **setting** of a story is presented effectively, it becomes easier for readers to believe in fictional characters and events.

For example, the realistic and recognizable streets of Dublin, described so vividly in "The Sniper" (page 213), help make the actions and characters of that story credible. The wholly imaginary setting of the planet Venus in "All Summer in a Day" (page 203) is presented so convincingly that we are willing to accept the existence of that alien world.

Setting may do more than create an illusion of reality. Setting may also be a means of revealing **character** to us. The environment in which a character lives may help us to understand that character's motives and behavior. In stories in which the primary conflict is internal rather than external, details of setting may reflect a character's state of mind.

In "The Wild Duck's Nest," the setting is a key to Colm's thoughts and feelings. At the opening of the story, we know how happy and carefree Colm is by his response to the setting. His race to the top of a hill where he watches a radiant sunset, his "exultant whoop," his delight in the lake and in the wild duck, all show us how sensitive Colm is to the beauty and wonder of nature. After he lifts the egg and feels that he has sinned against nature, the setting changes dramatically, signaling a change in Colm's state of mind. The "cold shiver of evening" surrounds him.

How does the setting reflect Colm's inner conflict on the following day? Find descriptive details that mirror his sadness and concern.

UNDERSTANDING THE WORDS IN THE STORY (Multiple-Choice)

1. The members of the winning soccer team walked *jauntily* onto the bus.
   a. carefully
   b. boldly
   c. cheerfully
2. Zeke was *exultant* when the Muskrats won the championship.
   a. disappointed
   b. understanding
   c. joyful

3. The students walked *languidly* into the classroom that hot Friday in June.
   a. sadly
   b. quickly
   c. lazily
4. Not convinced that the trip was a good idea, Yetta boarded the bus *reluctantly.*
   a. unwillingly
   b. slowly
   c. nervously
5. Boots the cat crept *stealthily* toward the unguarded turkey roast.
   a. steadily
   b. slowly
   c. slyly
6. His mind elsewhere, Carlo nibbled *indifferently* at the food on his plate.
   a. hungrily
   b. without interest
   c. slowly
7. Percy *meandered* through the mall, trying to kill time.
   a. moved slowly
   b. wandered aimlessly
   c. walked quickly
8. The toddler *peered* around the corner before taking cookies from the table.
   a. looked searchingly
   b. turned carefully
   c. walked on tiptoe
9. To Buchi, the new school building seemed a *maze* of hallways leading nowhere.
   a. complicated network
   b. large collection
   c. pleasing arrangement

10. Chuck knew that his muscles *tautened* whenever Rodman went to the foul line.
    a. tightened
    b. relaxed
    c. departed

(Matching Columns)

1. clambered	a. thickly covered
2. spattered	b. completely soaked
3. matted	c. made motionless
4. forsake	d. climbed with difficulty
5. vague	e. endlessly
6. vexation	f. became unsure
7. wavered	g. spotted
8. sodden	h. indefinite
9. interminably	i. desert
10. transfixed	j. annoyance

WRITING IT DOWN
A Description

Colm and Paddy are very much a part of the world in which they live. We learn from their conversation that they are familiar with different kinds of ducks and birds, and that the distinction between a gull's egg and a wild duck's egg is important to them. They also know how these creatures behave.

Think about the place where you live. What sights, sounds, and smells do you encounter every day? What birds or animals live in your backyard or in a nearby park? What kinds of streets run through your town?

Write two or three paragraphs describing your world. Add enough specific details so that someone from another kind of area, or even another country, would have a good understanding of your environment. You might find it helpful to begin by filling in a cluster diagram like the one on page 238.

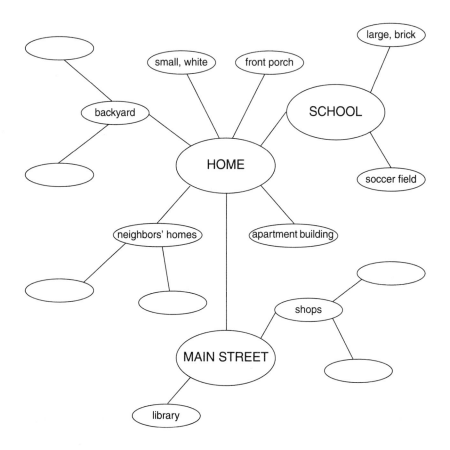

Sensory Images

Sensory images are word pictures that appeal to the senses—sight, hearing, touch, smell, and taste. Such images can help you portray a setting vividly in your writing. Notice, for example, how Michael McLaverty uses images that appeal to sight, hearing, and touch to describe Rathlin Island at sunset in the first paragraph of "The Wild Duck's Nest."

Make some notes for a short story setting of your own by filling out a chart like the one on page 239. List as many specific sensory images as you can.

TIME AND PLACE: _____

_____

SENSORY IMAGES

SIGHT: _____

_____

SOUND: _____

_____

TOUCH: _____

_____

SMELL: _____

_____

TASTE: _____

_____

ABOUT THE AUTHOR

Michael McLaverty (1904–1992) was born in County Monaghan, Ireland. He was headmaster of a secondary school in Belfast for many years. His first novel, *Call My Brother Back,* was published in 1939. "The Wild Duck's Nest" is from a collection called *The Game Cock and Other Stories.* While other Irish writers of his generation—like Liam O'Flaherty and Sean O'Faolain—became deeply involved in political struggles, McLaverty focused on the internal conflicts of his characters. The world of his native Northern Ireland—its people and its landscape—fills his novels and short stories.

LA PUERTA°

José Antonio Burciaga°

What is meant by the expression "so close yet so far?" Have you ever come close to reaching a goal only to meet with unexpected difficulty? If so, write down a few notes about your experience.

It had rained in thundering sheets every afternoon that summer. A dog-tired Sinesio returned home from his job in a mattress sweat shop. With a weary step from the *autobús*, Sinesio gathered the last of his strength and darted across the busy *avenida* into the ramshackle *colonia* where children played in the meandering pathways that would soon turn into a noisy *arroyo*[1] of rushing water. The rain drops striking the *barrio's*[2] tin, wooden and cardboard roofs would soon become a sheet of water from heaven.

Every afternoon Sinesio's muffled knock on their two-room shack was answered by Faustina, his wife. She would unlatch the door and return to iron more shirts and dresses of people who could afford the luxury. When thunder clapped, a frightened Faustina would quickly pull the electric cord, believing it would attract lightning. Then she would occupy herself with preparing dinner. Their three children would not arrive home for another hour.

On this day Sinesio laid down his tattered lunch bag, a lottery ticket and his week's wages on the oily tablecloth. Faustina threw a glance at the lottery ticket.

Sinesio's silent arrival always angered Faustina so she glared back at the lottery ticket, "Throwing money away! Buying paper dreams! We can't afford dreams, and you buy them!"

Sinesio ignored her anger. From the table, he picked up a letter, smelled it, studied the U.S. stamp, and with the emphatic opening of the envelope sat down at the table and slowly read aloud the letter from his brother Aurelio as the rain beat against the half tin, half wooden rooftop.

°**La Puerta** (lä pwĕr′tä): Spanish for "the door."
°**José Antonio Burciaga** (hō-sā′ än-tō′nyō bōōr-syä′gä).
1. *arroyo* (ə-roi′ō): a deep gully.
2. *barrio* (bä′ryō): a neighborhood or district in a Latin American country.

240

Dear Sinesio,
I write to you from this country of abundance, the first letter I write from los
Estados Unidos. After two weeks of nerves and frustration I finally have a job
at a canning factory. It took me that long only because I did not have the neces-
sary social security number. It's amazing how much money one can make, but
just as amazing how fast it goes. I had to pay for the social security number, two
weeks of rent, food, and a pair of shoes. The good pair you gave me wore out on
our journey across the border. From the border we crossed two mountains, and
the desert in between.
I will get ahead because I'm a better worker than the rest of my countrymen.
I can see that already and so does the "boss." Coming here will be hard for you,
leaving Faustina and the children. It was hard enough for me and I'm single
without a worry in life. But at least you will have me here if you come and I'm
sure I can get you a job. All you've heard about the crossing is true. Even the lies
are true. "Saludos" from your "compadres"[3] *Silvio and Ramiro. They are doing*
fine. They're already bothering me for the bet you made against the Dodgers.
Next time we get together I will relate my adventures and those of my
"compañeros" . . . things to laugh and cry about.

Aurelio signed the letter *Saludos y abrazo*. Sinesio looked off into
space and imagined himself there already. But this dreaming was interrupted by the pelting rain and Faustina's knife dicing *nopal*, cactus, on
the wooden board.

¿Qué crees?—"What do you think?" Faustina asked Sinesio.

¡No sé!—"I don't know," Sinesio responded with annoyance.

"But you do know, Sinesio. How could you not know? There's no
choice. We have turned this over and around a thousand times. That
miserable mattress factory will never pay you enough to eat with. We
can't even afford the mattresses you make!"

Sinesio's heart sank as if he was being pushed out or had already left
his home. She would join her *comadres*[4] as another undocumented
widow. Already he missed his three children, Celso, Jenaro, and Natasia
his eldest, a joy every time he saw her. "An absence in the heart is an
empty pain," he thought.

Faustina reminded Sinesio of the inevitable trip with subtle statements and proverbs that went straight to the heart of the matter.

3. **compadres** (kōm-pä′ thrĕs): close friends; companions.
4. **comadres** (kō-mä′ thrĕs): close women friends.

"Necessity knows no frontiers," she would say. The dicing of the *nopal* and onions took on the fast clip of the rain. Faustina looked up to momentarily study a trickle of water that had begun to run on the inside of a heavily patched glass on the door. It bothered her, but unable to fix it at the moment she went back to her cooking.

Sinesio accepted the answer to a question he wished he had never asked. The decision was made. There was no turning back. "I will leave for *el norte* in two weeks," he said gruffly and with authority.

Faustina's heart sank as she continued to make dinner. After the rain, Sinesio went out to help his *compadre* widen a ditch to keep the water from flooding in front of his door. The children came home, and it became Faustina's job to inform them that *Papá* would have to leave for a while. None of them said anything. Jenaro refused to eat. They had expected and accepted the news. From their friends, they knew exactly what it meant. Many of their friends' fathers had already left and many more would follow.

Throughout the following days, Sinesio continued the same drudgery at work but as his departure date approached he began to miss even that. He secured his family and home, made all the essential home repairs he had put off and asked his creditors for patience and trust. He asked his sisters, cousins and neighbors to check on his family. Another *compadre* lent him money for the trip and the coyote.[5] Sinesio did not know when he would return but told everyone "One year, no more. Save enough money, buy things to sell here and open up a *negocio*, a small business the family can help with."

The last trip home from work was no different except for the going-away gift, a bottle of *mezcal*,[6] and the promise of his job when he returned. As usual, the *autobús* was packed. And as usual, the only ones to talk were two loud young men, *sinvergüenzas*—without shame.

The two young men talked about the *Lotería Nacional* and a lottery prize that had gone unclaimed for a week. "*¡Cien millones de pesos!*—One hundred million pesos! *¡Caray!*" one of them kept repeating as he slapped the folded newspaper on his knees again and again. "Maybe the fool that bought it doesn't even know!"

---

5. **coyote:** a slang term for a smuggler.
6. *mezcal* (mĕs-kăl'): a liquor made from a type of desert cactus.

"Or can't read!" answered the other. And they laughed with open mouths.

This caught Sinesio's attention. Two weeks earlier he had bought a lottery ticket. "Could . . . ? No!" he thought. But he felt a slight flush of blood rush to his face. Maybe this was his lucky day. The one day out of the thousands that he had lived in poverty.

The two jumped off the bus, and Sinesio reached for the newspaper they had left behind. There on the front page was the winning number. At the end of the article was the deadline to claim the prize: 8 that night.

Sinesio did not have the faintest idea if his ticket matched the winning number. So he swung from the highest of hopes and dreams to resigned despair as he wondered if he had won one hundred million pesos.

Jumping off the bus, he ran home, at times slowing to a walk to catch his breath. The times he jogged, his heart pounded, the newspaper clutched in his hand, the heavy grey clouds ready to pour down.

Faustina heard his desperate knock and swung the door open.

"*¿Dónde está?*" Sinesio pleaded. "Where is the lottery ticket I bought?" He said it slowly and clearly so he wouldn't have to repeat himself.

Faustina was confused, "What lottery ticket?"

Sinesio searched the table, under the green, oily cloth, on top of the dresser and through his papers, all the while with the jabbing question, "What did you do with the *boleto de lotería?*"

Thunder clapped. Faustina quit ironing and unplugged the iron. Sinesio sounded off about no one respecting his papers and how no one could find anything in that house. *¿Dónde está el boleto de lotería?*— Where is the lottery ticket?

They both stopped to think. The rain splashed into a downpour against the door. Faustina looked at the door to see if she had fixed the hole in the glass.

¡La puerta!—"The door!" blurted Faustina, "I put it on the door to keep the rain from coming in!"

Sinesio turned to see the ticket glued on the broken window pane. It was light blue with red numbers and the letters "*Lotería Nacional.*" Sinesio brought the newspaper up to the glued lottery ticket and with his wife compared the numbers off one by one—*Seis - tres - cuatro - uno - ocho - nueve - uno - ¡SIETE-DOS!*—Sinesio yelled.

"¡No!" trembled a disbelieving and frightened Sinesio, "One hundred million pesos!" His heart pounded afraid this was all a mistake, a bad joke. They checked it again and again only to confirm the matching numbers.

Sinesio then tried to peel the ticket off. His fingernail slid off the cold, glued lottery ticket. Faustina looked at Sinesio's stubby fingernails and moved in. But Faustina's thinner fingernails also slid off the lottery ticket. Sinesio walked around the kitchen table looking, thinking, trying to remain calm.

Then he grew frustrated and angry. "What time is it?"

"A quarter to seven," Faustina said looking at the alarm clock above the dresser. They tried hot water and a razor blade with no success. Sinesio then lashed out at Faustina in anger, "You! I never answered your mockery! Your lack of faith in me! I played the lottery because I knew this day would come!" "¡*Por Dios Santo!*" and he swore and kissed his crossed thumb and forefinger. "And now? Look what you have done to me, to us, to your children!"

"We can get something at the *farmacia!* The doctor would surely have something to unglue the ticket."

"¡*Sí! ¡O sí!*" mocked Sinesio. "Sure! We have time to go there."

Time runs faster when there is a deadline. The last bus downtown was due in a few minutes. They tried to take the broken glass pane off the door but he was afraid the ticket would tear more. Sinesio's fear and anger mounted with each glance at the clock. In frustration, he pushed the door out into the downpour and swung it back into the house, cracking the molding and the inside hinges. One more swing, pulling, twisting, splintering, and Sinesio broke the door completely off.

Faustina stood back with hands over her mouth as she recited a litany to all the *santos* and virgins in heaven as the rain blew into their home and splashed her face wet.

Sinesio's face was also drenched. But Faustina could not tell if it was from the rain or tears of anger, as he put the door over his head and ran down the streaming pathway to catch the *autobús.*

First Response: *Do you think that Sinesio will succeed in claiming the lottery prize? Why or why not?*

CHECKING UP

1. When Sinesio returns from work, why is Faustina angry with him?
2. What decision does Sinesio make after reading his brother's letter?
3. How does Sinesio learn that a lottery prize has gone unclaimed?
4. What has Faustina done with the lottery ticket?
5. How does Sinesio finally manage to take the ticket downtown?

TALKING IT OVER

1. What details of the story's setting show that Sinesio and Faustina are poor even though they work very hard? How is the stormy weather an important part of the story?
2. What does the author's use of Spanish words and phrases contribute to the story?
3. Explain how Aurelio's letter prompts an internal conflict for Sinesio.
4. Why do you think Burciaga used the title "La Puerta" for this story? What is the significance of a door for Sinesio and Faustina?
5. Why do you think the story ends where it does? Why doesn't Burciaga tell us whether or not Sinesio succeeded in claiming his prize?

SETTING
Setting and Mood

Setting can be an important element in the creation of **mood,** or **atmosphere,** in short stories. The mood of a story is its overall feeling. Mood can be frightening, suspenseful, gloomy, peaceful—any aspect of their environment to which the characters react.

In "All Summer in a Day" (page 203) and "The Wild Duck's Nest" (page 230), rainy weather contributes to an atmosphere of frustration and tension. The inhospitable prairie and mountain country through which the family travels in "Too Soon a Woman" (page 221) is directly related to the story's atmosphere of desperation.

1. What mood is established by the setting of "La Puerta"?
2. How do the details about Sinesio's home and neighborhood contribute to the atmosphere of the story? How does the weather affect the mood of the story?
3. How does the stormy weather reflect the relationship between Sinesio and Faustina?

UNDERSTANDING THE WORDS IN THE STORY (Jumbles)

Use the clues to solve the jumble items. All the solutions are drawn from the glossary word bank below.

Glossary Word Bank

ramshackle	inevitable
tattered	momentarily
emphatic	drudgery
abundance	creditors
subtle	blurted

1. D B C N A N U E A   Great plenty; wealth

2. Y U R D D G E R   Hard, tiresome work

3. R U D L T B E   Spoke suddenly

4. H T M A E C P I   Pronounced; definite

5. V L E A I T N I B E   Unavoidable

WRITING IT DOWN
A Short Story

Using the notes and ideas you have accumulated in the course of this unit, write a short story of your own. As you plan your tale, you might find it helpful to fill in a chart like the Story Map below.

Pay special attention to the role of setting in your story. Begin by making a list of specific details and sensory images for the setting. Then decide how your story's setting will be related to plot, character, and atmosphere, or mood. When you have finished writing, get together with a small group of classmates and share your story.

STORY MAP

TITLE: _____

SETTING

  Time: _____

  Place: _____

  Sensory Images: _____

  Other Details: _____

MOOD: _____

_____

CHARACTERS: _____

_____

PLOT

  Exposition: _____

  Conflict: _____

  Event: _____

  Event: _____

  Event: _____

  Climax: _____

  Resolution: _____

ABOUT THE AUTHOR

José Antonio Burciaga was born in 1940 in El Paso, Texas. Storytelling was an important part of his family life as he grew up, and he was also an enthusiastic reader of biographies and newspapers.

After serving in the United States Air Force, Burciaga attended the University of Texas at El Paso. He received his bachelor's degree in fine arts in 1968 and began working as an illustrator and graphic artist. In 1974 he moved to California, where he added writing for local journals and newspapers to his repertoire.

Although known primarily as an illustrator and a journalist, Burciaga has written a great deal of fiction, poetry, and essays of social criticism. He approaches even serious subjects with satiric humor. His books include *Restless Serpents* (1976), a collection of poetry and short prose pieces; *Weedee Peepo: A Collection of Essays* (1988); *Undocumented Love* (1992), an award-winning poetry anthology; and *Drink Cultura* (1993).

Burciaga founded a publishing company, Diseños Literarios, in Menlo Park, California. He is currently teaching at Stanford University.

A DAY'S WAIT

Ernest Hemingway

What is a misunderstanding? How does a misunderstanding come about? Discuss your answers with a small group of classmates.

He came into the room to shut the windows while we were still in bed, and I saw he looked ill. He was shivering, his face was white, and he walked slowly as though it ached to move.

"What's the matter, Schatz?"[1]

"I've got a headache."

"You better go back to bed."

"No, I'm all right."

"You go to bed. I'll see you when I'm dressed."

But when I came downstairs he was dressed, sitting by the fire, looking a very sick and miserable boy of nine years. When I put my hand on his forehead I knew he had a fever.

"You go up to bed," I said, "you're sick."

"I'm all right," he said.

When the doctor came he took the boy's temperature.

"What is it?" I asked him.

"One hundred and two."

Downstairs, the doctor left three different medicines in different colored capsules with instructions for giving them. One was to bring down the fever, another a purgative, the third to overcome an acid condition. The germs of influenza can only exist in an acid condition, he explained. He seemed to know all about influenza and said there was nothing to worry about if the fever did not go above one hundred and four degrees. This was a light epidemic of flu and there was no danger if you avoided pneumonia.

Back in the room I wrote the boy's temperature down and made a note of the time to give the various capsules.

1. **Schatz** (shäts): an affectionate nickname taken from a German term.

"Do you want me to read to you?"

"All right. If you want to," said the boy. His face was very white and there were dark areas under his eyes. He lay still in the bed and seemed very detached from what was going on.

I read aloud from Howard Pyle's *Book of Pirates;* but I could see he was not following what I was reading

"How do you feel, Schatz?" I asked him.

"Just the same, so far," he said.

I sat at the foot of the bed and read to myself while I waited for it to be time to give another capsule. It would have been natural for him to go to sleep, but when I looked up he was looking at the foot of the bed, looking very strangely.

"Why don't you try to go to sleep? I'll wake you up for the medicine."

"I'd rather stay awake."

After a while he said to me, "You don't have to stay in here with me, Papa, if it bothers you."

"It doesn't bother me."

"No, I mean you don't have to stay if it's going to bother you."

I thought perhaps he was a little lightheaded and after giving him the prescribed capsules at eleven o'clock I went out for a while.

It was a bright, cold day, the ground covered with a sleet that had frozen so that it seemed as if all the bare trees, the bushes, the cut brush and all the grass and the bare ground had been varnished with ice. I took the young Irish setter for a little walk up the road and along a frozen creek, but it was difficult to stand or walk on the glassy surface, and the red dog stopped and slithered and I fell twice, hard, once dropping my gun and having it slide away over the ice.

We flushed a covey of quail under a high clay bank with overhanging brush and I killed two as they went out of sight over the top of the bank. Some of the covey lit in trees, but most of them scattered into brush piles and it was necessary to jump on the ice-coated mounds of brush several times before they would flush. Coming out while you were poised unsteadily on the icy, springy brush they made difficult shooting, and I killed two, missed five, and started back pleased to have found a covey close to the house and happy there were so many left to find on another day.

At the house they said the boy had refused to let anyone come into the room.

"You can't come in," he said. "You mustn't get what I have."

I went up to him and found him in exactly the position I had left him, white-faced, but with the tops of his cheeks flushed by the fever, staring still, as he had stared, at the foot of the bed.

I took his temperature.

"What is it?"

"Something like a hundred," I said. It was one hundred and two and four tenths.

"It was a hundred and two," he said.

"Who said so?"

"The doctor."

"Your temperature is all right," I said. "It's nothing to worry about."

"I don't worry," he said, "but I can't keep from thinking."

"Don't think," I said. "Just take it easy."

"I'm taking it easy," he said and looked straight ahead. He was evidently holding tight on to himself about something.

"Take this with water."

"Do you think it will do any good?"

"Of course it will."

I sat down and opened the *Pirate* book and commenced to read, but I could see he was not following, so I stopped.

"About what time do you think I'm going to die?" he asked.

"What?"

"About how long will it be before I die?"

"You aren't going to die. What's the matter with you?"

"Oh, yes, I am. I heard him say a hundred and two."

"People don't die with a fever of one hundred and two. That's a silly way to talk."

"I know they do. At school in France the boys told me you can't live with forty-four degrees. I've got a hundred and two."

He had been waiting to die all day, ever since nine o'clock in the morning.

"You poor Schatz," I said. "Poor old Schatz. It's like miles and kilometers. You aren't going to die. That's a different thermometer. On that thermometer thirty-seven is normal. On this kind it's ninety-eight."

"Are you sure?"

"Absolutely," I said. "It's like miles and kilometers. You know, like how many kilometers we make when we do seventy miles in the car?"

"Oh," he said.

But his gaze at the foot of the bed relaxed slowly. The hold over himself relaxed too, finally, and the next day it was very slack and he cried very easily at little things that were of no importance.

First Response: *What did you feel toward the boy in the story? compassion? admiration? Explain your answer.*

CHECKING UP

1. How does the father know that the boy is ill?
2. What is the doctor's diagnosis of the boy's illness?
3. How does the father pass the time as he sits in the boy's room?
4. What does the father do when he goes outside for a while?
5. Why doesn't the boy let anyone else into the room?

TALKING IT OVER

1. Why does the boy assume he is going to die before the day is over?
2. The story turns on a misunderstanding between the father and the boy. What does the boy mean when he tells the father ". . . you don't have to stay if it's going to bother you"?
3. How does the boy behave in the face of what he believes to be his own death? How does the father explain the boy's behavior?
4. How would you describe the relationship between the father and his son? How does each show concern for the other?
5. How does the boy's behavior change when he realizes he is not going to die?

POINT OF VIEW
First-Person Point of View

The person who tells a story is called the **narrator,** and the angle from which the story is told is called its **point of view.** A story can be told by someone who is a character in the story or by an outside observer.

"A Day's Wait" is told from the inside, through the words of one of the story's main characters. This point of view, in which the narrator speaks as "I," is known as the **first-person point of view.**

The first-person point of view has the advantage of adding immediacy to a story—we get the story directly from one of its characters. The first-person point of view also has some limitations. The reader sees the events from the vantage point of only one character. That character can reveal his or her own feelings, thoughts, and observations, but cannot get into the minds of other characters. As a result, the reader must determine what the other characters may be thinking, as well as whether the narrator's impressions are to be trusted.

1. The narrator in this story does not have all the facts. At what point in the story do you realize that his point of view is limited?
2. Imagine that the boy rather than the father is the narrator. How would the story be different?

UNDERSTANDING THE WORDS IN THE STORY (Analogy)

For instructions on completing analogies, see page 155.

1. sorrowful : joyful :: detached : _____
   a. separate   c. bored
   b. curious   d. involved

2. removed : took away :: flushed : _____
   a. drove out   c. pushed in
   b. moved away   d. grew dim

3. bounding : leaping :: slithering : _____
   a. crawling   c. hissing
   b. sliding   d. sneaking

4. kin : relatives :: covey : _____
   a. place   c. cave
   b. container   d. group

5. shaking : trembling :: poised _____
   a. falling   c. balanced
   b. motioned   d. confirmed

WRITING IT DOWN
A Letter

Imagine that you are the boy in the story and that you want to write a letter to one of your friends in France. You have decided to tell him or her about the day you thought you were going to die because your temperature was one hundred and two degrees. What details of the episode are you going to tell about? Will you describe how you felt that day?

ABOUT THE AUTHOR

Ernest Hemingway (1899–1961) was born in Oak Park, Illinois, and grew up hunting and fishing in the Michigan woods. He boxed and played football at Oak Park High School. He wrote poetry and short stories and a column for the school newspaper.

Shortly after the outbreak of the First World War, Hemingway became an ambulance driver for the Italian army. The job was short-lived, however, because Hemingway was soon seriously wounded by an artillery shell. The incident that caused the injury and the lengthy recovery that followed were to become a central force in both his life and his fiction.

Hemingway returned to Illinois where he again made a living by newspaper work. He befriended the writer Sherwood Anderson, who encouraged him to continue writing poetry and short stories. An assignment with the Toronto *Star* took Hemingway to Europe. In Paris he joined a community of Americans who had left the United States for Europe in search of personal and artistic fulfillment.

Hemingway's first novel, *The Sun Also Rises* (1926), yielded a new phrase to describe those who were disillusioned with the war and its ideals: "the lost generation." His next novel, *A Farewell to Arms* (1929), dealt with the war itself; it tells the story of a wounded ambulance driver and a nurse with whom he falls in love. These two novels, with their concentrated prose and stark dialogue, created a tone and a style that have had a strong influence on American literature.

After the success of *A Farewell to Arms,* Hemingway pursued a life of danger and excitement; he hunted in Africa, deep-sea fished in Florida waters, and followed bullfighting in Spain. Much of his work at this time consisted of nonfiction writing and war correspondence. His most popular novel, *For Whom the Bell Tolls* (1940), grew out of his experiences covering the Spanish Civil War in the 1930s.

In 1954, two years after the publication of his novel *The Old Man and the Sea,* Hemingway was awarded the Nobel Prize for Literature.

ZLATEH THE GOAT

Isaac Bashevis Singer

Do you think that animals and people can communicate with each other? Discuss your answer with a small group of classmates.

At Hanukkah[1] time the road from the village to the town is usually covered with snow, but this year the winter had been a mild one. Hanukkah had almost come, yet little snow had fallen. The sun shone most of the time. The peasants complained that because of the dry weather there would be a poor harvest of winter grain. New grass sprouted, and the peasants sent their cattle out to pasture.

For Reuven the furrier it was a bad year, and after long hesitation he decided to sell Zlateh the goat. She was old and gave little milk. Feyvel the town butcher had offered eight gulden[2] for her. Such a sum would buy Hanukkah candles, potatoes and oil for pancakes, gifts for the children, and other holiday necessaries for the house. Reuven told his oldest boy Aaron to take the goat to town.

Aaron understood what taking the goat to Feyvel meant, but he had to obey his father. Leah, his mother, wiped the tears from her eyes when she heard the news. Aaron's younger sisters, Anna and Miriam, cried loudly. Aaron put on his quilted jacket and a cap with earmuffs, bound a rope around Zlateh's neck, and took along two slices of bread with cheese to eat on the road. Aaron was supposed to deliver the goat by evening, spend the night at the butcher's, and return the next day with the money.

While the family said goodbye to the goat, and Aaron placed the rope around her neck, Zlateh stood as patiently and good-naturedly as ever. She licked Reuven's hand. She shook her small white beard. Zlateh trusted human beings. She knew that they always fed her and never did her any harm.

When Aaron brought her out on the road to town, she seemed

---

1. **Hanukkah** (ᴋʜä′nōō-kə): a Jewish holiday that falls in December and is celebrated for eight days.
2. **gulden** (gōōl′dən): coins used in several European countries.

somewhat astonished. She'd never been led in that direction before. She looked back at him questioningly, as if to say, "Where are you taking me?" But after a while she seemed to come to the conclusion that a goat shouldn't ask questions. Still, the road was different. They passed new fields, pastures, and huts with thatched roofs. Here and there a dog barked and came running after them, but Aaron chased it away with his stick.

The sun was shining when Aaron left the village. Suddenly the weather changed. A large black cloud with a bluish center appeared in the east and spread itself rapidly over the sky. A cold wind blew in with it. The crows flew low, croaking. At first it looked as if it would rain, but instead it began to hail as in summer. It was early in the day, but it became dark as dusk. After a while the hail turned to snow.

In his twelve years Aaron had seen all kinds of weather, but he had never experienced a snow like this one. It was so dense it shut out the light of the day. In a short time their path was completely covered. The wind became as cold as ice. The road to town was narrow and winding. Aaron no longer knew where he was. He could not see through the snow. The cold soon penetrated his quilted jacket.

At first Zlateh didn't seem to mind the change in weather. She too was twelve years old and knew what winter meant. But when her legs sank deeper and deeper into the snow, she began to turn her head and look at Aaron in wonderment. Her mild eyes seemed to ask, "Why are we out in such a storm?" Aaron hoped that a peasant would come along with his cart, but no one passed by.

The snow grew thicker, falling to the ground in large, whirling flakes. Beneath it Aaron's boots touched the softness of a plowed field. He realized that he was no longer on the road. He had gone astray. He could no longer figure out which was east or west, which way was the village, the town. The wind whistled, howled, whirled the snow about in eddies.[3] It looked as if white imps were playing tag on the fields. A white dust rose above the ground. Zlateh stopped. She could walk no longer. Stubbornly she anchored her cleft hooves in the earth and bleated as if pleading to be taken home. Icicles hung from her white beard, and her horns were glazed with frost.

---

3. **eddies** (ĕd′ēz): An *eddy* is a current of air or water moving circularly.

Aaron did not want to admit the danger, but he knew just the same that if they did not find shelter they would freeze to death. This was no ordinary storm. It was a mighty blizzard. The snowfall had reached his knees. His hands were numb, and he could no longer feel his toes. He choked when he breathed. His nose felt like wood, and he rubbed it with snow. Zlateh's bleating began to sound like crying. Those humans in whom she had so much confidence had dragged her into a trap. Aaron began to pray to God for himself and for the innocent animal.

Suddenly he made out the shape of a hill. He wondered what it could be. Who had piled snow into such a huge heap? He moved toward it, dragging Zlateh after him. When he came near it, he realized that it was a large haystack which the snow had blanketed.

Aaron realized immediately that they were saved. With great effort he dug his way through the snow. He was a village boy and knew what to do. When he reached the hay, he hollowed out a nest for himself and the goat. No matter how cold it may be outside, in the hay it is always warm. And hay was food for Zlateh. The moment she smelled it she became contented and began to eat. Outside the snow continued to fall. It quickly covered the passageway Aaron had dug. But a boy and an animal need to breathe, and there was hardly any air in their hideout. Aaron bored a kind of window through the hay and snow and carefully kept the passage clear.

Zlateh, having eaten her fill, sat down on her hind legs and seemed to have regained her confidence in man. Aaron ate his two slices of bread and cheese, but after the difficult journey he was still hungry. He looked at Zlateh and noticed her udders were full. He lay down next to her, placing himself so that when he milked her he could squirt the milk into his mouth. It was rich and sweet. Zlateh was not accustomed to being milked that way, but she did not resist. On the contrary, she seemed eager to reward Aaron for bringing her to a shelter whose very walls, floor, and ceiling were made of food.

Through the window Aaron could catch a glimpse of the chaos outside. The wind carried before it whole drifts of snow. It was completely dark, and he did not know whether night had already come or whether it was the darkness of the storm. Thank God that in the hay it was not cold. The dried hay, grass, and field flowers exuded the warmth of the summer sun. Zlateh ate frequently; she nibbled from above, below, from the left and right. Her body gave forth an animal warmth, and Aaron cuddled up to her. He had always loved Zlateh, but now she was like a sister. He was alone, cut off from his family, and wanted to talk. He began to talk to Zlateh. "Zlateh, what do you think about what has happened to us?" he asked.

"Maaaa," Zlateh answered.

"If we hadn't found this stack of hay, we would both be frozen stiff by now," Aaron said.

"Maaaa," was the goat's reply.

"If the snow keeps on falling like this, we may have to stay here for days," Aaron explained.

"Maaaa," Zlateh bleated.

"What does 'Maaaa' mean?" Aaron asked. "You'd better speak up clearly."

"Maaaa, Maaaa," Zlateh tried.

"Well, let it be 'Maaaa' then," Aaron said patiently. "You can't speak, but I know you understand. I need you and you need me. Isn't that right?"

"Maaaa."

Aaron became sleepy. He made a pillow out of some hay, leaned his head on it, and dozed off. Zlateh too fell asleep.

When Aaron opened his eyes, he didn't know whether it was morning or night. The snow had blocked up his window. He tried to clear it, but when he had bored through to the length of his arm, he still hadn't reached the outside. Luckily he had his stick with him and was able to break through to the open air. It was still dark outside. The snow continued to fall and the wind wailed, first with one voice and then with many. Sometimes it had the sound of devilish laughter. Zlateh too awoke, and when Aaron greeted her, she answered, "Maaaa." Yes, Zlateh's language consisted of only one word, but it meant many things. Now she was saying, "We must accept all that God gives us—heat, cold, hunger, satisfaction, light, and darkness."

Aaron had awakened hungry. He had eaten up his food, but Zlateh had plenty of milk.

For three days Aaron and Zlateh stayed in the haystack. Aaron had always loved Zlateh, but in these three days he loved her more and more. She fed him with her milk and helped him keep warm. She comforted him with her patience. He told her many stories, and she always cocked her ears and listened. When he patted her, she licked his hand and his face. Then she said, "Maaaa," and he knew it meant, I love you too.

The snow fell for three days, though after the first day it was not as thick and the wind quieted down. Sometimes Aaron felt that there could never have been a summer, that the snow had always fallen, ever since he could remember. He, Aaron, never had a father or mother or sisters. He was a snow child, born of the snow, and so was Zlateh. It was so quiet in the hay that his ears rang in the stillness. Aaron and Zlateh slept all night and a good part of the day. As for Aaron's dreams, they were all about warm weather. He dreamed of green fields, trees covered with blossoms, clear brooks, and singing birds. By the third night the snow had stopped, but Aaron did not dare to find his way home in the darkness. The sky became clear and the moon shone, casting silvery nets on the snow. Aaron dug his way out and looked at the world. It was all white, quiet, dreaming dreams of heavenly splendor. The stars were large and close. The moon swam in the sky as in a sea.

On the morning of the fourth day Aaron heard the ringing of sleigh bells. The haystack was not far from the road. The peasant who drove the sleigh pointed out the way to him—not to the town and Feyvel the butcher, but home to the village. Aaron had decided in the haystack that he would never part with Zlateh.

Aaron's family and their neighbors had searched for the boy and the goat but had found no trace of them during the storm. They feared they were lost. Aaron's mother and sisters cried for him; his father remained silent and gloomy. Suddenly one of the neighbors came running to their house with the news that Aaron and Zlateh were coming up the road.

There was great joy in the family. Aaron told them how he had found the stack of hay and how Zlateh had fed him with her milk. Aaron's sisters kissed and hugged Zlateh and gave her a special treat of chopped carrots and potato peels, which Zlateh gobbled up hungrily.

Nobody ever again thought of selling Zlateh, and now that the cold weather had finally set in, the villagers needed the services of Reuven the furrier once more. When Hanukkah came, Aaron's mother was able to fry pancakes every evening, and Zlateh got her portion too. Even though Zlateh had her own pen, she often came to the kitchen, knocking on the door with her horns to indicate that she was ready to visit, and she was always admitted. In the evening Aaron, Miriam, and Anna played dreidel.⁴ Zlateh sat near the stove watching the children and the flickering of the Hanukkah candles.

Once in a while Aaron would ask her, "Zlateh, do you remember the three days we spent together?"

And Zlateh would scratch her neck with a horn, shake her white bearded head and come out with the single sound which expressed all her thoughts, and all her love.

4. **dreidel** (drā'dəl): a game played with a four-sided top called a dreidel.

First Response: *Did you guess, as the story unfolded, that Zlateh would be saved? Explain your answer.*

CHECKING UP

1. What is Reuven's trade?
2. Why does Reuven decide to sell Zlateh?
3. What does Aaron dream about during the storm?
4. What decision does Aaron come to in the haystack?
5. How does the family celebrate Hanukkah?

TALKING IT OVER

1. In what way are Reuven and his family dependent on nature for their livelihood?
2. Aaron and the goat almost perish in the snowstorm. How does the storm ironically turn out to be a godsend for the family?
3. At one point in the story, Singer interprets Zlateh's thoughts: "We must accept all that God gives us." In what way does the story show that all the characters are in God's hands?
4. How are the bonds of the family strengthened by their hardships?

POINT OF VIEW
Third-Person Omniscient

The standpoint from which a writer tells a story is called **point of view**. In the **first-person point of view**, as you have seen, the narrative is told by a character in the story. This point of view is limited to what that one character sees, thinks, and feels.

In the **third-person point of view**, the narrator is an outside observer who does not play a role in the story. The narrator speaks from the vantage point of "he" or "she." The third-person narrator may be an **omniscient** (ŏm-nĭsh'ənt), or all-knowing, observer, who knows what *all* the characters can see, hear, think, and feel, and who comments on the action.

"Zlateh the Goat" is told from the omniscient point of view. We are allowed to know what all the characters, including Zlateh, think and feel:

> Aaron did not want to admit the danger, but he knew just the same that if they did not find shelter they would freeze to death.

> Zlateh trusted human beings. She knew that they always fed her and never did her any harm.

> Nobody ever again thought of selling Zlateh . . .

The author also comments on and interprets the events:

> Yes, Zlateh's language consisted of only one word, but it meant many things. Now she was saying, "We must accept all that God gives us—heat, cold, hunger, satisfaction, light, and darkness."

Find three other passages in the story that demonstrate Singer's use of the omniscient point of view.

UNDERSTANDING THE WORDS IN THE STORY
(Matching Columns)

1. necessaries	a. devilish spirits
2. dense	b. gave off
3. penetrated	c. coated
4. wonderment	d. thick
5. astray	e. cried
6. imps	f. surprise
7. glazed	g. disorder
8. chaos	h. essential items
9. exuded	i. out of the right way
10. wailed	j. got through

WRITING IT DOWN
Other Points of View

In the first-person point of view, one of the characters in a story tells everything in his or her own words, using the first-person pronouns *I, me, my, we,* and *our.* In the third-person point of view, an outside observer tells the story. This point of view uses pronouns such as *he, she, they, them,* and *their.*

Experiment with point of view by retelling passages from "Zlateh the Goat" from the point of view of some of the characters in the story. You might find it helpful to fill in a chart such as the one below.

REUVEN	AARON	ZLATEH
I didn't want to send Zlateh to Feyvel, but I was having a bad season and we needed money.	I felt sad taking Zlateh to Feyvel. Mom and my little sisters cried a lot.	I was very happy because Aaron was taking a walk with me.

An Informative Paper

Hanukkah, often called the Festival of Lights, is a holiday that celebrates the victory of Judah the Maccabee over the Syrians in 165 B.C. Consult some reference sources about Hanukkah or another holiday of your choice, and write a short, informative paper about it. Explain the historical background of the holiday and describe its traditional celebration, including the use of songs, candles, special foods, and decorations.

ABOUT THE AUTHOR

Isaac Bashevis Singer (1904–1991) was born in Radzymin, Poland, and educated in Warsaw. For a while he lived in Bilgoray, a Jewish village steeped in tradition. He returned to Warsaw, where he worked as a proofreader and editor for several literary magazines. He began writing stories in Hebrew, but then turned to Yiddish. For the rest of his life, Yiddish was the language of his writings.

In 1935 Singer left Poland for New York City, where he continued to publish articles, reviews, and works of fiction. He is best known for his stories of Jewish family life in Eastern Europe. Some of his best-known works are *The Family Moskat* (1950), *Gimpel the Fool* (1957), and the novel *Shosha* (1978). His story "Yentl the Yeshiva Boy" (1983) was made into a full-length motion picture.

In 1978 Singer was awarded the Nobel Prize for Literature, and in 1981 his *Collected Stories* won a Pulitzer Prize.

WHAT HAPPENED DURING THE ICE STORM

Jim Heynen

Sometimes one person in a group chooses a course of action, whether wise or foolish, that the rest follow unthinkingly. Have you ever witnessed or been involved in such a situation? If so, describe the episode to a small group of classmates.

One winter there was a freezing rain. How beautiful! people said when things outside started to shine with ice. But the freezing rain kept coming. Tree branches glistened like glass. Then broke like glass. Ice thickened on the windows until everything outside blurred. Farmers moved their livestock into the barns, and most animals were safe. But not the pheasants. Their eyes froze shut.

Some farmers went ice skating down the gravel roads with clubs to harvest the pheasants that sat helplessly in the roadside ditches. The boys went out into the freezing rain to find pheasants too. They saw dark spots along a fence. Pheasants, all right. Five or six of them. The boys slid their feet along slowly, trying not to break the ice that covered the snow. They slid up close to the pheasants. The pheasants pulled their heads down between their wings. They couldn't tell how easy it was to see them huddled there.

The boys stood still in the icy rain. Their breath came out in slow puffs of steam. The pheasants' breath came out in quick little white puffs. Some of them lifted their heads and turned them from side to side, but they were blindfolded with ice and didn't flush.

The boys had not brought clubs, or sacks, or anything but themselves. They stood over the pheasants, turning their own heads, looking at each other, each expecting the other to do something. To pounce on a pheasant, or to yell Bang! Things around them were shining and dripping with icy rain. The barbed wire fence. The fence posts. The broken stems of grass. Even the grass seeds. The grass seeds looked like little yolks inside gelatin whites. And the pheasants looked like unborn birds glazed in egg white. Ice was hardening on the boys' caps and coats. Soon they would be covered with ice too.

Then one of the boys said, Shh. He was taking off his coat, the thin layer of ice splintering in flakes as he pulled his arms from the sleeves. But the inside of the coat was dry and warm. He covered two of the crouching pheasants with his coat, rounding the back of it over them like a shell. The other boys did the same. They covered all the helpless pheasants. The small gray hens and the larger brown cocks. Now the boys felt the rain soaking through their shirts and freezing. They ran across the slippery fields, unsure of their footing, the ice clinging to their skin as they made their way toward the blurry lights of the house.

First Response: *How did you feel at the end of the story, when the boys covered the pheasants?*

CHECKING UP

1. What did the farmers do with their livestock during the ice storm?
2. Why were the pheasants helpless during the storm?
3. Where did the boys find the pheasants?
4. How did the boys save the pheasants?

TALKING IT OVER

1. The opening paragraph describes the effects of the ice storm. How did people react to the freezing rain at first? How does the story's atmosphere, or mood, change in the opening paragraph?
2. **Imagery** is descriptive language that appeals to the senses. To what is the freezing rain compared in the story's opening? How does the imagery in the third and fourth paragraphs contrast the boys with the pheasants? How does this imagery make you feel about the birds?

3. How does the author build suspense in the second paragraph?
4. What is going through the boys' minds as they look at each other, "each expecting the other to do something"?
5. What *did* happen during the ice storm? Why do you think the author felt that the boys' actions were worth reporting?

POINT OF VIEW
Objective Point of View

Sometimes a writer tells a story from the point of view of an observer who witnesses the action but offers no commentary or interpretation of the events. This observer tells us what the characters say and do but does not reveal their thoughts and feelings. We must draw our own conclusions about the characters from their dialogue and actions. This point of view is called the **objective** (or **dramatic) point of view** because the narrator maintains distance from the story in much the same way as a playwright does, letting the dialogue and action speak for themselves.

Heynen uses the objective point of view in "What Happened During the Ice Storm." His observer records external details with the accuracy of a camera. We see what the farmers and the boys are doing, but we do not enter their thoughts. We do not know what the author thinks of this incident. By remaining detached, Heynen allows us to experience the situation as a whole.

1. What do you think is gained by the objective point of view in this story? Do you think that the action requires direct commentary and interpretation, or are such conclusions better left to the individual reader?

2. The story has an unusual title. Whereas most story titles capture some key element of the story, the title "What Happened During the Ice Storm" is vague. Also, the characters are not described or named. Why are names not important in this story? How is the author's treatment of the title and the characters consistent with his use of the objective point of view?

WRITING IT DOWN
A Newspaper Article

In an objective account, the reader learns only the facts of an episode or an event; the writer's opinions do not show through. Certain types of writing—news stories, for example—require an objective point of view.

Get together with a group of classmates and think of an episode that you all have experienced. Imagine that you are newspaper reporters sent to "cover the story." Have each member of the group write an article on the event, trying to be as objective as possible. When you have finished writing, read one another's articles. How are the accounts similar? How are they different? Are they completely objective, or do they somehow reflect the opinions and interpretations of the writers?

SPEAKING AND LISTENING
Discussing Objectivity

Get together with a small group and discuss whether or not a writer or artist can ever be totally objective. Doesn't a journalist or photographer, for example, unavoidably give a certain slant to a story by choosing to include certain details and omit others? Doesn't the writer's choice of words have some effect on the reader's emotions? Appoint a group recorder and have the recorder take notes on your discussion.

ABOUT THE AUTHOR

Jim Heynen, who was born in 1940, is the author of several collections of poems and short stories, many of which are about rural life. "What Happened During the Ice Storm" is taken from a recent short-story collection, *The One-Room Schoolhouse* (1993). Heynen teaches creative writing and contemporary short fiction at St. Olaf College in Northfield, Minnesota.

The author has made the following comment on the story:

> Like most of my short short stories that include a group of farm boys, "What Happened During the Ice Storm" has a grain of truth to it. There really were some gorgeous but sometimes scary ice storms in the farm country where I grew up. The freezing rain made everything glisten beautifully, but for some creatures the beauty had a sharp and often fatal edge to it. As a kid, I thought only of the slippery fun you could get from a world covered with ice—until that day I heard some neighbors had gone out on ice skates with clubs to kill pheasants that were blinded by the ice. I was no goody-goody as a young farm kid: I had a BB gun and killed more birds with it than I'd like to admit. . . . But the idea of killing pheasants that couldn't even see you coming! That struck me as one of the cruelest, most unfair things a human being could do to an animal. At least the birds I shot with my BB gun could see me coming. I was on the helpless animals' side when I heard about those people going out to club pheasants that had their eyes frozen shut. I guess as a kid I identified with their helplessness against unfair odds. The story came out of the memory of that feeling.

THE PIECE OF YARN

Guy de Maupassant

Have you ever read about—or known of—someone who was accused of something he or she did not do? If so, describe the episode in a sentence or two.

On all the roads around Goderville, farmers and their wives were streaming into town, for this was market day. The men strode calmly along, their bodies hunching forward with each movement of their long, crooked legs, misshapen from hard labors—from leaning on the plow, which simultaneously elevated the left shoulder and threw the back out of line; from swinging the scythe, in which the need for a solid stance bowed the legs at the knees; from all the slow and laborious tasks of work in the field. Their blue smocks, starched until they glistened like varnish, embroidered at neck and wrist with a small design in white thread, puffed out around their bony chests like balloons about to take flight with a head, two arms, and two feet attached.

The men tugged after them, at the end of a rope, a cow or a calf. And their wives, behind the animal, tried to hasten it on by flicking its rump with a small branch still bearing leaves. In the crook of their arms they carried large covered baskets from which heads of chickens and ducks protruded here and there. They walked with shorter and more lively steps than their husbands; their figures lean, erect, and wrapped in a tightfitting shawl pinned together over their flat chests; their hair swathed in a piece of white linen and topped off by a tight brimless cap.

Now and then a farm wagon would overtake them, drawn at a brisk trot by a small sturdy horse, grotesquely jouncing two men side by side, and a woman in the back clinging to the frame to cushion the rough jolts.

What a milling around, what a jostling mob of people and animals there was on Goderville square! Above the surface of the assemblage protruded the horns of cattle, the high-crowned, long-furred hats of wealthy farmers, and the headdresses of their ladies. The bawling, shrill, piercing voices raised a continuous din, above which echoed an

270

occasional hearty laugh from the robust lungs of a merrymaking farmhand or the long lowing of a cow tied to a house wall.

Everything smelled of the stable, milk and manure, hay and sweat, and gave off the pungent, sour odor of man and beast so characteristic of those who work in the fields.

Maître Hauchecorne, of Bréauté,[1] had just reached Goderville and was making his way toward the square when he glimpsed a piece of yarn on the ground. Maître Hauchecorne, thrifty like the true Norman he was, thought it worthwhile to pick up anything that could be useful; and he stooped down painfully, for he suffered from rheumatism. He plucked up the thin piece of yarn and was just starting to wind it up carefully when he caught sight of Maître Malandain,[2] the harness maker, eyeing him from his doorstep. They had once disagreed over the price of a harness, and since both had a tendency to hold grudges, they had remained on bad terms with each other. Maître Hauchecorne felt a bit humiliated at having been seen by his enemy scrabbling in the dirt for a bit of yarn. He quickly thrust his find under his smock, then into his trousers pocket; afterwards he pretended to search the ground for something he had lost, and at last he went off toward the marketplace with his head bent forward and his body doubled over by his aches and pains.

He lost himself at once in the shrill and slow-moving crowd, keyed up by long-drawn-out bargaining. The farmers would run their hands over the cows, go away, come back, undecided, always in fear of being taken in, never daring to commit themselves, slyly watching the seller's eye, endlessly hoping to discover the deception in the man and the defect in the beast.

The women, after placing their baskets at their feet, had drawn out their poultry, which sprawled on the ground, their feet tied together, with fear-glazed eyes and scarlet combs.

Standing rigidly, their faces giving away nothing, the women would listen to offers and hold to their prices; or else, on impulse deciding to accept an offer, would shout after a customer who was slowly moving off: "All right, Maît' Anthime.[3] It's yours."

1. **Maître Hauchecorne, of Bréauté** (mā′trə ōsh′kôrn of brā′ō-tā′).
2. **Malandain** (mȧl′ȧN-dāN′).
3. **Maît' Anthime** (māt ȧN-tēm′).

Then, little by little, the square emptied, and as the bells rang the noonday angelus,[4] those who lived too far away scattered to the inns.

At Jourdain's the large hall was filled with diners just as the great courtyard was filled with vehicles of all descriptions: two-wheeled carts, buggies, farm wagons, carriages, nameless carryalls, yellow with mud, battered, patched together, with shafts raised heavenward like two arms or with front down and rear pointing upward.

Next to the seated diners the immense fireplace, flaming brightly, cast a lively warmth on the backs of the right-hand row. Three spits were turning, loaded with chickens, pigeons, and legs of mutton, and a delectable aroma of roasting meat and of juices trickling over the heat-browned skin wafted from the hearth, making hearts gay and mouths drool.

All the carriage aristocracy was eating here at the table of Maît' Jourdain, innkeeper and horse dealer, a sly man who had a knack for making money.

The dishes were passed and emptied, along with jugs of yellow cider. Each man told of his dealings, what he had bought and sold. They asked one another about how they thought the crops would do. The weather was fine for hay, but a bit damp for grain.

All of a sudden the rolling beat of a drum echoed in the courtyard before the inn. At once all the diners, except a few indifferent ones, leaped to their feet, and with mouths still full and napkins in hand, rushed to the door and windows.

When the drum roll ended, the town crier announced in a jerky voice, breaking his sentences in the wrong places:

"It is made known to the inhabitants of Goderville, and in general to all—the persons attending the market fair, that there was lost this morning, on the Beuzeville[5] road, between—nine and ten o'clock, a black leather pocketbook containing five hundred francs[6] and some business documents. It is requested that the finder return it—to the town hall, at once, or to Maître Fortuné Houlbrèque[7] of Manneville. There will be a reward of twenty francs."

---

4. **angelus** (ăn′jə-ləs): a prayer said at morning, noon, and evening.
5. **Beuzeville** (bœz′vēl′).
6. **five hundred francs:** about one hundred dollars, a considerable sum at that time.
7. **Fortuné Houlbrèque** (fôr-tü-nā′ ōol′brĕk).

The man then went off. Once more in the distance the beat of the drum rolled out hollowly, followed by the receding voice of the crier.

Now everyone began to discuss the announcement, weighing the chance Maître Houlbrèque had of getting his pocketbook back.

And the meal came to an end.

They were finishing coffee when the police sergeant appeared in the doorway.

He asked: "Is Maître Hauchecorne, of Bréauté, here?"

Maître Hauchecorne, sitting at the far end of the table, spoke up: "That's me!"

And the sergeant continued: "Maître Hauchecorne, please be good enough to come with me to the town hall. The mayor wants to talk with you."

The farmer, surprised and uneasy, gulped down his after-dinner glass of brandy, got up, and more stooped over than earlier in the morning, because his first steps after each meal were especially painful, started on his way, saying over and over:

"That's me! That's me!"

And he followed the sergeant out.

The mayor was waiting for him, presiding in an armchair. He was the local notary,[8] a large man, grave in manner and given to pompous phrases.

"Maître Hauchecorne," he said, "you were seen this morning on the Beuzeville road picking up the pocketbook lost by Maître Houlbrèque, of Manneville."

The old farmer, struck speechless, in a panic over being suspected and not understanding why, stared at the mayor:

"Me? Me? Me pick up that pocketbook?"

"Yes, you are indeed the one."

"I swear! I don't know anything at all about it."

"You were seen."

"Seen? Me? Who says he saw me?"

"Monsieur[9] Malandain, the harness maker."

Then the old man remembered, understood, and flushing with anger, said: "Hah! He saw me, that old good-for-nothing! He saw me

---

8. **notary:** a person authorized to certify documents.
9. **Monsieur** (mə-syœ′): French title equivalent to "Mr."

pick up this bit of yarn. Look, Mr. Mayor." And, fumbling in the depths of his pocket, he pulled out the little piece of yarn.

But the mayor, incredulous, shook his head: "You would have me to believe, Maître Hauchecorne, that Monsieur Malandain, who is a trustworthy man, mistook that piece of yarn for a pocketbook?"

The farmer, enraged, raised his hand, spit to one side to reinforce his word, and said again: "But it's God's honest truth, the sacred truth, Mister Mayor. There! On my soul and salvation, I swear."

The mayor resumed his accusation: "After having picked up the article, you kept on searching in the mud for some time to see if some coin might have slipped out."

The old man was choking with indignation and fear.

"How can anyone say such things! . . . How can anyone say such lies to ruin a man's good name! How can anyone . . ."

No matter how much he protested, no one believed him.

He was confronted by Monsieur Malandain, who repeated his statement under oath. They hurled insults at each other for a full hour. Maître Hauchecorne was searched at his own request. They found nothing on him.

Finally the mayor, completely baffled, sent him away with the warning that he was going to inform the public prosecutor and ask what should be done.

The news had spread. On leaving the town hall, the old man was surrounded and questioned with serious or good-humored curiosity, but without any hint of blame. He began to tell the story of the piece of yarn. They didn't believe him. They laughed.

He went here and there, stopped by everyone, buttonholing his acquaintances, beginning over and over again his story and his protestations, turning his pockets inside out to prove that he had nothing in them.

People said to him: "You sly old rascal, you!"

He got more and more annoyed, upset, feverish in his distress because no one believed him, not knowing what to do, and always telling his story.

Night came. It was time to go home. He set off with his three neighbors, showed them the place where he had picked up the piece of yarn, and all the way talked about his experience.

That evening he made the rounds of the village of Bréauté, telling his tale to everyone. He met no one who believed him.

He was sick about it all night.

The next day, about one in the afternoon, Marius Paumelle,[10] a farmhand working for Maître Breton, a landowner of Ymauville[11] returned the pocketbook and its contents to Maître Houlbrèque, of Manneville.

This man claimed he had actually found the article on the highway, but being unable to read, he had taken it home and given it to his employer.

The news spread through the neighborhood. Maître Hauchecorne was informed. He began immediately to make the rounds, telling his story all over again, including the ending. He was exultant.

"What made me mad" he said, "wasn't so much the accusation, you know; it was all that lying. Nothing burns you up as much as being hauled into court on the word of a liar."

All day he kept talking about his experience, retelling it on the street to passersby, in the tavern to people having a drink, outside the church on the following Sunday. He would stop complete strangers to tell them. He felt calm about it now, but something still bothered him that he could not quite figure out. People listening to him seemed to be amused. They didn't appear to be convinced. He sensed that they were making remarks behind his back.

On Tuesday of the following week he returned to the marketplace in Goderville, driven by his need to state his case.

Malandain, standing in his doorway, began to laugh when he saw him going by. Why?

He accosted a farmer from Criquetot,[12] who didn't let him finish but punched him in the pit of the stomach and shouted in his face: "Knock it off, you old rascal!" Then he turned on his heel and walked away.

Maître Hauchecorne was struck speechless and grew more and more upset. Why would anyone call him an "old rascal"?

When he had taken his usual place at Jourdain's table, he launched into another explanation of the incident.

10. **Marius Paumelle** (má-rē-ŭs′ pō-mĕl′).
11. **Breton . . . Ymauville** (brĕ-tôɴ′ ē′môv-vēl′).
12. **Criquetot** (krĭk′tō′).

A horse dealer of Montivilliers[13] shouted at him: "Oh, come off it! I'm wise to that old trick. We know all about your yarn!"

Hauchecorne stammered: "But they found the pocketbook!"

"Sure old man! Somebody found it, and somebody took it back. Seeing is believing. A real pretty tangle to unsnarl!"

The farmer was stunned. At last he understood. People were accusing him of having gotten an accomplice to return the pocketbook.

He tried to deny it. The whole table burst into laughter.

Unable to finish his dinner, he left, the butt of jokes and mockery.

He went home, feeling humiliated and indignant, strangled with anger and mental confusion, especially crushed because, as a shrewd Norman, he knew himself capable of doing what he was accused of, and even boasting about it as a good trick. In his confusion, he could not see how he could prove his innocence, since he was well known for driving a sharp bargain. He was heartsick over the injustice of being suspected.

He set about telling his experience all over again, each day embroidering his recital, with each retelling adding new reasons, more vigorous protestations, more solemn vows that he dreamed up and repeated during his hours alone, his whole mind occupied with the yarn. He was believed less and less as his defense became more and more intricate and his explanations more and more involved.

"Ha! With such an explanation, he must be lying!" they said behind his back. He sensed this, ate his heart out, and exhausted his strength in useless efforts. He visibly began to weaken.

Jokers now encouraged him, for their amusement, to tell "The yarn" as one encourages a soldier back from the wars to tell about his battles. His mind, hurt to the depths, began to weaken.

Toward the end of December he took to his bed.

He died during the early days of January, and, in his dying delirium, kept protesting his innocence, repeating:

"Just a bit of yarn . . . a little bit of yarn . . . see, Mr. Mayor, there it is!"

13. **Montivilliers** (môn′tə-vēl-yā′).

First Response: *What did you feel toward Maître Hauchecorne? amusement? sympathy? Explain your answer.*

CHECKING UP

1. Where does this story take place?
2. Why does Maître Hauchecorne pick up the piece of yarn?
3. Who accuses Hauchecorne of stealing the pocketbook?
4. Who makes the announcement about the missing pocketbook?
5. What happens to Hauchecorne in the end?

TALKING IT OVER

1. Why does Hauchecorne try to conceal the piece of yarn he picks up? How is this action important later in the story?
2. What aspects of the villagers' character do the opening paragraphs of the story reveal? How do these details prepare us for their behavior later in the story?
3. Guy de Maupassant was famous for his accurate observation of life. How does the description of the lunchtime scene at Jourdain's inn illustrate the author's careful attention to detail?
4. Despite his efforts, Hauchecorne cannot convince the villagers of his innocence. Why does he fail to clear his name?
5. **Situational irony** occurs when events turn out to be quite different from what we expect. What are some of the ironies that occur in this story? What do these ironies reveal about human nature?

POINT OF VIEW
Third-Person Limited Point of View

As you saw in Isaac Bashevis Singer's "Zlateh the Goat" (page 256), a story may be told in the third person by a narrator who is all-knowing, or **omniscient**. This kind of observer can enter into the minds and feelings of all the characters and can comment on or interpret events.

Sometimes an author tells a story in the third person from the point of view of only one character. Instead of learning what all the characters see, feel, and think, we see the story through the eyes of the one character. The **third-person limited point of view** brings us close to a character: we are allowed to feel that we are inside that character's mind.

In "The Piece of Yarn," Maupassant's use of the third-person limited point of view enables us to focus on Maître Hauchecorne's thoughts and feelings. Find several key passages in the story that offer insight into the motives for his actions and that explain his reactions to events.

UNDERSTANDING THE WORDS IN THE STORY
(Matching Columns)

1. stance	a. wrapped
2. laborious	b. huge
3. hasten	c. perplexed; confused
4. swathed	d. sharp; penetrating
5. immense	e. self-important
6. delectable	f. fading away
7. pungent	g. way of standing
8. baffled	h. involving hard work
9. receding	i. to cause to hurry
10. pompous	j. delicious

WRITING IT DOWN
An Advice Column

Imagine that you are an advice columnist from Goderville and that Maître Hauchecorne of Bréauté has written to you. He has described the trouble he has had in trying to convince the villagers that he is innocent; he says that the whole situation is making him crazy. He asks your thoughts on how he could best handle the situation.

    What advice can you offer Maître Hauchecorne? How could he go about putting this embarrassing episode behind him?

A Literary Analysis

In a **literary analysis,** you examine a literary work's separate elements, present a main idea about the work, and provide support for that idea with quotations and other details.

In a brief essay, develop and support the following statement about Maupassant's attitude toward his characters in "The Piece of Yarn":

> Close observation and irony are two of Guy de Maupassant's most important techniques for developing character in "The Piece of Yarn."

As you work on your essay, you may wish to follow an outline like the one below.

I. INTRODUCTION: State main idea

II. BODY: Support main idea with quotations and details
 A. Author's use of close observation
 Quotations and details: _____
 B. Author's use of irony
 Quotations and details: _____

III. CONCLUSION: Restate main idea and summarize major points

ABOUT THE AUTHOR

Guy de Maupassant (1850–1893) was born and raised in Normandy, a province in the northwest corner of France. He served in the French army during the Franco-Prussian war, and following the war he worked as a government clerk. With the success of his first story, *Boule de suif* ("Ball of Fat"), Maupassant was able to leave his government post to devote himself to writing. Although he produced novels, travel sketches, and poems, he is best known for his short stories. These tales reflect Maupassant's keen observation of human life, and many, like "The Piece of Yarn," have an ironic ending.

THE LADY, OR THE TIGER?

Frank R. Stockton

What kinds of entertainments bring large groups of people to stadiums, ballparks, and amphitheaters? What kinds of public entertainment were popular in ancient Rome? Get together with a small group of classmates to discuss how people behave at such events.

In the very olden time there lived a semi-barbaric king, whose ideas, though somewhat polished and sharpened by the progressiveness of distant Latin neighbors, were still large, florid, and untrammeled,[1] as became the half of him which was barbaric. He was a man of exuberant fancy, and, withal,[2] of an authority so irresistible that, at his will, he turned his varied fancies into facts. He was greatly given to self-communing; and when he and himself agreed upon anything, the thing was done. When every member of his domestic and political systems moved smoothly in its appointed course, his nature was bland and genial; but whenever there was a little hitch, and some of his orbs got out of their orbits, he was blander and more genial still, for nothing pleased him so much as to make the crooked straight, and crush down uneven places.

Among the borrowed notions by which his barbarism had become semified[3] was that of the public arena, in which, by exhibitions of manly and beastly valor, the minds of his subjects were refined and cultured.

But even here the exuberant and barbaric fancy asserted itself. The arena of the king was built not to give the people an opportunity of hearing the rhapsodies of dying gladiators, nor to enable them to view the inevitable conclusion of a conflict between religious opinions and hungry jaws, but for purposes far better adapted to widen and develop the mental energies of the people. This vast amphitheatre, with its encircling galleries, its mysterious vaults, and its unseen passages, was an agent of poetic justice, in which crime was punished, or virtue rewarded, by the decrees of an impartial and incorruptible chance.

1. **untrammeled** (ŭn-trăm′əld): not hindered or restrained.
2. **withal** (wĭth-ôl′): besides.
3. **semified:** reduced by half or made partial.

When a subject was accused of a crime of sufficient importance to interest the king, public notice was given that on an appointed day the fate of the accused person would be decided in the king's arena—a structure which well deserved its name; for, although its form and plan were borrowed from afar, its purpose emanated solely from the brain of this man, who, every barleycorn a king, knew no tradition to which he owed more allegiance than pleased his fancy, and who ingrafted on every adopted form of human thought and action the rich growth of his barbaric idealism.

When all the people had assembled in the galleries, and the king, surrounded by his court, sat high up on his throne of royal state on one side of the arena, he gave a signal, a door beneath him opened, and the accused subject stepped out into the amphitheatre. Directly opposite him, on the other side of the enclosed space, were two doors, exactly alike and side by side. It was the duty and the privilege of the person on trial to walk directly to these doors and open one of them. He could open either door he pleased: he was subject to no guidance or influence but that of the aforementioned impartial and incorruptible chance. If he opened the one, there came out of it a hungry tiger, the fiercest and most cruel that could be procured, which immediately sprang upon him and tore him to pieces, as a punishment for his guilt. The moment that the case of the criminal was thus decided, doleful iron bells were clanged, great wails went up from the hired mourners posted on the outer rim of the arena, and the vast audience, with bowed heads and downcast hearts, wended slowly their homeward way, mourning greatly that one so young and fair, or so old and respected, should have merited so dire a fate.

But if the accused person opened the other door, there came forth from it a lady, the most suitable to his years and station that his Majesty could select among his fair subjects; and to this lady he was immediately married, as a reward of his innocence. It mattered not that he might already possess a wife and family, or that his affections might be engaged upon an object of his own selection: the king allowed no such subordinate arrangements to interfere with his great scheme of retribution and reward. The exercises, as in the other instance, took place immediately, and in the arena. Another door opened beneath the king, and a priest, followed by a band of choristers, and dancing maidens blowing joyous airs on golden horns and treading an epithalamic measure,[4] advanced to where the pair stood side by side; and the wedding was promptly and cheerily solemnized. Then the gay brass bells rang forth their merry peals, the people shouted glad hurrahs, and the innocent man, preceded by children strewing flowers on his path, led his bride to his home.

This was the king's semi-barbaric method of administering justice. Its perfect fairness is obvious. The criminal could not know out of which door would come the lady: he opened either he pleased, without having the slightest idea whether, in the next instant, he was to be devoured or married. On some occasions the tiger came out of one door, and on some out of the other. The decisions of this tribunal were not only fair, they were positively determinate: the accused person was instantly punished if he found himself guilty; and if innocent, he was rewarded on the spot, whether he liked it or not. There was no escape from the judgments of the king's arena.

The institution was a very popular one. When the people gathered together on one of the great trial-days, they never knew whether they were to witness a bloody slaughter or a hilarious wedding. This element of uncertainty lent an interest to the occasion which it could not otherwise have attained. Thus the masses were entertained and pleased, and the thinking part of the community could bring no charge of unfairness against this plan; for did not the accused person have the whole matter in his own hands?

This semi-barbaric king had a daughter as blooming as his most florid fancies, and with a soul as fervent and imperious as his own. As is usual in such cases, she was the apple of his eye, and was loved by him above all humanity. Among his courtiers was a young man of that fineness of blood and lowness of station common to the conventional heroes of romance who love royal maidens. This royal maiden was well satisfied with her lover, for he was handsome and brave to a degree unsurpassed in all this kingdom; and she loved him with an ardor that had enough of barbarism in it to make it exceedingly warm and strong. This love affair moved on happily for many months, until one day the king happened to discover its existence. He did not hesitate nor waver

4. **treading an epithalamic** (ĕp′ə-thə-lā′mĭk) **measure:** performing a wedding dance.

in regard to his duty in the premises. The youth was immediately cast into prison, and a day was appointed for his trial in the king's arena. This, of course, was an especially important occasion; and his Majesty, as well as all the people, was greatly interested in the workings and development of this trial. Never before had such a case occurred; never before had a subject dared to love the daughter of a king. In after years such things became commonplace enough; but then they were, in no slight degree, novel and startling.

The tiger-cages of the kingdom were searched for the most savage and relentless beasts, from which the fiercest monster might be selected for the arena: and the ranks of maiden youth and beauty throughout the land were carefully surveyed by competent judges, in order that the young man might have a fitting bride in case fate did not determine for him a different destiny. Of course everybody knew that the deed with which the accused was charged had been done. He had loved the princess, and neither he, she, nor any one else thought of denying the fact; but the king would not think of allowing any fact of this kind to interfere with the workings of the tribunal, in which he took such a great delight and satisfaction. No matter how the affair turned out, the youth would be disposed of; and the king would take an aesthetic pleasure in watching the course of events, which would determine whether or not the young man had done wrong in allowing himself to love the princess.

The appointed day arrived. From far and near the people gathered, and thronged the great galleries of the arena; and crowds, unable to gain admittance, massed themselves against its outside walls. The king and his court were in their places, opposite the twin doors—those fateful portals, so terrible in their similarity.

All was ready. The signal was given. A door beneath the royal party opened, and the lover of the princess walked into the arena. Tall, beautiful, fair, his appearance was greeted with a low hum of admiration and anxiety. Half the audience had not known so grand a youth had lived among them. No wonder the princess loved him! What a terrible thing for him to be there!

As the youth advanced into the arena, he turned, as the custom was, to bow to the king: but he did not think at all of that royal personage; his eyes were fixed upon the princess, who sat to the right of her father.

Had it not been for the moiety[5] of barbarism in her nature it is probable that lady would not have been there; but her intense and fervid soul would not allow her to be absent on an occasion in which she was so terribly interested. From the moment that the decree had gone forth that her lover should decide his fate in the king's arena, she had thought of nothing, night or day, but this great event and the various subjects connected with it. Possessed of more power, influence, and force of character than any one who had ever before been interested in such a case, she had done what no other person had done—she had possessed herself of the secret of the doors. She knew in which of the two rooms that lay behind those doors stood the cage of the tiger, with its open front, and in which waited the lady. Through these thick doors, heavily curtained with skins on the inside, it was impossible that any noise or suggestion should come from within to the person who should approach to raise the latch of one of them; but gold, and the power of a woman's will, had brought the secret to the princess.

And not only did she know in which room stood the lady ready to emerge, all blushing and radiant, should her door be opened, but she knew who the lady was. It was one of the fairest and loveliest of the damsels of the court who had been selected as the reward of the accused youth, should he be proved innocent of the crime of aspiring to one so far above him; and the princess hated her. Often had she seen, or imagined that she had seen, this fair creature throwing glances of admiration upon the person of her lover, and sometimes she thought these glances were perceived and even returned. Now and then she had seen them talking together; it was but for a moment or two, but much can be said in a brief space; it may have been on most unimportant topics, but how could she know that? The girl was lovely, but she had dared to raise her eyes to the loved one of the princess; and, with all the intensity of the savage blood transmitted to her through long lines of wholly barbaric ancestors, she hated the woman who blushed and trembled behind that silent door.

When her lover turned and looked at her, and his eye met hers as she sat there paler and whiter than any one in the vast ocean of anxious faces about her, he saw, by that power of quick perception which is given to

5. **moiety** (moi′ə-tē): share.

those whose souls are one, that she knew behind which door crouched the tiger, and behind which stood the lady. He had expected her to know it. He understood her nature, and his soul was assured that she would never rest until she had made plain to herself this thing, hidden to all other lookers-on, even to the king. The only hope for the youth in which there was any element of certainty was based upon the success of the princess in discovering this mystery; and the moment he looked upon her, he saw she had succeeded, as in his soul he knew she would succeed.

Then it was that his quick and anxious glance asked the question, "Which?" It was as plain to her as if he shouted it from where he stood. There was not an instant to be lost. The question was asked in a flash; it must be answered in another.

Her right arm lay on the cushioned parapet before her. She raised her hand, and made a slight, quick movement toward the right. No one but her lover saw her. Every eye was fixed on the man in the arena.

He turned, and with a firm and rapid step he walked across the empty space. Every heart stopped beating, every breath was held, every eye was fixed immovably upon that man. Without the slightest hesitation, he went to the door on the right and opened it.

Now, the point of the story is this: Did the tiger come out of that door, or did the lady?

The more we reflect upon this question the harder it is to answer. It involves a study of the human heart which leads us through devious mazes of passion, out of which it is difficult to find our way. Think of it, fair reader, not as if the decision of the question depended on yourself, but upon that hot-blooded, semi-barbaric princess, her soul at a white heat beneath the combined fires of despair and jealousy. She had lost him, but who should have him?

How often, in her waking hours and in her dreams, had she started in wild horror and covered her face with her hands as she thought of her lover opening the door on the other side of which waited the cruel fangs of the tiger!

But how much oftener had she seen him at the other door! How in her grievous reveries had she gnashed her teeth and torn her hair when she saw his start of rapturous delight as he opened the door of the lady! How her soul had burned in agony when she had seen him rush to meet that woman, with her flushing cheek and sparkling eye of triumph; when she had seen him lead her forth, his whole frame kindled with the joy of recovered life; when she heard the glad shouts from the multitude, and the wild ringing of the happy bells; when she had seen the priest, with his joyous followers, advance to the couple, and make them man and wife before her very eyes; and when she had seen them walk away together upon their path of flowers, followed by the tremendous shouts of the hilarious multitude, in which her one despairing shriek was lost and drowned!

Would it not be better for him to die at once, and go to wait for her in the blessed regions of semi-barbaric futurity?

And yet, that awful tiger, those shrieks, that blood!

Her decision had been indicated in an instant, but it had been made after days and nights of anguished deliberation. She had known she would be asked, she had decided what she would answer, and, without the slightest hesitation, she had moved her hand to the right.

The question of her decision is one not to be lightly considered, and it is not for me to presume to set myself up as the one person able to answer it. And so I leave it with all of you: Which came out of the opened door—the lady, or the tiger?

First Response: *What is your answer to the author's question at the end of the story?*

CHECKING UP (True/False)

1. The king is stern and ill-tempered.
2. The arena is used to determine whether an accused person is guilty or innocent.
3. The people feel that the judgments of the arena are unfair.
4. The princess does not know which door holds the tiger.
5. The princess is jealous of the lady chosen for her lover.

TALKING IT OVER

1. What are some of the ironies of the king's system of justice?
2. Why is the institution of the arena so popular with the people?
3. What internal conflict is at the root of the princess's dilemma?
4. What is the reaction of the audience as the young man enters the arena?
5. How does the young man know that the princess has discovered the secret of the doors?
6. The author challenges you to guess the outcome of the story. From what you know of the princess, which door do you think she would point to—the one concealing the lady, or the one concealing the tiger? Give reasons to support your answer.

POINT OF VIEW
Self-conscious Point of View

The narrator of a story may address the audience directly, commenting on events and characters in the story or encouraging the reader's involvement. Such a narrator is considered **self-conscious** because he or she reminds the reader that what is being read is, after all, "only a story."

The narrator of "The Lady, or the Tiger?" can be considered self-conscious. As you read, you are quite aware that someone is telling the tale to you; the narrator's presence is felt throughout the story.

The narrator makes a direct comment on the king's system of justice when he says, "Its perfect fairness is obvious." How do you know that this statement is ironic? Find other passages in the story that demonstrate the presence of a self-conscious narrator.

UNDERSTANDING THE WORDS IN THE STORY
(Matching Columns)

1. florid	a. came forth
2. genial	b. court
3. valor	c. sad; melancholy
4. decrees	d. flowery; showy
5. incorruptible	e. secondary
6. emanated	f. official orders
7. doleful	g. courage
8. dire	h. dreadful; terrible
9. subordinate	i. friendly; cheerful
10. tribunal	j. unable to be bribed or tainted

(Multiple-Choice)

1. An *impartial* decision
   a. shows no favoritism
   b. is unfair
   c. is made quickly
2. Something *procured* is
   a. obtained
   b. well fed
   c. safe to eat
3. A scheme of *retribution*
   a. redistributes wealth
   b. asks questions
   c. punishes wrongdoing
4. A person with an *imperious* nature is
   a. arrogant
   b. heir to the throne
   c. soft-spoken
5. *Ardor* can be described as
   a. a love for trees
   b. burning resentment
   c. strong feeling

6. The *portals* of a building or structure are its
   a. windows
   b. doors
   c. roof lines
7. The *parapet* on which the princess's right arm lay was a
   a. cushion
   b. low railing
   c. desk
8. *Devious* paths are
   a. roundabout and winding
   b. long and exhausting
   c. clearly indicated and pleasant
9. *Reveries* are
   a. daydreams
   b. jealous rages
   c. wake-up calls
10. The *deliberation* that preceded the decision of the princess was marked by
    a. a hasty search for documents
    b. bitter arguments
    c. careful consideration

WRITING IT DOWN
Another Point of View

As you have seen, a story may be told in the **first-person point of view;** that is, by a narrator who is a character in the story. A story may be also be told in the **third-person point of view,** by an outside observer who is not a character in the story. The third-person point of view can be **omniscient, limited, objective,** or **self-conscious.** Choose one of the stories in this unit and rewrite a passage from that story using a different point of view.

ABOUT THE AUTHOR

Frank R. Stockton (1834–1902) was born in Philadelphia. He attended a small high school for boys, and while a student there he won a prize in a short-story contest. Although he began working as a wood engraver following high school, he continued to write stories. A number were published in magazines.

In 1873 Stockton was appointed assistant editor on *St. Nicholas,* a popular children's magazine. He contributed a number of stories and articles to the periodical and published books for both children and adults.

Stockton's reputation as a children's writer was based on the literary fairy tales he created. His witty, inventive stories were well liked by children, although his youthful readers didn't always grasp his gentle irony concerning society and human nature.

Stockton's most famous story, "The Lady, or the Tiger?" caused a sensation when it was published in *Century Magazine* in 1882. After receiving hundreds of queries about the story's ending, Stockton released the following statement: "If you decide which it was—the lady, or the tiger, you find out what kind of a person you are yourself."

THE CIRCUIT

Francisco Jiménez

Has your family—or the family of a close friend—ever had to pack up and move to a different city or state? Was that move an adventure or a hardship? Think for a moment and jot down your answer in a sentence or two.

It was that time of year again. Ito, the strawberry sharecropper, did not smile. It was natural. The peak of the strawberry season was over and the last few days the workers, most of them braceros,[1] were not picking as many boxes as they had during the months of June and July.

As the last days of August disappeared, so did the number of braceros. Sunday, only one—the best picker—came to work. I liked him. Sometimes we talked during our half-hour lunch break. That is how I found out he was from Jalisco,[2] the same state in Mexico my family was from. That Sunday was the last time I saw him.

When the sun had tired and sunk behind the mountains, Ito signaled us that it was time to go home. "Ya esora," he yelled in his broken Spanish. Those were the words I waited for twelve hours a day, every day, seven days a week, week after week. And the thought of not hearing them again saddened me.

As we drove home Papá did not say a word. With both hands on the wheel, he stared at the dirt road. My older brother, Roberto, was also silent. He leaned back and closed his eyes. Once in a while he cleared from his throat the dust that blew in from outside.

Yes, it was that time of year. When I opened the front door to the shack, I stopped. Everything we owned was neatly packed in cardboard boxes. Suddenly I felt even more the weight of hours, days, weeks, and months of work. I sat down on a box. The thought of having to move to Fresno and knowing what was in store for me there brought tears to my eyes.

---

1. **braceros** (brä-sĕr′ōs): Mexican farm laborers who are in the United States temporarily as migrant workers.
2. **Jalisco** (hä-lēs′kō).

That night I could not sleep. I lay in bed thinking about how much I hated this move.

A little before five o'clock in the morning, Papá woke everyone up. A few minutes later, the yelling and screaming of my little brothers and sisters, for whom the move was a great adventure, broke the silence of dawn. Shortly, the barking of the dogs accompanied them.

While we packed the breakfast dishes, Papá went outside to start the "Carcanchita." That was the name Papá gave his old '38 black Plymouth. He bought it in a used-car lot in Santa Rosa in the winter of 1949. Papá was very proud of his little jalopy. He had a right to be proud of it. He spent a lot of time looking at other cars before buying this one. When he finally chose the "Carcanchita," he checked it thoroughly before driving it out of the car lot. He examined every inch of the car. He listened to the motor, tilting his head from side to side like a parrot, trying to detect any noises that spelled car trouble. After being satisfied with the looks and sounds of the car, Papá then insisted on knowing who the original owner was. He never did find out from the car salesman, but he bought the car anyway. Papá figured the original owner must have been an important man because behind the rear seat of the car he found a blue necktie.

Papá parked the car out in front and left the motor running. "Listo,"[3] he yelled. Without saying a word, Roberto and I began to carry the boxes out to the car. Roberto carried the two big boxes and I carried the two smaller ones. Papá then threw the mattress on top of the car roof and tied it with ropes to the front and rear bumpers.

Everything was packed except Mamá's pot. It was an old large galvanized pot she had picked up at an army surplus store in Santa María the year I was born. The pot had many dents and nicks, and the more dents and nicks it acquired the more Mamá liked it. "Mi olla," she used to say proudly.

I held the front door open as Mamá carefully carried out her pot by both handles, making sure not to spill the cooked beans. When she got to the car, Papá reached out to help her with it. Roberto opened the rear car door and Papá gently placed it on the floor behind the front seat. All of us then climbed in. Papá sighed, wiped

---

3. **Listo** (lēs′tō): "Ready."

the sweat off his forehead with his sleeve, and said wearily: "Es todo."[4]

As we drove away, I felt a lump in my throat. I turned around and looked at our little shack for the last time.

At sunset we drove into a labor camp near Fresno. Since Papá did not speak English, Mamá asked the camp foreman if he needed any more workers. "We don't need no more," said the foreman, scratching his head. "Check with Sullivan down the road. Can't miss him. He lives in a big white house with a fence around it."

When we got there, Mamá walked up to the house. She went through a white gate, past a row of rose bushes, up the stairs to the front door. She rang the doorbell. The porch light went on and a tall husky man came out. They exchanged a few words. After the man went in, Mamá clasped her hands and hurried back to the car. "We have work! Mr. Sullivan said we can stay there the whole season," she said, gasping and pointing to an old garage near the stables.

The garage was worn out by the years. It had no windows. The walls, eaten by termites, strained to support the roof full of holes. The dirt floor, populated by earth worms, looked like a gray road map.

That night, by the light of a kerosene lamp, we unpacked and cleaned our new home. Roberto swept away the loose dirt, leaving the hard ground. Papá plugged the holes in the walls with old newspapers and tin can tops. Mamá fed my little brothers and sisters. Papá and Roberto then brought in the mattress and placed it on the far corner of the garage. "Mamá, you and the little ones sleep on the mattress. Roberto, Panchito, and I will sleep outside under the trees," Papá said.

Early next morning Mr. Sullivan showed us where his crop was, and after breakfast, Papá, Roberto, and I headed for the vineyard to pick.

Around nine o'clock the temperature had risen to almost one hundred degrees. I was completely soaked in sweat and my mouth felt as if I had been chewing on a handkerchief. I walked over to the end of the row, picked up the jug of water we had brought, and began drinking. "Don't drink too much; you'll get sick," Roberto shouted. No sooner had he said that than I felt sick to my stomach. I dropped to my knees and let the jug roll off my hands. I remained motionless with my eyes glued on the hot sandy ground. All I could hear was the drone of

4. **Es todo** (ĕs tō′*thō*): "That's all."

insects. Slowly I began to recover. I poured water over my face and neck and watched the dirty water run down my arms to the ground.

I still felt a little dizzy when we took a break to eat lunch. It was past two o'clock and we sat underneath a large walnut tree that was on the side of the road. While we ate, Papá jotted down the number of boxes we had picked. Roberto drew designs on the ground with a stick. Suddenly I noticed Papá's face turn pale as he looked down the road. "Here comes the school bus," he whispered loudly in alarm. Instinctively, Roberto and I ran and hid in the vineyards. We did not want to get in trouble for not going to school. The neatly dressed boys about my age got off. They carried books under their arms. After they crossed the street, the bus drove away. Roberto and I came out from hiding and joined Papá. "Tienen que tener cuidado,"[5] he warned us.

After lunch we went back to work. The sun kept beating down. The buzzing insects, the wet sweat, and the hot dry dust made the afternoon seem to last forever. Finally the mountains around the valley reached out and swallowed the sun. Within an hour it was too dark to continue picking. The vines blanketed the grapes, making it difficult to see the bunches. "Vámonos,"[6] said Papá, signaling to us that it was time to quit work. Papá then took out a pencil and began to figure out how much we had earned our first day. He wrote down numbers, crossed some out, wrote down some more. "Quince,"[7] he murmured.

When we arrived home, we took a cold shower underneath a water hose. We then sat down to eat dinner around some wooden crates that served as a table. Mamá had cooked a special meal for us. We had rice and tortillas with "carne con chile," my favorite dish.

The next morning I could hardly move. My body ached all over. I felt little control over my arms and legs. This feeling went on every morning for days until my muscles finally got used to the work.

It was Monday, the first week of November. The grape season was over and I could now go to school. I woke up early that morning and lay in bed, looking at the stars and savoring the thought of not going to work and of starting sixth grade for the first time that year. Since I could not sleep, I decided to get up and join Papá and Roberto at

5. **Tienen que tener cuidado:** "You have to be careful."
6. **Vámonos** (bä′mō-nōs): "Let's go."
7. **Quince** (kēn′sĕ): "Fifteen."

breakfast. I sat at the table across from Roberto, but I kept my head down. I did not want to look up and face him. I knew he was sad. He was not going to school today. He was not going tomorrow, or next week, or next month. He would not go until the cotton season was over, and that was sometime in February. I rubbed my hands together and watched the dry, acid-stained skin fall to the floor in little rolls.

When Papá and Roberto left for work, I felt relief. I walked to the top of a small grade next to the shack and watched the "Carcanchita" disappear in the distance in a cloud of dust.

Two hours later, around eight o'clock, I stood by the side of the road waiting for school bus number twenty. When it arrived I climbed in. Everyone was busy either talking or yelling. I sat in an empty seat in the back.

When the bus stopped in front of the school, I felt very nervous. I looked out the bus window and saw boys and girls carrying books under their arms. I put my hands in my pant pockets and walked to the principal's office. When I entered I heard a woman's voice say: "May I help you?" I was startled. I had not heard English for months. For a few seconds I remained speechless. I looked at the lady who waited for an answer. My first instinct was to answer her in Spanish, but I held back. Finally, after struggling for English words, I managed to tell her that I wanted to enroll in the sixth grade. After answering many questions, I was led to the classroom.

Mr. Lema, the sixth grade teacher, greeted me and assigned me a desk. He then introduced me to the class. I was so nervous and scared at that moment when everyone's eyes were on me that I wished I were with Papá and Roberto picking cotton. After taking roll, Mr. Lema gave the class the assignment for the first hour. "The first thing we have to do this morning is finish reading the story we began yesterday," he said enthusiastically. He walked up to me, handed me an English book, and asked me to read. "We are on page 125," he said politely. When I heard this, I felt my blood rush to my head; I felt dizzy. "Would you like to read?" he asked hesitantly. I opened the book to page 125. My mouth was dry. My eyes began to water. I could not begin. "You can read later," Mr. Lema said understandingly.

For the rest of the reading period I kept getting angrier and angrier with myself. I should have read, I thought to myself.

During recess I went into the restroom and opened my English book to page 125. I began to read in a low voice, pretending I was in class. There were many words I did not know. I closed the book and headed back to the classroom.

Mr. Lema was sitting at his desk correcting papers. When I entered he looked up at me and smiled. I felt better. I walked up to him and asked if he could help me with the new words. "Gladly," he said.

The rest of the month I spent my lunch hours working on English with Mr. Lema, my best friend at school.

One Friday during lunch hour Mr. Lema asked me to take a walk with him to the music room. "Do you like music?" he asked me as we entered the building.

"Yes, I like corridos,"[8] I answered. He then picked up a trumpet, blew on it and handed it to me. The sound gave me goose bumps. I knew that sound. I had heard it in many corridos. "How would you like to learn how to play it?" he asked. He must have read my face because before I could answer, he added: "I'll teach you how to play it during our lunch hours."

That day I could hardly wait to get home to tell Papá and Mamá the great news. As I got off the bus, my little brothers and sisters ran up to meet me. They were yelling and screaming. I thought they were happy to see me, but when I opened the door to our shack, I saw that everything we owned was neatly packed in cardboard boxes.

8. **corridos** (kō-rē′*th*ōs): Mexican folk ballads.

First Response: *How did the story's ending make you feel?*

CHECKING UP (True/False)

1. The story opens at the end of the strawberry season.
2. Panchito is unhappy about moving to Fresno.
3. Mamá is tired of her old, dented pot.

4. Roberto will go to school when the cotton season ends.
5. Panchito spends his lunch hours studying English.

TALKING IT OVER

1. What is the main external conflict that confronts the family in this story? How is this struggle related to Panchito's internal conflict?
2. What details in the story suggest that the family members remain strong and united despite the hardships that they face?
3. Why is Panchito unable to face his brother on his first morning of school?
4. How do you think Panchito feels at the end of the story, when he sees the packed boxes?
5. How is the story's plot structure reflected in its title?
6. What do you think will happen to the narrator? Will he complete his education?

TONE
Recognizing Tone

Tone is the attitude a writer takes toward the subject, characters, and readers of a literary work. To give you some examples, tone can be solemn, humorous, romantic, mocking, compassionate, bitter. If you have read Ruskin Bond's "A Tiger in the House" (page 1), you remember that the tone of that story is humorous. If you have read Ernest Hemingway's "A Day's Wait" (page 249), you recall that the tone of that story is compassionate. A writer's tone can shift within a work; for example, some stories that begin with a humorous, lighthearted tone become serious as they develop. However, most stories have a single, predominant tone.

It is important to recognize the tone of a story. If you fail to recognize tone, you may misunderstand the author's intention. If you were to take the story of "The Lady, or the Tiger?" (page 280) at face value, for example, you would miss the irony of the story and the point that Stockton is making about human nature.

"The Circuit" is a realistic story. Jiménez's narrator, Panchito, describes the harsh lives of the migrant workers—the endless "circuit" of hard work and relocation. Panchito is not bitter, angry, or mocking, however; he relates the events of the story with sadness and resignation. The story is written in a simple, direct style. We could say that the tone of this story is **serious.**

1. Find details in the story that reveal the hardships faced by workers and their families.
2. Locate some of the passages in the story that convey Panchito's feelings of sadness and resignation.

WRITING IT DOWN
An Analysis of Tone

Journalists usually try to remain objective about the events they report on. Nevertheless, many news stories in the print or broadcast media convey a certain tone, or attitude, toward their subject.

Select a news story from a subject area that appeals to you—sports, politics, entertainment, or the arts, for example. Make notes analyzing the story's tone—the attitude that the writer or broadcaster seems to take toward the material. Then summarize your results in a paragraph or two.

ABOUT THE AUTHOR

Francisco Jiménez was born in Mexico in 1943 and came to the United States with his family when he was four. Two years later, he began working in the fields of southern California. Because he was from a family of migrant workers, it was difficult for him to complete his education. However, he now holds a doctorate from Columbia University in New York City. A teacher since 1971, he is currently professor of

Spanish and director of Arts and Humanities at the University of Santa Clara in California.

Jiménez has edited several anthologies, including *Hispanics in the United States: An Anthology of Creative Culture.* He once said:

> My primary goal in writing both scholarly and creative works is to fill the need for cultural and human understanding, between the United States and Mexico in particular. I write in both English and Spanish. The language I use is determined by what period in my life I write about. Since Spanish was the dominant language during my childhood, I generally write about those experiences in Spanish. My scholarly research has been published in both English and Spanish. Because I am bilingual and bicultural, I can move in and out of both American and Mexican cultures with ease; therefore, I have been able to write stories in both languages. I consider that a privilege.

A SECRET FOR TWO

Quentin Reynolds

---

*People often develop strong attachments to animals. Have you ever
had a special feeling for an animal? If so, write down a few sentences
explaining why the animal was important to you.*

Montreal is a very large city, but, like all large cities, it has some
very small streets. Streets, for instance, like Prince Edward
Street, which is only four blocks long, ending in a cul-de-
sac.[1] No one knew Prince Edward Street as well as did Pierre Dupin,
for Pierre had delivered milk to the families on the street for thirty
years now.

During the past fifteen years the horse which drew the milk wagon
used by Pierre was a large white horse named Joseph. In Montreal, especially in that part of Montreal which is very French, the animals, like
children, are often given the names of saints. When the big white horse
first came to the Provincale Milk Company he didn't have a name. They
told Pierre that he could use the white horse henceforth. Pierre stroked
the softness of the horse's neck; he stroked the sheen of its splendid
belly and he looked into the eyes of the horse.

"This is a kind horse, a gentle and a faithful horse," Pierre said, "and
I can see a beautiful spirit shining out of the eyes of the horse. I will
name him after good St. Joseph, who was also kind and gentle and faithful and a beautiful spirit."

Within a year Joseph knew the milk route as well as Pierre. Pierre
used to boast that he didn't need reins—he never touched them. Each
morning Pierre arrived at the stables of the Provincale Milk Company
at five o'clock. The wagon would be loaded and Joseph hitched to it.
Pierre would call *"Bon jour, vieil ami,"*[2] as he climbed into his seat and
Joseph would turn his head and the other drivers would smile and say
that the horse would smile at Pierre. Then Jacques, the foreman, would
say, "All right, Pierre, go on," and Pierre would call softly to Joseph,

---

1. **cul-de-sac** (kŭl'dĭ-săk'): dead-end street.
2. *"Bon jour, vieil ami"* (bōn zhōōr' vyā á-mē'): French for "Good morning, old
   friend."

"Avance, mon ami,"[3] and this splendid combination would stalk proudly down the street.

The wagon, without any direction from Pierre, would roll three blocks down St. Catherine Street, then turn right two blocks along Roslyn Avenue; then left, for that was Prince Edward Street. The horse would stop at the first house, allow Pierre perhaps thirty seconds to get down from his seat and put a bottle of milk at the front door and would then go on, skipping two houses and stopping at the third. So down the length of the street. Then Joseph, still without any direction from Pierre, would turn around and come back along the other side. Yes, Joseph was a smart horse.

Pierre would boast at the stable of Joseph's skill. "I never touch the reins. He knows just where to stop. Why, a blind man could handle my route with Joseph pulling the wagon."

So it went on for years—always the same. Pierre and Joseph both grew old together, but gradually, not suddenly. Pierre's huge walrus mustache was pure white now and Joseph didn't lift his knees so high or raise his head quite as much. Jacques, the foreman of the stables, never noticed that they were both getting old until Pierre appeared one morning carrying a heavy walking stick.

"Hey, Pierre," Jacques laughed. "Maybe you got the gout, hey?"

"Mais oui,[4] *Jacques,"* Pierre said a bit uncertainly. "One grows old. One's legs get tired."

"You should teach that horse to carry the milk to the front door for you," Jacques told him. "He does everything else."

He knew every one of the forty families he served on Prince Edward Street. The cooks knew that Pierre could neither read nor write, so instead of following the usual custom of leaving a note in an empty bottle if an additional quart of milk was needed they would sing out when they heard the rumble of his wagon wheels over the cobbled street, "Bring an extra quart this morning, Pierre."

"So you have company for dinner tonight," he would call back gaily.

Pierre had a remarkable memory. When he arrived at the stable he'd always remember to tell Jacques, "The Paquins took an extra quart this morning; the Lemoines bought a pint of cream."

3. *"Avance, mon ami"* (à-väNs′ môN à-mē′): French for "Go ahead, my friend."
4. *"Mais oui"* (mā wē′): French for "But of course."

Jacques would note these things in a little book he always carried. Most of the drivers had to make out the weekly bills and collect the money, but Jacques, liking Pierre, had always excused him from this task. All Pierre had to do was to arrive at five in the morning, walk to his wagon, which was always in the same spot at the curb, and deliver his milk. He returned some two hours later, got down stiffly from his seat, called a cheery *"Au 'voir"* [5] to Jacques and then limped slowly down the street.

One morning the president of the Provincale Milk Company came to inspect the early morning deliveries. Jacques pointed Pierre out to him and said: "Watch how he talks to that horse. See how the horse listens and how he turns his head toward Pierre? See the look in that horse's eyes? You know, I think those two share a secret. I have often noticed it. It is as though they both sometimes chuckle at us as they go off on their route. Pierre is a good man, Monsieur[6] President, but he gets old. Would it be too bold of me to suggest that he be retired and be given perhaps a small pension?" he added anxiously.

"But of course," the president laughed. "I know his record. He has been on this route now for thirty years and never once has there been a complaint. Tell him it is time he rested. His salary will go on just the same."

But Pierre refused to retire. He was panic-stricken at the thought of not driving Joseph every day. "We are two old men," he said to Jacques. "Let us wear out together. When Joseph is ready to retire—then I, too, will quit."

Jacques, who was a kind man, understood. There was something about Pierre and Joseph which made a man smile tenderly. It was as though each drew some hidden strength from the other. When Pierre was sitting in his seat, and when Joseph was hitched to the wagon, neither seemed old. But when they finished their work, then Pierre would limp down the street slowly, seeming very old indeed, and the horse's head would drop and he would walk very wearily to his stall.

Then one morning Jacques had dreadful news for Pierre when he arrived. It was a cold morning and still pitch-dark. The air was like iced

---

5. *"Au 'voir":* "Au revoir" (ō r a̅/wär′), French for "Until we meet again."
6. **Monsieur** (mə-syœ′): a French title equivalent to "Mister" or "Sir."

wine that morning and the snow which had fallen during the night glistened like a million diamonds piled together.

Jacques said, "Pierre, your horse, Joseph, did not wake up this morning. He was very old, Pierre, he was twenty-five and that is like being seventy-five for a man."

"Yes," Pierre said, slowly. "Yes. I am seventy-five. And I cannot see Joseph again."

"Of course you can," Jacques soothed. "He is over in his stall, looking very peaceful. Go over and see him."

Pierre took one step forward then turned. "No . . . no . . . you don't understand, Jacques."

Jacques clapped him on the shoulder. "We'll find another horse just as good as Joseph. Why, in a month you'll teach him to know your route as well as Joseph did. We'll . . ."

The look in Pierre's eyes stopped him. For years Pierre had worn a heavy cap, the peak of which came low over his eyes, keeping the bitter morning wind out of them. Now Jacques looked into Pierre's eyes and he saw something which startled him. He saw a dead, lifeless look in them. The eyes were mirroring the grief that was in Pierre's heart and his soul. It was as though his heart and soul had died.

"Take today off, Pierre," Jacques said, but already Pierre was hobbling off down the street, and had one been near one would have seen tears streaming down his cheeks and have heard half-smothered sobs. Pierre walked to the corner and stepped into the street. There was a warning yell from the driver of a huge truck that was coming fast and there was the scream of brakes, but Pierre apparently heard neither.

Five minutes later an ambulance driver said, "He's dead. Was killed instantly."

Jacques and several of the milk-wagon drivers had arrived and they looked down at the still figure.

"I couldn't help it," the driver of the truck protested, "he walked right into my truck. He never saw it, I guess. Why, he walked into it as though he were blind."

The ambulance doctor bent down, "Blind? Of course the man was blind. See those cataracts? This man has been blind for five years." He turned to Jacques, "You say he worked for you? Didn't you know he was blind?"

"No . . . no . . ." Jacques said, softly. "None of us knew. Only one knew—a friend of his named Joseph. . . . It was a secret, I think, just between those two."

First Response: *Did you find the story believable? Explain your answer.*

CHECKING UP

1. What is Pierre Dupin's job?
2. Why does Pierre boast about Joseph?
3. How does Pierre explain his use of the walking stick?
4. From what task does Jacques regularly excuse Pierre?
5. How does Pierre die?

TALKING IT OVER

1. What does the "secret" in the title of the story refer to? Why are the two friends able to keep this secret from others?
2. What details of setting and language in the story help to create a sense of place?
3. What details in the story foreshadow Pierre's blindness?
4. How do you know that the author has a warmhearted view of his characters?

TONE
Sentimentalism

Short stories can arouse different feelings in readers. Some stories, like "Who's There?" (page 139), can cause us to experience suspense and excitement. Some stories, like "The Bracelet" (page 108), can make us feel sad. Still other stories, like "The Revolt of the Evil Fairies" (page 117), can make us laugh.

When the term **sentimentalism** is used of literature, it refers to the expression of gentle or tender feelings. Quentin Reynolds' tone in "A Secret for Two" is sentimental. His feelings toward his characters are warm and tender. He has affection for his characters and wants the reader to feel kindly and sympathetic toward them.

1. Note how Reynolds focuses on the relationship of Pierre and his horse. How does he develop the sense of a special bond between man and animal?
2. Note the reactions of other characters in the story. How do their comments and actions create sympathy for Pierre and Joseph?
3. Note the direct comments of the narrator. Find several examples that reveal his attitude toward the different characters.
4. How does the final episode in the story make you feel?

UNDERSTANDING THE WORDS IN THE STORY (Completion)

Choose one of the words in the following list to complete each of the sentences below. A word may be used only once.

hobbling	route
stalk	boast
protested	apparently
sheen	soothed
glistened	stall

1. When Pierre first saw the big white horse, he stroked the _____ of the horse's belly.
2. The horse was as familiar with the milk _____ as Pierre was.
3. After the wagon was loaded, the man and animal would _____ down the street.
4. At the stable, Pierre used to _____ of his horse's ability.
5. When they returned, Joseph would be put in his _____.
6. The snow that had fallen during the night _____ like diamonds.
7. Jacques _____ Pierre with the news that Joseph was looking peaceful.

8. After he left the stable, Pierre began _____ down the street.
9. Although the driver called a warning, Pierre _____ heard nothing.
10. The truck driver _____ that the accident was unavoidable.

WRITING IT DOWN
A Book Report

Think of another story or novel that focuses on the relationship between a person and an animal. Some examples are "Weep No More, My Lady" by James Street; "My Friend Flicka" by Mary O'Hara; *Lassie Come-Home* by Eric Knight; *National Velvet* by Enid Bagnold; *Born Free* by Joy Adamson; *Ring of Bright Water* by Gavin Maxwell.

Make some notes about the plot, characters, setting and tone of the story you choose. Then organize your notes into a brief book report. When you have finished writing, get together with a small group of classmates and take turns presenting your reports.

A Personal Account

Think of an experience that brought out tender or sentimental feelings in you. Write about that episode in a paragraph or two. Try to make the tone of your account convey your feelings toward the event.

ABOUT THE AUTHOR

Quentin Reynolds (1902–1965) served as a war correspondent in London, Paris, Italy, and the South Pacific during the Second World War. His experiences are described in *The Wounded Don't Cry* (1941). He wrote several biographies (his subjects included Winston Churchill and the Wright brothers) and a number of short stories.

THE PRINCESS
AND THE TIN BOX

James Thurber

---

*Think about how princesses in fairy tales are usually depicted. How
is the princess in this story different?*

O nce upon a time, in a far country, there lived a king whose
daughter was the prettiest princess in the world. Her eyes were
like the cornflower, her hair was sweeter than the hyacinth,
and her throat made the swan look dusty.

From the time she was a year old, the princess had been showered
with presents. Her nursery looked like Cartier's[1] window. Her toys were
all made of gold or platinum or diamonds or emeralds. She was not
permitted to have wooden blocks or china dolls or rubber dogs or linen
books, because such materials were considered cheap for the daughter
of a king.

When she was seven, she was allowed to attend the wedding of her
brother and throw real pearls at the bride instead of rice. Only the
nightingale, with his lyre of gold, was permitted to sing for the princess.
The common blackbird, with his boxwood flute, was kept out of the
palace grounds. She walked in silver-and-samite[2] slippers to a sapphire-
and-topaz bathroom and slept in an ivory bed inlaid with rubies.

On the day the princess was eighteen, the king sent a royal ambassador to the courts of five neighboring kingdoms to announce that he
would give his daughter's hand in marriage to the prince who brought
her the gift she liked the most.

The first prince to arrive at the palace rode a swift white stallion and
laid at the feet of the princess an enormous apple made of solid gold
which he had taken from a dragon who had guarded it for a thousand
years. It was placed on a long ebony table set up to hold the gifts of the
princess's suitors. The second prince, who came on a gray charger,
brought her a nightingale made of a thousand diamonds, and it was

---

1. **Cartier's** (kär-tyāz′): a store in New York City that sells very expensive jewelry.
2. **samite** (sā′mīt′): a heavy silk fabric, often interwoven with silver or gold threads.

placed beside the golden apple. The third prince, riding on a black horse, carried a great jewel box made of platinum and sapphires, and it was placed next to the diamond nightingale. The fourth prince, astride a fiery yellow horse, gave the princess a gigantic heart made of rubies and pierced by an emerald arrow. It was placed next to the platinum-and-sapphire jewel box.

Now the fifth prince was the strongest and handsomest of all the five suitors, but he was the son of a poor king whose realm had been overrun by mice and locusts and wizards and mining engineers so that there was nothing much of value left in it. He came plodding up to the palace of the princess on a plow horse and he brought her a small tin box filled with mica and feldspar and hornblende[3] which he had picked up on the way.

The other princes roared with disdainful laughter when they saw the tawdry gift the fifth prince had brought to the princess. But she examined it with great interest and squealed with delight, for all her life she had been glutted with precious stones and priceless metals, but she had never seen tin before or mica or feldspar or hornblende. The tin box was placed next to the ruby heart pierced with an emerald arrow.

"Now," the king said to his daughter, "you must select the gift you like best and marry the prince that brought it."

The princess smiled and walked up to the table and picked up the present she liked the most. It was the platinum-and-sapphire jewel box, the gift of the third prince.

"The way I figure it," she said, "is this. It is a very large and expensive box, and when I am married, I will meet many admirers who will give me precious gems with which to fill it to the top. Therefore, it is the most valuable of all the gifts my suitors have brought me and I like it the best."

The princess married the third prince that very day in the midst of great merriment and high revelry. More than a hundred thousand pearls were thrown at her and she loved it.

Moral: All those who thought the princess was going to select the tin box filled with worthless stones instead of one of the other gifts will kindly stay after class

---

3. **mica** (mī′kə) ... **feldspar** (fĕld′spär′, fĕl′) ... **hornblende** (hôrn′blĕnd′): common mineral substances found in rocks.

and write one hundred times on the blackboard "I would rather have a hunk of aluminum silicate than a diamond necklace."

First Response: *Were you surprised that the princess chose the platinum-and-sapphire jewel box?*

CHECKING UP (True/False)

1. The princess's toys were all made of precious metals and gems.
2. All the suitors' gifts were placed on the princess's ivory bed.
3. The first of the princess's suitors brought an enormous golden apple.
4. The princess made her choice on the basis of what was most valuable.
5. The princess in this story believes that it is better to give than to receive.

TALKING IT OVER

1. In fairy tales the beautiful princess and the handsome prince fall in love, marry, and live happily ever after. What has replaced the importance of love in Thurber's story?
2. Why does the princess choose the jewel box? What does this choice reveal about her values?
3. Do you think Thurber admires the princess, or do you think he is poking fun at her? Support your opinion with evidence from the story.
4. How does this story show Thurber's keen understanding of human nature?

TONE
Genial Satire

Sometimes a humorous story, such as Thurber's "The Princess and the Tin Box," mocks or ridicules certain weaknesses, follies, or vices in human nature and society. A literary work that pokes fun at some failing of human behavior is called **satire**. Satire is generally of two kinds: it can be gentle, amusing, and lighthearted, or it can be biting, bitter, even savage. Thurber's story is of the genial variety. This satiric work is not intended to insult or hurt anyone, but to point out the foolishness of certain attitudes and beliefs.

In a traditional fairy tale, the plot might go like this: The princess would prefer the poor but handsome prince above the other suitors and would choose his insignificant gift. As a reward, the prince would drop his disguise and announce that he assumed a humble appearance in order to test her, that in reality he is the richest prince of all the neighboring kingdoms.

Thurber's princess, however, is not an idealist who has noble spiritual goals and principles. She is a materialist who believes that wealth and pleasure are the chief goals and values to be concerned with.

Thurber seems to be saying that both extremes are laughable. The princess who would choose a "hunk of aluminum silicate" over a diamond necklace would be unbelievably foolish. Yet the princess in the story gets her share of ridicule, too. She is what is commonly referred to as a "gold digger," a woman whose chief interest in men is to get money and gifts from them. By exposing her for what she is, Thurber gets us to laugh at her and her shallow values.

1. One way Thurber achieves a satiric tone in this story is by using **exaggeration**. Note, for example, Thurber's account of the privileged childhood of the princess. Which details are particularly absurd?
2. Another technique Thurber uses in this tale is **incongruity** (ĭn'kŏng-grōo'ə-tē, ĭn'kən-), the pairing of opposites to create an

unexpected contrast. Note the princess's manner of speaking. How is her speech *incongruous,* or inconsistent, with the traditional image of a storybook princess?

UNDERSTANDING THE WORDS IN THE STORY (Multiple-Choice)

1. The *hyacinth* is a
   a. small, furry animal
   b. precious gem
   c. plant with sweet-smelling flowers
2. The *lyre* is used to
   a. make music
   b. weave precious cloth
   c. house birds
3. An *ambassador* is
   a. a representative of one country to another
   b. an official who arranges royal weddings
   c. a servant in charge of palace expenses
4. An *ebony* table is made of
   a. precious jewels
   b. wood
   c. stone
5. One rides a *charger*
   a. at a carnival
   b. into battle
   c. to deliver mail
6. One rides *astride* when one sits
   a. with one leg on each side of a horse
   b. with both legs on one side of a saddle
   c. on a horse with no saddle
7. One is *disdainful* when feeling
   a. ill at ease in someone's presence
   b. talkative and friendly
   c. superior to someone or something

8. An example of *tawdry* jewelry is a
   a. string of cultured pearls
   b. rope of flashy glass beads
   c. diamond engagement ring
9. To be *glutted* is to
   a. have just enough
   b. experience hunger
   c. be filled beyond the point of satisfaction
10. One expects *revelry* during a
    a. feast
    b. concert
    c. test

WRITING IT DOWN
A Satirical Retelling

Work with a partner or a small group of classmates to develop a satirical version of a well-known fairy tale or children's story. Use the elements of exaggeration and incongruity in your tale. For example, you might choose to update a story such as "Goldilocks and the Three Bears" by placing it in an incongruous, modern setting. You may write your satire as a story or as a short play. Try to match James Thurber's humorous tone in your writing.

ABOUT THE AUTHOR

James Thurber (1894–1961), one of America's finest humorists, was born in Columbus, Ohio. For more than thirty years he contributed hundreds of stories, essays, and articles to *The New Yorker* magazine. He was also a talented cartoonist, and he illustrated many of his own works.

Thurber lost an eye in a childhood accident and was completely blind when he died. In "University Days" he described, with whimsical humor, his predicament in trying to use a microscope.

Thurber used incidents from his childhood to create *My Life and Hard Times,* his most famous collection of stories. In "The Secret Life of Walter Mitty," he created his most memorable character, a man who lives a double life. Thurber rewrote that story fifteen times before he felt satisfied with the result. Of his rewrites he once said, "With humor you have to look out for traps. You're likely to be very gleeful with what you've first put down, and you think it's fine, very funny. One reason you go over and over it is to make the piece sound less as if you were having a lot of fun with yourself. You try to play it down."

Writing about himself in the third person, Thurber said, "He never listens when anybody else is talking, preferring to keep his mind a blank until they get through, so he can talk. . . . He wears excellent clothes very badly and can never find his hat. He is Sagittarius with the moon in Aries and gets along fine with persons born between the 20th and 24th of August."

TOP OF THE FOOD CHAIN

T. Coraghessan Boyle

What is "the balance of nature"? Can you recall any instances in which human carelessness caused an environmental disaster? Get together with a small group of classmates to discuss your answers.

The thing was, we had a little problem with the insect vector[1] there, and believe me, your tamer stuff, your malathion[2] and pyrethrum[3] and the rest of the so-called environmentally safe products, didn't begin to make a dent in it, not a dent, I mean it was utterly useless—we might as well have been spraying Chanel No. 5[4] for all the good it did. And you've got to realize these people were literally covered with insects day and night—and the fact that they hardly wore any clothes just compounded the problem. Picture if you can, gentlemen, a naked little two-year-old boy so black with flies and mosquitoes it looks like he's wearing long johns, or the young mother so racked with the malarial shakes she can't even lift a Diet Coke to her lips—it was pathetic, just pathetic, like something out of the Dark Ages . . . Well, anyway, the decision was made to go with DDT. In the short term. Just to get the situation under control, you understand.

Yes, that's right, Senator, *DDT:* dichlorodiphenyltrichloroethane.

Yes, I'm well aware of that fact, sir. But just because *we* banned it domestically, under pressure from the bird-watching contingent and the hopheads down at the EPA,[5] it doesn't necessarily follow that the rest of the world—especially the developing world—was about to jump on the bandwagon. And that's the key word here, Senator, "developing." You've got to realize this is Borneo[6] we're talking about here, not Port Townsend or Enumclaw. These people don't know from square one about sanitation, disease control, pest eradication—or even personal

---

1. **vector:** disease carrier.
2. **malathion** (măl′ə-thī′ŏn′, -ən): an insecticide that has relatively low toxicity for mammals.
3. **pyrethrum** (pī-rĕth′rəm): an insecticide made from dried chrysanthemums.
4. **Chanel No. 5**: a famous French perfume.
5. **EPA:** Environmental Protection Agency.
6. **Borneo** (bôr′nē-ō′): a large island in the Malay archipelago of the southwest Pacific. Most of the island is part of Indonesia.

314

hygiene, if you want to come right down to it. It rains 120 inches a year, minimum. They dig up roots in the jungle. They've still got head-hunters along the Rajang River, for God's sake.

And please don't forget they *asked* us to come in there, practically begged us—and not only the World Health Organization but the Sultan of Brunei[7] and the government in Sarawak[8] too. We did what we could to accommodate them and reach our objective in the shortest period of time and by the most direct and effective means. We went to the air. Obviously. And no one could have foreseen the consequences, no one, not even if we'd gone out and generated a hundred environmental impact statements—it was just one of those things, a freak occurrence, and there's no defense against that. Not that I know of, anyway . . .

Caterpillars? Yes, Senator, that's correct. That was the first sign: caterpillars.

But let me backtrack a minute here. You see, out in the bush they have these roofs made of thatched palm leaves—you'll see them in the towns too, even in Bintulu or Brunei—and they're really pretty effective, you'd be surprised. A hundred and twenty inches of rain, they've got to figure a way to keep it out of the hut, and for centuries, this was it. Palm leaves. Well, it was about a month after we sprayed for the final time and I'm sitting at my desk in the trailer thinking about the drainage project at Kuching, enjoying the fact that for the first time in maybe a year I'm not smearing mosquitoes all over the back of my neck, when there's a knock at the door. It's this elderly gentleman, tattooed from head to toe, dressed only in a pair of running shorts—they love those shorts, by the way, the shiny material and the tight machine-stitching, the whole country, men and women both, they can't get enough of them . . . Anyway, he's the headman of the local village and he's very excited, something about the roofs—*atap*, they call them. That's all he can say, *atap, atap*, over and over again.

It's raining, of course. It's always raining. So I shrug into my rain slicker, start up the 4 × 4, and go have a look. Sure enough, all the *atap* roofs are collapsing, not only in his village but throughout the target area. The people are all huddled there in their running shorts, looking

---

7. **Brunei** (broo-nī′): a small, independent state on the northern coast of Borneo.
8. **Sarawak** (sə-rä′wäk): a state or administrative division of Malaysia, located in north-western Borneo.

pretty miserable, and one after another the roofs keep falling in, it's bewildering, and gradually I realize the headman's diatribe has begun to feature a new term I was unfamiliar with at the time—the word for caterpillar, as it turns out, in the Iban dialect. But who was to make the connection between three passes with the crop duster and all these staved-in roofs?

Our people finally sorted it out a couple weeks later. The chemical, which, by the way, cut down the number of mosquitoes exponentially, had the unfortunate side effect of killing off this little wasp—I've got the scientific name for it somewhere in my report here, if you're interested—that preyed on a type of caterpillar that in turn ate palm leaves. Well, with the wasps gone, the caterpillars hatched out with nothing to keep them in check and chewed the roofs to pieces, which was unfortunate, we admit it, and we had a real cost overrun on replacing those roofs with tin . . . but the people were happier, I think, in the long run, because, let's face it, no matter how tightly you weave those palm leaves, they're just not going to keep the water out like tin. Of course, nothing's perfect, and we had a lot of complaints about the rain drumming on the panels, people unable to sleep, and what have you . . .

Yes, sir, that's correct—the flies were next.

Well, you've got to understand the magnitude of the fly problem in Borneo, there's nothing like it here to compare it with, except maybe a garbage strike in New York. Every minute of every day you've got flies everywhere, up your nose, in your mouth, your ears, your eyes, flies in your rice, your Coke, your Singapore sling, and your gin rickey. It's enough to drive you to distraction, not to mention the diseases these things carry, from dysentery to typhoid to cholera and back round the loop again. And once the mosquito population was down, the flies seemed to breed up to fill in the gap—Borneo wouldn't be Borneo without some damned insect blackening the air.

Of course, this was before our people had tracked down the problem with the caterpillars and the wasps and all of that, and so we figured we'd had a big success with the mosquitoes, why not a series of ground sweeps, mount a fogger in the back of a Suzuki Brat, and sanitize the huts, not to mention the open sewers, which as you know are nothing but a breeding ground for flies, chiggers, and biting insects of every sort—at least it was an error of commission rather than omission. At least we were trying.

I watched the flies go down myself. One day they were so thick in the trailer I couldn't even *find* my paperwork, let alone attempt to get through it, and the next they were collecting on the windows, bumbling around like they were drunk. A day later they were gone. Just like that. From a million flies in the trailer to none . . .

Well, no one could have foreseen that, Senator.

The geckos ate the flies, yes. You're all familiar with geckos, I assume, gentlemen? These are the lizards you've seen during your trips to Hawaii, very colorful, patrolling the houses for roaches and flies, almost like pets, but of course they're wild animals, never lose sight of that, and just about as unsanitary as anything I can think of, except maybe flies.

Yes, well don't forget, sir, we're viewing this with twenty-twenty hindsight, but at the time no one gave a thought to geckos or what they ate—they were just another fact of life in the tropics. Mosquitoes, lizards, scorpions, leeches—you name it, they've got it. When the flies began piling up on the windowsills like drift, naturally the geckos feasted on them, stuffing themselves till they looked like sausages crawling up the walls. Whereas before they moved so fast you could never be sure you'd seen them, now they waddled across the floor, laid around in the corners, clung to the air vents like magnets—and even then no one paid much attention to them till they started turning belly-up in the streets. Believe me, we confirmed a lot of things there about the buildup of these products as you move up the food chain and the efficacy—or lack thereof—of certain methods, no doubt about that . . .

The cats? That's where it got sticky, really sticky. You see, nobody really lost any sleep over a pile of dead lizards—though we did tests routinely and the tests confirmed what we'd expected, that is, the product had been concentrated in the geckos because of the number of contaminated flies they consumed. But lizards are one thing and cats are another. These people really have an affection for their cats—no house, no hut, no matter how primitive, is without at least a couple of them. Mangy-looking things, long-legged and scrawny, maybe, not at all the sort of animal you'd see here, but there it was: they loved their cats. Because the cats were functional, you understand—without them, the place would have been swimming in rodents inside of a week.

You're right there, Senator, yes—that's exactly what happened.

You see, the cats had a field day with these feeble geckos—you can imagine, if any of you have ever owned a cat, the kind of joy these animals must have experienced to see their nemesis, this ultra-quick lizard, and it's just barely creeping across the floor like a bug. Well, to make a long story short, the cats ate up every dead and dying gecko in the country, from snout to tail, and then the cats began to die . . . which to my mind would have been no great loss if it wasn't for the rats. Suddenly there were rats everywhere—you couldn't drive down the street without running over half a dozen of them at a time. They fouled the grain supplies, fell in the wells and died, bit infants as they slept in their cradles. But that wasn't the worst, not by a long shot. No, things really went down the tube after that. Within the month we were getting scattered reports of bubonic plague, and of course we tracked them all down and made sure the people got antibiotics, but still we lost a few and the rats kept coming . . .

It was my plan, yes. I was brainstorming one night, rats scuttling all over the trailer like something out of a cheap horror film, the villagers in a panic over the threat of the plague and the stream of nonstop hysterical reports from the interior—people were turning black, swelling up and bursting, that sort of thing—well, as I say, I came up with a plan, a stopgap, not perfect, not cheap, but at this juncture, I'm sure you'll agree, something had to be done.

We wound up going as far as Australia for some of the cats, cleaning out the S.P.C.A.[9] facilities and what have you, though we rounded most of them up in Indonesia and Singapore—approximately 14,000 in all. And yes, it cost us—cost us up-front purchase money and aircraft fuel and pilots' overtime and all the rest of it—but we really felt there was no alternative. It was like all nature had turned against us.

And yet, all things considered, we made a lot of friends for the U.S.A. the day we dropped those cats, and you should have seen them, gentlemen, the little parachutes and harnesses we'd tricked up, 14,000 of them, cats in every color of the rainbow, cats with one ear, no ears, half a tail, three-legged cats, cats that could have taken pride of show in Springfield, Massachusetts, and all of them twirling down out of the sky like great big oversized snowflakes . . .

It was something. It was really something.

---

9. **S.P.C.A.:** Society for the Prevention of Cruelty to Animals.

Of course, you've all seen the reports. There were other factors we hadn't counted on, adverse conditions in the paddies and manioc[10] fields—we don't to this day know what predatory species were inadvertently killed off by the initial sprayings, it's just a mystery—but the weevils and whatnot took a pretty heavy toll on the crops that year, and by the time we dropped the cats, well—the people were pretty hungry, and I suppose it was inevitable that we lost a good proportion of them right then and there. But we've got a CARE program going there now and something hit the rat population—we still don't know what, a virus, we think—and the geckos, they tell me, are making a comeback.

So what I'm saying is it could be worse, and to every cloud a silver lining, wouldn't you agree, gentlemen?

10. **manioc** (măn′ē-ŏk′): cassava, a plant with an edible, starchy root.

First Response: *Would you agree with the speaker's final comment?*

CHECKING UP

1. Where do the events described by the speaker take place?
2. Why, according to the speaker, was DDT used?
3. What happened to the caterpillars when the wasps were killed off?
4. Why did the cats begin to die?
5. What plan was devised to control the rats?

TALKING IT OVER

1. Boyle plunges right into the story without identifying either the speaker or the setting. Who is the speaker? On what occasion is he reporting these events?
2. This story involves a cause-and-effect chain that threatens to spiral out of control. How did the seemingly simple act of

spraying for the flies and mosquitoes turn out to have such far-reaching consequences?

3. What is the climax of the story?

4. The term "food chain" refers to the earth's cycle of food and energy. The chain begins with inorganic substances (like water and certain minerals), continues with food producers such as trees and plants, and then culminates in two levels of "consumers." Primary consumers (such as rabbits and squirrels) eat plants, grass, seeds, and nuts. Secondary consumers (such as hawks and foxes) eat smaller animals. Human beings are considered to be at the "top of the food chain." Why is the title of the story ironic?

5. How would you describe the attitude of the speaker toward his job and the people he is supposed to be helping?

6. A **dramatic monologue** is a narrative in which a single character speaks to one or more listeners whose replies are not given. Why do you think Boyle chose to write his story as a monologue?

TONE
Forceful Satire

As you have seen, recognizing an author's **tone** is crucial to understanding a literary work. To say that "Top of the Food Chain" is about the ineffectiveness of pesticides is to miss the point of the story. Boyle is trying to show how the folly of human beings—their reckless disregard for the ecosystem—can have disastrous consequences. His tone, like Thurber's in "The Princess and the Tin Box (page 307), is **satirical**. However, unlike Thurber's satire, which is gentle and lighthearted, Boyle's satire is forceful and sarcastic.

1. One clue to Boyle's tone is his use of **irony,** a technique commonly used in satire. What is ironic about the speaker's statement, "It was like all nature had turned against us"?

2. **Exaggeration** and **understatement** are other techniques commonly used in satire. How does the author use exaggeration in the story's climax?

How does the speaker use understatement, or deliberate restraint, when he describes the collapse of the thatched palm-leaf roofs? when he refers to the fate of the plague victims?
3. Another clue to Boyle's attitude toward his subject is the way in which he depicts the character in the story. By having the speaker use almost nothing but **jargon** and **cliché,** we see that he has little understanding of ecology.

Jargon is specialized or technical language used in a particular trade or profession. An example of jargon in the story is the term "insect vector" in the first sentence. Find other examples of jargon in the story.

A cliché is an expression that has lost its meaning through excessive use. "Jump on the bandwagon" and "know from square one" are examples of cliché. List other examples of cliché in the story.

UNDERSTANDING THE WORDS IN THE STORY (Multiple-Choice)

1. Something that has *compounded* a problem has
   a. eliminated it
   b. made it worse
   c. caused it
2. A *contingent* is
   a. part of a larger group
   b. always well informed
   c. usually stingy
3. The *eradication* of pests refers to their
   a. elimination
   b. breeding
   c. multiplying
4. A *diatribe* is a long speech of
   a. praise
   b. criticism
   c. explanation
5. The *magnitude* of a problem refers to its
   a. extent
   b. location
   c. causes

6. The *efficacy* of a plan refers to its
   a. logic
   b. economy
   c. effectiveness
7. Your *nemesis* always seems to
   a. get the better of you
   b. ignore you
   c. help you
8. When the rats were *scuttling* all over the narrator's trailer, they were
   a. scurrying
   b. creeping
   c. falling
9. *Adverse* conditions are
   a. unexpected
   b. unfavorable or harmful
   c. well recognized
10. An action performed *inadvertently* is
   a. inexcusable
   b. irrational
   c. unintentional

WRITING IT DOWN
Dialogue

What do you think the senators said when the speaker testified at this hearing? Using clues from the story as well as your imagination, fill in the questions and comments of the senators. As you write, consider the tone of their remarks. Are the senators impatient? detached? angry? skeptical? As you write, try to suggest the senators' attitudes toward the witness and the events he describes.

Another Tone

Although the incidents in the story may be exaggerated and comical, the point that Boyle makes is a serious one. What tone, do you suppose, might a journalist adopt in reporting the events of the story? What tone would an environmentalist use? Rewrite the story in a tone that would be used by a different kind of narrator.

A Research Report

A number of environmental catastrophes—oil spills, for example—have occurred over the last few years. Read about one of these incidents in newspapers and magazines and summarize your findings in a brief report. Think about your attitude toward the episode. What will be the tone of your summary?

SPEAKING AND LISTENING
Preparing an Oral Interpretation

Get together with a small group of classmates and exchange ideas about how the monologue in this story would sound when delivered orally. Plan an oral reading of the story, dividing the monologue into parts to be read by different group members. As you practice reading, pay attention to volume, rate, pitch, and tone. Then take turns presenting your oral interpretation of the story to the class.

ABOUT THE AUTHOR

T. Coraghessan Boyle was born Thomas John Boyle in 1948 in Peekskill, New York. His parents were Irish immigrants. When he turned seventeen he took the middle name of Coraghessan, the surname of one of his ancestors. Although he did not read books until the age of eighteen, he recalls being fascinated with newspaper stories that his mother read to him. Boyle received his M.A. and his Ph.D. from the University of

Iowa, and he now teaches English at the University of Southern California in Los Angeles.

Boyle has become one of the most acclaimed satirical writers in the United States. His books include *Without a Hero, Greasy Lake and Other Stories,* and *Budding Prospects: A Pastoral.* He has been a recipient of the creative writing fellowship from the National Endowment for the Arts. He has said, "I don't want to do something small. I want to stretch as much as possible. . . . You think of these guys who burn out and you wonder if it's going to happen to you, and you pray it doesn't. I'd like to have a career like [John] Updike's . . . where you keep getting better all the time, keep changing and doing different things."

JUST LATHER, THAT'S ALL

Hernando Téllez

A dilemma *is a situation in which someone is forced to choose between two alternatives. Have you ever faced a dilemma? If so, write about your experience in a sentence or two.*

He said nothing when he entered. I was passing the best of my razors back and forth on a strop. When I recognized him I started to tremble. But he didn't notice. Hoping to conceal my emotion, I continued sharpening the razor. I tested it on the meat of my thumb, and then held it up to the light.

At that moment he took off the bullet-studded belt that his gun holster dangled from. He hung it up on a wall hook and placed his military cap over it. Then he turned to me, loosening the knot of his tie, and said, "It's hot as hell. Give me a shave." He sat in the chair.

I estimated he had a four-day beard—the four days taken up by the latest expedition in search of our troops. His face seemed reddened, burned by the sun. Carefully, I began to prepare the soap. I cut off a few slices, dropped them into the cup, mixed in a bit of warm water, and began to stir with the brush. Immediately the foam began to rise.

"The other boys in the group should have this much beard, too," he remarked. I continued stirring the lather.

"But we did all right, you know. We got the main ones. We brought back some dead, and we got some others still alive. But pretty soon they'll all be dead."

"How many did you catch?" I asked.

"Fourteen. We had to go pretty deep into the woods to find them. But we'll get even. Not one of them comes out of this alive, not one."

He leaned back on the chair when he saw me with the lather-covered brush in my hand. I still had to put the sheet on him. No doubt about it, I was upset. I took a sheet out of a drawer and knotted it around his neck. He wouldn't stop talking. He probably thought I was in sympathy with his party.

"The town must have learned a lesson from what we did," he said.

"Yes," I replied, securing the knot at the base of his dark, sweaty neck. "That was a fine show, eh?"

"Very good," I answered, turning back for the brush.

The man closed his eyes with a gesture of fatigue and sat waiting for the cool caress of the soap. I had never had him so close to me. The day he ordered the whole town to file into the patio of the school to see the four rebels hanging there, I came face to face with him for an instant. But the sight of the mutilated bodies kept me from noticing the face of the man who had directed it all, the face I was now about to take into my hands.

It was not an unpleasant face, and the beard, which made him look a bit older than he was, didn't suit him badly at all. His name was Torres—Captain Torres. A man of imagination, because who else would have thought of hanging the naked rebels and then holding target practice on their bodies?

I began to apply the first layer of soap. With his eyes closed, he continued. "Without any effort I could go straight to sleep," he said, "but there's plenty to do this afternoon."

I stopped the lathering and asked with a feigned lack of interest, "A firing squad?"

"Something like that, but a little slower."

I got on with the job of lathering his beard. My hands started trembling again. The man could not possibly realize it, and this was in my favor. But I would have preferred that he hadn't come. It was likely that many of our faction had seen him enter. And an enemy under one's roof imposes certain conditions.

I would be obliged to shave that beard like any other one, carefully, gently, like that of any customer, taking pains to see that no single pore emitted a drop of blood. Being careful to see that the little tufts of hair did not lead the blade astray. Seeing that his skin ended up clean, soft, and healthy, so that passing the back of my hand over it I couldn't feel a hair. Yes, I was secretly a rebel, but I was also a conscientious barber, and proud of the precision required of my profession.

I took the razor, opened up the two protective arms, exposed the blade, and began the job—from one of the sideburns downward. The razor responded beautifully. His beard was inflexible and hard, not too long, but thick. Bit by bit the skin emerged. The razor rasped along, making its customary sound as fluffs of lather, mixed with bits of hair, gathered along the blade.

I paused a moment to clean it, then took up the strop again to sharpen the razor, because I'm a barber who does things properly. The man, who had kept his eyes closed, opened them now, removed one of his hands from under the sheet, felt the spot on his face where the soap had been cleared off, and said, "Come to the school today at six o'clock."

"The same thing as the other day?" I asked, horrified.

"It could be even better," he said.

"What do you plan to do?"

"I don't know yet. But we'll amuse ourselves." Once more he leaned back and closed his eyes. I approached with the razor poised.

"Do you plan to punish them all?" I ventured timidly.

"All."

The soap was drying on his face. I had to hurry. In the mirror I looked towards the street. It was the same as ever—the grocery store with two or three customers in it. Then I glanced at the clock—2:20 in the afternoon.

The razor continued on its downward stroke. Now from the other sideburn down. A thick, blue beard. He should have let it grow like some poets or priests do. It would suit him well. A lot of people wouldn't recognize him. Much to his benefit, I thought, as I attempted to cover the neck area smoothly.

There, surely, the razor had to be handled masterfully, since the hair, although softer, grew into little swirls. A curly beard. One of the tiny pores could open up and issue forth its pearl of blood, but a good barber prides himself on never allowing this to happen to a customer.

How many of us had he ordered shot? How many of us had he ordered mutilated? It was better not to think about it. Torres did not know that I was his enemy. He did not know it nor did the rest. It was a secret shared by very few, precisely so that I could inform the revolutionaries of what Torres was doing in the town and of what he was planning each time he undertook a rebel-hunting excursion.

So it was going to be very difficult to explain that I had him right in my hands and let him go peacefully—alive and shaved.

The beard was now almost completely gone. He seemed younger, less burdened by years than when he had arrived. I suppose this always happens with men who visit barber shops. Under the stroke of my razor Torres was being rejuvenated—rejuvenated because I am a good barber, the best in the town, if I may say so.

How hot it is getting! Torres must be sweating as much as I. But he is a calm man, who is not even thinking about what he is going to do with the prisoners this afternoon. On the other hand I, with this razor in my hands—I stroking and restroking this skin, can't even think clearly.

Damn him for coming! I'm a revolutionary, not a murderer. And how easy it would be to kill him. And he deserves it. Does he? No! What the devil! No one deserves to have someone else make the sacrifice of becoming a murderer. What do you gain by it? Nothing. Others come along and still others, and the first ones kill the second ones, and they the next ones—and it goes on like this until everything is a sea of blood.

I could cut this throat just so—*zip, zip!* I wouldn't give him time to resist and since he has his eyes closed he wouldn't see the glistening blade or my glistening eyes. But I'm trembling like a real murderer. Out of his neck a gush of blood would spout onto the sheet, on the chair, on my hands, on the floor. I would have to close the door. And the blood would keep inching along the floor, warm, ineradicable, uncontainable, until it reached the street, like a little scarlet stream.

I'm sure that one solid stroke, one deep incision, would prevent any pain. He wouldn't suffer. But what would I do with the body? Where would I hide it? I would have to flee, leaving all I have behind, and take refuge far away. But they would follow until they found me. "Captain Torres' murderer. He slit his throat while he was shaving him—a coward." And then on the other side. "The avenger of us all. A name to remember. He was the town barber. No one knew he was defending our cause."

Murderer or hero? My destiny depends on the edge of this blade. I can turn my hand a bit more, press a little harder on the razor, and sink it in. The skin would give way like silk, like rubber. There is nothing more tender than human skin and the blood is always there, ready to pour forth.

But I don't want to be a murderer. You came to me for a shave. And I perform my work honorably . . . I don't want blood on my hands. Just lather, that's all. You are an executioner and I am only a barber. Each person has his own place in the scheme of things.

Now his chin had been stroked clean and smooth. The man sat up and looked into the mirror. He rubbed his hands over his skin and felt it fresh, like new.

"Thanks," he said. He went to the hanger for his belt, pistol, and cap. I must have been very pale; my shirt felt soaked. Torres finished adjusting the buckle, straightened his pistol in the holster, and after automatically smoothing down his hair, he put on the cap. From his pants pocket he took out several coins to pay me for my services and then headed for the door.

In the doorway he paused for a moment and said, "They told me that you'd kill me. I came to find out. But killing isn't easy. You can take my word for it." And he turned and walked away.

First Response: *What was your reaction to the story's ending?*

CHECKING UP (True/False)

1. The captain has been searching for rebel troops.
2. The barber takes pride in his work.
3. The barber is an informer for the rebels.
4. The barber has killed many of Torres's men.
5. Torres does not know that the barber is a rebel.

TALKING IT OVER

1. We learn from the narrator's opening comments that the customer's presence is making him nervous. When does it become clear that the two characters are on opposite sides of a political struggle?

2. Why does the barber feel it would be wrong to let Torres go? Why, on the other hand, does he believe it would be wrong to take the captain's life? In what way can the decision he makes affect the course of his own life?
3. What, in the end, is the barber's reason for sparing Torres?
4. Near the end of the story, the narrator makes the surprising suggestion that there is a fine line between a reputation as a hero and a reputation as a murderer. Do you agree or disagree with this opinion? Can you give some examples from real life to support your view?

TONE
Irony

You have seen that a story can have elements of **irony** (see pages 5, 26, and 128). Sometimes the tone of an entire story can be ironic.

Irony involves a difference or contrast between appearance and reality—that is, a discrepancy between what is expected or considered appropriate and what actually happens. Irony reminds us that many of life's situations are filled with incongruities, or inconsistencies. Irony can make us smile or wince. Irony can be genial or bitter.

In "Just Lather, That's All" there are three kinds of irony.

1. **Irony of situation,** in which the story's circumstances are the opposite of what would be expected or considered appropriate. In "Just Lather, That's All" it is ironic that a barber is taking pains not to spill a drop of blood from a man who is an executioner. Find passages in the story that illustrate this ironic situation.

2. **Verbal irony,** in which a character says one thing and means something entirely different. What is ironic about the barber's claim that he is a revolutionary and not a murderer?

3. **Dramatic irony,** in which the reader knows something that a character in the story does not know. For example, the narrator and the reader know that the barber is one of the revolutionaries, but they believe that Torres does not know. How is this dramatic

irony turned around, or ironically reversed, in the last paragraph of the story?

UNDERSTANDING THE WORDS IN THE STORY
(Matching Columns)

1. caress		a. gave forth; discharged
2. feigned		b. short trip
3. faction		c. permanent; irremovable
4. obliged		d. gentle touch
5. emitted		e. made youthful again
6. conscientious		f. shining; sparkling
7. excursion		g. pretended
8. rejuvenated		h. careful; responsible
9. glistening		i. dissenting group
10. ineradicable		j. compelled; forced

WRITING IT DOWN
An Opinion

In facing the dilemma of whether to take his enemy's life or let him leave peacefully, the barber takes many factors into consideration and makes several points about right and wrong.

Do you agree with his decision? Do you think that he took the honorable course of action? Write your answer to these questions in a brief essay. Begin by summarizing the barber's arguments for and against each course of action.

A Defense

Imagine that you are the barber in the story. Your fellow revolutionaries have discovered that Torres was in your hands and that you let him go peacefully. What will you say to them? How will you defend your decision? Write down your answer in a paragraph or two.

SPEAKING AND LISTENING
Discussing a Comment

At the end of the story, Torres says to the barber, ". . . killing isn't easy. You can take my word for it."

Does this statement in any way change your opinion of the captain? What do you think he means by this comment? Does it suggest that he might have some redeeming qualities, or does it reveal something else about him? Think about these questions for a few minutes and discuss your answers with your classmates.

ABOUT THE AUTHOR

Hernando Téllez (1908–1966) was born in Bogotá, Colombia. When he was not yet seventeen, he became a contributor to the weekly *Mundo al Día*. Two years later, he began to write for the magazine *Universidad*, which attracted many talented writers. By the age of twenty-one, Téllez had become a member of the staff of *El Tiempo*, one of the biggest newspapers in Latin America. In the following years he also became a political worker, and in 1934 he entered the City Council of Bogotá. In 1937 he was named Colombian consul in Marseilles, and in 1943 and 1944 he was a Colombian senator.

Téllez's books began to appear in 1943, and in 1950 his most famous collection of stories, *Cenizas para el viento*, was published. In 1959 he was named Colombian Ambassador to UNESCO in Paris. Téllez once said, "Grammar, rhetoric, literary composition, gave me generous compensation for what to me was the tacit cruelty of studying mathematics. . . . One day, my teacher of rhetoric, who was a young cleric who 'made' verses, hiding from his superiors, while the students were busy copying long segments of the *Aeneid* or the *Odyssey*, told me: 'Thank God, you are a terrible mathematics student. You have no recourse but to make a living through literature. Learn how to write.' These words did not impress me then. I have later understood how much they meant in [determining] the path of my vocation. . . ."

THE EMPEROR'S NEW CLOTHES

Hans Christian Andersen

How are swindlers and con artists able to get what they want from people? Think for a moment and then discuss this question with your classmates.

Many years ago there lived an Emperor who was so exceedingly fond of fine new clothes that he spent all his money on being elaborately dressed. He took no interest in his soldiers, no interest in the theater, nor did he care to drive about in his state coach, unless it were to show off his new clothes. He had different robes for every hour of the day, and just as one says of a King that he is in his Council Chamber, people always said of him, "The Emperor is in his wardrobe!"

The great city in which he lived was full of gaiety. Strangers were always coming and going. One day two swindlers arrived; they made themselves out to be weavers, and said they knew how to weave the most magnificent fabric that one could imagine. Not only were the colors and patterns unusually beautiful, but the clothes that were made of this material had the extraordinary quality of becoming invisible to everyone who was either unfit for his post, or inexcusably stupid.

"What useful clothes to have!" thought the Emperor. "If I had some like that, I might find out which of the people in my Empire are unfit for their posts. I should also be able to distinguish the wise from the fools. Yes, that material must be woven for me immediately!" Then he gave the swindlers large sums of money so that they could start work at once.

Quickly they set up two looms and pretended to weave, but there was not a trace of anything on the frames. They made no bones about demanding the finest silk and the purest gold thread. They stuffed everything into their bags, and continued to work at the empty looms until late into the night.

"I'm rather anxious to know how much of the material is finished," thought the Emperor, but to tell the truth, he felt a bit uneasy, remembering that anyone who was either a fool or unfit for his post would never be able to see it. He rather imagined that he need not have any fear for himself, yet he thought it wise to send someone else first to see how things were going. Everyone in the town knew about the exceptional powers of the material, and all were eager to know how incompetent or how stupid their neighbors might be.

"I will send my honest old Chamberlain[1] to the weavers," thought the Emperor. "He will be able to judge the fabric better than anyone else, for he has brains, and nobody fills his post better than he does."

So the nice old Chamberlain went into the hall where the two swindlers were sitting working at the empty looms.

"Upon my life!" he thought, opening his eyes very wide, "I can't see anything at all!" But he didn't say so.

Both the swindlers begged him to be good enough to come nearer, and asked how he liked the unusual design and the splendid colors. They pointed to the empty looms, and the poor old Chamberlain opened his eyes wider and wider, but he could see nothing, for there was nothing. "Heavens above!" he thought, "could it possibly be that I am stupid? I have never thought that of myself, and not a soul must know it. Could it be that I am not fit for my post? It will never do for me to admit that I can't see the material!"

"Well, you don't say what you think of it," said one of the weavers.

"Oh, it's delightful—most exquisite!" said the old Chamberlain, looking through his spectacles. "What a wonderful design and what beautiful colors! I shall certainly tell the Emperor that I am enchanted with it."

"We're very pleased to hear that," said the two weavers, and they started describing the colors and the curious pattern. The old Chamberlain listened carefully in order to repeat, when he came home to the Emperor, exactly what he had heard, and he did so.

The swindlers now demanded more money, as well as more silk and gold thread, saying that they needed it for weaving. They put everything

---

1. **Chamberlain** (chām′bər-lĭn): a high official at court.

into their pockets and not a thread appeared upon the looms, but they kept on working at the empty frames as before.

Soon after this, the Emperor sent another nice official to see how the weaving was getting on, and to inquire whether the stuff would soon be ready. Exactly the same thing happened to him as to the Chamberlain. He looked and looked, but as there was nothing to be seen except the empty looms, he could see nothing.

"Isn't it a beautiful piece of material?" said the swindlers, showing and describing the pattern that did not exist at all.

"Stupid I certainly am not," thought the official; "then I must be unfit for my excellent post, I suppose. That seems rather funny—but I'll take great care that nobody gets wind of it." Then he praised the material he could not see, and assured them of his enthusiasm for the gorgeous colors and the beautiful pattern. "It's simply enchanting!" he said to the Emperor.

The whole town was talking about the splendid material.

And now the Emperor was curious to see it for himself while it was still upon the looms.

Accompanied by a great number of selected people, among whom were the two nice old officials who had already been there, the Emperor went forth to visit the two wily swindlers. They were now weaving madly, yet without a single thread upon the looms.

"Isn't it magnificent?" said the two nice officials. "Will your Imperial Majesty deign to look at this splendid pattern and these glorious colors?" Then they pointed to the empty looms, for each thought that the others could probably see the material.

"What on earth can this mean?" thought the Emperor. "I don't see anything! This is terrible. Am I stupid? Am I unfit to be Emperor? That would be the most disastrous thing that could possibly befall me.—Oh, it's perfectly wonderful!" he said. "It quite meets with my Imperial approval." And he nodded appreciatively and stared at the empty looms—he would not admit that he saw nothing. His whole suite looked and looked, but with as little result as the others; nevertheless, they all said, like the Emperor, "It's perfectly wonderful!" They advised him to have some new clothes made from this splendid stuff and to wear them for the first time in the next great procession.

"Magnificent!" "Excellent!" "Prodigious!"[2] went from mouth to mouth, and everyone was exceedingly pleased. The Emperor gave each of the swindlers a decoration to wear in his buttonhole, and the title of "Knight of the Loom."

Before the procession they worked all night, burning more than sixteen candles. People could see how busy they were finishing the Emperor's new clothes. They pretended to take the material from the looms, they slashed the air with great scissors, they sewed with needles without any thread, and finally they said, "The Emperor's clothes are ready!"

Then the Emperor himself arrived with his most distinguished courtiers, and each swindler raised an arm as if he were holding something, and said, "These are Your Imperial Majesty's knee breeches. This is Your Imperial Majesty's robe. This is Your Imperial Majesty's mantle," and so forth. "It is all as light as a spider's web, one might fancy one had nothing on, but that is just the beauty of it!"

"Yes, indeed," said all the courtiers, but they could see nothing, for there was nothing to be seen.

"If Your Imperial Majesty would graciously consent to take off your clothes," said the swindlers, "we could fit on the new ones in front of the long glass."

So the Emperor laid aside his clothes, and the swindlers pretended to hand him, piece by piece, the new ones they were supposed to have made, and they fitted him round the waist, and acted as if they were fastening something on—it was the train;[3] and the Emperor turned round and round in front of the long glass.

"How well the new robes suit Your Imperial Majesty! How well they fit!" they all said. "What a splendid design! What gorgeous colors! It's all magnificently regal!"

"The canopy which is to be held over Your Imperial Majesty in the procession is waiting outside," announced the Lord High Chamberlain.

"Well, I suppose I'm ready," said the Emperor. "Don't you think they are a nice fit?" And he looked at himself again in the glass, first on one side and then the other, as if he really were carefully examining his handsome attire.

2. **prodigious** (prə-dĭj'əs): amazing.
3. **train:** the part of the robe that trails behind.

The courtiers who were to carry the train groped about on the floor with fumbling fingers, and pretended to lift it; they walked on, holding their hands up in the air; nothing would have induced them to admit that they could not see anything.

And so the Emperor set off in the procession under the beautiful canopy, and everybody in the streets and at the windows said, "Oh! how superb the Emperor's new clothes are! What a gorgeous train! What a perfect fit!" No one would acknowledge that he didn't see anything, so proving that he was not fit for his post, or that he was very stupid.

None of the Emperor's clothes had ever met with such a success.

"But he hasn't got any clothes on!" gasped out a little child.

"Good heavens! Hark at the little innocent!" said the father, and people whispered to one another what the child had said. "But he hasn't got any clothes on! There's a little child saying he hasn't got any clothes on!"

"But he hasn't got any clothes on!" shouted the whole town at last. The Emperor had a creepy feeling down his spine, because it began to dawn upon him that the people were right. "All the same," he thought to himself, "I've got to go through with it as long as the procession lasts."

So he drew himself up and held his head higher than before, and the courtiers held on to the train that wasn't there at all.

First Response: *How did you feel toward the people who were deceived by the swindlers?*

CHECKING UP (True/False)

1. The swindlers in this story take advantage of the Emperor's vanity.
2. The swindlers claim that their fabric is invisible to anyone who is dishonest or cowardly.

3. The old Chamberlain pretends to admire the fabric because he wishes to trap the swindlers.

4. The only honest person in the story is a little child.

5. At the end of the story, the people of the town admit that the Emperor hasn't got any clothes on.

TALKING IT OVER

1. What does the Emperor's obsession with fine clothes reveal about his character?

2. Why are the swindlers able to dupe the Emperor, the Chamberlain, the courtiers, and the people watching the procession?

3. How does the child's innocence expose the folly and deceitfulness of the other people in the story?

4. At the end of the story, the Emperor realizes that he has been tricked. Why does he decide, nevertheless, to go through with the procession?

5. The swindlers claim that people who cannot see the cloth are stupid or unfit for their posts. How do the events of the story show, ironically, that this judgment is true?

THEME
Understanding Theme

Is "The Emperor's New Clothes" really about clothes?

Although clothes—real or imaginary—are the focus of the story, we sense that the events in the tale are meant to illustrate something about human nature. The Emperor and all his subjects are willing to agree to an outrageous falsehood rather than risk being accused of stupidity or incompetence. The clothes in the story are central to the underlying notion that people need a flattering image of themselves. This is the central idea, or **theme,** that is developed in the story.

Not every story can be said to have a theme. Mysteries and adventure stories are told mainly for entertainment, and theme is generally of little or no significance in them. Theme is an important element in those stories that offer insight into human behavior.

Sometimes theme is expressed directly in a story. Most of the time, however, the theme must be inferred from other elements in the story.

How would you state the theme, or central idea, of "The Emperor's New Clothes"?

UNDERSTANDING THE WORDS IN THE STORY (Completion)

suite	induced
wily	exquisite
dawn	attire
imperial	deign
regal	acknowledge

1. The old Chamberlain told the two swindlers that their work was _____.
2. The Emperor finally went in person to see what the two _____ swindlers had woven.
3. They asked if the Emperor would _____ to examine the cloth.
4. The Emperor nodded and said that the fabric had his _____ approval.
5. The Emperor's entire _____ looked at the empty looms and said that the material was wonderful.
6. The courtiers praised the splendor of the _____ robes.
7. The Emperor looked at himself in the mirror, pretending to admire his _____.
8. The courtiers could not be _____ to admit that they could not see the cloth.
9. The people watching the procession would not _____ that they could not see the Emperor's new clothes.
10. Finally, it began to _____ upon the Emperor that he had been swindled.

WRITING IT DOWN
Ideas for a Theme

Get together with your classmates and compile a list of well-known sayings and proverbs. Choose three that you find especially appealing. Here are some examples:

> A fool and his money are soon parted.
> A penny saved is a penny earned.
> The bigger they come, the harder they fall.
> Don't be penny-wise and pound-foolish.
> People who live in glass houses shouldn't throw stones.
> The early bird gets the worm.

Think about the sayings that you have chosen and make sure you understand what each means. Then think of stories or incidents from your experience that could illustrate the sayings, and jot down a few notes about the plot, characters, and setting for each story. When you have finished writing, get together with a small group to discuss your notes. Which sayings seem to function best as themes for stories?

ABOUT THE AUTHOR

Hans Christian Andersen (1805–1875) was born in Odense, a small fishing village in Denmark. His parents were very poor—his father was a shoemaker—but they managed to take him to the theater when he was seven years old. After this experience Andersen yearned to be an actor and a dramatist. When he was eleven years old his father died, and Andersen left school. In 1819 he ran away to Copenhagen, Denmark's capital, where he drifted in and out of theatrical and musical circles.

Andersen published his first book, *The Ghost at Palnatoke's Grave*, in 1822. His work came to the attention of the Danish king, and he received a royal scholarship, which allowed him to continue his education for the next six years.

Andersen released his *Fairy Tales* in installments beginning in 1835 and stretching over the next thirty-seven years. Although he considered himself a novelist, poet, and playwright, Andersen has always been known primarily for his fairy tales. Along with much of his other work, they found a warmer reception abroad than in Denmark. Some of Andersen's best-known tales are "The Ugly Duckling," "The Red Shoes," "The Nightingale," and "The Princess and the Pea."

A NINCOMPOOP

Anton Chekhov°

Are there times when a harsh lesson is more effective than a gentle one? Can you think of any examples? Discuss your answer with a small group of classmates.

A few days ago I asked my children's governess, Julia Vassilyevna,[1] to come into my study.

"Sit down, Julia Vassilyevna," I said. "Let's settle our accounts. Although you most likely need some money, you stand on ceremony and won't ask for it yourself. Now then, we agreed on thirty rubles a month. . . ."

"Forty."

"No, thirty. I made a note of it. I always pay the governess thirty. Now then, you've been here two months, so . . ."

"Two months and five days."

"Exactly two months. I made a specific note of it. That means you have sixty rubles coming to you. Subtract nine Sundays . . . you know you didn't work with Kolya[2] on Sundays, you only took walks. And three holidays . . ."

Julia Vassilyevna flushed a deep red and picked at the flounce of her dress, but—not a word.

"Three holidays, therefore take off twelve rubles. Four days Kolya was sick and there were no lessons, as you were occupied only with Vanya.[3] Three days you had a toothache and my wife gave you permission not to work after lunch. Twelve and seven—nineteen. Subtract . . . that leaves . . . hmm . . . forty-one rubles. Correct?"

Julia Vassilyevna's left eye reddened and filled with moisture. Her chin trembled; she coughed nervously and blew her nose, but—not a word.

"Around New Year's you broke a teacup and saucer: take off two

---

°**Chekhov** (chĕk′ôf′).

1. **Vassilyevna** (vä-sēl′yĕv-nä).

2. **Kolya** (kôl′yä): short for Nikolai.

3. **Vanya** (vän′yä): short for Ivan.

rubles. The cup cost more, it was an heirloom, but—let it go. When didn't I take a loss! Then, due to your neglect, Kolya climbed a tree and tore his jacket: take away ten. Also due to your heedlessness the maid stole Vanya's shoes. You ought to watch everything! You get paid for it. So, that means five more rubles off. The tenth of January I gave you ten rubles. . . ."

"You didn't," whispered Julia Vassilyevna.

"But I made a note of it."

"Well . . . all right."

"Take twenty-seven from forty-one—that leaves fourteen."

Both eyes filled with tears. Perspiration appeared on the thin, pretty little nose. Poor girl!

"Only once was I given any money," she said in a trembling voice, "and that was by your wife. Three rubles, nothing more."

"Really? You see now, and I didn't make a note of it! Take three from fourteen . . . leaves eleven. Here's your money, my dear. Three, three, three, one and one. Here it is!"

I handed her eleven rubles. She took them and with trembling fingers stuffed them into her pocket.

"*Merci*,"[4] she whispered.

I jumped up and started pacing the room. I was overcome with anger.

"For what, this—'*merci*'?" I asked.

"For the money."

"But you know I've cheated you—robbed you! I have actually stolen from you! *Why* this '*merci*'?"

"In my other places they didn't give me anything at all."

"They didn't give you anything? No wonder! I played a little joke on you, a cruel lesson, just to teach you. . . . I'm going to give you the entire eighty rubles! Here they are in an envelope all ready for you. . . . Is it really possible to be so spineless? Why don't you protest? Why be silent? Is it possible in this world to be without teeth and claws—to be such a nincompoop?"

She smiled crookedly and I read in her expression: "It is possible."

---

4. *Merci* (mâr-sē´): French for "Thank you." During the nineteenth century in czarist Russia, French was spoken by the upper classes.

I asked her pardon for the cruel lesson and, to her great surprise, gave her the eighty rubles. She murmured her little *"merci"* several times and went out. I looked after her and thought: "How easy it is to crush the weak in this world!"

_____

First Response: *How did you feel about the girl in the story? Did you find her foolish or did you feel sympathy for her?*

CHECKING UP (True/False)

1. The person telling the story is Julia Vassilyevna's employer.
2. The narrator wishes to cheat the girl.
3. Julia Vassilyevna works as a maid.
4. Julia Vassilyevna is used to being cheated.
5. At the end of the story, the girl decides to leave her job.

TALKING IT OVER

1. Why is the narrator "overcome with anger" at the girl's passive acceptance of the eleven rubles?
2. The speaker says he wants to teach the girl "a cruel lesson." What is the lesson he wishes her to learn?
3. In your opinion, does Julia Vassilyevna learn the lesson? Give reasons for your answer.
4. Do you think that the speaker learns another lesson from this episode? Explain your answer.
5. Do the lessons in this story have any application in today's world? Support your answer with some examples from your own experience or from your reading.

THEME
Explicit Theme

A **theme** is the controlling idea behind a story. It expresses a point of view about life or gives us insight into human behavior. Sometimes an author makes the theme of a story **explicit,** or plain, through direct statement. The last sentence of "A Nincompoop" leaves no doubt about the meaning of Chekhov's story. His tale of the pathetic governess, who can be so easily bullied, dramatizes his compassion for weak and defenseless creatures in society.

Cite some specific passages in the story that help to create sympathy for Julia Vassilyevna.

UNDERSTANDING THE WORDS IN THE STORY
(Matching Columns)

1. governess
2. ceremony
3. flushed
4. flounce
5. heirloom
6. heedlessness
7. spineless
8. protest
9. nincompoop
10. expression

a. turned red
b. object to
c. look
d. precious possession
e. cowardly
f. fool
g. ruffle
h. instructor
i. carelessness
j. formal act

WRITING IT DOWN
A Story Map

If you have completed Ideas for a Theme on page 340, choose one of the story ideas that you have developed to illustrate a proverb or saying. Add characters, situations, and other details to the story idea by filling out a story map such as the one on page 346.

STORY MAP

TITLE: _____

POINT OF VIEW: _____

TONE: _____

THEME: _____

SETTING
  Time: _____
  Place: _____

CHARACTERS:
_____
_____
_____

PLOT
  Exposition: _____
  Conflict: _____
  Event: _____
  Event: _____
  Event: _____
  Climax: _____
  Resolution: _____

ABOUT THE AUTHOR

Anton Chekhov (1860–1904), the son of a failed shopkeeper and the grandson of a serf, was born in Taganrog, a tiny Russian town on the Sea of Azov. He is the only great Russian writer of the nineteenth century to have received a public school education; all the others—Tolstoy and Dostoevsky among them—were tutored privately.

While he was in medical school in Moscow, Chekhov supported his family by writing one story a day. By the time he was twenty-seven he had written more than six hundred stories. Although increasingly admired and respected for his stories and powerful plays, Chekhov considered himself a hack writer. It was not until 1888, when he won the Pushkin Prize, that he began to take his writing seriously. "A Nincompoop," like many of Chekhov's works, portrays characters trapped in situations from which they cannot escape. Julia Vassilyevna's meek resignation illustrates Chekhov's compassion for the humble and powerless, a compassion borne out by his free treatment of a thousand patients a year at his home outside Moscow. While providing care to those in need, however, he ignored his own battle with tuberculosis.

When he was thirty, Chekhov journeyed five thousand miles to investigate the treatment of prisoners in a Siberian penal colony. There he interviewed 160 prisoners each day and deepened his understanding of human strengths and weaknesses. By the time he died at Yalta, at age forty-four, he had changed the short story forever.

AMBUSH

Tim O'Brien

Recall an event from your experience that you wish had ended differently. In a brief paragraph write the ending that you wish had taken place.

When she was nine, my daughter Kathleen asked if I had ever killed anyone. She knew about the war; she knew I'd been a soldier. "You keep writing these war stories," she said, "so I guess you must've killed somebody." It was a difficult moment, but I did what seemed right, which was to say, "Of course not," and then to take her onto my lap and hold her for a while. Someday, I hope, she'll ask again. But here I want to pretend she's a grown-up. I want to tell her exactly what happened, or what I remember happening, and then I want to say to her that as a little girl she was absolutely right. This is why I keep writing war stories:

He was a short, slender young man of about twenty. I was afraid of him—afraid of something—and as he passed me on the trail I threw a grenade that exploded at his feet and killed him.

Or to go back:

Shortly after midnight we moved into the ambush site outside My Khe. The whole platoon was there, spread out in the dense brush along the trail, and for five hours nothing at all happened. We were working in two-man teams—one man on guard while the other slept, switching off every two hours—and I remember it was still dark when Kiowa shook me awake for the final watch. The night was foggy and hot. For the first few moments I felt lost, not sure about directions, groping for my helmet and weapon. I reached out and found three grenades and lined them up in front of me; the pins had already been straightened for quick throwing. And then for maybe half an hour I kneeled there and waited. Very gradually, in tiny slivers, dawn began to break through the fog, and from my position in the brush I could see ten or fifteen meters up the trail. The mosquitoes were fierce. I remember slapping at them, wondering if I should wake up Kiowa and ask for some repellent, then thinking it was a bad idea, then looking up and seeing the young man come out of the fog. He wore black clothing and rubber sandals and a gray ammunition belt. His shoulders were slightly stooped, his head cocked to the side as if listening for something. He seemed at ease. He carried his weapon in one hand, muzzle down, moving without any hurry up the center of the trail. There was no sound at all—none that I can remember. In a way, it seemed, he was part of the morning fog, or my own imagination, but there was also the reality of what was happening in my stomach. I had already pulled the pin on a grenade. I had come up to a crouch. It was entirely automatic. I did not hate the young man; I did not see him as the enemy; I did not ponder issues of morality or politics or military duty. I crouched and kept my head low. I tried to swallow whatever was rising from my stomach, which tasted like lemonade, something fruity and sour. I was terrified. There were no thoughts about killing. The grenade was to make him go away—just evaporate—and I leaned back and felt my mind go empty and then felt it fill up again. I had already thrown the grenade before telling myself to throw it. The brush was thick and I had to lob it high, not aiming, and I remember the grenade seeming to freeze above me for an instant, as if a camera had clicked, and I remember ducking down and holding my breath and seeing little wisps of fog rise from the earth. The grenade bounced once and rolled across the trail. I did not hear it, but there must've been a sound, because the young man dropped his weapon and began to run, just two or three quick steps, then he hesitated, swiveling to his right, and he glanced down at the grenade and tried to cover his head but never did. It occurred to me then that he was about to die. I wanted to warn him. The grenade made a popping noise—not soft but not loud either—not what I'd expected—and there was a puff of dust and smoke—a small white puff—and the young man seemed to jerk upward as if pulled by invisible wires. He fell on his back. His rubber sandals had been blown off. There was no wind. He lay at the center of the trail, his right leg bent beneath him, his one eye shut, his other eye a huge star-shaped hole.

It was not a matter of live or die. There was no real peril. Almost certainly the young man would have passed by. And it will always be that way.

Later, I remember, Kiowa tried to tell me that the man would've died anyway. He told me that it was a good kill, that I was a soldier and this was a war, that I should shape up and stop staring and ask myself what the dead man would've done if things were reversed.

None of it mattered. The words seemed far too complicated. All I could do was gape at the fact of the young man's body.

Even now I haven't finished sorting it out. Sometimes I forgive myself, other times I don't. In the ordinary hours of life I try not to dwell on it, but now and then, when I'm reading a newspaper or just sitting alone in a room, I'll look up and see the young man coming out of the morning fog. I'll watch him walk toward me, his shoulders slightly stooped, his head cocked to the side, and he'll pass within a few yards of me and suddenly smile at some secret thought and then continue up the trail to where it bends back into the fog.

First Response: *How did you feel toward the narrator at the end of the story?*

CHECKING UP (Multiple-Choice)

1. The narrator recounts the episode to
   a. protest the war
   b. show how brave he was
   c. explain why he keeps writing war stories
2. The episode takes place on a
   a. sunny day
   b. windy night
   c. foggy morning
3. As the young man moved up the trail, the narrator felt
   a. courageous
   b. terrified
   c. angry

4. After the grenade landed, the narrator
   a. wanted to warn the young man
   b. wanted to run away
   c. felt great relief
5. Kiowa told the narrator that
   a. they had been in peril
   b. his act was courageous
   c. he had done the right thing

TALKING IT OVER

1. At the beginning of the story, the narrator does not want to answer his daughter's question. Why does he hope that she will ask him the same question again when she is older?
2. What kind of atmosphere, or mood, does the story's setting help create?
3. Just as the grenade was about to land, the narrator realized that he had made a mistake. How does he explain his action? What internal conflict did he face after the incident occurred? How did his fellow soldier, Kiowa, try to justify the action?
4. The title refers to the narrator's "ambush" of his unsuspecting enemy. How does the ending suggest that, long after the episode, the young man would, in a sense, "ambush" the narrator?

THEME
Implied Theme

Writers seldom express their themes directly. Most of the time, the theme of a story is **implied**—that is, readers have to work out the theme on their own.

Sometimes one or two key passages will point the way to the theme. In O'Brien's story, the narrator says:

> I did not hate the young man; I did not see him as the enemy; I did not ponder issues of morality or politics or military duty.

None of it mattered. The words seemed far too complicated. All I could do was gape at the fact of the young
man's body.
Even now I haven't finished sorting it out. . . .

The narrator is saying that although various moral, political, and
logical arguments are given to justify war, the fact remains that
when war is waged, people lose their lives.

Why does the narrator keep writing war stories?

WRITING IT DOWN
A Comparison

If you have read "War" on page 70, you will recall that Pirandello's
story also explores the way in which war affects people's lives. What
is the theme of that story? In a brief essay compare the messages
about war conveyed in the stories by Pirandello and O'Brien.

SPEAKING AND LISTENING
Comparing Two Works

Many writers have addressed the theme of war and its effects on
those who participate in it. One example is the following poem,
which was written by the English novelist and poet Thomas Hardy
(1840–1928). After you have read the poem, hold a class discussion. Compare the thoughts expressed by the speaker in Hardy's
poem with the comments of the narrator in O'Brien's story.

THE MAN HE KILLED

"Had he and I but met
By some old ancient inn,
We should have sat us down to wet
Right many a nipperkin!°

4. **nipperkin:** a small cup or glass for drinking beer and wine.

    "But ranged as infantry,   5
     And staring face to face,
 I shot at him as he at me,
     And killed him in his place.

    "I shot him dead because—
     Because he was my foe,   10
 Just so: my foe of course he was;
     That's clear enough; although

    "He thought he'd 'list,° perhaps,
     Offhand like—just as I—
Was out of work—had sold his traps—   15
     No other reason why.

    "Yes; quaint and curious war is!
     You shoot a fellow down
You'd treat if met where any bar is,
     Or help to half-a-crown."°   20

13. **'list:** enlist.   20. **help to half-a-crown:** lend a coin worth two and a half shillings.

ABOUT THE AUTHOR

Tim O'Brien was born in Austin, Minnesota, in 1946. After his graduation from Macalester College, he was drafted into the army and sent to Vietnam, even though he believed that the war was wrong and had protested against it. He has said that he went to war to stay loved by his family and not to disappoint the people of his town, and this inclination toward goodness—good actions, good words, good hearts—is at the heart of his writing. In the stories he has written of his war experiences, O'Brien conveys the complexity of human feelings and behavior.

If I Die in a Combat Zone, Box Me Up and Ship Me Home (1973) was O'Brien's first work on the theme of life and war. The book drew high praise not only from critics, but also from Vietnam veterans. O'Brien has also written three novels, *Northern Lights* (1974), *Going After Cacciato* (1978), and *In the Lake of the Woods* (1994). "Ambush" is taken from a book called *The Things They Carried* (1990), a collection of fictional episodes.

A GAME OF CATCH

Richard Wilbur

What sports do you enjoy playing or watching? Jot down a few words that come to mind when you think of that sport.

Monk and Glennie were playing catch on the side lawn of the firehouse when Scho caught sight of them. They were good at it, for seventh-graders, as anyone could see right away. Monk, wearing a catcher's mitt, would lean easily sidewise and back, with one leg lifted and his throwing hand almost down to the grass, and then lob the white ball straight up into the sunlight. Glennie would shield his eyes with his left hand and, just as the ball fell past him, snag it with a little dart of his glove. Then he would burn the ball straight toward Monk, and it would spank into the round mitt and sit, like a still-life apple on a plate,[1] until Monk flipped it over into his right hand and, with a negligent flick of his hanging arm, gave Glennie a fast grounder.

They were going on and on like that, in a kind of slow, mannered,[2] luxurious dance in the sun, their faces perfectly blank and entranced, when Glennie noticed Scho dawdling along the other side of the street and called hello to him. Scho crossed over and stood at the front edge of the lawn, near an apple tree, watching.

"Got your glove?" asked Glennie after a time. Scho obviously hadn't.

"You could give me some easy grounders," said Scho. "But don't burn 'em."

"All right," Glennie said. He moved off a little, so the three of them formed a triangle, and they passed the ball around for about five minutes, Monk tossing easy grounders to Scho, Scho throwing to Glennie, and Glennie burning them in to Monk. After a while, Monk began to throw them back to Glennie once or twice before he let Scho have his grounder, and finally Monk gave Scho a fast, bumpy grounder that hopped over his shoulder and went into the brake on the other side of the street.

---

1. **still-life . . . plate:** A still life is a painting that uses objects such as fruit or flowers as its subject.
2. **mannered** (măn′ərd): having specified movements.

"Not so hard," called Scho as he ran across to get it.

"You should've had it," Monk shouted.

It took Scho a little while to find the ball among the ferns and dead leaves, and when he saw it, he grabbed it up and threw it toward Glennie. It struck the trunk of the apple tree, bounced back at an angle, and rolled steadily and stupidly onto the cement apron in front of the firehouse, where one of the trucks was parked. Scho ran hard and stopped it just before it rolled under the truck, and this time he carried it back to his former position on the lawn and threw it carefully to Glennie.

"I got an idea," said Glennie. "Why don't Monk and I catch for five minutes more, and then you can borrow one of our gloves?"

"That's all right with me," said Monk. He socked his fist into his mitt, and Glennie burned one in.

"All right," Scho said, and went over and sat under the tree. There in the shade he watched them resume their skillful play. They threw lazily fast or lazily slow—high, low, or wide—and always handsomely, their expressions serene, changeless and forgetful. When Monk missed a low backhand catch, he walked indolently after the ball and, hardly even looking, flung it sidearm for an imaginary putout. After a good while of this, Scho said, "Isn't it five minutes yet?"

"One minute to go," said Monk, with a fraction of a grin.

Scho stood up and watched the ball slap back and forth for several minutes more, and then he turned and pulled himself up into the crotch of the tree.

"Where you going?" Monk asked.

"Just up the tree," Scho said.

"I guess he doesn't want to catch," said Monk.

Scho went up and up through the fat light-gray branches until they grew slender and bright and gave under him. He found a place where several supple branches were knit to make a dangerous chair, and sat there with his head coming out of the leaves into the sunlight. He could see the two other boys down below, the ball going back and forth between them as if they were bowling on the grass, and Glennie's crewcut head looking like a sea urchin.

"I found a wonderful seat up here," Scho said loudly. "If I don't fall out." Monk and Glennie didn't look up or comment, and so he began jouncing gently in his chair of branches and singing "Yo-ho, heave ho" in an exaggerated way.

"Do you know what, Monk?" he announced in a few minutes. "I can make you two guys do anything I want. Catch that ball, Monk! Now you catch it, Glennie!"

"I was going to catch it anyway," Monk suddenly said. "You're not making anybody do anything when they're already going to do it anyway."

"I made you say what you just said," Scho replied joyfully.

"No, you didn't," said Monk, still throwing and catching but now less serenely absorbed in the game.

"That's what I wanted you to say," Scho said.

The ball bounded off the rim of Monk's mitt and plowed into a gladiolus bed beside the firehouse, and Monk ran to get it while Scho jounced in his treetop and sang, "I wanted you to miss that. Anything you do is what I wanted you to do."

"Let's quit for a minute," Glennie suggested.

"We might as well, until the peanut gallery[3] shuts up," Monk said.

They went over and sat cross-legged in the shade of the tree. Scho looked down between his legs and saw them on the dim, spotty ground, saying nothing to one another. Glennie soon began abstractedly spinning his glove between his palms; Monk pulled his nose and stared out across the lawn.

"I want you to mess around with your nose, Monk," said Scho, giggling. Monk withdrew his hand from his face.

"Do that with your glove, Glennie," Scho persisted. "Monk, I want you to pull up hunks of grass and chew on it."

Glennie looked up and saw a self-delighted, intense face staring down at him through the leaves. "Stop being a dope and come down and we'll catch for a few minutes," he said.

Scho hesitated, and then said, in a tentatively mocking voice, "That's what I wanted you to say."

"All right, then, nuts to you," said Glennie.

3. **peanut gallery:** the topmost section of the balcony in a theater, where the cheaper seats are found.

"Why don't you keep quiet and stop bothering people?" Monk asked.

"I made you say that," Scho replied, softly.

"Shut up," Monk said.

"I made you say that, and I want you to be standing there looking sore. And I want you to climb up the tree. I'm making you do it!"

Monk was scrambling up through the branches, awkward in his haste, and getting snagged on twigs. His face was furious and foolish, and he kept telling Scho to shut up, shut up, shut up, while the other's exuberant and panicky voice poured down upon his head.

"*Now* you shut up or you'll be sorry," Monk said, breathing hard as he reached up and threatened to shake the cradle of slight branches in which Scho was sitting.

"I *want*——" Scho screamed as he fell. Two lower branches broke his rustling, crackling fall, but he landed on his back with a deep thud and lay still, with a strangled look on his face and his eyes clenched. Glennie knelt down and asked breathlessly, "Are you O.K., Scho? Are you O.K.?" while Monk swung down through the leaves crying that honestly he hadn't even touched him, the crazy guy just let go. Scho doubled up and turned over on his right side, and now both the other boys knelt beside him, pawing at his shoulder and begging to know how he was.

Then Scho rolled away from them and sat partly up, still struggling to get his wind but forcing a species of smile onto his face.

"I'm sorry, Scho," Monk said. "I didn't mean to make you fall."

Scho's voice came out weak and gravelly, in gasps. "I meant—you to do it. You—had to. You can't do—anything—unless—I want—you to."

Glennie and Monk looked helplessly at him as he sat there, breathing a bit more easily and smiling fixedly, with tears in his eyes. Then they picked up their gloves and the ball, walked over to the street, and went slowly away down the sidewalk, Monk punching his fist into the mitt, Glennie juggling the ball between glove and hand.

From under the apple tree, Scho, still bent over a little for lack of breath, croaked after them in triumph and misery, "I want you to do whatever you're going to do for the whole rest of your life!"

___

First Response: *Did your opinion of any of the characters change as the story developed? Explain your answer.*

CHECKING UP

Arrange the following events in the order in which they occur in the story.

> Scho begins singing in an exaggerated way.
> Monk and Glennie kneel beside Scho, asking how he is.
> Scho falls from the tree and lands on his back.
> Monk throws a bumpy grounder to Scho.
> Monk begins to climb the apple tree.
> Glennie asks Scho if he has his glove.
> Scho stands on the lawn watching Monk and Glennie play catch.
> Scho throws a ball that strikes the trunk of the apple tree and bounces onto the sidewalk in front of the firehouse.
> Scho pulls himself up into the apple tree.
> Monk and Glennie stop the game and sit down under the apple tree.

TALKING IT OVER

1. The game of catch between Monk and Glennie is described as a kind of "dance in the sun." What features of dancing does the narrator have in mind?
2. What problem does Scho's presence introduce? Why do you suppose Monk and Glennie ease Scho out of the game?
3. Some people react to rejection by withdrawing or showing anger. How does Scho get even with the other boys? What makes his "game" effective?
4. At the end of the story, is the conflict between Scho and the other boys resolved? Or does it take another form?
5. Why do children's games often end in conflicts or broken friendships? What insight does this story offer into the relationships and motivations of young people?

THEME
Theme and Conflict

A story that offers insight into human behavior has a **theme**. One way to uncover the theme of a story is to examine the **conflict** faced by its characters. If you have read "Ambush" (page 348), you have seen how the narrator's comments reveal his internal conflict—the guilt he struggles with after having taken the young man's life. His comments are the key to the story's theme.

In "A Game of Catch," conflict develops when Monk and Glennie stop including Scho in their game; it worsens as Scho begins to feel hurt and rejected. The story offers a glimpse of human interaction.

How would you state the theme of "A Game of Catch"?

UNDERSTANDING THE WORDS IN THE STORY (Multiple-Choice)

1. When Monk would *lob* the ball, he would
   a. throw it in a high, arching curve
   b. bounce it along the ground
   c. throw it overhand
2. When Glennie would *burn* the ball, he would
   a. catch the ball on the fly
   b. throw it very hard
   c. pitch the ball in a curve
3. A *negligent* movement is
   a. unskillful
   b. careless
   c. dangerous
4. The boys are *entranced,* or
   a. competing with one another
   b. enclosed on all sides
   c. filled with delight

5. Glennie notices Scho *dawdling*, or
   a. smiling
   b. idling
   c. moving restlessly
6. The *brake* is
   a. an area covered with bushes
   b. a recess from the game
   c. a wall around the firehouse
7. When Scho spoke *tentatively*, he sounded
   a. stubborn
   b. uncertain
   c. angry
8. Scho's voice was *mocking*, because he was
   a. making fun of the boys
   b. laughing
   c. talking loudly
9. When Scho's voice was *exuberant*, it was
   a. gleeful
   b. annoying
   c. hushed
10. Something *clenched* is
   a. opened wide
   b. gathered closely
   c. shut tightly

(Matching Columns)

1. resume	a. bouncing
2. serene	b. serious; earnest
3. indolently	c. completely involved in
4. supple	d. climbing hastily
5. jouncing	e. continued stubbornly
6. absorbed	f. lazily
7. abstractedly	g. bending easily
8. persisted	h. absent-mindedly
9. intense	i. begin again
10. scrambling	j. calm; peaceful

WRITING IT DOWN
Another Point of View

"A Game of Catch" is written from the **objective point of view** (see page 267). Wilbur remains detached as he records the details of the story and does not let us know what he thinks of the incident.

Rewrite a part of this story in the first person, from the point of view of one of its characters—Monk, Glennie, or Scho. Have your narrator reveal his thoughts and feelings.

ABOUT THE AUTHOR

Richard Wilbur was born in New York City in 1921 and grew up in the suburbs of New Jersey. He is best known for his poetry, which he began writing while serving in the army during the Second World War. Wilbur's wartime experience of the destruction of order became a strong current in his work, flowing through his poetry and into his prose.

Wilbur has published several collections of poetry, among them *Things of This World* (1956), which received both the Pulitzer Prize and the National Book Award. In 1957 Wilbur collaborated on the Broadway musical *Candide* with Leonard Bernstein and Lillian Hellman. He has also written verse translations of *The Misanthrope* and *Tartuffe* by the French dramatist Molière. Wilbur was honored as Poet Laureate of the United States in 1987.

THE RETURN

Ngugi wa Thiong'o°

The stories "War" (page 70) and "Ambush" (page 348) show how people's lives are affected by war and its aftermath. Think of some movies and television programs that have addressed this theme, and discuss them with a small group of classmates.

The road was long. Whenever he took a step forward, little clouds of dust rose, whirled angrily behind him, and then slowly settled again. But a thin train of dust was left in the air, moving like smoke. He walked on, however, unmindful of the dust and ground under his feet. Yet with every step he seemed more and more conscious of the hardness and apparent animosity of the road. Not that he looked down; on the contrary, he looked straight ahead as if he would, any time now, see a familiar object that would hail him as a friend and tell him that he was near home. But the road stretched on.

He made quick, springing steps, his left hand dangling freely by the side of his once white coat, now torn and worn out. His right hand, bent at the elbow, held onto a string tied to a small bundle on his slightly drooping back. The bundle, well wrapped with a cotton cloth that had once been printed with red flowers now faded out, swung from side to side in harmony with the rhythm of his steps. The bundle held the bitterness and hardships of the years spent in detention camps.[1] Now and then he looked at the sun on its homeward journey. Sometimes he darted quick side-glances at the small hedged strips of land which, with their sickly-looking crops, maize, beans, and peas, appeared much as everything else did—unfriendly. The whole country was dull and seemed weary. To Kamau, this was nothing new. He remembered that, even before the Mau Mau emergency,[2] the overtilled Gikuyu[3] holdings wore haggard looks in contrast to the sprawling green fields in the settled area.

°**Ngugi wa Thiong'o** (n-go͞o'ge͞ wä the͞-ŏn'go͞).
1. **detention camps:** camps where political prisoners are confined.
2. **Mau Mau** (mou'mou) **emergency:** a conflict between whites and blacks over land ownership in the 1950s.
3. **Gikuyu** also spelled *Kikuyu* (kĭ-ko͞o'yo͞o): an agricultural people of Kenya.

A path branched to the left. He hesitated for a moment and then made up his mind. For the first time, his eyes brightened a little as he went along the path that would take him down the valley and then to the village. At last home was near and, with that realization, the faraway look of a weary traveler seemed to desert him for a while. The valley and the vegetation along it were in deep contrast to the surrounding country. For here green bush and trees thrived. This could mean only one thing: Honia River still flowed. He quickened his steps as if he could scarcely believe this to be true till he had actually set his eyes on the river. It was there; it still flowed. Honia, where so often he had taken a bath, plunging stark naked into its cool living water, warmed his heart as he watched its serpentine movement around the rocks and heard its slight murmurs. A painful exhilaration passed all over him, and for a moment he longed for those days. He sighed. Perhaps the river would not recognize in his hardened features that same boy to whom the riverside world had meant everything. Yet as he approached Honia, he felt more akin to it than he had felt to anything else since his release.

A group of women were drawing water. He was excited, for he could recognize one or two from his ridge. There was the middle-aged Wanjiku, whose deaf son had been killed by the Security Forces just before he himself was arrested. She had always been a darling of the village, having a smile for everyone and food for all. Would they receive him? Would they give him a "hero's welcome?" He thought so. Had he not always been a favorite all along the ridge? And had he not fought for the land? He wanted to run and shout: "Here I am. I have come back to you." But he desisted. He was a man.

"Is it well with you?" A few voices responded. The other women, with tired and worn features, looked at him mutely as if his greeting was of no consequence. Why! Had he been so long in the camp? His spirits were damped as he feebly asked: "Do you not remember me?" Again they looked at him. They stared at him with cold, hard looks; like everything else, they seemed to be deliberately refusing to know or own him. It was Wanjiku who at last recognized him. But there was neither warmth nor enthusiasm in her voice as she said, "Oh, is it you, Kamau? We thought you—" She did not continue. Only now he noticed something else—surprise? fear? He could not tell. He saw their quick glances dart at him and he knew for certain that a secret from which he was excluded bound them together.

"Perhaps I am no longer one of them!" he bitterly reflected. But they told him of the new village. The old village of scattered huts spread thinly over the ridge was no more.

He left them, feeling embittered and cheated. The old village had not even waited for him. And suddenly he felt a strong nostalgia for his old home, friends and surroundings. He thought of his father, mother and—and—he dared not think about her. But for all that, Muthoni, just as she had been in the old days, came back to his mind. His heart beat faster. He felt desire and a warmth thrilled through him. He quickened his step. He forgot the village women as he remembered his wife. He had stayed with her for a mere two weeks; then he had been swept away by the colonial forces. Like many others, he had been hurriedly screened and then taken to detention without trial. And all that time he had thought of nothing but the village and his beautiful woman.

The others had been like him. They had talked of nothing but their homes. One day he was working next to another detainee from Muranga. Suddenly the detainee, Njoroge, stopped breaking stones. He sighed heavily. His worn-out eyes had a faraway look.

"What's wrong, man? What's the matter with you?" Kamau asked.

"It is my wife. I left her expecting a baby. I have no idea what has happened to her."

Another detainee put in: "For me, I left my woman with a baby. She had just been delivered. We were all happy. But on the same day, I was arrested . . ."

And so they went on. All of them longed for one day—the day of their return home. Then life would begin anew.

Kamau himself had left his wife without a child. He had not even finished paying the bride price.[4] But now he would go, seek work in Nairobi,[5] and pay off the remainder to Muthoni's parents. Life would indeed begin anew. They would have a son and bring him up in their own home. With these prospects before his eyes, he quickened his steps. He wanted to run—no, fly to hasten his return. He was now

4. **bride price:** money or property customarily paid by the husband-to-be to the bride's family.
5. **Nairobi** (nī-rō′bē): the capital of Kenya.

nearing the top of the hill. He wished he could suddenly meet his brothers and sisters. Would they ask him questions? He would, at any rate, not tell them all: the beating, the screening and the work on roads and in quarries with an askari[6] always nearby ready to kick him if he relaxed. Yes. He had suffered many humiliations, and he had not resisted. Was there any need? But his soul and all the vigor of his manhood had rebelled and bled with rage and bitterness.

One day these wazungu would go!

One day his people would be free! Then, then—he did not know what he would do. However, he bitterly assured himself no one would ever flout his manhood again.

He mounted the hill and then stopped. The whole plain lay below. The new village was before him—rows and rows of compact mud huts, crouching on the plain under the fast-vanishing sun. Dark blue smoke curled upward from various huts, to form a dark mist that hovered over the village. Beyond, the deep, blood-red sinking sun sent out fingerlike streaks of light that thinned outward and mingled with the gray mist shrouding the distant hills.

In the village, he moved from street to street, meeting new faces. He inquired. He found his home. He stopped at the entrance to the yard and breathed hard and full. This was the moment of his return home. His father sat huddled up on a three-legged stool. He was now very aged and Kamau pitied the old man. But he had been spared—yes, spared to see his son's return—

"Father!"

The old man did not answer. He just looked at Kamau with strange vacant eyes. Kamau was impatient. He felt annoyed and irritated. Did he not see him? Would he behave like the women Kamau had met by the river?

In the street, naked and half-naked children were playing, throwing dust at one another. The sun had already set and it looked as if there would be moonlight.

"Father, don't you remember me?" Hope was sinking in him. He felt tired. Then he saw his father suddenly start and tremble like a leaf. He saw him stare with unbelieving eyes. Fear was discernible in those eyes.

---

6. **askari** (äs′kä-rē): an African soldier who works for a European power.

His mother came, and his brothers too. They crowded around him. His aged mother clung to him and sobbed hard.

"I knew my son would come. I knew he was not dead."

"Why, who told you I was dead?"

"That Karanja, son of Njogu."

And then Kamau understood. He understood his trembling father. He understood the women at the river. But one thing puzzled him: he had never been in the same detention camp with Karanja. Anyway he had come back. He wanted now to see Muthoni. Why had she not come out? He wanted to shout, "I have come, Muthoni; I am here." He looked around. His mother understood him. She quickly darted a glance at her man and then simply said:

"Muthoni went away."

Kamau felt something cold settle in his stomach. He looked at the village huts and the dullness of the land. He wanted to ask many questions but he dared not. He could not yet believe that Muthoni had gone. But he knew by the look of the women at the river, by the look of his parents, that she was gone.

"She was a good daughter to us," his mother was explaining. "She waited for you and patiently bore all the ills of the land. Then Karanja came and said that you were dead. Your father believed him. She believed him too and keened[7] for a month. Karanja constantly paid us visits. He was of your Rika, you know. Then she got a child. We could have kept her. But where is the land? Where is the food? Ever since land consolidation, our last security was taken away. We let Karanja go with her. Other women have done worse—gone to town. Only the infirm and the old have been left here."

He was not listening; the coldness in his stomach slowly changed to bitterness. He felt bitter against all, all the people including his father and mother. They had betrayed him. They had leagued against him, and Karanja had always been his rival. Five years was admittedly not a short time. But why did she go? Why did they allow her to go? He wanted to speak. Yes, speak and denounce everything—the women by the river, the village and the people who dwelled there. But he could not. This bitter thing was choking him.

---

7. **keened:** lamented.

"You—you gave my own away?" he whispered.

"Listen, child, child . . ."

The big yellow moon dominated the horizon. He hurried away bitter and blind, and only stopped when he came to the Honia River.

And standing at the bank, he saw not the river, but his hopes dashed on the ground instead. The river moved swiftly, making ceaseless monotonous murmurs. In the forest the crickets and other insects kept up an incessant buzz. And above, the moon shone bright. He tried to remove his coat, and the small bundle he had held on to so firmly fell. It rolled down the bank and before Kamau knew what was happening, it was floating swiftly down the river. For a time he was shocked and wanted to retrieve it. What would he show his—Oh, had he forgotten so soon? His wife had gone. And the little things that had so strangely reminded him of her and that he had guarded all those years, had gone! He did not know why, but somehow he felt relieved. Thoughts of drowning himself dispersed. He began to put on his coat, murmuring to himself, "Why should she have waited for me? Why should all the changes have waited for my return?"

First Response: *How did you feel when Kamau learned that Muthoni was gone?*

CHECKING UP (True/False)

1. Kamau is returning home after five years of military service.
2. The river that Kamau played in as a child has dried up.
3. The village women give Kamau a hero's welcome.
4. Kamau's mother and father were told that Kamau was dead.
5. Kamau throws his bundle into the river.

TALKING IT OVER

1. Kamau quickens his step as he approaches the river. Why is the Honia River so important to him?
2. Why does Kamau receive a cold reception from the villagers? What was your reaction to their treatment of him?
3. Like Kamau, many men were swept away by the colonial forces and taken to detention camps. What did they talk about constantly?
4. What are Kamau's hopes for the future?
5. What reasons do Kamau's parents give for allowing Muthoni to leave?
6. Kamau returns to the river with thoughts of taking his life, but he does not. Why does watching his little bundle float down the river cause him to change his mind?

THEME
Theme and Symbol

In "The Return" Ngugi wa Thiong'o tells the moving story of a man's return home after spending several years in detention camps. The feeling of betrayal by his own family and townspeople is worse for him than the pain and humiliation he has suffered at the hands of enemy forces. The **theme** of the story is that we must go on living despite the painful blows that life may deal us. Central to Ngugi's theme is the **symbol** of Kamau's bundle.

A symbol is any person, place, object, or event that has meaning in itself and also stands for something larger than itself. Early in "The Return" Kamau is carrying a bundle that holds "the bitterness and hardships of the years spent in detention camps." The bundle holds real objects, yet it symbolizes the bitter past that is burdening Kamau.

1. Reread the passage in which Kamau decides that he will not share the details of his suffering with his brothers and sisters. How does this passage show that he is burdened by the events of his recent past?

2. At the end of the story, what is symbolic about Kamau's little bundle floating swiftly down the river? How does this episode become a "turning point" for Kamau?

In the midst of all the unpleasant changes Kamau faces, the Honia River has remained constant. As Kamau takes the path toward his village, he is glad to see the river. He recalls the happiness he felt as a child playing there, and he feels a certain kinship with it. Later, when Kamau has received all of the bitter news he can bear, it is to the river that he runs. His bundle of "hardships" is then carried away by the river.

3. What might the river symbolize?

UNDERSTANDING THE WORDS IN THE STORY
(Matching Columns)

1. animosity	a. mock; make fun of
2. exhilaration	b. scattered
3. desisted	c. continuous; unending
4. nostalgia	d. political prisoner
5. detainee	e. resided; lived at
6. flout	f. stopped
7. discernible	g. hostility; hatred
8. dwelled	h. joyfulness
9. incessant	i. longing for the past
10. dispersed	j. able to be seen

WRITING IT DOWN
A Story

Write a story of your own called "The Return." Think about the point of view from which you would like to relate the narrative. Your story can be either humorous or serious; it can be purely entertaining, or it can be insightful and thought-provoking.

ABOUT THE AUTHOR

Ngugi wa Thiong'o, born James T. Ngugi in Kenya in 1938, is considered East Africa's foremost writer. Through his fiction, nonfiction, and plays, he has tried to make his fellow Kenyans—and the rest of the world—aware of the effects of colonialism on their culture.

In the early 1970s Ngugi changed his Christian name, James, to a Gikuyu name. In 1977 Ngugi began writing in Gikuyu and Swahili only; he believes that a people's culture and values are carried by their language.

Ngugi has often criticized and run into trouble with the Kenyan government. He was imprisoned for a year without a trial, and on his release in 1978, lost his professorship at the University of Nairobi. In 1982 his theater group was banned by the Kenyan government and, fearing further problems, Ngugi left Kenya. He now lives in London.

THE TELL-TALE HEART

Edgar Allan Poe

Read the first paragraph of this story. Then stop and jot down a few notes giving your impressions of the narrator who is telling the tale.

True!—nervous—very, very dreadfully nervous I had been and am; but why *will* you say that I am mad? The disease had sharpened my senses—not destroyed—not dulled them. Above all was the sense of hearing acute. I heard all things in the heaven and in the earth. I heard many things in hell. How, then, am I mad? Hearken![1] and observe how healthily—how calmly I can tell you the whole story.

It is impossible to say how first the idea entered my brain; but once conceived, it haunted me day and night. Object there was none. Passion there was none. I loved the old man. He had never wronged me. He had never given me insult. For his gold I had no desire. I think it was his eye! yes, it was this! One of his eyes resembled that of a vulture—a pale blue eye, with a film over it. Whenever it fell upon me, my blood ran cold; and so by degrees—very gradually—I made up my mind to take the life of the old man, and thus rid myself of the eye forever.

Now this is the point. You fancy[2] me mad. Madmen know nothing. But you should have seen *me*. You should have seen how wisely I proceeded—with what caution—with what foresight—with what dissimulation[3] I went to work! I was never kinder to the old man than during the whole week before I killed him. And every night, about midnight, I turned the latch of his door and opened it—oh, so gently! And then, when I had made an opening sufficient for my head, I put in a dark lantern,[4] all closed, closed, so that no light shone out, and then I thrust in my head. Oh, you would have laughed to see how cunningly I thrust it in! I moved it slowly—very, very slowly, so that I might not

1. **Hearken** (här′kən): Listen.
2. **fancy** (făn′sē): imagine; suppose.
3. **dissimulation** (dĭ-sĭm′yə-lā′shən): concealment of intentions.
4. **dark lantern:** a lantern with a panel or shutter to block its light.

disturb the old man's sleep. It took me an hour to place my whole head within the opening so far that I could see him as he lay upon his bed. Ha!—would a madman have been so wise as this? And then, when my head was well in the room, I undid the lantern cautiously—oh, so cautiously—cautiously (for the hinges creaked)—I undid it just so much that a single thin ray fell upon the vulture eye. And this I did for seven long nights—every night just at midnight—but I found the eye always closed; and so it was impossible to do the work; for it was not the old man who vexed me, but his Evil Eye. And every morning, when the day broke, I went boldly into the chamber, and spoke courageously to him, calling him by name in a hearty tone, and inquiring how he had passed the night. So you see he would have been a very profound old man, indeed, to suspect that every night, just at twelve, I looked in upon him while he slept.

Upon the eighth night I was more than usually cautious in opening the door. A watch's minute hand moves more quickly than did mine. Never before that night had I *felt* the extent of my own powers—of my sagacity.[5] I could scarcely contain my feelings of triumph. To think that there I was, opening the door, little by little, and he not even to dream of my secret deeds or thoughts. I fairly chuckled at the idea; and perhaps he heard me; for he moved on the bed suddenly, as if startled. Now you may think that I drew back—but no. His room was as black as pitch with the thick darkness (for the shutters were close fastened, through fear of robbers), and so I know that he could not see the opening of the door, and I kept pushing it on steadily, steadily.

I had my head in, and was about to open the lantern, when my thumb slipped upon the tin fastening, and the old man sprang up in the bed, crying out—"Who's there?"

I kept quite still and said nothing. For a whole hour I did not move a muscle, and in the meantime I did not hear him lie down. He was still sitting up in the bed listening—just as I have done, night after night, hearkening to the deathwatches[6] in the wall.

Presently I heard a slight groan, and I knew it was the groan of

---

5. **sagacity** (sə-găs′ə-tē): shrewdness.
6. **deathwatches** (dĕth′wŏch′əs): beetles that make a clicking sound when they strike their heads against wood. According to superstition, they are a forewarning of death.

mortal terror. It was not a groan of pain or of grief—oh, no!—it was the low stifled sound that arises from the bottom of the soul when overcharged with awe. I knew the sound well. Many a night, just at midnight, when all the world slept, it has welled up from my own bosom, deepening, with its dreadful echo, the terrors that distracted me. I say I knew it well. I knew what the old man felt, and pitied him, although I chuckled at heart. I knew that he had been lying awake ever since the first slight noise, when he had turned in the bed. His fears had been ever since growing upon him. He had been trying to fancy them causeless, but could not. He had been saying to himself—"It is nothing but the wind in the chimney—it is only a mouse crossing the floor," or "It is merely a cricket which has made a single chirp." Yes, he had been trying to comfort himself with these suppositions;[7] but he had found all in vain. *All in vain;* because Death, in approaching him, had stalked with his black shadow before him, and enveloped the victim. And it was the mournful influence of the unperceived[8] shadow that caused him to feel—although he neither saw nor heard—to *feel* the presence of my head within the room.

When I had waited a long time, very patiently, without hearing him lie down, I resolved to open a little—a very, very little crevice[9] in the lantern. So I opened it—you cannot imagine how stealthily, stealthily—until, at length, a single dim ray, like the thread of the spider, shot from out the crevice and full upon the vulture eye.

It was open—wide, wide open—and I grew furious as I gazed upon it. I saw it with perfect distinctness—all a dull blue, with a hideous veil over it that chilled the very marrow in my bones; but I could see nothing else of the old man's face or person: for I had directed the ray as if by instinct, precisely upon the damned spot.

And now have I not told you that what you mistake for madness is but overacuteness of the senses?—now, I say, there came to my ears a low, dull, quick sound, such as a watch makes when enveloped in cotton. I knew *that* sound well too. It was the beating of the old man's heart. It increased my fury, as the beating of a drum stimulates the soldier into courage.

7. **suppositions** (sŭp′ə-zĭsh′əns): ideas accepted without proof.
8. **unperceived** (ŭn′pər-sēvd′): unseen and unheard.
9. **crevice** (krĕv′ĭs): a narrow opening, like a slit or crack.

But even yet I refrained and kept still. I scarcely breathed. I held the lantern motionless. I tried how steadily I could maintain the ray upon the eye. Meantime the hellish tattoo[10] of the heart increased. It grew quicker and quicker, and louder and louder every instant. The old man's terror *must* have been extreme! It grew louder, I say, louder every moment!—do you mark[11] me well? I have told you that I am nervous: so I am. And now at the dead hour of the night, amid the dreadful silence of that old house, so strange a noise as this excited me to uncontrollable terror. Yet, for some minutes longer I refrained and stood still. But the beating grew louder, louder! I thought the heart must burst. And now a new anxiety seized me—the sound would be heard by a neighbor! The old man's hour had come! With a loud yell, I threw open the lantern and leaped into the room. He shrieked once—once only. In an instant I dragged him to the floor, and pulled the heavy bed over him. I then smiled gaily, to find the deed so far done. But, for many minutes, the heart beat on with a muffled sound. This, however, did not vex me; it would not be heard through the wall. At length it ceased. The old man was dead. I removed the bed and examined the corpse. Yes, he was stone, stone dead. I placed my hand upon the heart and held it there many minutes. There was no pulsation. He was stone dead. His eye would trouble me no more.

If still you think me mad, you will think so no longer when I describe the wise precautions I took for the concealment of the body. The night waned,[12] and I worked hastily, but in silence. First of all I dismembered the corpse. I cut off the head and the arms and the legs.

I then took up three planks from the flooring of the chamber, and deposited all between the scantlings.[13] I then replaced the boards so cleverly, so cunningly, that no human eye—not even *his*—could have detected anything wrong. There was nothing to wash out—no stain of any kind—no blood spot whatever. I had been too wary for that. A tub had caught all—ha! ha!

When I had made an end of these labors, it was four o'clock—still dark as midnight. As the bell sounded the hour, there came a

10. **tattoo** (tă-tōō'): a continuous, even beating.
11. **mark**: pay attention to.
12. **waned** (wānd): drew to an end.
13. **scantlings** (skănt'lĭngz): small upright pieces beneath the floorboards.

knocking at the street door. I went down to open it with a light heart—for what had I *now* to fear? There entered three men, who introduced themselves, with perfect suavity,[14] as officers of the police. A shriek had been heard by a neighbor during the night; suspicion of foul play had been aroused; information had been lodged at the police office, and they (the officers) had been deputed[15] to search the premises.

I smiled—for *what* had I to fear? I bade the gentlemen welcome. The shriek, I said, was my own in a dream. The old man, I mentioned, was absent in the country. I took my visitors all over the house. I bade them search—search *well*. I led them, at length, to *his* chamber. I showed them his treasures, secure, undisturbed. In the enthusiasm of my confidence, I brought chairs into the room, and desired them *here* to rest from their fatigues, while I myself, in the wild audacity[16] of my perfect triumph, placed my own seat upon the very spot beneath which reposed the corpse of the victim.

The officers were satisfied. My *manner* had convinced them. I was singularly at ease. They sat, and while I answered cheerily, they chatted familiar things. But, ere long, I felt myself getting pale and wished them gone. My head ached, and I fancied a ringing in my ears: but still they sat and still chatted. The ringing became more distinct—it continued and became more distinct; I talked more freely to get rid of the feelings, but it continued and gained definitiveness—until, at length, I found that the noise was *not* within my ears.

No doubt I now grew *very* pale—but I talked more fluently, and with a heightened voice. Yet the sound increased—and what could I do? It was *a low, dull, quick sound—much such a sound as a watch makes when enveloped in cotton.* I gasped for breath—and yet the officers heard it not. I talked more quickly—more vehemently;[17] but the noise steadily increased. I arose and argued about trifles, in a high key and with violent gesticulations,[18] but the noise steadily increased. Why *would* they not be gone? I paced the floor to and fro with heavy strides, as if excited to fury by the observation of the men—but the noise steadily increased. Oh what *could* I do? I foamed—I raved—I swore! I swung the chair

14. **suavity** (swäv'ə-tē, swāv-): graciousness, refinement.
15. **deputed** (dĭ-pyōō'təd): assigned.
16. **audacity** (ô-dăs'ə-tē): boldness.
17. **vehemently** (vē'ə-mənt-lē): forcefully.
18. **gesticulations** (jĕ-stĭk'yə-lā'shənz): vigorous movements of the limbs or body.

upon which I had been sitting, and grated it upon the boards, but the noise arose over all and continually increased. It grew louder—louder—*louder!* And still the men chatted pleasantly, and smiled. Was it possible they heard not? No, no! They heard!—they suspected!—they *knew!* they were making a mockery of my horror!—this I thought, and this I think. But anything was better than this agony! Anything was more tolerable than this derision![19] I could bear those hypocritical smiles no longer! I felt that I must scream or die!—and now—again!—hark! louder! louder! louder! *louder!*—

"Villains!" I shrieked, "dissemble[20] no more! I admit the deed!—tear up the planks!—here, here!—it is the beating of his hideous heart!"

19. **derision** (dĭ-rĭzh'ən): ridicule.
20. **dissemble** (dĭ-sĕm'bəl): pretend.

First Response: *On a scale of 1 to 5 (with 5 being the most scary), how would you rate this horror tale?*

CHECKING UP (Multiple-Choice)

1. The narrator claims that his keenest sense is his sense of
   a. smell
   b. touch
   c. hearing
2. The narrator admits to being
   a. mad
   b. nervous
   c. depressed
3. His object in killing the old man is
   a. to possess his gold
   b. to revenge an insult
   c. to get rid of an obsession

4. The narrator is most pleased by his own
  a. cleverness
  b. strength
  c. courage
5. The sight of the old man's eye arouses the narrator's
  a. fear
  b. fury
  c. curiosity
6. Before he kills the old man, the narrator is aware of
  a. the ticking of a clock
  b. the sound of a drum
  c. the beating of a human heart
7. The narrator hides the body in
  a. the old man's room
  b. the parlor
  c. the bathroom
8. A neighbor reports hearing a
  a. loud shriek
  b. drumbeat
  c. ringing noise
9. When the police first arrive, the narrator feels
  a. vaguely uneasy
  b. very angry
  c. completely confident
10. The narrator suspects the police of
  a. brutality
  b. cunning
  c. hypocrisy

TALKING IT OVER

1. At the opening of the story, the narrator is trying to convince someone of his sanity. What examples does he use to demonstrate that he is in his right mind? To whom do you think he is speaking?
2. What is the narrator's motive for killing the old man? Why does he wait until the eighth night to commit the murder?

3. Poe uses the first-person point of view in this story. At what points in the tale did your interpretations of the action differ from those of the narrator?
4. Point out several instances of dramatic irony, when you were aware of things that the narrator did not notice.
5. What causes the narrator to lose control at the end of the story?

TOTAL EFFECT

The **total effect** of a story is the central impression or impact it makes on its readers. In a famous comment, Edgar Allan Poe asserted that all the words and incidents in a short story should directly contribute to a single, overall effect or "pre-established design."

Elements that contribute to a story's total effect include its **plot, characterization, setting, point of view, tone,** and **theme.** The author's **diction,** or choice of words, and use of elements such as **imagery** can also contribute to a story's total effect.

1. How would you describe the total effect of "The Tell-Tale Heart"? List some words in the story that contribute to this effect.
2. What image does the narrator use to describe the old man's eye? How does it contribute to the effect of the story?
3. What instances does the narrator give of his sensitivity to sound? How do these instances reveal that he is insane?

UNDERSTANDING THE WORDS IN THE STORY (Multiple-Choice)

1. The narrator claims that his sense of hearing is *acute.*
   a. serious
   b. sharp
   c. painful

2. Once the idea of murder was *conceived,* he was haunted by it.
   a. imagined
   b. declared
   c. confided
3. He opened the door and *thrust* his head into the room.
   a. slipped
   b. poked
   c. crammed
4. He was *vexed* by the Evil Eye.
   a. delayed
   b. irritated
   c. enchanted
5. Only a *profound* person could have suspected his plan.
   a. suspicious
   b. highly intelligent
   c. sane
6. The old man *stifled* a groan.
   a. smothered
   b. grumbled
   c. uttered
7. The narrator often felt his soul filled with *awe.*
   a. grief and pain
   b. rage and jealousy
   c. wonder and fear
8. Dreadful sounds would *well up* from his soul at midnight.
   a. come
   b. fall
   c. rise
9. He was *distracted* by terrors.
   a. confused
   b. entertained
   c. frightened
10. The victim tried to imagine that all his fears were *causeless.*
    a. unnecessary
    b. unfounded
    c. silly

(Matching Columns)

1. stalked	a. showing grief
2. enveloped	b. cut into pieces
3. mournful	c. very careful
4. resolved	d. held back
5. refrained	e. care taken beforehand
6. precaution	f. covered or surrounded
7. dismembered	g. set down
8. deposited	h. cleverly
9. cunningly	i. approached secretly
10. wary	j. determined

(Completion)

lodged	grated
premises	mockery
reposed	agony
fluently	tolerable
heightened	hypocritical

1. At first the narrator spoke _____ while the police sat and listened.
2. The police made a search of the _____.
3. After hearing a shriek, a neighbor had _____ a complaint with the police.
4. The narrator believed that the police knew the truth and were making a (an) _____ of his feelings.
5. He _____ a chair against the floor.
6. The remains of the victim _____ under the planks.
7. He was unable to endure the _____ any longer.
8. He spoke in a (an) _____ voice.
9. He could not bear their false, _____ smiles.
10. He decided that anything would be more _____ than their pretense.

WRITING IT DOWN
An Account

Imagine that you are one of the police officers sent to investigate the suspected foul play. Write an eyewitness account of what you observe.

SPEAKING AND LISTENING
Discussing an Answer

To whom is the narrator telling this story? Is he talking to the police? to his lawyer? to a doctor? to a cell mate? Or is he ranting to himself? Discuss your opinion with your classmates.

Comparing Narrators

Comparison focuses on the similarities of two or more subjects, whereas **contrast** focuses on the differences. Join with a small group of classmates and organize a round-table discussion to compare and contrast the first-person narrator in James Gould Cozzens's "Success Story" (page 83) with the narrator in Poe's "The Tell-Tale Heart." In your discussion, focus especially on the question of each narrator's reliability. Can the narrators of these stories be trusted to give a reasonably objective, accurate account of the events in which they took part? If not, why not?

ABOUT THE AUTHOR

Edgar Allan Poe (1809–1849), a major American writer, left a substantial legacy of poetry, fiction, and literary criticism. He was born in Boston to traveling actors. His father deserted the family, and Poe's mother died when he was two. He was then taken in by John Allan, a wealthy tobacco merchant in Virginia, but he was never formally adopted. It was from his foster family that he took his middle name.

Poe's relations with his guardian were always strained. When he contracted huge debts at the University of Virginia, John Allan refused to pay them, and Poe had to leave the university. Poe entered the army and spent several months as a cadet at West Point in an effort to please his guardian, but all attempts at reconciliation failed.

Finally, Poe turned to writing to earn a living. For a time he lived in Baltimore with his aunt, Maria Clemm, and his cousin, Virginia, whom he married when she was thirteen. During the decade of their married life, Virginia was ill much of the time, and Poe, depressed and given to drink, was unable to keep a job. After her death, he tried unsuccessfully to set up his own magazine. Perhaps seeking to find both financial and emotional security, he courted several wealthy women.

The circumstances of Poe's death remain a mystery. On a business trip, Poe stopped off in Baltimore. Several days later he was found lying unconscious on a sidewalk, and he died without regaining consciousness.

The despair that marked Poe's life appears in his poems and stories. Some of his best-known stories are "The Fall of the House of Usher," "The Cask of Amontillado," "The Masque of the Red Death," and "The Murders in the Rue Morgue."

AUGUST HEAT

William Fryer Harvey

In stories such as "Appointment in Samarra" (page xi) and "The Colomber" (page 28), a character confronts his or her own fate or destiny. Can you think of other stories that are similar? Think about why such stories are appealing.

PENISTONE ROAD, CLAPHAM,
20*th August*, 19—.

I have had what I believe to be the most remarkable day in my life, and while the events are still fresh in my mind, I wish to put them down on paper as clearly as possible.

Let me say at the outset that my name is James Clarence Withencroft.

I am forty years old, in perfect health, never having known a day's illness.

By profession I am an artist, not a very successful one, but I earn enough money by my black-and-white work to satisfy my necessary wants.

My only near relative, a sister, died five years ago, so that I am independent.

I breakfasted this morning at nine, and after glancing through the morning paper I lighted my pipe and proceeded to let my mind wander in the hope that I might chance upon some subject for my pencil.

The room, though door and windows were open, was oppressively hot, and I had just made up my mind that the coolest and most comfortable place in the neighborhood would be the deep end of the public swimming bath, when the idea came.

I began to draw. So intent was I on my work that I left my lunch untouched, only stopping work when the clock of St. Jude's struck four.

The final result, for a hurried sketch, was, I felt sure, the best thing I had done.

It showed a criminal in the dock[1] immediately after the judge had pronounced sentence. The man was fat—enormously fat. The flesh hung in rolls about his chin; it creased his huge, stumpy neck. He was

---

1. **dock** (dŏk): in English criminal courts, the place where a defendant sits or stands.

cleanshaven (perhaps I should say a few days before he must have been cleanshaven) and almost bald. He stood in the dock, his short, stumpy fingers clasping the rail, looking straight in front of him. The feeling that his expression conveyed was not so much one of horror as of utter, absolute collapse.

There seemed nothing in the man strong enough to sustain that mountain of flesh.

I rolled up the sketch, and without quite knowing why, placed it in my pocket. Then with the rare sense of happiness which the knowledge of a good thing well done gives, I left the house.

I believe that I set out with the idea of calling upon Trenton, for I remember walking along Lytton Street and turning to the right along Gilchrist Road at the bottom of the hill where the men were at work on the new tram[2] lines.

From there onward I have only the vaguest recollections of where I went. The one thing of which I was fully conscious was the awful heat, that came up from the dusty asphalt pavement as an almost palpable wave. I longed for the thunder promised by the great banks of copper-colored cloud that hung low over the western sky.

I must have walked five or six miles, when a small boy roused me from my reverie by asking the time.

It was twenty minutes to seven.

When he left me I began to take stock of my bearings. I found myself standing before a gate that led into a yard bordered by a strip of thirsty earth, where there were flowers, purple stock and scarlet geranium. Above the entrance was a board with the inscription—

CHAS. ATKINSON

MONUMENTAL MASON

WORKER IN ENGLISH AND ITALIAN MARBLES

From the yard itself came a cheery whistle, the noise of hammer blows, and the cold sound of steel meeting stone.

A sudden impulse made me enter.

A man was sitting with his back toward me, busy at work on a slab

2. **tram** (trăm): streetcar.

of curiously veined marble. He turned round as he heard my steps and stopped short.

It was the man I had been drawing, whose portrait lay in my pocket.

He sat there, huge and elephantine,[3] the sweat pouring from his scalp, which he wiped with a red silk handkerchief. But though the face was the same, the expression was absolutely different.

He greeted me smiling, as if we were old friends, and shook my hand.

I apologized for my intrusion.

"Everything is hot and glary outside," I said. "This seems an oasis in the wilderness."

"I don't know about the oasis," he replied, "but it certainly is hot. Take a seat, sir!"

He pointed to the end of the gravestone on which he was at work, and I sat down.

"That's a beautiful piece of stone you've got hold of," I said.

He shook his head. "In a way it is," he answered; "the surface here is as fine as anything you could wish, but there's a big flaw at the back, though I don't expect you'd ever notice it. I could never make really a good job of a bit of marble like that. It would be all right in a summer like this; it wouldn't mind the blasted heat. But wait till the winter comes. There's nothing quite like frost to find out the weak points in stone."

"Then what's it for?" I asked.

The man burst out laughing.

"You'd hardly believe me if I was to tell you it's for an exhibition, but it's the truth. Artists have exhibitions: so do grocers and butchers; we have them too. All the latest little things in headstones, you know."

He went on to talk of marbles, which sort best withstood wind and rain, and which were easiest to work; then of his garden and a new sort of carnation he had bought. At the end of every other minute he would drop his tools, wipe his shining head, and curse the heat.

I said little, for I felt uneasy. There was something unnatural, uncanny, in meeting this man.

---

3. **elephantine** (ĕl′ə-făn′tēn, -tīn′, ĕl′ə-fən-): huge and heavy-footed.

I tried at first to persuade myself that I had seen him before, that his face, unknown to me, had found a place in some out-of-the-way corner of my memory, but I knew that I was practicing little more than a plausible piece of self-deception.

Mr. Atkinson finished his work, spat on the ground, and got up with a sigh of relief.

"There! What do you think of that?" he said, with an air of evident pride.

The inscription which I read for the first time was this—

SACRED TO THE MEMORY

OF

JAMES CLARENCE WITHENCROFT.

BORN JAN. 18TH, 1860.

HE PASSED AWAY VERY SUDDENLY

ON AUGUST 20TH, 190—

"In the midst of life we are in death."

For some time I sat in silence. Then a cold shudder ran down my spine. I asked him where he had seen the name.

"Oh, I didn't see it anywhere," replied Mr. Atkinson. "I wanted some name, and I put down the first that came into my head. Why do you want to know?"

"It's a strange coincidence, but it happens to be mine."

He gave a long, low whistle.

"And the dates?"

"I can only answer for one of them, and that's correct."

"It's a rum go!"[4] he said.

But he knew less than I did. I told him of my morning's work. I took the sketch from my pocket and showed it to him. As he looked, the expression of his face altered until it became more and more like that of the man I had drawn.

"And it was only the day before yesterday," he said, "that I told Maria there were no such things as ghosts!"

---

4. **It's a rum go:** British slang with the general meaning of "It's a strange business."

Neither of us had seen a ghost, but I knew what he meant.

"You probably heard my name," I said.

"And you must have seen me somewhere and have forgotten it! Were you at Clacton-on-Sea last July?"

I had never been to Clacton in my life. We were silent for some time. We were both looking at the same thing, the two dates on the gravestone, and one was right.

"Come inside and have some supper," said Mr. Atkinson.

His wife is a cheerful little woman, with the flaky red cheeks of the country-bred. Her husband introduced me as a friend of his who was an artist. The result was unfortunate, for after the sardines and watercress had been removed, she brought out a Doré[5] Bible, and I had to sit and express my admiration for nearly half an hour.

I went outside, and found Atkinson sitting on the gravestone smoking.

We resumed the conversation at the point we had left off.

"You must excuse my asking," I said, "but do you know of anything you've done for which you could be put on trial?"

He shook his head.

"I'm not a bankrupt, the business is prosperous enough. Three years ago I gave turkeys to some of the guardians[6] at Christmas, but that's all I can think of. And they were small ones, too," he added as an afterthought.

He got up, fetched a can from the porch, and began to water the flowers. "Twice a day regular in the hot weather," he said, "and then the heat sometimes gets the better of the delicate ones. And ferns, they could never stand it. Where do you live?"

I told him my address. It would take an hour's quick walk to get back home.

"It's like this," he said. "We'll look at the matter straight. If you go back home tonight, you take your chance of accidents. A cart may run over you, and there's always banana skins and orange peel, to say nothing of fallen ladders."

He spoke of the improbable with an intense seriousness that would have been laughable six hours before. But I did not laugh.

5. **Doré:** (Paul) Gustave Doré (dô-rā´), a French artist and illustrator (1832–1883).
6. **guardians:** members of a board that cares for the poor within a parish or district.

"The best thing we can do," he continued, "is for you to stay here till twelve o'clock. We'll go upstairs and smoke; it may be cooler inside."

To my surprise I agreed.

We are sitting now in a long, low room beneath the eaves. Atkinson has sent his wife to bed. He himself is busy sharpening some tools at a little oilstone, smoking one of my cigars the while.

The air seems charged with thunder. I am writing this at a shaky table before the open window. The leg is cracked, and Atkinson, who seems a handy man with his tools, is going to mend it as soon as he has finished putting an edge on his chisel.

It is after eleven now. I shall be gone in less than an hour.

But the heat is stifling.

It is enough to send a man mad.

***

First Response: *What would you do if you were in the narrator's predicament?*

CHECKING UP

Arrange the following events in the order in which they occur in the story.

Withencroft hears the noise of hammer blows.
Atkinson greets Withencroft with a smile.
Withencroft draws a sketch of a criminal.
Atkinson waters his flowers.
Withencroft goes for a walk.
Atkinson sharpens his chisel.
Withencroft sees the inscription on the monument.
Mrs. Atkinson shows Withencroft an illustrated Bible.
A boy asks Withencroft the time.
Atkinson invites Withencroft to supper.

TALKING IT OVER

1. This story takes place during the *dog days,* the hot, uncomfortable part of summer between mid-July and September. People in ancient times reckoned this period from the rising of Sirius, the Dog Star. During this time, dogs were supposed to be especially apt to go mad. What is the connection between this belief and the events of the story?
2. The narrator says that a "sudden impulse" makes him enter the yard. What evidence is there that the characters have no control over what is taking place?
3. What rational explanations do the two men offer for the strange coincidences of the story? Why are these explanations rejected?
4. Judging from clues in the last part of the story, what do you think will be the final outcome?
5. The background of this story is ordinary and familiar. There are references to the asphalt pavement, streetcars, and the front yard and garden of a house. Why does this naturalistic setting make the events of the story more terrifying?

TOTAL EFFECT

"August Heat" is clearly intended to arouse horror and create suspense. All the elements in the story contribute to the total effect of chilling terror.

The story presents a fascinating mystery that has no rational explanation. The reader responds to the mounting horror of coincidence and irony. A murder is about to be committed. Both the victim and the murderer have an uncanny foreknowledge of each other and are drawn together by some mysterious power. Yet, ironically, they remain ignorant of precisely what is going to happen.

1. The narrator tells the story in a completely serious and naturalistic manner. How does the narrator convince us that the events he records are true?
2. How does the setting make the action believable?

UNDERSTANDING THE WORDS IN THE STORY (Multiple-Choice)

1. The *outset* of something is its
   a. beginning
   b. middle
   c. end
2. An *oppressively* hot day is
   a. rainy
   b. unbearable
   c. pleasant
3. An *intent* gaze is
   a. earnest
   b. curious
   c. angry
4. *Stumpy* fingers are
   a. thick
   b. graceful
   c. bony
5. An *utter* surprise is
   a. total
   b. expected
   c. imaginative
6. To *sustain* something is to give it
   a. attention
   b. support
   c. understanding
7. A *recollection* is a
   a. memory
   b. fund
   c. book
8. Something that is *palpable* is experienced by the
   a. senses
   b. mind
   c. subconscious
9. When one is *roused,* one
   a. sleeps
   b. dreams
   c. stirs

10. To be lost in *reverie* is to
    a. forget
    b. travel
    c. daydream

(Matching Columns)

1. inscription	a. not likely
2. intrusion	b. well-off
3. flaw	c. weird; mysterious
4. uncanny	d. writing on a surface
5. plausible	e. edges on a roof
6. coincidence	f. smothering
7. prosperous	g. uninvited entry
8. improbable	h. seemingly true
9. eaves	i. chance occurrence
10. stifling	j. defect

WRITING IT DOWN
A Plan

At the end of the story, it appears that time is running out for the narrator. What action would you take if you were in his situation? Would you remain in the room or would you try to escape?

SPEAKING AND LISTENING
Comparing Stories

Hold a round-table discussion to explore the techniques that Edgar Allan Poe and William Fryer Harvey use to create and sustain suspense in "The Tell-Tale Heart" (page 375) and "August Heat." Which horror tale is more suspenseful, in your group's judgment?

LUCK

Mark Twain

Which is more important to achieving success—luck or hard work?
Summarize your opinion in two or three sentences.

It was at a banquet in London in honor of one of the two or three conspicuously illustrious English military names of this generation. For reasons which will presently appear, I will withhold his real name and titles and call him Lieutenant-General Lord Arthur Scoresby, Y.C., K.C.B.,[1] etc., etc., etc. What a fascination there is in a renowned name! There sat the man, in actual flesh, whom I had heard of so many thousands of times since that day, thirty years before, when his name shot suddenly to the zenith from a Crimean[2] battlefield, to remain forever celebrated. It was food and drink to me to look, and look, and look at that demigod; scanning, searching, noting: the quietness, the reserve, the noble gravity of his countenance; the simple honesty that expressed itself all over him; the sweet unconsciousness of his greatness—unconsciousness of the hundreds of admiring eyes fastened upon him, unconsciousness of the deep, loving, sincere worship welling out of the breasts of those people and flowing toward him.

The clergyman at my left was an old acquaintance of mine— clergyman now, but had spent the first half of his life in the camp and field and as an instructor in the military school at Woolwich. Just at the moment I have been talking about a veiled and singular light glimmered in his eyes and he leaned down and muttered confidentially to me—indicating the hero of the banquet with a gesture:

"Privately—he's an absolute fool."

This verdict was a great surprise to me. If its subject had been Napoleon, or Socrates, or Solomon,[3] my astonishment could not have

---

1. **Y.C.:** Yeomanry Cavalry. **K.C.B.:** Knight Commander of the Order of the Bath.
2. **Crimean** (krī-mē′ən): In the Crimean War (1854–1856), Russia was defeated by England, France, Turkey, and Sardinia.
3. **Napoleon . . . Solomon:** famous men noted for their military leadership or wisdom. Napoleon Bonaparte (bō′nə-pärt′) (1769–1821) became Emperor of France; Socrates (sŏk′rə-tēz′) was a Greek philosopher and teacher (470?–399 B.C.); Solomon, King of Israel in the tenth century B.C., was known for his wisdom.

been greater. Two things I was well aware of: that the Reverend was a man of strict veracity and that his judgment of men was good. Therefore I knew, beyond doubt or question, that the world was mistaken about this hero: he *was* a fool. So I meant to find out, at a convenient moment, how the Reverend, all solitary and alone, had discovered the secret.

Some days later the opportunity came, and this is what the Reverend told me:

About forty years ago I was an instructor in the military academy at Woolwich. I was present in one of the sections when young Scoresby underwent his preliminary examination. I was touched to the quick with pity, for the rest of the class answered up brightly and handsomely, while he—why, dear me, he didn't know *anything*, so to speak. He was evidently good, and sweet, and lovable, and guileless; and so it was exceedingly painful to see him stand there, as serene as a graven image,[4] and deliver himself of answers which were veritably miraculous for stupidity and ignorance. All the compassion in me was aroused in his behalf. I said to myself, when he comes to be examined again he will be flung over, of course; so it will be simply a harmless act of charity to ease his fall as much as I can. I took him aside and found that he knew a little of Caesar's history;[5] and as he didn't know anything else, I went to work and drilled him like a galley-slave on a certain line of stock questions concerning Caesar which I knew would be used. If you'll believe me, he went through with flying colors on examination day! He went through on that purely superficial "cram," and got compliments, too, while others, who knew a thousand times more than he, got plucked.[6] By some strangely lucky accident—an accident not likely to happen twice in a century—he was asked no question outside of the narrow limits of his drill.

It was stupefying. Well, all through his course I stood by him, with something of the sentiment which a mother feels for a crippled child; and he always saved himself, just by miracle apparently.

4. **graven image:** an idol carved in wood or stone.
5. **Caesar's history:** Julius Caesar (100–44 B.C.) wrote military narratives that are still studied by students of Latin as well as by military leaders.
6. **plucked:** British slang, meaning "rejected as candidates."

Now, of course, the thing that would expose him and kill him at last was mathematics. I resolved to make his death as easy as I could; so I drilled him and crammed him, and crammed him and drilled him, just on the line of questions which the examiners would be most likely to use, and then launched him on his fate. Well, sir, try to conceive of the result: to my consternation, he took the first prize! And with it he got a perfect ovation in the way of compliments.

Sleep? There was no more sleep for me for a week. My conscience tortured me day and night. What I had done I had done purely through charity, and only to ease the poor youth's fall. I never had dreamed of any such preposterous results as the thing that had happened. I felt as guilty and miserable as Frankenstein.[7] Here was a woodenhead whom I had put in the way of glittering promotions and prodigious responsibilities, and but one thing could happen: he and his responsibilities would all go to ruin together at the first opportunity.

The Crimean War had just broken out. Of course there had to be a war, I said to myself. We couldn't have peace and give this donkey a chance to die before he is found out. I waited for the earthquake. It came. And it made me reel when it did come. He was actually gazetted[8] to a captaincy in a marching regiment! Better men grow old and gray in the service before they climb to a sublimity like that. And who could ever have foreseen that they would go and put such a load of responsibility on such green and inadequate shoulders? I could just barely have stood it if they had made him a cornet;[9] but a captain—think of it! I thought my hair would turn white.

Consider what I did—I who so loved repose and inaction. I said to myself, I am responsible to the country for this, and I must go along with him and protect the country against him as far as I can. So I took my poor little capital that I had saved up through years of work and grinding economy, and went with a sigh and bought a cornetcy in his regiment, and away we went to the field.

And there—oh, dear, it was awful. Blunders?—why, he never did anything *but* blunder. But, you see, nobody was in the fellow's secret.

---

7. **Frankenstein:** the creator of the famous monster in *Frankenstein,* a novel by Mary Shelley.
8. **gazetted** (gə-zĕt'əd): appointed.
9. **cornet** (kôr'nĭt): the fifth commissioned officer in a cavalry troop.

Everybody had him focused wrong, and necessarily misinterpreted his performance every time. Consequently they took his idiotic blunders for inspirations of genius. They did, honestly! His mildest blunders were enough to make a man in his right mind cry; and they did make me cry—and rage and rave, too, privately. And the thing that kept me always in a sweat of apprehension was the fact that every fresh blunder he made always increased the luster of his reputation! I kept saying to myself, he'll get so high that when discovery does finally come it will be like the sun falling out of the sky.

He went right along up, from grade to grade, over the dead bodies of his superiors, until at last, in the hottest moment of the battle of ——— down went our colonel, and my heart jumped into my mouth, for Scoresby was next in rank! Now for it, said I; we'll all land in Sheol[10] in ten minutes, sure.

The battle was awfully hot; the allies were steadily giving way all over the field. Our regiment occupied a position that was vital; a blunder now must be destruction. At this crucial moment, what does this immortal fool do but detach the regiment from its place and order a charge over a neighboring hill where there wasn't a suggestion of an enemy! "There you go!" I said to myself; "this *is* the end at last."

And away we did go, and were over the shoulder of the hill before the insane movement could be discovered and stopped. And what did we find? An entire and unsuspected Russian army in reserve! And what happened? We were eaten up? That is necessarily what would have happened in ninety-nine cases out of a hundred. But no; those Russians argued that no single regiment would come browsing around there at such a time. It must be the entire English army, and that the sly Russian game was detected and blocked; so they turned tail, and away they went, pell-mell, over the hill and down into the field, in wild confusion, and we after them; they themselves broke the solid Russian center in the field, and tore through, and in no time there was the most tremendous rout you ever saw, and the defeat of the allies was turned into a sweeping and splendid victory! Marshal Canrobert looked on, dizzy with astonishment, admiration, and delight; and sent right off for Scoresby,

10. **Sheol** (shē'ōl'): in the Old Testament, a place described as the dwelling place of the dead.

and hugged him, and decorated him on the field in presence of all the armies!

And what was Scoresby's blunder that time? Merely the mistaking his right hand for his left—that was all. An order had come to him to fall back and support our right; and instead, he fell *forward* and went over the hill to the left. But the name he won that day as a marvelous military genius filled the world with his glory, and that glory will never fade while history books last.

He is just as good and sweet and lovable and unpretending as a man can be, but he doesn't know enough to come in when it rains. Now that is absolutely true. He is the supremest ass in the universe; and until half an hour ago nobody knew it but himself and me. He has been pursued, day by day and year by year, by a most phenomenal and astonishing luckiness. He has been a shining soldier in all our wars for a generation; he has littered his whole military life with blunders, and yet has never committed one that didn't make him a knight or a baronet or a lord or something. Look at his breast; why, he is just clothed in domestic and foreign decorations. Well, sir, every one of them is the record of some shouting stupidity or other; and, taken together, they are proof that the very best thing in all this world that can befall a man is to be born lucky. I say again, as I said at the banquet, Scoresby's an absolute fool.

First Response: *Do you think this story has a theme or serious message? Or is Mark Twain's purpose simply to entertain the reader?*

CHECKING UP (True/False)

1. At the opening of the story, the Reverend is attending a banquet to honor a former pupil.
2. Scoresby passed his examinations at the military academy by cheating.

3. Scoresby took first prize in mathematics.
4. Scoresby's stunning military victories were actually blunders.
5. During the Crimean War, Scoresby put the entire English army to flight.

TALKING IT OVER

1. The story has two narrators. What impression do you form of the first narrator? What is his attitude toward Lord Arthur Scoresby?
2. How does Twain convince you that his second narrator, the Reverend, is someone who can be trusted to tell the truth?
3. What are the Reverend's motives for helping Scoresby?
4. Why do you suppose that only the Reverend is aware of Scoresby's "secret"?
5. What is the point of Twain's satire in this story?

TOTAL EFFECT

The **tall tale** was a popular form of humor in American folklore of the nineteenth century. Folk heroes like Paul Bunyan and Pecos Bill performed superhuman feats. Like the tall tale, Twain's story contains elements of outlandish exaggeration.

1. Twain achieves his effects through a combination of exaggeration and comic deflation. Find examples of language in the first paragraph that glorify the figure of Lord Arthur Scoresby. Why do you suppose Twain emphasizes the narrator's reverence for this man?
2. How does the Reverend's tale deflate this image of Scoresby?
3. Which events in the Reverend's tale are improbable or comically absurd?
4. Some readers think that Twain's satire is aimed at debunking a military hero. Other readers think that Twain is expressing a cynical attitude toward life. What is your opinion of Twain's intention? Give evidence from the story to support your opinion.

UNDERSTANDING THE WORDS IN THE STORY (Completion)

conspicuous   gravity
illustrious   countenance
renowned   welling
zenith   singular
demigod   glimmer

1. At high noon the sun is said to be at its _____.
2. Character can be read in a person's _____.
3. An idea is beginning to _____ in your eyes.
4. A person who stands out in a crowd is _____.
5. A _____ seems to be superhuman.
6. Scoresby had enjoyed a (an) _____ career.
7. Tears began _____ in the eyes of the audience.
8. Despite the _____ of his expression, Scoresby was a fool.
9. Scoresby was _____ for his military victories.
10. The Reverend had a _____ look on his face.

(Matching Columns)

1. veracity   a. authentic
2. preliminary   b. commonly used
3. guileless   c. awaken or excite
4. veritable   d. determine
5. compassion   e. coming before
6. arouse   f. understand; imagine
7. stock   g. truthfulness
8. superficial   h. pity or sympathy
9. resolve   i. innocent
10. conceive   j. on the surface

(Multiple-Choice)

1. The Reverend found, to his *consternation,* that Scoresby had passed his examinations.
   a. pleasure
   b. amusement
   c. dismay

2. The *ovation* Scoresby received was for achieving the highest score on his mathematics examination.
   a. prize
   b. reward
   c. expression of approval

3. The Reverend found the outcome of the examinations *preposterous*.
   a. ridiculous
   b. frightening
   c. prejudiced

4. Scoresby was given *prodigious* responsibilities.
   a. unusual
   b. huge
   c. professional

5. Scoresby achieved a *sublimity* denied to other men of greater talent.
   a. supreme honor
   b. command
   c. reputation

6. The Reverend gave up a life of *repose* in order to protect the country against Scoresby.
   a. calmness
   b. simplicity
   c. idleness

7. The Reverend was in a constant state of *apprehension*.
   a. controlled anger
   b. worried expectation
   c. intense fascination

8. The Russians did not expect a regiment to come *browsing* around.
   a. spying
   b. charging
   c. looking casually

9. Scoresby was responsible for the *rout* of the Russian army.
   a. blunder
   b. disastrous defeat
   c. loss

10. Scoresby was blessed with *phenomenal* luck.
    a. extraordinary
    b. absolute
    c. repeated

WRITING IT DOWN
Notes on Literature and History

Use a history book or an encyclopedia to learn the details of the Battle of Balaklava, which took place in 1854 during the Crimean War. Pay special attention to the actions of the Light Cavalry Brigade. What aspects of this battle might Twain have had in mind when he created the character of Scoresby and the events in "Luck"? Jot down some notes.

A Comparison

Read the poem "The Charge of the Light Brigade" by Alfred, Lord Tennyson. In a brief essay, compare Tennyson's attitude toward this historical event with Twain's attitude toward Scoresby's charge in "Luck."

ABOUT THE AUTHOR

Mark Twain is the pen name of Samuel Langhorne Clemens (1835–1910), who grew up in Hannibal, Missouri, a small town on the Mississippi River. He worked on a newspaper, then became a riverboat pilot. He may have taken his pen name from a cry used by the riverboatmen, "By the mark, twain!" This cry meant that the river's depth was two fathoms, a depth safe for navigation. After a trip to Europe and Palestine, Twain wrote *Innocents Abroad* (1869), a humorous travelogue that met with popular success. His other works include *The Adventures of Tom Sawyer* (1876), *Life on the Mississippi* (1883), and his masterpiece, *Adventures of Huckleberry Finn* (1884). Many critics consider Twain to be the greatest humorist this country has produced.

THE GIFT OF THE MAGI
O. Henry

Do you agree with the saying "It is better to give than to receive"?
Explain your answer in a sentence or two.

One dollar and eighty-seven cents. That was all. And sixty cents of it was in pennies. Pennies saved one and two at a time by bulldozing the grocer and the vegetable man and the butcher until one's cheek burned with the silent imputation of parsimony[1] that such close dealing implied. Three times Della counted it. One dollar and eighty-seven cents. And the next day would be Christmas.

There was clearly nothing to do but flop down on the shabby little couch and howl. So Della did it. Which instigates[2] the moral reflection that life is made up of sobs, sniffles, and smiles, with sniffles predominating.

While the mistress of the home is gradually subsiding from the first stage to the second,[3] take a look at the home. A furnished flat at eight dollars per week. It did not exactly beggar description, but it certainly had that word on the lookout for the mendicancy squad.[4]

In the vestibule below was a letter box into which no letter would go, and an electric button from which no mortal finger could coax a ring. Also appertaining thereunto[5] was a card bearing the name "Mr. James Dillingham Young."

The "Dillingham" had been flung to the breeze during a former period of prosperity when its possessor was being paid thirty dollars per week. Now, when the income was shrunk to twenty dollars, the letters of "Dillingham" looked blurred, as though they were thinking seriously of contracting to a modest and unassuming *D*. But whenever Mr. James Dillingham Young came home and reached his flat above he was called

---

1. **imputation** (ĭm′pyōō-tā′shən) **of parsimony** (pär′sə-mō′nē): charge or accusation of stinginess.
2. **instigates** (ĭn′stĭ-gāts′): provokes.
3. **first . . . second:** from sobs to sniffles.
4. **mendicancy** (mĕn′dĭ-kən′sē) **squad:** a police squad that picked up beggars. O. Henry means that the apartment is shabby.
5. **appertaining thereunto:** belonging to.

"Jim" and greatly hugged by Mrs. James Dillingham Young, already introduced to you as Della. Which is all very good.

Della finished her cry and attended to her cheeks with the powder rag. She stood by the window and looked out dully at a gray cat walking a gray fence in a gray backyard. Tomorrow would be Christmas Day, and she had only one dollar and eighty-seven cents with which to buy Jim a present. She had been saving every penny she could for months, with this result. Twenty dollars a week doesn't go far. Expenses had been greater than she had calculated. They always are. Only one dollar and eighty-seven cents to buy a present for Jim. Her Jim. Many a happy hour she had spent planning for something nice for him. Something fine and rare and sterling—something just a little bit near to being worthy of the honor of being owned by Jim.

There was a pier glass[6] between the windows of the room. Perhaps you have seen a pier glass in an eight-dollar flat. A very thin and very agile person may, by observing his reflection in a rapid sequence of longitudinal strips, obtain a fairly accurate conception of his looks. Della, being slender, had mastered the art.

Suddenly she whirled from the window and stood before the glass. Her eyes were shining brilliantly, but her face had lost its color within twenty seconds. Rapidly she pulled down her hair and let it fall to its full length.

Now there were two possessions of the James Dillingham Youngs in which they both took a mighty pride. One was Jim's gold watch that had been his father's and his grandfather's. The other was Della's hair. Had the Queen of Sheba[7] lived in the flat across the air shaft, Della would have let her hair hang out the window someday to dry, just to depreciate Her Majesty's jewels and gifts. Had King Solomon been the janitor, with all his treasures piled up in the basement, Jim would have pulled out his watch every time he passed, just to see him pluck at his beard from envy.

So now Dell's beautiful hair fell about her, rippling and shining like a cascade of brown waters. It reached below her knee and made itself almost a garment for her. And then she did it up again nervously and

6. **pier glass:** a long narrow mirror that fits between two windows.
7. **Queen of Sheba** (shē′bə): in the Bible, a woman famous for her wealth and beauty. She visited King Solomon in order to test his wisdom.

quickly. Once she faltered for a minute and stood still while a tear or two splashed on the worn red carpet.

On went her old brown jacket; on went her old brown hat. With a whirl of skirts and with the brilliant sparkle still in her eyes, she fluttered out the door and down the stairs to the street.

Where she stopped the sign read: "Mme. Sofronie. Hair Goods of All Kinds." One flight up Della ran—and collected herself, panting. Madame, large, too white, chilly, hardly looked the "Sofronie."

"Will you buy my hair?" asked Della.

"I buy hair," said Madame. "Take yer hat off and let's have a sight at the looks of it."

Down rippled the brown cascade.

"Twenty dollars," said Madame, lifting the mass with a practiced hand.

"Give it to me quick," said Della.

Oh, and the next two hours tripped by on rosy wings. Forget the hashed metaphor.[8] She was ransacking the stores for Jim's present.

She found it at last. It surely had been made for Jim and no one else. There was no other like it in any of the stores, and she had turned all of them inside out. It was a platinum fob chain simple and chaste in design, properly proclaiming its value by substance alone and not by meretricious[9] ornamentation—as all good things should do. It was even worthy of The Watch. As soon as she saw it she knew that it must be Jim's. It was like him. Quietness and value—the description applied to both. Twenty-one dollars they took from her for it, and she hurried home with the eighty-seven cents. With that chain on his watch Jim might be properly anxious about the time in any company. Grand as the watch was, he sometimes looked at it on the sly on account of the old leather strap that he used in place of a chain.

When Della reached home her intoxication gave way a little to prudence and reason. She got out her curling irons and lighted the gas and went to work repairing the ravages made by generosity added to love. Which is always a tremendous task, dear friends—a mammoth task.

Within forty minutes her head was covered with tiny, close-lying curls

---

8. **hashed metaphor** (mĕt′ə-fôr′, -fər): A metaphor is a comparison between two unlike things. O. Henry's metaphor is "mixed" for comic effect. He describes Time as both walking ("tripped by") and flying ("on rosy wings").

9. **meretricious** (mĕr′ə-trĭsh′əs): attractive but cheap and flashy.

that made her look wonderfully like a truant schoolboy. She looked at her reflection in the mirror long, carefully, and critically.

"If Jim doesn't kill me," she said to herself, "before he takes a second look at me, he'll say I look like a Coney Island chorus girl. But what could I do—oh! what could I do with a dollar and eighty-seven cents?"

At seven o'clock the coffee was made and the frying pan was on the back of the stove hot and ready to cook the chops.

Jim was never late. Della doubled the fob chain in her hand and sat on the corner of the table near the door that he always entered. Then she heard his step on the stair away down on the first flight, and she turned white for just a moment. She had a habit of saying little silent prayers about the simplest everyday things, and now she whispered, "Please, God, make him think I am still pretty."

The door opened and Jim stepped in and closed it. He looked thin and very serious. Poor fellow, he was only twenty-two—and to be burdened with a family! He needed a new overcoat and he was without gloves.

Jim stopped inside the door, as immovable as a setter at the scent of quail. His eyes were fixed upon Della; and there was an expression in them that she could not read, and it terrified her. It was not anger, nor surprise, nor disapproval, nor horror, nor any of the sentiments that she had been prepared for. He simply stared at her fixedly with that peculiar expression on his face.

Della wriggled off the table and went to him.

"Jim, darling," she cried, "don't look at me that way. I had my hair cut off and sold it because I couldn't have lived through Christmas without giving you a present. It'll grow out again—you won't mind, will you? I just had to do it. My hair grows awfully fast. Say 'Merry Christmas!' Jim, and let's be happy. You don't know what a nice—what a beautiful, nice gift I've got for you."

"You've cut off your hair?" asked Jim laboriously, as if he had not arrived at that patent fact yet even after the hardest mental labor.

"Cut if off and sold it," said Della. "Don't you like me just as well, anyhow? I'm me without my hair, ain't I?"

Jim looked about the room curiously.

"You say your hair is gone?" he said, with an air almost of idiocy.

"You needn't look for it," said Della. "It's sold, I tell you—sold and gone, too. It's Christmas Eve, boy. Be good to me, for it went for you.

Maybe the hairs of my head were numbered," she went on with a sudden serious sweetness, "but nobody could ever count my love for you. Shall I put the chops on, Jim?"

Out of his trance Jim seemed quickly to wake. He enfolded his Della. For ten seconds let us regard with discreet scrutiny some inconsequential object in the other direction. Eight dollars a week or a million a year—what is the difference? A mathematician or a wit would give you the wrong answer. The Magi[10] brought valuable gifts, but that was not among them. This dark assertion will be illuminated later on.

Jim drew a package from his overcoat pocket and threw it upon the table.

"Don't make any mistake, Dell," he said, "about me. I don't think there's anything in the way of a haircut or a shave or a shampoo that could make me like my girl any less. But if you'll unwrap that package you may see why you had me going awhile at first."

White fingers and nimble tore at the string and paper. And then an ecstatic scream of joy; and then, alas! a quick feminine change to hysterical tears and wails, necessitating the immediate employment of all the comforting powers of the lord of the flat.

For there lay The Combs—the set of combs, side and back, that Della had worshipped for long in a Broadway window. Beautiful combs, pure tortoise shell, with jeweled rims—just the shade to wear in the beautiful vanished hair. They were expensive combs, she knew, and her heart had simply craved and yearned over them without the least hope of possession. And now they were hers, but the tresses that should have adorned the coveted adornments were gone.

But she hugged them to her bosom, and at length she was able to look up with dim eyes and a smile and say, "My hair grows so fast, Jim!"

And then Della leaped up like a little singed cat and cried, "Oh, oh!"

Jim had not yet seen his beautiful present. She held it out to him eagerly upon her open palm. The dull precious metal seemed to flash with a reflection of her bright and ardent spirit.

"Isn't it a dandy, Jim? I hunted all over town to find it. You'll have to look at the time a hundred times a day now. Give me your watch. I want to see how it looks on it."

10. **Magi** (mā′jī′).

Instead of obeying, Jim tumbled down on the couch and put his hands under the back of his head and smiled.

"Della," said he, "let's put our Christmas presents away and keep 'em awhile. They're too nice to use just at present. I sold the watch to get the money to buy your combs. And now suppose you put the chops on."

The Magi, as you know, were wise men—wonderfully wise men—who brought gifts to the Babe in the manger. They invented the art of giving Christmas presents. Being wise, their gifts were no doubt wise ones, possibly bearing the privilege of exchange in case of duplication. And here I have lamely related to you the uneventful chronicle of two foolish children in a flat who most unwisely sacrificed for each other the greatest treasures of their house. But in a last word to the wise of these days let it be said that of all who give gifts these two were the wisest. Of all who give and receive gifts, such as they are wisest. Everywhere they are wisest. They are the Magi.

First Response: *Did you consider the story's surprise ending a trick or the logical conclusion of events?*

CHECKING UP

1. When does the action of the story take place?
2. What is Della's proudest possession?
3. What does Della buy for Jim?
4. What has happened to Jim's watch?
5. What is Jim's gift for Della?

TALKING IT OVER

1. Which details in the story tell you that the events take place early in the twentieth century?

2. This story is famous for its ironic plot. How do the actions of the characters bring about unexpected results? Are these actions consistent with the nature of the characters?
3. What is the tone of the story? Is O. Henry's attitude toward his characters sympathetic? mocking? amused? or something else?
4. Locate the statement in this story that best expresses its theme.
5. Explain the title of the story. What is the "gift" associated with the Magi? What has this gift to do with Jim and Della?

TOTAL EFFECT

Throughout his story O. Henry emphasizes the way that money, or the lack of it, affects the lives of Jim and Della. We know the exact amounts of things. They live in a furnished flat that costs eight dollars a week. Della has saved one dollar and eighty-seven cents. Jim's income is twenty dollars a week. Della sells her hair for twenty dollars and spends twenty-one dollars on a chain for Jim's watch. Yet, O. Henry means to show us that however deprived they may be of domestic comforts and possessions, Jim and Della are rich in what they bring to each other.

In the last paragraph, O. Henry appears to contradict himself. He refers to Jim and Della as "two foolish children . . . who most unwisely sacrificed for each other the greatest treasures of their house." In the very next sentence, however, he claims that of all gift givers, these two were "the wisest." It is clear that O. Henry is playing on the meaning of *wise* in order to make a point. To those people who attach value chiefly to money and material things, the sacrifice of Jim and Della must seem foolish and wasteful. To others, like the author, Jim and Della are wisest because their gift of love and sacrifice is far more important than any material gift.

The reader knows that far from narrating an "uneventful chronicle," O. Henry succeeds in giving meaning to the story of two ordinary people whose love for one another transforms them into the Magi—the wisest.

1. How does the title of the story reveal O. Henry's purpose?
2. The Magi were wise men who brought three gifts to Bethlehem. Why does O. Henry's title refers to a single gift?

UNDERSTANDING THE WORDS IN THE STORY
(Matching Columns)

1. reflection	a. wealth and success
2. vestibule	b. excellent
3. prosperity	c. hesitated
4. unassuming	d. quick
5. sterling	e. entranceway
6. agile	f. running lengthwise
7. longitudinal	g. belittle or lessen
8. depreciate	h. searching
9. faltered	i. serious thought
10. ransacking	j. modest

(Completion)

chaste	scrutiny
prudence	inconsequential
mammoth	adornment
laborious	ardent
patent	chronicle

1. Something that is evident or clear is said to be _____.
2. An object used to decorate or ornament something is a (an) _____.
3. A(n) _____ style is restrained and simple.
4. A narrative or history is known as a(n) _____.
5. Something of little significance is _____.
6. Impulsive people tend to act without _____.
7. A(n) _____ love is intense in feeling.
8. That which calls for hard work is _____.
9. To be subjected to _____ is to be examined carefully.
10. A(n) _____ undertaking is very big.

WRITING IT DOWN
A Comparison/Contrast Essay

Write a brief essay comparing and contrasting "The Gift of the Magi" by O. Henry and "Three Wise Guys" by Sandra Cisneros (page 39). Discuss the stories in terms of setting, plot, and theme. You may want to use a chart like the one below to organize details for your essay.

	"Three Wise Guys"	"The Gift of the Magi"
SETTING		
PLOT		
THEME		

When you draft your essay, include a statement of your **main idea** in the first paragraph. In this statement, identify the subjects for your comparison and tell whether you will emphasize similarities, differences, or both in your essay.

In the body of your paper, be sure to discuss your details in a logical order. If you use the *block method,* for example, you present your discussion of all three elements for one story. You then present your discussion of all three elements for the second story in the same order.

In a brief concluding paragraph, restate your main idea and sum up your reactions to both stories. Below is an outline to follow when you write your essay.

Paragraph 1: Introduction—State main idea
Paragraph 2: Body—Discuss "Three Wise Guys"
    A. Setting _____
    B. Plot _____
    C. Theme _____

Paragraph 3: Body—Discuss "The Gift of the Magi"
  A. Setting _____
  B. Plot _____
  C. Theme _____
Paragraph 4: Conclusion—Restate main idea and sum up reactions to both stories

ABOUT THE AUTHOR

O. Henry is the pen name of William Sydney Porter (1862–1910), who grew up in Greensboro, North Carolina. He took the name O. Henry after he had served a term in jail for embezzling money from a Texas bank. In 1902 he moved to New York City and became famous for his short stories. Some of his collections are *The Four Million* (1906), *Heart of the West* (1907), *The Voice of the City* (1908), *The Gentle Grafter* (1908), and *Whirligigs* (1910). The trademark of an O. Henry story is its surprise ending. "The Gift of the Magi" is probably O. Henry's most famous story. Other well-known stories are "The Ransom of Red Chief," "A Retrieved Reformation," "After Twenty Years," and "The Furnished Room."

HALF A DAY

Naguib Mahfouz°

---

*The passage of time is a common theme in literature. Think of books
you have read or movies you have seen that deal with time travel or
some other type of twist involving time.*

I proceeded alongside my father, clutching his right hand, running
to keep up with the long strides he was taking. All my clothes were
new: the black shoes, the green school uniform, and the red tarboosh.[1] My delight in my new clothes, however, was not altogether
unmarred, for this was no feast day but the day on which I was to be
cast into school for the first time.

My mother stood at the window watching our progress, and I would
turn toward her from time to time, as though appealing for help. We
walked along a street lined with gardens; on both sides were extensive
fields planted with crops, prickly pears, henna trees, and a few date
palms.

"Why school?" I challenged my father openly. "I shall never do
anything to annoy you."

"I'm not punishing you," he said, laughing. "School's not a punishment. It's the factory that makes useful men out of boys. Don't you want
to be like your father and brothers?"

I was not convinced. I did not believe there was really any good to
be had in tearing me away from the intimacy of my home and throwing me into this building that stood at the end of the road like some
huge, high-walled fortress, exceedingly stern and grim.

When we arrived at the gate we could see the courtyard, vast and
crammed full of boys and girls. "Go in by yourself," said my father, "and
join them. Put a smile on your face and be a good example to others."

I hesitated and clung to his hand, but he gently pushed me from
him. "Be a man," he said. "Today you truly begin life. You will find me
waiting for you when it's time to leave."

I took a few steps, then stopped and looked but saw nothing. Then

---

°**Naguib Mahfouz** (nä-gēb′ mä-fōōz′).
1. **tarboosh** (tär-bōōsh′): a cone-shaped cloth cap worn by Muslim men.

414   HALF A DAY

the faces of boys and girls came into view. I did not know a single one of them, and none of them knew me. I felt I was a stranger who had lost his way. But glances of curiosity were directed toward me, and one boy approached and asked, "Who brought you?"

"My father," I whispered.

"My father's dead," he said quite simply.

I did not know what to say. The gate was closed, letting out a pitiable screech. Some of the children burst into tears. The bell rang. A lady came along, followed by a group of men. The men began sorting us into ranks. We were formed into an intricate pattern in the great courtyard surrounded on three sides by high buildings of several floors; from each floor we were overlooked by a long balcony roofed in wood.

"This is your new home," said the woman. "Here too there are mothers and fathers. Here there is everything that is enjoyable and beneficial to knowledge and religion. Dry your tears and face life joyfully."

We submitted to the facts, and this submission brought a sort of contentment. Living beings were drawn to other living beings, and from the first moments my heart made friends with such boys as were to be my friends and fell in love with such girls as I was to be in love with, so that it seemed my misgivings had had no basis. I had never imagined school would have this rich variety. We played all sorts of different games: swings, the vaulting horse, ball games. In the music room we chanted our first songs. We also had our first introduction to language. We saw a globe of the Earth, which revolved and showed the various continents and countries. We started learning the numbers. The story of the Creator of the universe was read to us, we were told of His present world and of His Hereafter, and we heard examples of what He said. We ate delicious food, took a little nap, and woke up to go on with friendship and love, play and learning.

As our path revealed itself to us, however, we did not find it as totally sweet and unclouded as we had presumed. Dust-laden winds and unexpected accidents came about suddenly, so we had to be watchful, at the ready, and very patient. It was not all a matter of playing and fooling around. Rivalries could bring about pain and hatred or give rise to fighting. And while the lady would sometimes smile, she would often scowl and scold. Even more frequently she would resort to physical punishment.

In addition, the time for changing one's mind was over and gone and there was no question of ever returning to the paradise of home. Nothing lay ahead of us but exertion, struggle, and perseverance. Those who were able took advantage of the opportunities for success and happiness that presented themselves amid the worries.

The bell rang announcing the passing of the day and the end of work. The throngs of children rushed toward the gate, which was opened again. I bade farewell to friends and sweethearts and passed through the gate. I peered around but found no trace of my father, who had promised to be there. I stepped aside to wait. When I had waited for a long time without avail, I decided to return home on my own. After I had taken a few steps, a middle-aged man passed by, and I realized at once that I knew him. He came toward me, smiling, and shook me by the hand, saying, "It's a long time since we last met—how are you?"

With a nod of my head, I agreed with him and in turn asked, "And you, how are you?"

"As you can see, not all that good, the Almighty be praised!"

Again he shook me by the hand and went off. I proceeded a few steps, then came to a startled halt. Good Lord! Where was the street lined with gardens? Where had it disappeared to? When did all these vehicles invade it? And when did all these hordes of humanity come to rest upon its surface? How did these hills of refuse come to cover its sides? And where were the fields that bordered it? High buildings had taken over, the street surged with children, and disturbing noises shook the air. At various points stood conjurers showing off their tricks and making snakes appear from baskets. Then there was a band announcing the opening of a circus, with clowns and weight lifters walking in front. A line of trucks carrying central security troops crawled majestically by. The siren of a fire engine shrieked, and it was not clear how the vehicle would cleave its way to reach the blazing fire. A battle raged between a taxi driver and his passenger, while the passenger's wife called out for help and no one answered. Good God! I was in a daze. My head spun. I almost went crazy. How could all this have happened in half a day, between early morning and sunset? I would find the answer at home with my father. But where was my home? I could see only tall buildings and hordes of people. I hastened on to the crossroads between the gardens and Abu Khoda.[2] I had to cross Abu Khoda to reach my house, but the stream of cars would not let up. The fire engine's siren was shrieking at full pitch as it moved at a snail's pace, and I said to myself, "Let the fire take its pleasure in what it consumes."[3] Extremely irritated, I wondered when I would be able to cross. I stood there a long time, until the young lad employed at the ironing shop on the corner came up to me. He stretched out his arm and said gallantly, "Grandpa, let me take you across."

2. **Abu Khoda** (ä-bōō′ kō′dä).
3. **Let the fire . . . consumes:** an Egyptian proverb.

First Response: *Were you completely surprised by the ending of the story? Explain your answer.*

CHECKING UP (True/False)

1. The narrator is eager to begin school.
2. The narrator's father encourages the boy to smile and be a good example.
3. The narrator finds school surprisingly varied and interesting.
4. The narrator tries to return home on his own.
5. The narrator is delighted by the changes he encounters.

TALKING IT OVER

1. What is the narrator's attitude toward his first day at school?
2. According to his father, why is he being sent to school?
3. What lessons about life does the narrator learn at "school"?
4. What is the significance of the narrator's encounter with the middle-aged man? What does this meeting suggest about the passage of time?
5. As the narrator walks home from school, he notices changes in the landscape. What kinds of changes have taken place?

TOTAL EFFECT

An **allegory** is a tale in which characters, actions, or settings represent abstract ideas or moral qualities. In an allegorical short story, many of the story's principal elements are symbolic. The characters, setting, and events in this kind of story have meaning in themselves, but they also stand for something larger than themselves. The total effect of Naguib Mahfouz's haunting story "Half a Day" depends largely on the author's use of allegory.

1. What has happened to the narrator, in a sense, over the course of the story? What does the "half a day" represent?
2. What is the significance of the father's statement, "Today you truly begin life"?
3. The narrator describes his lessons and other school experiences in three paragraphs, beginning with the words, "We submitted to the facts" (page 414). What details in this passage hint that the narrator is really talking about more than his first day at school and that his words apply to life as a whole?
4. What do you think is the **theme,** or underlying message, of this story? Explain your answer.

UNDERSTANDING THE WORDS IN THE STORY
(Matching Columns)

1. unmarred
2. exceedingly
3. grim
4. beneficial
5. contentment
6. presumed
7. rivalries
8. exertion
9. perseverance
10. hastened

a. determination; endurance
b. disputes; competition
c. hurried
d. assumed
e. great effort
f. very; extremely
g. stern; harsh
h. unspoiled
i. satisfaction
j. helpful

WRITING IT DOWN
A Story

Write a story of your own about a day in which time passes in a strange way. Be creative with your choice of plot, characters, setting, and tone.

A Literary Analysis

In a **literary analysis** of a short story, you examine at least one of the story's major elements, present a main idea or thesis about it, and support that idea with quotations and other details from the story.

Write a literary analysis of "Half a Day." Start your prewriting by jotting down your personal responses to the story. Then move on to a more objective examination of the story's major elements. Consider some or all of the following:

    plot
    character
    setting
    point of view
    tone
    theme
    imagery

As you consider these elements, jot down notes to identify a main idea or overall thesis for your essay. Ask yourself: What are the most important elements in this story's total effect? What techniques does the author use to communicate his underlying message? State your main idea clearly in one or two sentences.

Collect support for your main idea by rereading the story and gathering specific details. Then organize these details logically and write a first draft of your literary analysis. Here is an outline that you may find helpful.

I. Introduction
  A. Capture reader's attention
  B. Identify title and author of the story
  C. State main idea

II. Body
  Support main idea with details, quotations, and other evidence

III. Conclusion
  A. Summarize major points
  B. Restate main idea

When you have finished writing a first draft of your essay, exchange papers with a peer reader and offer each other suggestions for the revision of your work. Make sure that you have presented your material in a logical way and that you have used appropriate transitional words to help the reader see the relationships of ideas in your writing.

Next, proofread your essay to correct any errors in grammar, usage, and mechanics. Prepare a final version of your literary analysis by making a clean copy, and then share your essay with the class as a whole.

ABOUT THE AUTHOR

Naguib Mahfouz was born around 1911 in the Gamaliyya quarter of Cairo, Egypt, which later became a favorite setting for many of his works. He is referred to as "Al-Sabir" or "the patient one" by his friends, because he labored in obscurity for many years.

Mahfouz had many interests as a teenager. He liked to read Egyptian detective novels, go to the movies, play soccer, listen to music, and visit friends. He has said, "To be able to do all that, I had to divide my time very carefully. . . . I wanted to be brilliant so I had to work hard."

Mahfouz attended the University of Cairo. He worked in the Ministry of Religious Affairs for fifteen years until he transferred to a post in the Arts Administration. During these years he continued to write fiction and successful screenplays. The breakthrough in his career came in 1956 with the publication of *Between the Two Palaces,* which is now the most famous novel in the Arabic language. Since his retirement in 1972, Mahfouz has written prolifically, producing fourteen novels and five short-story collections. *Arabian Nights and Days,* a collection of seventeen interconnected tales first published in Arabic in 1979, has recently been translated into English. Mahfouz received the Nobel Prize for Literature in 1988.

GLOSSARY OF LITERARY TERMS

Allegory A tale in which characters, actions, or settings have symbolic meanings. This type of narrative is most often used to convey ideas or moral principles.

See page 417.

Anecdote A very short humorous or entertaining incident, often from personal experience.

See page 138.

Atmosphere The overall feeling of a work of literature.

See **Mood.**
See pages 17, 80, 226, 245.

Character A person—or animal or thing presented as a person—appearing in a work of literature. In order to be believable a character must have credibility, consistency, and motivation.

See **Static** and **Dynamic Character.**
See **Stock Character.**
See pages 163, 199, 235.

Characterization The methods used to present a character in a short story. A writer can create character by *direct* and *indirect* methods.

See **Direct and Indirect Characterization.**
See pages 163, 170, 199.

Cliché An expression that has become trite from excessive use.

See page 321.

Climax The point of greatest excitement or intensity in a story.

See pages 74, 122, 128.

Coincidence The accidental coming together of things or events in a seemingly planned or arranged way.

See page 154.

Conflict A problem or a struggle of some kind. Conflict may be *external* or *internal.* In a story there may be one conflict or several conflicts.

See pages 61, 74, 122, 124, 144, 360.

Dialogue In literature, the conversation of characters. The use of dialogue can add to the realistic quality of a story.

See page 61.

Direct and Indirect Characterization. Methods of presenting a character in a short story. In *direct characterization,* a writer *tells* what a character is like by means of direct comment. In *indirect characterization,* a writer *shows* what a character is like by 1) giving a physical description of the character; 2) relating the character's actions and words; 3) revealing the character's thoughts and feelings; and 4) making clear what others in the story think about the character.

See page 163.

Dramatic Irony A type of irony in which the reader knows something that a character in the story does not know.

See page 330.

Dramatic Monologue An extended speech delivered by a character to listeners whose replies are not given.

See pages 75, 320.

Dramatic Point of View

See **Objective Point of View.**

Dynamic Character A character who undergoes an important change.

See page 180.

Exaggeration Overstatement or overemphasis, often with comic effect.

See pages 320, 399.

Explicit Theme A statement that directly expresses the central meaning of a story.

See page 345.

Exposition The part of a story giving background information.

See pages 25, 122, 144, 154.

Fantasy   A form of fiction that deals with unreal or fantastic things.

See page 35.

Fiction   A narrative that is invented or imagined. A work of fiction may be based on true events, but the final product has been shaped and reformed by the writer.

See page 5.

First-Person Point of View   The vantage point in which the narrator is a character in the story and uses the pronoun "I."

See pages 253, 262, 289, 380.

Flashback   An interruption in a narrative to relate an action that has already occurred.

See page 137.

Forceful Satire   A type of satire employing a bitter or sarcastic tone.

See page 320.

Foreshadowing   The method of building in clues or hints about what is to come in a story.

See pages 18, 26, 67, 145.

Genial Satire   A type of satire that makes use of a humorous or light-hearted tone.

See page 310.

Humor   An amusing or funny element that is warm and genial rather than critical in tone.

See pages 5, 122.

Imagery   Descriptive language that appeals to the senses and creates pictures or images in the reader's mind.

See page 266.

Implied Theme The central meaning that must be inferred from the characters and events in a story.

See page 351.

Incongruity A technique of pairing opposites to create unexpected contrast.

See page 310.

Irony A difference or contrast between appearance and reality. The types of irony include *irony of situation, dramatic irony,* and *verbal irony.*

See **Dramatic Irony.**
See **Irony of Situation.**
See **Verbal Irony.**
See pages 5, 26, 87, 105, 113, 128, 277, 320, 330.

Irony of Situation A type of irony in which there is a contrast between what is expected and what actually happens.

See pages 227, 330.

Jargon A specialized vocabulary used by those of a particular trade or profession.

See page 321.

Mood The emotional quality in a piece of literature.

See **Atmosphere.**
See pages 80, 226, 245.

Narrator The person who tells a story.

See pages 87, 253, 262, 287.

Objective Point of View A third-person point of view in which the observer records events without offering commentary or interpretation. Also called the *dramatic point of view.*

See pages 267, 362.

Oral Tradition Storytelling used for passing tales from one generation to the next.

See page 18.

Parable   A short, simple tale that illustrates a moral or spiritual lesson.

See page 45.

Personification   The presentation of an abstract quality, object, or idea as a person.

See page 191.

Plot   The sequence of related events or actions in a story.

See pages 122, 227.

Point of View   The angle from which a story is told.

See pages 200, 253, 262, 267, 277, 287, 360.

Protagonist   The main character in a story.

See page 163.

Realism   A type of fiction that deals with everyday characters and events.

See page 61.

Resolution   The final part of a story that makes clear the outcome of the conflict.

See page 129.

Revelation   A dramatic moment that reveals something important to a character.

See page xi.

Satire   A literary work that pokes fun at some weakness or vice of human nature or society. Satire can be gentle and lighthearted, or savage and bitter.

See **Forceful Satire.**
See **Genial Satire.**
See pages 310, 320.

Self-conscious Point of View   A point of view in which the narrator addresses the reader directly and comments on the story.

See page 287.

Sentimentalism   The expression of warm and tender feelings often used to describe *tone.*

See page 304.

Setting   The time, place, and circumstances that form the background of a story.

See pages 74, 97, 210, 218, 227, 234, 245.

Sketch   A short, informal piece of prose, most often used for description.

See page 80.

Static Character   A character who does not change in any significant way.

See page 180.

Stereotype

See **Stock Character.**

Stock Character   A character who conforms to a familiar and predictable formula, also known as a **stereotype.**

See page 191.

Surprise Ending   A conclusion to a work of literature, usually a short story, that is unexpected. Such endings often involve some sort of "twist."

See page 26.

Suspense   The element that keeps readers guessing about the outcome of events.

See pages 122, 145, 391.

Symbol   A person, object, or event that has meaning in itself and also stands for something else.

See pages 97, 113, 369.

Tall Tale   A narrative relating superhuman feats or comically exaggerated and improbable events.

See page 399.

Theme   The central idea or underlying meaning about human nature that is developed in a story. A theme may be expressed directly or indirectly.

See **Explicit Theme.**
See **Implied Theme.**
See pages 115, 338, 345, 351, 360, 369.

Third-Person Limited Point of View   A point of view that focuses on one character's thoughts, feelings, and actions.

See page 277.

Third-Person Omniscient Point of View   A point of view in which the narrator is an all-knowing observer who knows what all the characters can see, hear, think, and feel.

See page 262.

Tone   The attitude a writer takes toward the subject, characters, and readers of a work.

See pages 5, 122, 297, 320.

Total Effect   The central impression or impact that a literary work has on its readers.

See pages 380, 391, 399, 409, 417.

Understatement   A restrained form of expression, in which less is said than is meant.

See page 320.

Verbal Irony   A type of irony in which a writer or character says one thing and means something entirely different.

See page 330.

Verisimilitude   The appearance of reality in fiction.

See page 218.

GLOSSARY

The words listed in the glossary on the following pages are found in the short stories in this textbook. In this glossary, the meanings given are the ones that apply to the words as they are used in the selections. Words closely related in form and meaning are generally listed together in one entry (**abrupt** and **abruptly**) and the definition is given for the first form. Regular adverbs (ending in *-ly*) are defined in their adjective form, with the adverb form shown at the end of the definition.

The following abbreviations are used:

adj., adjective	*n.*, noun
adv., adverb	*v.*, verb

For more information about the words in this glossary, consult a dictionary.

A

abrupt (ə-brŭpt′) *adj.* Happening suddenly; unexpected.—**abruptly** *adv.*

absorbed (ăb-sôrbd′, -zôrbd′) *adj.* Completely attentive; wholly involved in.

abstracted (ăb-străk′tid) *adj.* Absent-minded.—**abstractedly** *adv.*

abundance (ə-bŭn′dəns) *n.* Wealth; plenty.

acceleration (ăk-sĕl′ə-rā′shən) *n.* An increase in speed.

acknowledge (ăk-nŏl′ĭj) *v.* To admit.

acquiesce (ăk′wē-ĕs′) *v.* To agree with; comply.

acute (ə-kyo͞ot′) *adj.* **1.** Sensitive. **2.** Sharp; intense. **3.** Keen; perceptive.

adobe (ə-dō′bē) *adj.* Made of unburnt, sun-dried brick.

adorn (ə-dôrn′) *v.* To add beauty to.—**adornment** *n.*

adverse (ăd-vûrs′, ăd′vûrs′) *adj.* Causing harm; unfavorable.

affable (ăf′ə-bəl) *adj.* Pleasant; good-natured.

agile (ăj′əl, ăj′īl) *adj.* Quick and light in movement.

agony (ăg′ə-nē) *n.* Intense suffering.

The pronunciation system in this glossary is from *The American Heritage Dictionary of the English Language.* Copyright © 1981 by Houghton Mifflin Company. Reprinted by permission of ***Houghton Mifflin Company.***

ă pat / ā pay / âr care / ä father / b bib / ch church / d deed / ĕ pet / ē be / f fife / g gag /
h hat / hw which / ĭ pit / ī pie / îr pier / j judge / k kick / l lid, needle / m mum / n no,
sudden / ng thing / ŏ pot / ō toe / ô paw, for / oi noise / ou out / o͞o took / o͞o boot / p pop /
r roar / s sauce / sh ship, dish / t tight / th thin, path / *th* this, bathe / ŭ cut / ûr urge / v valve /
w with / y yes / z zebra, size / zh vision / ə about, item, edible, gallop, circus / à *Fr.* ami / œ *Fr.*
feu, *Ger.* schön / ü *Fr.* tu, *Ger.* über / ᴋʜ *Ger.* ich, *Scot.* loch / ɴ *Fr.* bon.

ambassador (ăm-băs′ə-dər, -dôr′) *n.* An official messenger or representative of a country.

animosity (ăn-ə-mŏs′ə-tē) *n.* Hatred; bitter hostility.

anxiety (ăng-zī′ə-tē) *n.* Restless eagerness.

apparent (ə-păr′ənt, -pâr′) *adj.* Plain; obvious.—**apparently** *adv.*

apprehension (ăp′rĭ-hĕn′shən) *n.* Dread; uneasiness.

ardent (är′dənt) *adj.* Warm; passionate.

ardor (är′dər) *n.* Intense emotion.

aristocratic (ə-rĭs′tə-krăt′ĭk) *adj.* Having the manners of the upper class; exclusive or snobbish.

arouse (ə-rouz′) *v.* To stimulate or stir up.

arrogant (ăr′ə-gənt) *adj.* Proud; disdainful.—**arrogantly** *adv.*

articulate (är-tĭk′yə-lāt) *v.* To express clearly.

ascetic (ə-sĕt′ĭk) *adj.* Self-denying; strictly self-disciplined.

asinine (ăs′ə-nīn′) *adj.* Stupid or silly.

assured (ə-shoŏrd′) *adj.* Confident.

astern (ə-stûrn′) *adj.* Toward the rear of a ship.

astray (ə-strā′) *adv.* Away from the right direction.

astride (ə-strīd′) *prep.* With a leg on each side of.

attire (ə-tīr′) *n.* Clothing.

awe (ô) *n.* A feeling of wonder and dread. *v.* To inspire with fear or wonder.

B

baffle (băf′əl) *v.* To confuse.

bayonet (bā′ə-nĭt, -nĕt′, bā′ə-nĕt′) *n.* A blade attached to the end of a rifle for use in close combat.

beleaguer (bĭ-lē′gər) *v.* To lay siege to by surrounding with troops.

beneficial (bĕn′ə-fĭsh′əl) *adj.* Helpful; advantageous.

bleak (blēk) *adj.* Harsh and barren.

blurt (blûrt) *v.* To speak suddenly or thoughtlessly.

bluster (blŭs′tər) *v.* To speak boastfully or scornfully.

boast (bōst) *v.* To speak with pride.

bound (bound) *v.* **1.** To bounce. **2.** To enclose.

bounder (boun′dər) *n.* Someone whose behavior is coarse and ungentlemanly.

brake (brāk) *n.* An area covered with dense growth such as bushes.

brier (brī′ər) *n.* A prickly or thorny bush.

broach (brōch) *v.* To bring up; introduce.

browse (brouz) *v.* To look over carefully.

brusque (brŭsk) *adj.* Abrupt in speech or manner.—**brusquely** *adv.*

burden (bûrd′n) *n.* A heavy weight; trouble.

burn (bûrn) *v.* To throw a ball very hard.

bygone (bī′gôn′, -gŏn′) *adj.* Past; former.

C

cad (kăd) *n.* An ill-bred man.

canteen (kăn-tēn′) *n.* A small container for drinking water.

caress (kə-rĕs′) *n.* A gentle stroke or touch.

causeless (kôz′ləs) *adj.* Without basis.

ceremony (sĕr′ə-mō′nē) *n.* A formal or conventional act.—**stand on ceremony.** Behave in an extremely formal way.

chaos (kā′ŏs) *n.* Confusion; complete disorder.

charger (chär′jər) *n.* A horse trained for battle.

charity (chăr′ĭ-tē) *n.* **1.** A feeling of good will; benevolence. **2.** The voluntary giving of money or other help to those in need.

chaste (chāst) *adj.* Simple in style.

chastise (chăs′tīz) *v.* To scold severely.

chronicle (krŏn′ĭ-kəl) *n.* A record.

cinch (sĭnch) *v.* Tightened or fastened, as a saddle or belt.

clamber (klăm′ər, klăm′bər) *v.* To climb with effort, using hands and feet.

clench (klĕnch) *v.* To close tightly.

coincidence (kō′ĭn′sə-dəns, -dĕns) *n.* An instance of two things appearing at the same place or time purely by chance.

commotion (kə-mō′shən) *n.* A noisy disturbance; confusion.

compassion (kəm-păsh′ən) *n.* Sympathy.

composure (kəm-pō′zhər) *n.* Calmness.

compound (kŏm-pound′, kəm-, kŏm′pound′) *v.* To add to or intensify.

conceive (kən-sēv′) *v.* **1.** To form an idea. **2.** To imagine.

concussion (kən-kŭsh′ən) *n.* A shock; violent jolt from impact.

condolence (kən-dō′ləns) *n.* An expression of sympathy.

confirm (kən-fûrm′) *v.* To make certain of; verify.

conscientious (kŏn′shē-ĕn′shəs) *adj.* **1.** Given to doing what is right; principled. **2.** Careful; thorough.

consequence (kŏn′sə-kwĕns) *n.* Importance.

ă pat / ā pay / âr care / ä father / b bib / ch church / d deed / ĕ pet / ē be / f fife / g gag / h hat / hw which / ĭ pit / ī pie / îr pier / j judge / k kick / l lid, needle / m mum / n no, sudden / ng thing / ŏ pot / ō toe / ô paw, for / oi noise / ou out / ŏŏ took / ōō boot / p pop / r roar / s sauce / sh ship, dish / t tight / th thin, path / *th* this, bathe / ŭ cut / ûr urge / v valve / w with / y yes / z zebra, size / zh vision / ə about, item, edible, gallop, circus / à *Fr.* ami / œ *Fr.* feu, *Ger.* schön / ü *Fr.* tu, *Ger.* über / KH *Ger.* ich, *Scot.* loch / N *Fr.* bon.

console (kən-sōl´) *v.* To comfort.

conspicuous (kən-spĭk´yōō-əs) *adj.* Noticeable; attracting attention.—
conspicuously *adv.*

consternation (kŏn´stər-nā´shən) *n.* Amazement; confusion; alarm.

contempt (kən-tĕmpt´) *n.* Strong disdain; scorn.

contentment (kən-tĕnt´mənt) *n.* Satisfaction.

contingent (kən-tĭn´jənt) *n.* A small group that is part of a larger one.

contract (kən-trăkt´) *v.* To pull or draw together.

cordiality (kôr-jăl´ə-tē) *n.* A friendly act or comment.

countenance (koun´tə-nəns) *n.* Facial expression.

covey (kŭv´ē) *n.* A small group.

crafty (krăf´tē) *adj.* Cleverly deceitful; cunning.

creditor (krĕd´ĭ-tər) *n.* A person to whom money or some type of payment
is owed.

crisp (krĭsp) *adj.* Short and forceful; sharp.—**crisply** *adv.*

cunning (kŭn´ĭng) *adj.* Shrewd.—**cunningly** *adv.*

cynical (sĭn´i-kəl) *adj.* Distrustful of the motives of others.—**cynically** *adv.*

D

dawdle (dôd´l) *v.* To linger; loiter.

dawn (dôn) *v.* To begin to be understood.

dazzle (dăz´əl) *v.* To overwhelm or amaze with light or splendor.

deceitful (dĭ-sēt´fəl) *adj.* Given to lying or misleading.

declaim (dĭ-klām´) *v.* To speak passionately or eloquently.

decree (dĭ-krē´) *n.* An official ruling or order.

deign (dān) *v.* To come down to the level of someone considered to be
inferior.

delectable (dĭ-lĕk´tə-bəl) *adj.* Delicious.

deliberation (dĭ-lĭb´ə-rā´shən) *n.* Careful decision making; consideration.

demigod (dĕm´ē-gŏd´) *n.* A godlike human being.

denigrate (dĕn´ĭ-grāt´) *v.* To blacken the reputation of; belittle.

dense (dĕns) *adj.* Thick.

deposit (dĭ-pŏz´ĭt) *v.* To put down carefully.

depreciate (dĭ-prē´shē-āt) *v.* To lessen or diminish in value.

deprive (dĭ-prīv´) *v.* To take away; deny.

descend (dĭ-sĕnd´) *v.* To move from a higher to a lower place.

designate (dĕz´ĭg-nāt´) *v.* To assign to an office or duty; appoint.

desist (dĭ-zĭst´, -sĭst´) *v.* To stop doing something; cease.

detached (dĭ-tăcht´) *adj.* Not emotionally involved; aloof.

detainee (dē′tā-nē′, dĭ-tā′-) *n.* A person held in custody, usually for political reasons.

detour (dē′tŏor′, dĭ-tŏor′) *n.* A temporary alternate route.

devious (dē′vē-əs) *adj.* Not direct; roundabout.

diatribe (dī′ə-trīb′) *n.* A bitter criticism or denunciation; tirade.

dire (dīr) *adj.* Having terrible consequences; dreadful.

discern (dĭ-sûrn′, -zûrn′) *v.* To recognize or see clearly.

disdainful (dĭs-dān′fəl) *adj.* Scornful; haughty.

dismember (dĭs-mĕm′bər) *v.* To take off the arms and legs.

disperse (dĭ-spûrs′) *v.* To scatter in different directions.

dissuade (dĭ-swād′) *v.* To discourage someone's course of action by means of persuasion.

distinction (dĭ-stĭngk′shən) *n.* The condition of being different or set apart.

distort (dĭs-tôrt′) *v.* To twist or pull out of shape.

distract (dĭs-trăkt′) *v.* **1.** To draw the attention away toward a different direction; divert. **2.** To disturb; trouble.

distracted (dĭs-trăk′tĭd) *adj.* Having the attention drawn in another direction; diverted.

dogged (dôg′ĭd, dŏg′ĭd) *adj.* Stubborn; determined.—**doggedly** *adv.*

doleful (dōl′fəl) *adj.* Sad; mournful.

dominant (dŏm′ə-nənt) *adj.* Most important or influential.

downcast (doun′căst′) *adj.* Sad; discouraged.

drudgery (drŭj′ə-rē) *n.* Work that is hard, tiresome, or unpleasant.

dwell (dwĕl) *v.* To live in a place; reside; inhabit.

E

eaves (ēvz) *n.* Overhang at the lower edge of a roof.

ebony (ĕb′ə-nē) *adj.* Black.

efficacy (ĕf′ĭ-kə-sē) *n.* Effectiveness.

elite (ĭ-lēt′, ā-lēt′) *n.* A small, privileged group regarded as the best or the most distinguished.

emanate (ĕm′ə-nāt′) *v.* To flow out or come forth.

embed (ĕm-bĕd′) *v.* To fix firmly in something.

embrace (ĕm-brās′) *v.* **1.** To hug. **2.** To provide support and comfort.

ă pat / ā pay / âr care / ä father / b bib / ch church / d deed / ĕ pet / ē be / f fife / g gag / h hat / hw which / ĭ pit / ī pie / îr pier / j judge / k kick / l lid, needle / m mum / n no, sudden / ng thing / ŏ pot / ō toe / ô paw, for / oi noise / ou out / ŏŏ took / ōō boot / p pop / r roar / s sauce / sh ship, dish / t tight / th thin, path / *th* this, bathe / ŭ cut / ûr urge / v valve / w with / y yes / z zebra, size / zh vision / ə about, item, edible, gallop, circus / à *Fr.* ami / œ *Fr.* feu, *Ger.* schön / ü *Fr.* tu, *Ger.* über / KH *Ger.* ich, *Scot.* loch / N *Fr.* bon.

emerge (ĭ-mûrj′) *v.* To come into view.

emit (ĭ-mĭt′) *v.* To give forth; discharge.

emphatic (ĕm-făt′ĭk) *adj.* **1.** Definite. **2.** Striking. **3.** With emphasis.—
emphatically *adv.*

enhance (ĕn-hăns′) *v.* To make greater or increase.

entranced (ĕn-trănsd′, -tränsd′, ĭn-) *adj.* Filled with pleasure.

envelop (ĕn-vĕl′əp, ĭn-) *v.* To encircle or cover completely.

era (îr′ə, ĕr′ə) *n.* A distinctive period of time.

eradicate (ĭ-răd′ĭ-kāt′) *v.* To eliminate completely; abolish.

ermine (ûr′mĭn) *n.* Valuable white fur of a weasel.

evacuate (ĭ-văk′yo͞o-āt′) *v.* To remove people from where they are living.

eventual (ĭ-vĕn′cho͞o-əl) *adj.* Final; ultimate.—**eventually** *adv.*

ewer (yo͞o′ər) *n.* Pitcher.

exceedingly (ĭk-sē′dĭng-lē) *adv.* Extremely; very.

excessive (ĕk-sĕs′ĭv, ĭk-) *adj.* Beyond a normal limit or amount.

excursion (ĕk-skûr′zhən, ĭk-) *n.* A short trip.

exertion (ĭg-zûr′shən) *n.* Strenuous effort.

exhilaration (ĭg-zĭl′ə-rā′shən) *n.* A feeling of liveliness.

expedient (ĭk-spē′dē-ənt) *n.* A means to an end; something that aids in
achievement of a goal.

expire (ĭk-spīr′) *v.* To die.

expression (ĕk-sprĕsh′ən, ĭk-) *n.* A look.

exquisite (ĕks-kwĭ′zĭt) *adj.* Extremely beautiful. ⸱

extension (ĕk-stĕn′shən, ĭk-) *n.* A period of extra time.

exuberant (ĕg-zo͞o′bər-ənt, ĭg′) *adj.* Joyful; full of high spirits.

exude (ĕg-zo͞od′, ĭg-, ĕk-so͞od′, ĭk-) *v.* To give off in abundant quantity.

exultant (ĕg-zŭl′tənt, ĭg-) *adj.* Joyful.

F

faction (făk′shən) *n.* A small party or subgroup, usually in conflict with a
larger group.

falter (fôl′tər) *v.* To hesitate.

fanatic (fə-năt′ĭk) *n.* Someone with unreasonable attachment to a cause,
often a political or religious extremist.

feign (fān) *v.* To make a false show; pretend.

fidget (fĭj′ĭt) *v.* To move nervously or restlessly.

flat (flăt) *n.* An apartment.

flaw (flô) *n.* A defect; imperfection.

florid (flôr′id, flŏr-) *adj.* Elaborately decorated; showy; gaudy.

flounce (flouns) *n.* A piece of pleated or gathered material used to trim a garment; ruffle.

flout (flout) *v.* Mock; ridicule.

fluent (floo′ənt) *adj.* Smooth; flowing easily.—**fluently** *adv.*

flush (flŭsh) *v.* **1.** To turn red; blush. **2.** To drive from cover, as game birds.

forage (fŏr′ĭj, fôr′-) *n.* Food for animals.

forbidding (fər-bĭd′ĭng, fôr-) *adj.* Appearing disagreeable or threatening.

foresight (fôr′sīt′, fŏr′-) *n.* **1.** Ability to see or to know beforehand. **2.** Preparation for the future.

forfeit (fôr′fĭt) *v.* To surrender as a penalty.

formality (fôr-măl′ĭ-tē) *n.* A customary act or ritual.

forsake (fôr-sāk′, fər-) *v.* To abandon; desert.

G

garb (gärb) *n.* Style of dressing; clothing.

gaunt (gônt) *adj.* Thin and exhausted; bony.

gelding (gĕl′dĭng) *n.* A castrated animal, especially a male horse.

genial (jēn′yəl) *adj.* Pleasant; friendly.

glaze (glāz) *adj.* To cover a surface with a thin layer of ice.

gleam (glēm) *n.* Brightness; shining light.

glimmer (glĭm′ər) *v.* To appear faintly.

glisten (glĭs′ən) *v.* To shine by reflection.

glossy (glŏs′ē, glôs′ē) *adj.* Slick and shiny.

glut (glŭt) *v.* To supply with too much.

gnarled (närld) *adj.* Knotty and twisted; misshapen.

governess (gŭv′ər-nĭs) *n.* A woman who works as a teacher in a private household.

grate (grāt) *v.* To make a harsh sound by scraping.

gratify (grăt′ə-fī′) *adj.* To please or satisfy.

grave (grāv) *adj.* Very serious.—**gravely** *adv.*

gravity (grăv′ə-tē) *n.* Dignity.

grim (grĭm) *adj.* Stern or uninviting; severe.

grope (grōp) *v.* To search for uncertainly.

gruff (grŭf) *adj.* Rough or harsh in speech.—**gruffly** *adv.*

ă pat / ā pay / âr care / ä father / b bib / ch church / d deed / ĕ pet / ē be / f fife / g gag / h hat / hw which / ĭ pit / ī pie / îr pier / j judge / k kick / l lid, needle / m mum / n no, sudden / ng thing / ŏ pot / ō toe / ô paw, for / oi noise / ou out / ŏŏ took / ōō boot / p pop / r roar / s sauce / sh ship, dish / t tight / th thin, path / *th* this, bathe / ŭ cut / ûr urge / v valve / w with / y yes / z zebra, size / zh vision / ə about, item, edible, gallop, circus / à *Fr.* ami / œ *Fr.* feu, *Ger.* schön / ü *Fr.* tu, *Ger.* über / KH *Ger.* ich, *Scot.* loch / N *Fr.* bon.

guileless (gīl'lĭs) *adj.* Simple.

gyrate (jī'rāt') *v.* To turn or revolve.

H

haggard (hăg'ərd) *adj.* Tired and worn out.

harrowing (hăr'ō-ĭng) *adj.* Distressing; tormenting.

hasten (hā'sən) *v.* To hurry.

haughty (hô'tē) *adj.* Proud and vain.—**haughtily** *adv.*

headland (hĕd'lənd, -lănd') *n.* A point of high land extending out into a body of water.

heartily (här'tĭl-ē) *adv.* Enthusiastically.

heedlessness (hēd'lĭs-nĭs) *n.* Carelessness.

heighten (hīt'n) *v.* **1.** To be raised. **2.** To make higher.

heirloom (âr'lōōm') *n.* A treasured possession passed down through generations.

hobble (hŏb'əl) *v.* To move with difficulty; limp.

humility (hyōō-mĭl'ə-tē) *n.* Modesty; humbleness.

hurtle (hûr'tl) *v.* To move speedily and forcefully.

hyacinth (hī'ə-sĭnth) *n.* A plant with fragrant, bell-shaped flowers.

hypocritical (hĭp'ə-krĭt'ə-kəl) *adj.* False; insincere.

I

illustrious (ĭ-lŭs'trē-əs) *adj.* Famous.

immense (ĭ-mĕns') *adj.* Huge.

imp (ĭmp) *n.* A young devil; mischievous spirit.

impartial (ĭm-pär'shəl) *adj.* Without prejudice; just; fair.

impending (ĭm-pĕn'dĭng) *adj.* Likely to happen soon.

imperial (ĭm-pîr'ē-əl) *adj.* Relating to an emperor.

imperil (ĭm-pĕr'əl) *v.* To put in danger.

imperious (ĭm-pîr'ē-əs) *adj.* Domineering; arrogant.

improbable (ĭm-prŏb'ə-bəl) *adj.* Doubtful or unlikely.

impromptu (ĭm-prŏmp'tōō, -tyōō) *adj.* Spontaneous; unrehearsed.

improvise (ĭm'prə-vīz') *v.* To create on the spur of the moment, usually to fill a need.

inadvertent (ĭn'əd-vûr'tnt) *adj.* Accidental; unintentional.—**inadvertently** *adv.*

incessant (ĭn-sĕs'ənt) *adj.* Uninterrupted; continuous.

incompetent (ĭn-kŏm'pə-tənt) *adj.* Not capable.

incongruous (ĭn-kŏng'grōō-əs) *adj.* Unsuitable; not appropriate.

inconsequential (ĭn-kŏn'sə-kwen'shəl) *adj.* Of little importance.

inconspicuous (ĭn'kən-spĭk'-yōō-əs) *adj.* Not attracting attention.

incorruptible (ĭn´kə-rŭp´tə-bəl) *adj.* Incapable of being wrong; reliable.

incredulous (ĭn-krĕj´ə-ləs) *adj.* Disbelieving.—**incredulously** *adv.*

indefinable (ĭn´dĭ-fī´nə-bəl) *adj.* That which cannot be described.

indifferent (ĭn-dĭf´ər-ənt) *adj.* Without particular interest or concern.— **indifferently** *adv.*

indignation (ĭn´dĭg-nā´shən) *n.* Anger caused by something that is unjust, unfair, or wrong.

indistinct (ĭn´dĭ-stĭngkt´) *adj.* Not well marked; unclear.

indolent (ĭn´də-lənt) *adj.* Lazy.—**indolently** *adv.*

induce (ĭn-do͞os´, -dyo͞os´) *v.* To influence; prevail upon.

ineradicable (ĭn´ĭ-răd´ĭ-kə-bəl) *adj.* Incapable of being eradicated or eliminated; indestructible.

inevitable (ĭn-ĕv´ə-tə-bəl) *adj.* Certain to happen; not capable of being prevented.

informer (ĭn-fôr´mər) *n.* Someone who gives information against others for reward.

innumerable (ĭ-no͞o´mər-ə-bəl, ĭ-nyo͞o´) *adj.* Countless.

inscription (ĭn-skrĭp´shən) *n.* The writing carved or engraved on a monument.

insolent (ĭn´sə-lənt) *adj.* Insulting; disrespectful.—**insolently** *adv.*

institution (ĭn´stə-to͞o´-shən, -tyo͞o´shən) *n.* An established feature.

intense (ĭn-tĕns´) *adj.* Showing concentration.

intent (ĭn-tĕnt´) *adj.* **1.** Firmly directed; attentive. **2.** Concentrated; intense.

interloper (ĭn´tər-lōp´ər, ĭn´tər-lōp´ər) *n.* A meddler; intruder.

interminable (ĭn-tûr´mə-nə-bəl) *adj.* Endless.—**interminably** *adv.*

intermittent (ĭn´tər-mĭt´nt) *adj.* Occurring at intervals; irregular.—**intermittently** *adv.*

intern (ĭn-tûrn´) *v.* To confine, as a prisoner.

intervene (ĭn´tər-vēn´) *v.* To come, or lie, between two things.

intricate (ĭn´trĭ-kĭt) *adj.* Complex; containing elaborate detail.

intrusion (ĭn-tro͞o´zhən) *n.* Entry without invitation.

J

jaunt (jônt, jänt) *n.* A short trip.

jaunty (jôn´tē, jän´-) *adj.* Carefree; cheerful.—**jauntily** *adv.*

jounce (jouns) *v.* To bounce.

ă pat/ā pay/âr care/ä father/b bib/ch church/d deed/ĕ pet/ē be/f fife/g gag/ h hat/hw which/ĭ pit/ī pie/îr pier/j judge/k kick/l lid, needle/m mum/n no, sudden/ng thing/ŏ pot/ō toe/ô paw, for/oi noise/ou out/o͝o took/o͞o boot/p pop/ r roar/s sauce/sh ship, dish/t tight/th thin, path/ *th* this, bathe/ŭ cut/ûr urge/v valve/ w with/y yes/z zebra, size/zh vision/ə about, item, edible, gallop, circus/à *Fr.* ami/œ *Fr.* feu, *Ger.* schön/ü *Fr.* tu, *Ger.* über/кн *Ger.* ich, *Scot.* loch/N *Fr.* bon.

K

kin (kĭn) *n.* Relatives.

L

laborious (lə-bôr′ē-əs) *adj.* Requiring great effort.
languid (lăng′gwĭd) *adj.* Slow of movement; sluggish.—**languidly** *adv.*
languor (lăng′gər, lăng′ər) *n.* Tiredness; drowsiness.
livid (lĭv′ĭd) *adj.* Pale or ashen.
lob (lŏb) *v.* To throw a ball in a slow, high arc.
lodge (lŏj) *v.* To register a charge or complaint.
lofty (lŏf′tē, lôf′-) *adj.* **1.** High; towering. **2.** Overproud; haughty.
longitudinal (lŏn′jə-tōōd′n-əl, -tyood′n-əl) *adj.* Running lengthwise.
loom (lōōm) *v.* To come into view as a threatening image.
lunge (lŭnj) *v.* To move forward suddenly.
lyre (līr) *n.* An ancient stringed instrument similar to the harp, used to accompany singing.

M

magnitude (măg′nĭ-tōōd′, tyōōd′) *n.* Extent; breadth.
mammoth (măm′əth) *adj.* Gigantic.
maraud (mə-rôd′) *v.* To raid; loot.
matted (măt′ĭd) *adj.* Covered densely.
maze (māz) *n.* An intricate network or pattern.
meander (mē-ăn′dər) *v.* To wander aimlessly.
mesa (mā′sə) *n.* A high plateau with steep sides.
moat (mōt) *n.* A deep ditch surrounding a fortress as protection.
mockery (mŏk′ə r-ē) *n.* Ridicule; a scornful action.—**mocking** *adj.* In a scornful manner; expressing ridicule.
momentary (mō′mən-tĕr′ē) *adj.* Not lasting long; brief.—**momentarily** *adv.*
monitor (mŏn′ĭ-tər) *v.* To check on; keep watch over.
mournful (môrn′fəl, mōrn′-) *adj.* Sorrowful.
muffle (mŭf′əl) *v.* To deaden a sound.

N

necessaries (nĕs′ə-sĕr′ēz) *n. pl.* Whatever is needed, such as food.
negligent (nĕg′lĭ-jənt) *adj.* Unconcerned; careless.
negotiation (nĭ-gō′shē-ā′shən) *n.* Bargaining; the act of coming to an agreement.

nemesis (nĕm′ĭ-sĭs) *n.* An undefeatable rival.

nincompoop (nĭn′kəm-po͞op′, nĭng′-) *n.* A stupid person; fool.

nominal (nŏm′ə-nəl) *adj.* Minimal in value.—**nominally** *adv.*

nostalgia (nŏ-stăl′jə, nə-) *n.* A longing for the past.

O

oblige (ə-blīj′) *v.* To require; necessitate.

obsession (əb-sĕsh′ən, ŏb-) *n.* A persistent idea or desire that cannot be gotten rid of.

obstinate (ŏb′stə-nĭt) *adj.* Stubborn; difficult to control.

obstruct (əb-strŭkt′, ŏb-) *v.* To block or cut off from sight.

ominous (ŏm′ə-nəs) *adj.* Threatening; sinister.—**ominously** *adv.*

oppressive (ə-prĕs′ĭv) *adj.* Burdensome; difficult to bear.—**oppressively** *adv.*

ordeal (ôr-dēl′) *n.* A difficult experience.

outmoded (out-mō′dĭd) *adj.* No longer usable; out-of-date.

outset (out′sĕt′) *n.* The beginning of something.

ovation (ō-vā′shən) *n.* Triumph; enthusiastic reception.

P

palpable (păl′pə-bəl) *adj.* Capable of being touched or felt.

parapet (păr′ə-pĭt, -pĕt) *n.* A low protective wall along the edge of a roof.

patent (păt′ənt) *adj.* Obvious.

paternal (pə′tûr′nəl) *adj.* Fatherly.

patronize (pā′trə-nīz) *v.* To treat in an offensive way as an inferior.

peer (pîr) *v.* To look closely, as with difficulty.

penetrate (pĕn′ə-trāt′) *v.* To get in or through something.

perception (pər-sĕp′shən) *n.* Insight; understanding.

perseverance (pûr′sə-vîr′əns) *n.* Persistence; determination.

persist (pər-sĭst′, -zĭst′) *v.* To continue to do; refuse to stop.

perverse (pər-vûrs′, pûr′vûrs′) *adj.* Deviating from what is right; stubbornly oppositional; contrary.

pestilential (pĕs′tə-lĕn′shəl) *adj.* Dangerous; deadly.

phenomenal (fĭ-nŏm′ə-nəl) *adj.* Remarkable.

ă pat / ā pay / âr care / ä father / b bib / ch church / d deed / ĕ pet / ē be / f fife / g gag / h hat / hw which / ĭ pit / ī pie / îr pier / j judge / k kick / l lid, needle / m mum / n no, sudden / ng thing / ŏ pot / ō toe / ô paw, for / oi noise / ou out / o͝o took / o͞o boot / p pop / r roar / s sauce / sh ship, dish / t tight / th thin, path / *th* this, bathe / ŭ cut / ûr urge / v valve / w with / y yes / z zebra, size / zh vision / ə about, item, edible, gallop, circus / à *Fr.* ami / œ *Fr.* feu, *Ger.* schön / ü *Fr.* tu, *Ger.* über / KH *Ger.* ich, *Scot.* loch / N *Fr.* bon.

pillar (pĭl′ər) *n.* A column in a building used for support or decoration.

pious (pī′əs) *adj.* Devout; religious.

pique (pēk) *v.* To offend or make resentful.

pivotal (pĭv′ə-təl) *adj.* Crucial; central.

plaintive (plān′tĭv) *adj.* Mournful.—**plaintively** *adv.*

plausible (plô′zə-bəl) *adj.* Seemingly true; deceptive.

plea (plē) *n.* A sincere or urgent request; appeal.

plight (plīt) *n.* Difficult situation.

poised (poizd) *adj.* Balanced.

pomp (pŏmp) *n.* Splendor; magnificent display.

pompous (pŏm′pəs) *adj.* Self-important; pretentious.

ponderous (pŏn′dər-əs) *adj.* Heavy; labored.

portable (pôr′tə-bəl) *adj.* Easily carried or moved.

portal (pôr′tl, pōr′-) *n.* A doorway or entrance.

possessive (pə-zĕs′ĭv) *adj.* Showing a desire to control or own.—**possessively** *adv.*

precaution (prĭ-kô′shən) *n.* Safeguard; caution taken in advance.

preliminary (prĭ-lĭm′ə-nĕr-ē) *adj.* Introductory or preparatory.

premises (prĕm′ĭs-ĭs) *n. pl.* An area of land and the buildings on it.

preposterous (prĭ-pŏs′tər-əs) *adj.* Absurd.

presume (prĭ-zo͞om′) *v.* To assume; presuppose.

pretext (prē′tĕkst′) *n.* An excuse.

prim (prĭm) *adj.* Precise and proper.—**primly** *adv.*

procure (prō-kyo͞or′, prə-) *v.* To get; obtain.

prodigious (prə-dĭj′əs) *adj.* Enormous.

profound (prə-found′, prō-) *adj.* Of deep knowledge or intellect.

prolong (prə-lông′, -lŏng′) *v.* To extend the time of; continue.

prophecy (prŏf′ĭ-sē) *n.* A prediction.—**prophetic** *adj.*

proprietor (prə-prī′ə-tər) *n.* The owner and operator of a business.

prosperity (prŏs-pĕr′ə-tē) *n.* Financial success.—**prosperous** *adj.*

protest (pr ə-tĕst′, prō-tĕst′, prō′tĕst′) *v.* To object to. *n.* (prō′tĕst′) Objection.

prudence (pro͞od′əns) *n.* Caution; good judgment.

punctual (pŭngk′cho͞o-əl) *adj.* Prompt; arriving at the appointed time.— **punctually** *adv.*

pungent (pŭn′jənt) *adj.* Harsh or sharp to the taste or smell.

purloin (pər-loin′, pûr′loin) *v.* To steal.

Q

quaint (kwānt) *adj.* **1.** Old-fashioned. **2.** Unusual in a pleasing way.

R

rafter (răf′tər, räf′-) *n.* A sloping beam used to support a roof.

ramshackle (răm′shăk′əl) *adj.* Rickety; shaky; likely to fall apart.

rank (răngk) *adj.* Weedy; overgrown.

ransack (răn′săk′) *v.* To search carefully.

rationalize (răsh′ə-nə-līz′) *v.* To make explanations or excuses for one's behavior.

raucous (rô′kəs) *adj.* **1.** Harsh and rough. **2.** Loud and boisterous.

real property *n.* Landed property.

recede (rē-sēd′) *adj.* To become distant.

reckless (rĕk′lĭs) *adj.* Careless.

recline (rē-klīn′) *v.* To lean back or lie down.

recoil (rē′koil′, rĭ-koil′) *n.* The movement of a gun as it springs back when fired.

recollection (rĕk′ə-lĕk′shən) *n.* Something remembered.

reconcile (rĕk′ən-sīl′) *v.* To settle a dispute.

reek (rēk) *n.* A strong odor.

reel (rēl) *v.* To stagger or sway.

reflection (rĭ-flĕk′shən) *n.* Careful consideration.

reformation (rĕf′ər-mā′shən) *n.* A change for the better.

refrain (rĭ-frān′) *v.* To hold back.

regal (rē′gəl) *adj.* Royal.

register (rĕj′ĭ-stər) *v.* To realize; understand.

reimburse (rē′ĭm-bûrs′) *v.* To pay back.

rejuvenate (rĭ-jōō′və-nāt′) *v.* To restore the feeling or appearance of youthfulness.

relish (rĕl′ĭsh) *n.* Enjoyment; pleasure.

reluctant (rĭ-lŭk′tənt) *adj.* Unwilling.—**reluctantly** *adv.*

remorse (rĭ-môrs′) *n.* Regret for some action.

renounce (rĭ-nouns′) *v.* To give up completely.

renowned (rĭ-nound′) *adj.* Widely honored; famous.

repercussion (rē′pər-kŭsh′ən) *n.* Reflection of sound.

repose (rĭ-pōz′) *n.* Rest; peace of mind. *v.* To lie at rest.

reserves (rĭ-zûrvz′) *n.* Items stored or set aside for the future.

resilient (rĭ-zĭl′yənt) *adj.* Leaping back; able to return to its original shape.

resolute (rĕz′ə-lōōt′) *adj.* Determined; having a firm purpose.—**resolutely** *adv.*

ă pat / ā pay / âr care / ä father / b bib / ch church / d deed / ĕ pet / ē be / f fife / g gag / h hat / hw which / ĭ pit / ī pie / îr pier / j judge / k kick / l lid, needle / m mum / n no, sudden / ng thing / ŏ pot / ō toe / ô paw, for / oi noise / ou out / ŏŏ took / ōō boot / p pop / r roar / s sauce / sh ship, dish / t tight / th thin, path / *th* this, bathe / ŭ cut / ûr urge / v valve / w with / y yes / z zebra, size / zh vision / ə about, item, edible, gallop, circus / ä *Fr.* ami / œ *Fr.* feu, *Ger.* schön / ü *Fr.* tu, *Ger.* über / KH *Ger.* ich, *Scot.* loch / N *Fr.* bon.

resolve (rĭ-zŏlv′) *v.* **1.** To bring to a conclusion. **2.** To decide.

resume (rē-zo͞om′) *v.* To begin again after interruption.

retribution (rĕt-rə-byo͞o′shən) *n.* Punishment.

revelry (rĕv′əl-rē) *n.* Noisy merrymaking.

reverberate (rĭ′vûr′bə-rāt) *v.* To reecho; resound.

reverie (rĕv′ər-ē) *n.* Daydream.

revolt (rĭ-vōlt′) *v.* To turn away in disgust or shock.

rivalry (rī′vəl-rē) *n.* A struggle to equal or surpass another; competition.

rouse (rouz) *v.* To cause someone or something to stir or wake up.

rout (rout) *n.* A complete defeat.

route (ro͞ot, rout) *n.* A fixed course.

rummage (rŭm′ĭj) *v.* To search thoroughly.

ruse (ro͞oz) *n.* A trick; an action intended to create a false impression in order to mislead.

S

sashay (să-shā′) *v.* To walk or dance in a casual way.

savor (sā′vər) *n.* To enjoy wholeheartedly.

scan (skăn) *v.* To look over quickly.

scion (sī′ən) *n.* A descendant or heir; offspring.

scornful (skôrn′fəl) *n.* Having a feeling of extreme distaste; contempt.

scowl (skoul) *n.* An angry or disapproving look. *v.* To frown in disapproval or anger.

scramble (skrăm′bəl) *v.* To move quickly, on hands and knees.

scrutiny (skro͞ot′n-ē) *n.* Close observation or careful study.—**scrutinize** *v.*

scuttle (skŭt′l) *v.* To run hurriedly.

seclusion (sĭ-klo͞o′zhən) *n.* Solitude or privacy.

sedate (sĭ-dāt′) *adj.* Calm; serious.—**sedately** *adv.*

serene (sĭ-rēn′) *adj.* Calm and peaceful.—**serenely** *adv.*

shaft (shăft, shäft) *n.* A ray of light.

sheen (shēn) *n.* Shininess.

shrewd (shro͞od) *adj.* Cunning; clever in dealing with others.

shunt (shŭnt) *v.* To turn aside or move out of the way.

shy (shī) *v.* To draw back suddenly, as from fright.

simultaneously (sī′məl-tā′nē-əs-lē) *adj.* At the same time.

sinewy (sĭn′yo͞o-ē) *adj.* Strong; tough.

singular (sĭng′gyə-lər) *adj.* Rare; extraordinary.

skirt (skûrt) *v.* To pass around.

slacken (slăk′ən) *v.* To slow down.

slither (slĭ*th*′ər) *v.* To move in a sliding or gliding motion, as a snake.

snub (snŭb) *v.* To behave coldly toward; treat with scorn or contempt.

sodden (sŏd′n) *adj.* Thoroughly soaked.

solemn (sŏl′əm) *adj.* Serious.

soothe (so͞o*th*) *v.* To calm; bring comfort.

spacious (spā′shəs) *adj.* Large and roomy.

spatter (spăt′ər) *v.* To spot or soil, as in a shower of drops.

spawn (spôn) *n.* Eggs.

spineless (spīn′lĭs) *adj.* Lacking in courage.

spirited (spĭr′ĭ-tĭd) *adj.* Lively and vigorous.

spurt (spûrt) *v.* To come out suddenly and forcibly.

squabble (skwŏb′əl) *v.* To quarrel.

squall (skwôl) *v.* To scream or cry loudly.

squat (skwät) *adj.* Short and thick.

staccato (stə-kä′tō) *adj.* Short and abrupt.

stalk (stôk) *v.* **1.** To advance in a stealthy way. **2.** To walk with a noble bearing.

stall (stôl) *n.* A cubicle in a barn.

stammer (stăm′ər) *v.* To stutter; speak stumblingly.

stance (stăns) *n.* The way a person stands; posture.

stealthy (stĕl′thē) *adj.* Sly; secretive.—**stealthily** *adv.*

sterling (stûr′lĭng) *adj.* Of the highest quality.

stifle (stī′fəl) *v.* To smother; choke.—**stifling** *adj.*

stock (stŏk) *adj.* Ordinary. *n.* Supply; supplies of goods kept for sale.—**to take stock.** To make a careful examination.

stoical (stō′ĭ-kəl) *adj.* Seemingly indifferent to pain.—**stoically** *adv.*

stout (stout) *adj.* Fat; bulky.

stumpy (stŭmp′ē) *adj.* Short and thick.

sublimity (sə-blĭm′ə-tē) *n.* The quality of being supreme or impressive.

subordinate (sə-bôr′də-nĭt) *adj.* Of lesser rank; secondary.

subtle (sŭt′l) *adj.* Not obvious; indirect.

succour (sŭk′ər) *n.* Relief from distress; aid.—**succor** *American spelling.*

suite (swēt) *n.* A train of followers.

summon (sŭm′ən) *v.* To call or send for.

superficial (so͞o′pər-fĭsh′əl) *adj.* Trivial; obvious.

supple (sŭp′əl) *adj.* Easily bent.

ă pat / ā pay / âr care / ä father / b bib / ch church / d deed / ĕ pet / ē be / f fife / g gag / h hat / hw which / ĭ pit / ī pie / îr pier / j judge / k kick / l lid, needle / m mum / n no, sudden / ng thing / ŏ pot / ō toe / ô paw, for / oi noise / ou out / o͞o took / o͞o boot / p pop / r roar / s sauce / sh ship, dish / t tight / th thin, path / *th* this, bathe / ŭ cut / ûr urge / v valve / w with / y yes / z zebra, size / zh vision / ə about, item, edible, gallop, circus / à *Fr.* ami / œ *Fr.* feu, *Ger.* schön / ü *Fr.* tu, *Ger.* über / KH *Ger.* ich, *Scot.* loch / N *Fr.* bon.

survey (sər-vā′, sûr′vā′) *v.* To determine land boundaries.

suspect (sŭs′pĕkt′) *adj.* Open to suspicion.

suspend (sə-spĕnd′) *v.* To hold in a fixed state.

sustain (sə-stān′) *v.* To support.

swagger (swăg′ər) *v.* To brag; behave in an insolent way.—**swaggering** *adj.*

swathe (swä*th*) *v.* To wrap.

T

tact (tăkt) *adj.* The ability to say or do the appropriate thing in a delicate situation.—**tactfully** *adv.*

tarp (tärp) *n.* A waterproof covering. [Short for *tarpaulin*]

tattered (tăt′ərd) *adj.* Shredded or torn; ragged.

tauten (tôt′n) *v.* To grow tense.

tawdry (tô′drē) *adj.* Cheap and showy in a tasteless way.

tentative (tĕn′tə-tĭv) *adj.* Uncertain.—**tentatively** *adv.*

terrain (tə-rān′, tĕ-) *n.* An area of land or ground, especially with regard to its natural features.

thoroughfare (thûr′ō-fâr′, thûr′ə-) *n.* A public road; main highway.

thrust (thrŭst) *v.* To push or shove with force.

tolerable (tŏl′ər-ə-bəl) *adj.* Able to be endured; bearable.

tolerance (tŏl′ər-əns) *n.* Respect for the beliefs and actions of others.

transfix (trăns-fĭks′) *v.* To make motionless, as in amazement or fear.

tribunal (trī-byoo′nəl, trĭ-) *n.* A seat of justice.

tumultuous (too-mul′choo-əs, -tyoo-) *adj.* Riotous; disorderly.—**tumultuously** *adv.*

turret (tûr′ĭt) *n.* On a tank, a rotating structure with mounted guns.

U

unassuming (ŭn′ə-soo′mĭng) *adj.* Modest; not boastful.

uncanny (ŭn-kăn′ē) *adj.* Weird and mysterious; not possible to explain.

unfailing (ŭn-fā′lĭng) *adj.* Consistent; reliable.

unmarred (ŭn-märd′) *adj.* Unspoiled.

unsettle (ŭn′sĕt′l) *v.* To disturb; upset.

utter (ŭt′ər) *v.* To speak. *adj.* Total; complete.

V

vague (vāg) *adj.* Indefinite; not distinct.

valor (văl′ər) *n.* Courage; bravery.

vendor (vĕn´dər) *n.* One who sells.

veracity (və-răs´ə-tē) *n.* Honesty; truth.

veranda (və-răn´də) *n.* A roofed balcony or porch, partly enclosed, along the outside of a building.

veritable (vĕr´ə-tə-bəl) *adj.* Actual; real.—**veritably** *adv.*

vestibule (vĕs´tə-byo͞ol´) *n.* An entrance hall or lobby.

vexation (vĕk-sā´shən) *n.* Annoyance.

vexed (vĕks) *v.* To irritate; pester.

villainous (vĭl´ə-nəs) *adj.* Wicked; evil; criminal.

void (void) *n.* An empty space.

W

wail (wāl) *v.* To make a sad sound; cry.

wake (wāk) *n.* The trail left in water by a moving vessel.

wary (wâr´ē) *adj.* Cautious; watchful.—**warily** *adv.*

waver (wā´vər) *v.* To sway; become unsteady.

well (wĕl) *v.* To rise to the surface.—**well up.** To rise from some inner source.

whimper (hwĭm´pər) *v.* To cry in soft, broken sounds.

wily (wī´lē) *adj.* Sly.

wonderment (wŭn´dər-mənt) *n.* Astonishment; surprise.

wrath (răth, räth) *n.* Anger; rage.

wrest (rĕst) *v.* To take by force.

writhe (rīth) *v.* To twist or squirm, as in pain.

Z

zeal (zēl) *n.* Enthusiasm.

zenith (zē´nĭth) *n.* Peak; highest point.

ă pat/ā pay/âr care/ä father/b bib/ch church/d deed/ĕ pet/ē be/f fife/g gag/ h hat/hw which/ĭ pit/ī pie/îr pier/j judge/k kick/l lid, needle/m mum/n no, sudden/ng thing/ŏ pot/ō toe/ô paw, for/oi noise/ou out/o͝o took/o͞o boot/p pop/ r roar/s sauce/sh ship, dish/t tight/th thin, path/ *th* this, bathe/ŭ cut/ûr urge/v valve/ w with/y yes/z zebra, size/zh vision/ə about, item, edible, gallop, circus/à *Fr.* ami/œ *Fr.* feu, *Ger.* schön/ü *Fr.* tu, *Ger.* über/KH *Ger.* ich, *Scot.* loch/N *Fr.* bon.

INDEX OF AUTHORS AND TITLES

Numbers in italics refer to the pages on which author biographies appear.